Out of Harmony

Patti Frazee

© 2012 by Patti Frazee. All rights reserved.

First edition: January 2012

ISBN: 978-1467909181

Cover photo: Jacque Wikowsky
Author photo: Janet Mills
Back cover image: Sandhill Cranes in Flight ©iStockphoto.com/TheRealDarla

Cover Design: Patti Frazee and Marian Martin-Moran
Interior Book Design: Patti Frazee

Song lyrics of "Last Words" ©The Hippie Employed (a.k.a Jamie Willan), used with permission from Richard and Lindsay Willan.

All characters in this book are fictitious. Any resemblance to real individuals—either living or dead—is strictly coincidental.

To Marian,
for love and laughter

Chapter One

Sometimes ghosts live in your head. They rattle around, moving things from one side of your brain to the other, or appearing from the shadows at the least expected times.

"Alison?" Mom's voice comes from the phone.

My eyes are fixed on my reflection, a headset on my ear, as audience members stare at me from the other side of the glass. My eyes refocus and I see myself, *Alison Bullshit*, dressed in black as if waiting for a funeral.

"Did you hear me?" Mom talks louder like we have a bad connection. "Jude is dead."

I have to swallow down the dryness in my mouth, "Yeah."

"I've been trying to get a hold of you for a few days, but you never answer the phone."

I let guilt wash over me, but I don't say a word. I just twist the phone cord around my finger.

Mom breaks the silence, "They found her in old Emma's barn, well, they found Emma first. Neighbors saw her car sitting in the driveway for awhile with leaves all over it, not like Emma, you know. So they called the police to check on her because god forbid anyone would knock on Emma's door without the police. Anyway, you wouldn't believe the smell…"

Smell? I stop Mom's monologue. "What?!? When did Jude die?"

"No, not Jude, honey, Emma. Emma smelled. Jude died—what? Twenty-some years ago—when you were running around with her."

I blush when Mom says "running around with her."

"So wait—" I try to sort my thoughts, "Emma died?"

"Yes," Mom sounds frustrated, but then she softens her voice, "Honey, I'm sorry. They found Jude there in Emma's barn, but Jude died years ago. It's because Emma died that they found her."

Jesus, thousand-year-old Emma just died? And Jude...? Of all the places I imagined Jude to go, Emma's barn was not on the list. I feel Jude's breath on my ear, "I'm gonna get the fuck outta this town Ally...go to New Orleans or New York or San Francisco. Someplace I can disappear." Her syllables pop on my eardrum.

Mom interrupts my thought, "I helped them figure out who she was."

"What?" I'm only half-listening. Did Mom say *she* helped *them*?

"A couple officers were at the restaurant the other day, telling me about it, how they found this skeleton in old Emma's barn. They said the skeleton looked like a young girl, but she'd been dead a long time. I told them, I said, 'my daughter, she used to run with Emma's relative back in high school,' and so they asked me all sorts of questions about Jude. I told them her name."

"So wait," I pull the headset off my ear and look around at the crowds walking past the box office, smiling at me through the glass. "They don't know for sure that it's Jude." I feel hopeful.

"Oh no, it's Jude. They got her dental records. Matt and Ben, they told me today."

"Matt and Ben?" I take a deep breath, "Who...?"

"The officers that always come in. They told me."

"Mom," I really wish my mother could speak in complete thoughts. I try to lead her into a normal way of communicating, even though my heart is thumping in my chest and the lump in my throat is growing. Mom's been better at speaking her thoughts since Dad died, but I still have to coax the facts out of her from time to time. "They told you..."

"That it was Jude."

"You're sure it was Jude they found in old Emma's barn?"

"Yes, honey, I told you. I was the one that gave them her name."

"I understand, Mom," but I really don't. "Mom, I just want to make sure that it actually is Jude."

"Oh yeah. It's Jude. Those people, the ones that do the autopsies like them people on tv, they figured it out from the dental records. You haven't returned my calls, but I thought you'd want to know."

I look down at the phone cord twisted around my finger. It's wrapped so tight that the tip of my finger is bright red.

"They want to talk to you," my mom quickly grows tired of the silence.
"Who?"
"Matt and Ben. They want to ask you some questions."
"Me?" Oh god, what if they ask about the last time I saw her?

I squeeze my eyes shut as if that will take away the image of Jude, walking away from me, her shoulders slumped. Jesus, why was I so scared? No, there was nothing else I could do. Nothing else I could say.

Mom continues. "They want to know if you know anyone."

Know anyone? "Anyone who—what? Who murdered her?"

"No honey," Mom let's out a little nervous laugh, "if you know any relatives. She killed herself."

Killed herself? I try to pull my finger out of the twisted phone cord.

"She practically shot her head off."

I massage my eyes, eyebrows, and forehead to try to get those words out of my head.

Through the headset, the house manager asks if we're ready for the ten-minute warning. "Mom, I have to go back to work. I'll call you tomorrow." I hang up, happy I had some way to get back into my life again.

I move up the stairs, through the greenroom, don't look at the stunned actors, through the darkness of the wings; I get into my seat just in time. I put my headset on and don't even have time to look over the prompt script. I know this show back and forth, but I feel like I'm looking at a foreign language. "Warning Lights 86 through 89."

I take a deep breath and try to focus. "Standby Lights 90 through 94."

The stage is dark. Actors stand in the wings, listening for their cues. As I wait for the music to fade out, I mouth the words "she killed herself." I try to take the words in. Of course she killed herself; who was I kidding all these years thinking she'd just run away?

I used to look for her face when I travelled. New Orleans. San Francisco. New York. But there she was all this time in Emma's barn. She probably just plopped down on the dirt floor—resigned, ready. Where did she get the gun? Knowing Jude, she was probably determined when she put the barrel in her mouth and pulled the trigger. She did it quick. She didn't cry.

A shiver runs through me.

The music stops. I blink my eyes at the page under the white light in front of me and my left eye waters. "Go lights 86 and 87," I say quickly as I wipe the drip from my eye. A light slowly comes up on stage right. Two actors are set on stage as Jessie, the lead actress, enters upstage right.

I wonder if Emma had ever walked out to the barn and found Jude. Maybe when she went to feed the cats or something.

"Go lights 88."

Emma must've seen Jude at some point. Wouldn't she have at least smelled that kind of death? But Emma would never have called the police. She would have been too afraid of losing everything she had. Too afraid of people thinking she was somehow involved. So she probably just walked past the body, day after day, and then she walked past the skeleton, frozen in time, wearing bell bottoms and high-top sneakers.

"Ally!" Jeff, the lighting guy, whispers into his headset. Then he says, "Go lights 90. Standby lights 91," as if he's repeating something I've just said.

The lights come up on Jessie, standing stage left, already a few sentences into talking to another actor. The lights slowly rise on her. Jesus! She is not happy. I can tell by the tension in her hands.

Okay, I really have to get back into this show.

"Go lights 91."

The lights dim stage left and I'm back in control. At least for now.

As I wait for the bus, I take out my house keys. I look at them in my hand and wonder what I'm doing. I put them back in my pocket. Am I even at the right bus stop? I look at my watch, but I mean to look at the bus sign. *God, Ally, focus.* Yeah, the 6 and the 12. I'm here.

Eli hates it that I take the bus to and from the theatre, but I like the feeling of being connected to the city this way. Besides, it's a fifteen-minute bus ride from the front of the theatre to the corner by our condo. Eli says it's too late for a woman to take the bus in downtown. Too dangerous.

Well, I guess I like the danger.

It's cool tonight and I'm badly underdressed. Thankfully, I don't wait long for the bus to pull up to the curb. I see myself in the glass of the door. I always think of myself as the younger Alison Bouchard, the one Jude knew. I look older than I think of myself to be. Middle aged (but I feel young), middle class (but Eli's rich), middle American (but I take the bus at midnight). And now I see the weird cowlick the headset left at the back of my head. I try to smooth down my short brown hair. The door opens with a whoosh of air. Warmth seeps out of the bus.

I look out the dingy window and watch downtown pass by. A gay bar, a strip club, a parking ramp. I hate this part of downtown, it's so outside my life.

I close my eyes. I'm suddenly tired, the eyes-so-heavy-I-can't-keep-them-open tired. The bus jumps and my head bounces, but I keep my eyes closed. It just feels good.

She's dead honey.

Dead.

Jude has felt dead to me for a long time, but now she feels more alive than ever. It's like the memory of her settled inside me, tucked safely between my spleen and stomach. But now that memory is dislodged and creeps up into my chest like a pill that won't go down.

"Alison Bullshit," she whispers in my ear.

I haven't thought of how she called me that in a long time. She gave me that nickname the first night we talked to each other at the grocery store where I worked. It was September, and cold and rainy. Very cold for Harmony, Nebraska at that time of year. Jude came into the store —her clothes heavy and wet, hair dripping water, shoes squeaking on the linoleum. She was shivering under her usual "I don't give a shit" attitude.

I recognized her from school, but we had never talked before. I had never noticed the dark circles beneath her eyes or even how slender she was—her shoulder blades and hip bones stuck out through her wet clothes.

I think in some ways she always scared me—she looked tough and angry. Everyone stayed out of her way at school—she was there, but she wasn't there. We noticed her, but we didn't acknowledge her. After she and I became friends, I understood it—she didn't want anyone to notice her—not her bruises, her scars, her tears. She wanted to disappear.

And I was all innocent with my little fantasy life. The fantasy life that spilled into my real life as I introduced myself with my full name: "I'm Alison Bouchaaar." I'd say it proudly, my voice taking on all of my French ancestry. My family pronounced our last name like any good midwesterner, with a hard "r" and a hard "d": "BouchaRD." It was in my freshman year French class that I learned how to say the family name properly. "I'm Alison Booooshaaar." It was as if my name cancelled out my reality.

Booooshaaar was not the name of a family who lived in a rundown house on a gravel road by the railroad tracks at the edge of town. I was not the girl who had to call the truck stop in the middle of her mother's workday to report that the electricity was shut off again. I was not the girl who had to pick up the phone and lie to bill collectors, telling them my parents weren't home. Eric Bouchard, my father, was not the man who worked forty-plus hours a week at the slaughterhouse, picking up overtime whenever he could. And my mother, Mary Bouchard, was not the woman who dropped out of high school because she just gave up. The Bouchard children, my two younger siblings and I, did not make sport of banging on the ceiling with a broom handle to listen to rats scurry around in the attic. We were not the family who frantically placed pots and pans around the second floor of the house when it rained, listening to the ping ping ping of water dripping through the stormy night.

No, "I am Alison Booooshaaar" conveyed the person I wanted to be—the person whose life I dreamed about. Alison Bouchard was the daughter of Eric and Mary Bouchard, whose family came over from France long ago to live in New Orleans. (I spent hours at the library constructing this story—pouring over books on New Orleans history—reinventing myself.)

"I am Alison Booooshaaar" was the girl who lived in a fine mansion off Prytania Street in the Garden District of New Orleans. My mother was an interior decorator (just like Doris Day in *Pillow Talk*) and my father was a judge who worked with the civil rights movement in the 60s.

Our house had a cornstalk fence—it's the famous Short-Favrot House, but I recreated it as the Perrier-Bouchard House. (I wasn't very inventive with my French names.) My parents entertained often and guests would lounge around on either the front porch or the second-floor porch on hot summer nights in their fine white pressed linens. The men would smoke cigars while the women sipped on mint juleps.

At the side of the house were these huge semicircle balconies, upstairs and downstairs. That's where my siblings and friends liked to play when we weren't playing on the tire swing hanging from the huge magnolia tree out back. The house had 500 bedrooms (a random number) and 31 bathrooms (because I was born on the 31st).

Everyday, my father would walk me to the private school I attended just three blocks from home. Then he would walk one more block to catch the St. Charles Streetcar to go to work at the U.S. District Courthouse, Eastern District of Louisiana on Poydras Street. He was very much an Atticus Finch in his ethics as a lawyer.

On Sunday mornings, my parents and all four of us kids would pile onto the St. Charles Streetcar and take it all the way to Canal Street. We'd walk the length of the French Quarter along Bourbon Street (which, as an adult, I understood smelled of stale beer and fresh urine), then we made a turn onto Orleans Avenue, walked past Tennessee Williams's former apartment, turned right on Royal Street, took a few steps to go down Pirate's Alley where William Faulkner used to live, then walked through Jackson Square to cross Decatur and ended up at Café du Monde. (I had a photocopied map of the French Quarter that I kept in a cardboard box beneath my bed.) My family sat outside and listened to street musicians while we ate beignets (I imagined these to be like the funnel cakes at the State Fair). Then we would walk over to the French Market where my mother looked at linens and fabrics, my father searched for the best hot sauce, and us kids looked through stacks and stacks of t-shirts.

The one memory I convinced myself was true, was one of Martin Luther King Jr. holding me in his arms as he talked with my father about Ruby Bridges and how she was one of the first black children to go to an all-white school. I vividly remembered how Dr. King smelled of sweet cologne and how he had the softest hands I'd ever felt in my life.

My mother loved Dr. King too. But she liked to tell the story about how John F. Kennedy came to stay at our house while he was campaigning. Jackie Kennedy was impressed with our two kitchens and she and mom sat at the dining room table laughing themselves to tears.

I created such a history, I had almost convinced myself that Eric and Mary Bouchard and their three children lived in the Garden District in a fine mansion built by their ancestors. The mansion had pillars and a massive front porch. There were magnolias in the yard and a sturdy cast iron fence in the back where morning glories bloomed like crazy. We were the Bouchard family of the Garden District of New Orleans.

So on that rainy night in September when Jude came into the grocery store, I introduced myself to her. "I'm Alison Boooshaaar," I said, just as I had a million times before.

The corners of Jude's mouth twitched. She looked me in the eye for a moment, as if waiting for me to say more. My hand was suspended in front of her, waiting for her to shake it. Instead, she squinted and said, "Bullshit."

Her eyes bore into me. I took a step back, at least I felt like I did, and looked at her, but she didn't blink. I fumbled with her change, the receipt tape ran out on my machine. "Oh, ah, I…just a second…" I opened the machine and pulled out the old roll. My hands shook as I tried to begin the new tape roll. I couldn't find the damned start, everything was glued so well. "I'll get you, ah, that receipt."

"Don't bother, Alison Bouchaaaaaaaaaar," her voice lilted on the last word and I felt heat rise into my face.

Who was I kidding? Jude saw right through me. I was the daughter of Eric Bouchard, with a hard "r" and a hard "d." The same Eric Bouchard who came home at night with pig blood dried to his boots, smelling of pig shit and hay. He was the man who steadied a shotgun on his shoulder, aiming for that spot between the pig's eyes. "Dead Shot Bouchard" is what his coworkers called him and he hated that. "It's my job," he'd whisper nearly in tears at the dinner table. And after dinner, he'd open a beer and another and another and another. I think it was the only way he could forget.

My mother, Mary Bouchard was the woman who dropped out of high school because she couldn't read well enough to feel good about herself. She was the woman who wore baggy clothing to hide her young figure and then put her energy into standing her ground all day so that by the time she came home, there was nothing left for us.

And me, Alison Bouchard, was the girl trapped in a small Nebraska town, turning over an occasional paycheck to her parents so they could pay rent on the crappy three-bedroom house where she and her two siblings shared rooms. Alison Bouchard was the daughter who woke up to hear pigs screaming as they were led to her father, who worked across the railroad tracks at the slaughterhouse. "Bam. Bam. Bam." She heard the repetition of his daily existence. She dreamed about pigs squealing, falling in mud, their brains splattered next to them.

I can still smell the yards across the track—the piss of fear and the shit of terror.

But that was a long time ago and Jude happened to me a long time ago.

"Hey, it's okay," her voice was soft as she held my hand in her cold, dry hand. "I don't need a receipt."

Then she let go of my hand and I looked her dead in the eye. Surprisingly, she had kind eyes.

Now the bus driver's voice rumbles through the scratchy PA system, "Twelfth Street."

I quickly pull the cord. I jump up and go to the doors at the back. The bus slows, then jerks, I fall forward and catch myself with one of the poles by the door. Do I have everything? Bag, gloves. The door opens and I step out.

I pull my jacket up around my neck in an attempt to break the chill.

I go into the mini-mart.

Before I know it, I'm staring at the frozen pot pies. Chicken pot pie. Turkey pot pie. Beef pot pie.

I look at my watch. 11:45 p.m.

I can't decide which pot pies to get. Pot pies. Jesus, how did it come to this?

Okay, chicken for me; beef for Eli.

I put them in my basket and then go to the back of the store for a half gallon of milk. That'll get us through.

"Hey, Ally."

Softie, one of the techies, moves behind me. I don't know why they call her Softie. She's tattooed all down her arms, has a couple of piercings—that I know about anyway—and dreads. I don't even know her real name.

"Hey." I try to hide my pot pies from her and head toward the checkout line. Softie walks with me.

"Jessie was pissed about that third act tonight," she kind of laughs.

"Oh, yeah," I feel myself blush. "Dropped a cue. My bad."

My bad? That sounded stupid coming from my mouth. My face burns hotter.

Softie smiles. "Yeah, well it's good to know it happens to the old pros too."

Ouch.

Softie pays for her soda and pizza rolls. "See you tomorrow." She winks and I feel myself blush again.

"That's $5.63," the clerk says.

Buck-twenty pot pies and milk. Pathetic.

I used to cook for Eli. He'd chop and I'd cook before I went to the theatre; before he went to the orchestra. Then, we'd come home and have dinner together. A nice dinner—at midnight or 1:00. We'd stay up 'til three and watch a movie.

We haven't done that in awhile.

Fuck the bus, I'm walking home from here. Yeah, I know it's not the safest thing to walk along the park, but fuck it. I wear Jude's attitude and I feel like no one can touch me.

I walk fast to stay warm.

We moved into the condo three months ago. It doesn't feel like home to me. Not yet anyway. But I do like this part of town—the Basilica, Loring Park, the Sculpture Garden, the Walker. Still, I really miss our apartment in Uptown. We lived there for fifteen years, ever since we came to Minneapolis.

I switch the grocery bag from my right arm to my left arm to shift the weight around. My upper arm aches. From a half gallon of milk. It sucks getting older.

My cell phone rings. I frantically look through my pockets. It rings two times, three times—shit—where is it?

"Hello?"

It's Eli. "Hey Al, where are you?"

"Walking along Loring Park, heading for the bridge," I say it automatically, but know it's a bad choice as it's coming out of my mouth.

"Ally!" Eli has an amazing way of sounding upset and disappointed all at the same time. "How many times have I asked you not to walk alone at night. Jesus!"

"I'm sorry, I just—I stopped to get some groceries and I was going to walk home faster than the bus was going to come." Great timing; the second bus passes me and I hope Eli doesn't hear it.

Eli sighs deeply. "Would you?" I can hear him gritting his teeth. Was he going to say "get a cab"? He knows that's impossible in Minneapolis unless you call ahead. Besides, I'm only a few blocks from home. "Fuck, just get home fast and watch out; don't walk through the Sculpture Garden, walk along Hennepin. Jesus."

"Yes, Mom."

"Ally! I'm not kidding!"

"Okay, okay." God, I'm a grown woman.

Another deep sigh. "I'm going to grab a bite with some of the guys from the orchestra. Call me when you get home so I know you're okay, okay?"

The pot pies suddenly feel heavier. "Yeah, sure. I'll see you later."

"But call me when you get home."

"Yes!" I try to soften my voice, but I still sound angry. "Yeah, I will."

He hangs up with just a quick "bye."

Fucking pot pies. He could have at least asked if I wanted to join them. "Hey Ally, we're all going out and since there's nothing to eat at home…"

I look around to make sure no one is close by. You know what? I dare someone to attack me right now. I'll kick their sorry ass.

I'm walking so fast now and swinging the pot pies strongly enough no one will fuck with me.

Chapter Two

"Eli?" My voice echoes in the unlit condo. I don't know why I called his name out anyway; I know he's not home.

The Minneapolis skyline buzzes outside the window, just beyond the Cherry and Spoon Bridge. Lights from the Sculpture Garden give the room a soft glow.

Mozart comes to the door to meet me. Her purr is audible as she stretches out her front paws then falls to her side, begging me to pet her. I drop my keys in the ceramic dish by the door and kick off my shoes.

That's when I catch a slight movement from the corner of my eye and suddenly feel uneasy. "Hello?" I call out again. I stare into the darkness waiting for someone to come out of the shadows.

Mozart meows. Okay, my imagination is really getting away with me. The skyline lights are simply making shadows play in the room. I flip the light switch. The apartment is empty, and now bright.

"It's just me and you, huh Mozart?" I reach down to scratch her belly, but a creepy feeling rolls down my spine. I look across the empty room again.

"Geez, Ally, you should be a writer," Jude used to say with a little nudge of her shoulder whenever I made up stories. Stories of what might be crawling in the darkness around us, or of the spirits that lived in the Harmony Opera House, or of my pretend life in New Orleans.

I've never shared any of my stories with Eli.

I flick open my cell phone and push the speed dial. No. I click the cell phone shut. He can call me if he's that concerned.

An ache rises in my throat. I try to swallow it down, but it remains. I just want to drop. To stop moving. To fall into something different. So I throw the pot pies onto the kitchen counter with a solid thunk, I dim the lights as low as they go, then I fall into Eli's new couch—our new couch. I stare at the skyline.

Our new place is part of a recent condo development intended for "elegant urban living." Eli chose the unit. I helped him choose the maple hardwood floors, the marble countertops, and the jacuzzi versus the twenty-head shower (or some obnoxious number like that). It's Eli's mortgage; I could never afford this on a stage manager's budget. Even on Equity wages. So I help with the association dues and monthly bills, and chip in a few hundred for the I-don't-even-want-to-know-how-much monthly mortgage.

His condo was architecturally designed on rectangles. That's what the interior designer Eli hired told us. Well, some such thing as that—I don't remember her exact words. She said something like, "See how the windows are floor-to-ceiling rectangles and how the area with the piano is a rectangular stage: the living room is a rectangle; the fireplace a rectangle; the dining room a rectangle; the kitchen—" She was very excited about the rectangles.

I wanted to say, "The litterbox—a rectangle!" with the same dramatic flair she showed as she walked through the condo the first time.

After months of dealing with the woman, she's finally done. So now we have round paintings, round rugs, a curved couch, etc., etc., to offset all the rectangles. Well, at least I didn't have to do the work.

Eli thought I would, and that I'd like it. After the closing (I was there for moral support), he hugged me and said, "And you can decorate it any way you want!"

I pulled back from him. "What? You want me to decorate it?"

"Well, yeah. Don't you want to?"

"Okay," I said, "don't you know me better after all these years?"

He dropped his arms and I know he wanted to say, "Oh, here we go," but I didn't give him the chance.

I went off about how just because I'm a woman doesn't mean I like shopping and decorating and putting colors together and nesting and all that crap. And why would he just assume that I was going to put this place together?

"Okay, okay," he said and we didn't talk about it any more. I think I went a little overboard, because suddenly one day, after living out of boxes and using our crappy old furniture that was too small for his new home, Eleanor showed up with her colorologist and her gay assistant, Charles, and they swept through the place glorifying the almighty rectangle.

I just sat silently and watched my new home with Eli take shape. Now I sit on this overstuffed red couch that seems to want to consume me and I look out the rectangular floor-to-ceiling windows that make up one wall of our living room.

It's quiet until Mozart meows again.

"Come here," I wave my fingers and Mozart comes to me. She jumps up on the couch next to me and continues purring. "You still need me, don't you?" I rub behind her ears and she sits on my lap; her constant purring softly rumbles in the room.

I look out on the city lights. I wonder where Eli went. I should call him. But I'm not going to. If he's really worried he can call me.

"You're so stubborn, Alison Bullshit." The voice is soft, distant. It's Jude's voice.

"Yes." I say to it. "I am."

And why is she taking his side anyway?

Okay, wait, now I've lost it. Why am I responding to a voice that isn't here?

I stare at that one red light on the top of the IDS tower as I think of all the questions I'd like to ask the detectives like, where is Jude now? Where did she get the gun? How do you know it was suicide? When's the funeral? Where will she be buried? How long has she been dead? Was there a suicide note?

Jesus. Was there a suicide note? What if there was? Did it say anything about me?

Now I've been staring at that little red light so long I have to close my eyes to take away the burning. I swallow the dryness in my throat. It goes down hard.

I wonder if those detectives in Harmony really want to talk to me. Or did Mom just offer me up while pouring their coffee. "Ally would love to talk to you," she'd say, "You really should call her. She doesn't even work during the day so you could call her anytime."

My heart is pounding.

Then the words wash over me like a breeze, "No more."

If Jude would have left a suicide note, that's what it would have said. Simply, "No more."

Out of Harmony

She told me what she had done in the countless hours we spent together. Now I try to imagine how she felt—what could've led to her putting a gun into her mouth. Anything to keep from thinking it was because of me. It was because of what I did to Jude.

And so I think back to that first time we met and I see her, as she stepped into the grocery store, only a few dollars left in the pocket of her flannel shirt. She assessed the situation. Only Beth and I were working up front, plus one guy in the back stocking shelves. I imagine her, ducking over to the canned goods aisle. Her stomach must've growled when she picked up a can of tuna, a can of chicken noodle soup, and a can of pineapple slices. Who knows how long it had been since she'd eaten, but I know she looked thin. Very thin.

I can see her, putting her head down and walking back to the baked goods aisle, shivering from the warmth in the store. She looked both directions. From the front, we didn't notice her, but she could hear the guy stocking shelves a few aisles over. She took a small can opener off the shelf. $1.19. She would only have about 50¢ left after she paid for the rest. She quickly walked to the back of the store, ducking behind an endcap. She kept an ear out for the guy putting jars of pickles on the shelf, listening to him cut open boxes and jiggling the jars around. She shoved the can opener down the back of her pants, where her butt curved out from her low back and left a gap in the fabric, then she tugged her soaking army jacket down over her butt. Stealing was her only option.

Then with water dripping off the ends of her hair, Jude came over to my register and we had our little bullshit exchange. She may have even remembered we were in gym class together once—in seventh grade.

Jude paid for her stuff and started for the door. The rain was still coming down hard. Her stomach was growling, but the warmth of the store felt good. She backed away from the door and leaned up against a stack of water softener salt.

She looked out the big plate glass windows, but she could see in the reflection of the glass that Beth was staring at her. That's when she turned around and confronted Beth, "Mind if I wait it out in here?" She said it more as a statement than a question. Beth shrugged and turned away. I tried to stay out of it.

Jude held the three cans close to her chest. Her body shivered. Her wet clothes were feeling colder now that she was in the heat. Her underwear felt itchy, the elastic on her bra was pasted to her flesh. The small can opener was digging into the small of her back. And I imagine that, every now and then, Jude thought about her father. She wondered if he missed her. Really missed her. Like he missed her mom after she died.

But then Jude thought about the nights that she lay in bed thinking *no more*. She repeated those words day after day, night after night, until she could feel them enter her body. She knew for sure the words were part of her, that they had seeped into her brain, her tissue, her blood. She knew it the day she pulled a knife from the drawer in the kitchen and felt the blade with her thumb. It was sharp and gleaming. Jude softly rubbed the blade across her wrist, whispering "no more" as the blade pulled and stretched her skin. Then she changed directions, remembering that suicide was successful by slashing from wrist toward elbow. Three slices, three deep wounds. But she couldn't seem to let the knife pierce her flesh so she put it back in the drawer and made a promise to herself. A seemingly simple promise. *No more.*

"NO MORE!" Jude screamed at her father as he lay on the floor, calling her words that a father should never call his daughter. He was crying and yelling, but she refused to cry. She only yelled those two words that she had practiced for weeks, months, years before she ever got the courage to speak them aloud. *No more.*

When Jude left the house, with $52 she stole from her father and the clothes on her back, she promised herself that she would leave all these feelings, all these thoughts behind. No more.

That was two weeks before the rain began to fall.

"Hey, you!" Jude called out to me. "You get paid much here?"

"What?"

Jude softened her tone as I approached, "You get paid much working here?"

"It's okay. Better than McDonalds."

"Yeah? You think I could get a job here?"

For a minute, Jude thought I was going to laugh. But it wasn't in my nature to laugh at someone else's expense. "Yeah. Sure. You want an application?"

"Yeah." Jude thought why not? It was someplace to be. If she got a job, then she'd have some money to buy food. Maybe even get a place of her own. No more sleeping in random stairways.

Thunder rumbled outside. "Here you go. Do you want a pen?"

Jude patted her clothes, acting like she was looking for a pen she didn't have. "Yeah." Jude looked over the application, her eyes resting on the address line. I handed her a pen. "Thanks, uh…"

"Alison."

"Oh yeah," Jude suddenly got awkward, "Alison. Thanks."

Address. Jude tapped her pen on the lined page. She looked out the window. She didn't want to write down her father's address. That was her old life; this was her new life. But should she just leave it blank? Maybe make up an address? What did they want an address for anyway?

"You can fill it out over here if you want," I said, pointing to one of the checkout lanes. "I mean, if you want a hard surface to write on."

But I didn't know Beth was standing behind me, glaring at Jude. "That's okay," Jude said. She rolled up the two pages. "I think I'll take it with me." She walked toward me and gave back the pen.

As I took the pen from her, I asked if she was okay.

"Yeah." Jude swallowed hard. "I should..." she backed away toward the door.

"You can stay inside until the rain stops if you want."

"No, I've gotta...go...you know?"

She backed away and thought, *Man, this girl is trouble.* ("You're trouble, Alison Bullshit," that's what she used to say to me.) The automatic door jumped behind her. "See ya."

Jude stepped outside before I had a chance to say a word. Sheets of rain blanketed the parking lot. She stayed under the overhang of the grocery store front and walked to the edge of the sidewalk, away from the large windows where Beth or I might watch her. She sat on the sidewalk and took out her can opener and her three cans: pineapple slices, tuna, and chicken noodle soup. She opened the soup first, pulling the top off completely. She drank it, cold and salty, right from the can.

"Ally?" Eli's voice comes from the entryway.

It takes a moment for me to get away from Jude.

"Al-ly?" His voice is more singsong this time.

"Here!" I say as if attendance is being taken.

He turns up the dimmer so the lights in the room are bright again. "Why are you sitting in the dark?"

I clear my throat. "Just watching the city lights." I squint, trying to readjust my eyes.

I see him staring at his cell phone. "You didn't call." I don't like his accusatory tone.

"Guess I forgot." Sometimes it's easier not to argue.

He sighs, shuts off his cell phone, and takes off his coat. I don't move.

"It's beautiful isn't it," he says, squeezing my shoulders too hard. A pain shoots through my left shoulder blade.

I see his reflection in the glass looking out over the city and I wish he hadn't come home yet. He leans down and kisses my neck. He smells sweaty under his musky cologne.

"How was rehearsal?" I ask, but my mind wants to go back to Jude.

He sits next to me and takes my hand. "That freaking violinist is going to drive me nuts. She's such a prima donna."

I give an uncomfortable laugh. His leg is hot next to mine and it feels like the material of my pant leg is stuck beneath his thigh. I pull my leg away and lean toward the arm of the couch. "I'm glad you have one of them this time." We always commiserate about the artists we have to manage from time to time.

Sweat breaks out along my hairline. Jesus, am I going through menopause at age forty-two? My hand is burning where he holds it. My spine is curved awkwardly as I lean half away from Eli. I pull my hand from him. He tries to reach to take my hand back, but I pull it further away.

Eli takes a deep breath. It appears he doesn't know what to do now, so he just looks down and acts as if he's picking dead skin off the rejected hand. "How was your night?" He asks softly.

"Fine. Just fine." I swallow hard.

"But?" Eli knows me too well after all these years, and he almost looks hopeful, as if he will finally find some reason for my behavior.

I sigh and exhale, "Nothing."

He shakes his head, then asks, "Anything else happen today?"

"Um," I don't want to share Jude with him. I've always kept that time in my life to myself. "No, not really."

Another resigning nod. Then he goes back to the table by the door and picks up the mail.

"Just the usual, you know." I say quickly, trying to heal something between us. Trying to take back what just happened.

He doesn't say anything. He seems focused on sorting the mail.

I look back out to the city lights. I slouch down into the sofa. "God, I'm tired."

"Really? I'm wide awake." I'm not sure, but I think there's some sarcasm in his tone, as if to say, *Imagine that! We want different things.*

I choose to ignore it. "I think I'll go to sleep."

"I'm gonna stay up and watch tv for awhile." He points the remote at the tv.

"Okay, good night sweetie," he can't hear me over the surround sound—at least I think that's why he doesn't respond. I leave him with his eyes fixed on the changing screen as he clicks the remote over and over again.

"Ally?" he says just as I go into the bedroom. I'm not in the mood for a talk right now.

"What?" I sound more disturbed than I intend to.

"Your mom called me tonight." I can hear the stations changing on the television. I go back into the living room.

"What?"

"Your mom called me tonight." He mutes the tv and puts the remote down. "She told me about your friend."

"She shouldn't have done that," I say, then quickly cover myself by saying, "I mean, bother you at rehearsal."

"She called after rehearsal and why didn't you tell me?"

I feel set up. "Why didn't you ask?"

"I did. 'How was your night?' 'Anything else happen today?'"

"Eli, I'm not in the mood to argue. I'm tired. My friend died." I walk back toward the bedroom.

"Ally!" My name echoes with these high ceilings. I stop walking, but I don't turn around.

He doesn't say anything for a long time, but I'm not going to turn toward him. I'm not getting into an argument this late at night.

His voice becomes soft. "I'm here if you want to talk. Okay?"

I just nod and the volume on the tv comes back up. Time for bed. I leave Eli in the living room with his remote.

I lie in bed looking up at the ceiling. As tired as I am, I can't seem to fall asleep. Mr. Concerned out there seems to have turned up the volume.

I wish Mom wouldn't have told him. I know she did it out of concern, but still...

I can't tell Eli about Jude. It would just complicate our current situation. We haven't gotten along for a couple of months now; ever since Eli bought the condo. Damned rectangles.

That's it, I'll blame it on the rectangles.

"Bullshit," Jude whispers again.

I turn over and pull the covers up under my chin. I close my eyes and a tear breaks free and rolls onto my pillow.

She practically shot her head off. A shiver runs through my body. A part of me always thought that might have happened to her, but I wanted to dream. I wanted to think that she had escaped.

Why would Jude go to Emma's barn?

Well, Emma was Jude's aunt. And Jude always thought she might turn out like Emma someday. But I never saw that.

Now I remember that my run-in with Emma happened the night I first met Jude. I haven't thought of that incident in a long time.

But Jude was there and she told me how she saw the event unfold and why she was lurking in the shadows. She watched Emma just sitting there, resting her head on the steering wheel. Jude watched Emma sleep through heavy downpours and she watched Emma move around as the rain subsided. Jude wondered, just like I did, what Emma did in her car all that time.

Everyone in Harmony knew Emma. We would spend hours at the grocery store telling stories about Emma sightings, or about what we knew of her. Jude was never part of the story. Instead, we wondered what were in the bags piled on top of bags in Emma's backseat. We knew about her addiction to Listerine. And somehow we knew about the farm and about the dominating mother she took care of most of her life.

I always thought Emma spent all that time in her car just forgetting. Maybe she thought if she could just close her eyes, just for one moment, she would feel better. Maybe Emma and Jude had more in common than I thought.

But Emma had her farm and her car. I bet she used to escape to her car, sitting in the driveway, just to listen to rain tapping on the roof. And I imagine that she'd sit for hours and hours until her mother found her and pulled her back into the house. But in that car, she must have found sanctuary, and on rainy days she sat, listening to the tap tap tapping. Yeah, I bet Emma could always drift away into a deep sleep when the rain came.

And maybe in her sleep, she was normal. Maybe she had dreams. Dreams of being a ballerina, flitting across a stage—her toes pointed, her arms held out in a circle. And she could fly—drift up across the stage on pointed toes, spinning, spinning. But then maybe her mother appeared, bouncing a stick on the stage. "ONE, TWO, THREE, FOUR, ONE, TWO, THREE, FOUR." The stick hit her on the back of the head and Emma woke up. This was the kind of sleep she would have had. Just minutes at a time. Momentary happiness disrupted by her reality. And when she couldn't sleep, she would feel beneath the car seat, her arthritic fingers reaching out for the bag she thought she put there. But she wouldn't find it so she'd take a deep breath.

She'd look in the rearview mirror at the bags stacked up to the ceiling of her car. Little bags, medium-sized bags—all containing her life. She still had the farm, but these bags held her present; the farm held her past.

And on that night I met Jude, when the rain stopped, Emma opened the car door and swung her feet outside. She looked toward the sky and squinted her eyes into the lights of the parking lot. She sat like that for awhile, her legs sticking out of the car, her dress twisted beneath her butt. Her mother wouldn't have liked this manner of sitting. "Unladylike," she would have tsk'ed at Emma, and then smacked her legs with a yardstick or broom handle, whatever was closest. Emma still had an indentation on her kneecap from where her mother hit her so hard that she limped for two weeks. (Another tidbit I gained from Jude.)

Emma dozed off again, even in that awkward, painful position. She woke moments later. The rain had lightened. She pulled the plastic rain bonnet over her head. She pushed herself out of the car and shuffled her clunky shoes through a puddle to the back door of the car. She began sifting through the bags on the seat until she remembered what she was looking for. *No, that would be on the floor of the car.* Rain pelted the back of her jacket as she bent down and touched the bags on the floor. She couldn't see anything in this light. She felt each bag and noted their contents: cat food, canned tuna, laundry soap, canned fruit… AH! She found it. She pulled out the bag and held it to her chest. She shut the back door and shuffled into the driver's seat. Squinting her eyes against the rain, she shut the door and looked around the dark parking lot for anyone who might be watching her, but she didn't see Jude. Drips of water rolled down the bridge of Emma's nose. Her night vision was so bad, she couldn't see beyond the headlights of her still-running car. (Of course, this didn't stop her from driving.) Her hands shook as she unwrapped the bottle. Her heart pounded. This would make her feel so much better.

Her fingers struggled with the wrapping on the bottle. *Why did they have to wrap a bottle in brown cardboard anyway?* She finally managed to get the top exposed. She twisted the cap and pain shot up her forearms, but it would be worth it soon enough.

The intoxicating smell burned in her nose. She cupped the 64-ounce bottle of mouthwash with her right hand and steadied it with her left. She pushed the bottle to her lips and drank, drank, drank, drank. The mintyhot liquid burned as it went down deep into her chest, her belly, her bladder. She felt the burning fill up her torso and pass through her system.

Mmmmmm. She moaned to herself, wiping some of the liquid from her mouth. She leaned her head back on the headrest and closed her eyes. Her hands clutched the bottle that sat in her lap. She again drifted into a dream. Her mother lay in a coffin in a funeral home. No flowers surrounded her. A man vacuumed the floor below the coffin and Emma felt a moment of satisfaction. Satisfaction from knowing her mother was dead—

once and for all. As the man turned his head, Emma saw her mother's mouth move. Unmistakably, her mouth was moving, as if she was talking, talking, talking. Then she sat up in the coffin and looked at Emma, her mouth moving, moving, but no words came out. Emma couldn't yell at the man because the vacuum was too loud.

Emma woke with a start. The bottle of mouthwash tumbled to the side. She didn't even know that her precious liquid was escaping until she smelled the pungent odor rising in her car. She let out a gasp and picked the bottle up. Mouthwash ran down the side of her hand and she licked it off.

"Unladylike," she said to herself. She looked around the parking lot again, but couldn't see into the shadows beyond the parking lot lights.

She cleared her throat, tucked the bottle under her car seat, and opened the door. She swung her legs out of the car and sat there for awhile, her skirt again twisted beneath her butt. She then realized that the car was still running. *Stupid!* She swung her legs back into the car, grabbed hold of the massive set of keys, and turned it off. Damn! She still couldn't understand this button she had to push to get her keys out. Now what was it that man at the car lot said? She played with the button, pushing it in, pulling it out, moving it up and down, and she finally managed to release the keys. She slowly and painfully swung her legs outside the car once again.

Eli climbs into bed next to me and disturbs my imaginings. I pretend I'm asleep. I should've told him about Jude. I should've told him years ago. But I didn't want to mess things up between us. How do you tell the man you fall in love with that you once had a female lover?

He places a soft kiss on my cheek.

It makes me feel bad for being so cool to him earlier. I pretend to wake up. "Eli?" I whisper as if in a half-dream state. (What an actress!)

"Yeah, baby?" His hands move down along the curve of my hip.

"Tell me about your rehearsal tonight."

He gives a small laugh. "What do you want to know? It was a rehearsal."

"Yeah," I say as I close my eyes. Now I realize how heavy my eyelids feel.

"Go to sleep, baby." He kisses me on the forehead this time, then turns his back to me and adjusts the pillow beneath his head.

I try to lie still as he falls asleep, so I drift back into a daydream. I fast forward through Emma's shopping trip, which always took several hours. Fifteen minutes to get into the store and another two hours for her to shop. We could always tell where she was in the store by the hum of her hearing aid. And we could always tell where she had fallen asleep with her head resting on the bar of the cart. Eventually, she shuffled her way to the checkout lane, leaning most of her weight onto her shopping cart. Emma was an extremely frail woman. She was all stooped over (osteoporosis, I'm sure) and petite—4'11' and not more than ninety pounds. It took a lot of patience to wait on her because she methodically and slowly put her groceries on the conveyor belt. It would take five seconds to ring up her items, which were always four cans of cat food, two cans of tuna, gum, a 64-ounce bottle of mouthwash, two candy bars (O Henry and Hershey's chocolate), and chicken livers.

Of course, we always wondered about this purchase. But even more intriguing to the employees of the Super Valu were the bags. Emma had a very particular way that her groceries were to be put into bags. This method was handed down from bagger to bagger, cashier to cashier. The method was this: four cans of cat food in one bag, two cans of tuna in another bag, 64-ounce bottle of mouthwash in another bag, chicken livers wrapped in a plastic bag then double wrapped in another bag, candy bars in another bag, gum handed to Emma to put in her purse.

It was easy for multiple people to work together to get this right because it took Emma a good fifteen minutes to pay for her purchase. Her arthritic fingers dug the coin purse out of her handbag. She pulled out a wad of cash and peeled the money from it like pulling paper towels off the roll. She'd rub each bill between her thumb and index finger to make sure she was handing over only one bill to the cashier. Bill by bill, the cashier stood there, watching and waiting. Then she'd get to the coin. She always had exact change and her fingers would dig deep down into that beaded coin purse, jiggling all the change around. She'd pull out each penny, each nickel, each dime, one at a time, her fingers lunging back in after each coin.

So obviously, all of this time in the store gave Jude enough time outside the store to carry out her own plan. She told me about it once. About how she devised this plan to live on her own. Jude knew Emma well. She knew because she'd heard the stories in her family—of old Aunt Emma who took care of her mother for too many years and went crazy in the process. Jude's father had very little to do with his father's sister, but every now and then, he was called upon to help her.

Just the year before, Jude and her father had to go out to the farm to help Emma. (She was one of the few people of Harmony who locked her car doors.) Emma had locked her keys in the car, so Jude's father took a wire hanger, bent it out of shape. and jimmied open the car door for Emma.

"If you're going to be locking your doors, you need to get a magnetic key holder," Jude's father had said. Emma had looked puzzled, so Jude's dad said it louder, "A MAGNETIC KEY HOLDER. THEN PUT YOUR SPARE KEY HERE," he pointed to the wheel well, "SO THAT YOU HAVE A SPARE KEY WHENEVER YOU NEED IT."

Emma still looked puzzled, so Jude and her father had to drive back into town, to the drugstore, where her dad had bought a magnetic key holder. Then they drove back out to the farm and her father showed Emma what he was talking about.

Emma didn't say much, she just raised her finger, indicating she finally understood and it seemed to be a very good idea.

So on that night of the cold rain, Jude snuck over to the beat-up car, looking around to see if anyone was watching. She felt under the front wheel well and found the tiny box with the spare key. She looked in the back seat as she unlocked the door on the passenger side—the side of the car hidden from view of the front of the store.

She started going through the bags, quickly but gently. Trying not to tear the brown paper; trying not to misplace any of the bags. Her Aunt Emma was fussy, she knew that much. Jude opened one bag after the other, looking toward the store between bags to make sure no one saw her. Her heart raced. Each bag held something more disturbing than the bag before it. Her aunt truly was crazy.

Jude didn't want much, just twenty or thirty dollars to hold her over for another week. Until she figured out what to do. Jude kept searching, finding empty bottles of mouthwash, neatly wrapped. Photographs, magazine articles, newspaper clippings, yellow page ads, mysterious drawings, and some kind of animal fur (it looked like road kill). Jude felt like throwing up. This was her blood. This was her life.

Jude looked back toward the grocery store. Emma was in line, paying for her groceries. Jude closed her eyes and thought, Where would Emma hide her money? Jude knelt down on the floor and felt under the front seat. There were several paper bags tucked beneath there, lined up from one door across the car to the other door. She didn't have much time, so she quickly, and as gently as she could, opened one after the other. More mouthwash bottles, ripped pages from library books, illegible pages of written words, and *yes*! Several bags of cash. Jude took two tens and three fives. She knew her aunt would eventually notice; she could tell by the way the cash was organized. Ones, fives, tens, twenties, a few hundreds, all facing the same direction, all face-up, all crisp, new bills.

Jude shoved the bills in her pocket, tried to place each bag exactly the way she'd found it, and quickly got out of the car. Emma was making her way to the automatic door, with me trailing behind, a collection of small paper bags on the cart we used to carry out groceries. Jude quickly replaced the key and ran across the parking lot.

Jude leaned against the white wall of the gas station directly across the parking lot from the store. She watched as Emma shuffled toward the car and I followed behind. Jude told me that she tried to think of my name—Bullsha? Booshay? She couldn't remember, so she just stuck with Bullshit.

Emma jiggled her keys, going through them one by one, trying to find the one that would unlock the door. I followed behind silently pushing the carry-out cart. It squeaked, squeaked, squeaked as we slowly walked toward the car. No words were exchanged.

Emma opened the back door of the car and Jude's heart pounded, wondering if Emma would notice anything unusual.

As I carefully put the bags in the backseat (no small task since bags spilled out when I opened the door; all of them felt like they contained nothing but air), Emma positioned herself back into the driver's seat. She started the car before I finished putting all of the bags in; Jude told me it was the fastest she had ever seen her aunt move. I panicked as the car started. I didn't want Emma taking my head off. I quickly shouted "thank you" and shut Emma's door. The car rolled forward as I took one step away from it. And then everything happened so quickly, but in slow motion at the same time. My carry-out cart started moving, rolling sideways right in front of me. I tried to grab it, but it was attached to Emma's bumper. My grip on the cart failed and I yelled for Emma to stop, but of course she couldn't hear me. Her car was driving through the lot with a cart attached to the back. One wheel of the cart came off, then two. Sparks flew everywhere as both Jude and I watched in stunned amazement. The cart made the loudest, god-awful screeching we'd ever heard. We were surprised Emma couldn't hear it at all. It didn't even appear that Emma looked in her rearview mirror to see the sparks flying from the back of her car. When Emma passed a light post at the end of the parking lot, the grocery cart slammed into it and Emma's bumper flew up into the air. I tried again to yell for Emma, but her bumperless car was already turning onto the street.

Jude would have liked to laugh at the scene, but it was her crazy aunt who caused it. Her flesh and blood.

* * * * * * *

Eli is snoring, a soft, purring kind of snore. Mozart is lying between us, her paws stretched out as far as they can go. I reach out and pet her head. She matches Eli's purr.

I stare up at the ceiling.. The city lights still glow inside our condo, even in the middle of the night. I'm wide awake. I wish I could sleep. Eli stirs as I turn to readjust myself. Trying to free myself from the feel of blankets wrapped around my legs. Mozart stands and stretches into a full arch, then leaves the bed. I pull on the covers but only grab the blanket, the sheet feels tied around my knee. I kick and twist to try to remove that tied-up feeling. Eli mumbles, "What's wrong?"

"Nothing." I tug the sheet and the whole bed jerks as my legs are freed. Eli wraps his arm around my chest and drapes his leg over my hip. Now I really feel trapped. He's snoring again. I can't believe how he falls asleep so easily. Sweat beads on my chest. Mozart is lucky; she can just stand up and leave. I wriggle my way out from under Eli's arm and leg—maybe too forcefully—but he doesn't wake.

I stare up at the ceiling again as Eli snores, his elbow is lodged in my arm.

Okay, I've got to settle down. I think of the sparks coming off of the grocery cart again and stifle a laugh. Jude and I did laugh about that later. "You should write it all down, Ally." She said to me once.

My arm feels bruised where Eli's elbow digs in. I pull away even more and now I'm right at the edge of the bed. I could just roll off the edge and leave him here sleeping.

It's harder to stay.

So many times I want to roll off the edge.

Eli tugs the covers away from me so I'm halfway exposed. He's turned over on his side. Mozart is on the floor below me, begging for my hand. I let it drop. Mozart rubs her whiskers against my fingers.

I swing my feet over the side of the bed and stare back at Eli. He has turned over on his side, his back to me.

Mozart runs out ahead of me to the living room.

It seems easy to leave Eli now.

Chapter Three

The living room is freezing cold when I open my eyes. The room is dark and it's quiet outside so it must be early. My eyes can't adjust to the glowing numbers on the dvd player.

I pull my hands to my face and blow warmth into them. I swear I can see my own breath as a mist rises in front of me. A heavy, dull ache sits in my head. I shove my hands under the thin blanket on top of me. I have to decide, feet or neck? If I pull the blanket up under my neck, my feet are exposed; if I pull it down over my feet, it only covers me up to my breasts. A shiver runs through me as I decide on feet.

I blow my breath out and watch for the mist again.

This is what Jude and I used to do on cold nights. Our hands would be tucked into the sleeping bag and we would release our misty breath out into the cold air; we'd try to form smoke rings.

My mind seems to fire off all sorts of random memories. Even though I close my heavy eyelids, nothing settles in my mind to let me sleep.

I turn over and the new couch barely gives beneath me.

Tell me about the Victorian lady, Alison Bullshit.

Now Jude's voice is stuck in my head. It's so clear.

Part of me wants it to go away. But only part of me.

The Victorian lady that made you forget about the pigs.

When I was young, before I met Jude, I used to lay in bed making up stories about a long-ago ancestor. I was trying to block out the sound of the animals, squealing and grunting, as they were being led to slaughter.

The Victorian lady.

I close my eyes and think beyond the rectangles of Eli's house. The Victorian lady was my great-great-great grandmother, Elizabeth Perrier. Jude used to settle in, excited to hear these stories. I always had to remind her that Elizabeth was made up.

"Just tell me the story," Jude insisted.

Tell me the story.

Okay. Here goes, I answer the voice again. I try to relax my back and arms and jaw. I try to block out the cold and tell the story the way I used to.

Elizabeth was born in France and lived there until her seventeenth year when her father tired of her ways. Unlike me, she was a defiant little girl, disobeying her father from a very early age. She hated the gowns that her mother made her wear; she hated the bodice, the fringe, the lace, the fine silk—she hated it all. At the age of sixteen, she began to leave the house at night without her parents' knowledge.

Elizabeth had a friend named Jacqueline Montalban (*Fantasy Island* hit the air in 1978, the year this story was created), Jacqueline was a well-known seamstress who, at twenty-two, was five years older than young Elizabeth.

It was while strolling down Boulevard Monmartre in Paris that Elizabeth met Jacqueline.

Jude always laughed at my choice of street names. I found Monmartre while looking through books at the library and spent hours trying to pronounce it: moan-mar-tra, light on the last syllable just like my French teacher said, moan-mar-tra.

Moan-mar-tra.

Elizabeth was taken with the gown Jacqueline was wearing and innocently commented on its craftsmanship. Jacqueline invited Elizabeth into her shop to see her latest projects. It was no coincidence that Elizabeth began to make frequent stops at Jacqueline's shop. Soon enough, Elizabeth snuck out of her parents' house in the late evening to meet Jacqueline.

It was there, in the nighttime hours, that Elizabeth Perrier redesigned herself—she took off her dress, her bodice, her slip, and flung them over the partition (just like in the movies). Jacqueline took out her finest clothing—it was the clothing she made for princes and governors, for nobility and dukes. It was in Jacqueline's shop that Elizabeth could live exactly as she wanted—dressed in the fashion of the day for men.

First, there was the tailored pant that rose up to her waist with clean lines, neatly pressed. Then there was the crisp white shirt with a high collar. Elizabeth pulled a black tie around the high collar and closed her eyes as Jacqueline tied a perfect bow.

Now the rest. Jude used to say this with me.

"Now the rest," Jacqueline held out the powder blue vest, signaling for Elizabeth to hold out her arms. She complied. Jacqueline slipped the vest over one shoulder, then the other. She buttoned it up for Elizabeth.

And the coat.

"And the coat." This was the final transformation for Elizabeth. She slipped on the coat, the front line came down to her waist and cut back toward her hips, then one long, solid piece streamed down to the back of her knees. Elizabeth held the shorter front in her hands and tugged.

Jacqueline turned Elizabeth to the mirror and admired how well it fit. She placed a tall top hat on Elizabeth's head but it sank down to her eyes.

Maybe we don't need the hat.

"Maybe we don't need the hat," Elizabeth said.

Jacqueline took it off Elizabeth's head and brushed loose strands of hair over Elizabeth's ears, gently so that her fingertips slightly grazed Elizabeth's ears.

And it was in that room that Elizabeth and Jacqueline…

Would dance.

…would dance. They danced like they were at a great ball, thrown by King Louis-Philippe. Elizabeth and Jacqueline held each other and danced around the room—Elizabeth guiding Jacqueline, strong but gentle. Elizabeth's left hand splayed across Jacqueline's petite right shoulder, they turned around and around, giggling at times—waltzing, ballroom dancing, close but not too close.

Elizabeth and Jacqueline simply danced—enjoying the appropriate touch, excited merely by the fact that Elizabeth dressed as a male—her naked hand touching the silk-gloved hand of Miss Jacqueline Montalban.

Now I feel my heart pounding in my chest as all these familiar feelings rise in me once again. I kick the blanket off my feet. It's the same feeling I had in that moment when Jude's hand touched mine as we both reached to pick up Emma's bumper. My heart raced. I gulped down the thrill of that moment. And when Jude's hand seemed to grasp my hand, her fingers resting in my palm and, as my eyes met hers, I felt her hand squeeze mine—it was in that moment all of my fantasies seemed to be playing out and I felt so wrong.

I sit up on the couch and rub my eyes with my fingertips; I move into massaging my temples to try to take the ache away. I take a deep breath.

What's wrong, Ally?

No. I have to try to let these childhood fantasies rest. That's not the Alison Bouchard I am now. I'm with Eli now.

Don't be embarrassed…

"Don't be embarrassed," that's what Jude said as she examined the wheel of my broken grocery cart and my eyes rested on her for a moment. "That woman's a little crazy, you know?"

I just nodded. "Yeah." Her shoulder-length hair hung down in her eyes and she'd often take a moment to push it back behind her ears. She glanced at me once as she tried to bend the wheel back into place. She had these amazing green eyes.

My mind is churning out memories so rapidly I'm feeling dizzy. I can't seem to stop it.

Write it down, Ally.

Maybe a glass of warm milk will help me get to sleep. I go to the kitchen and get a mug out of the cupboard. I shut the refrigerator door too hard. I worry about waking Eli as the numbers on the microwave beep too loudly when I punch each button. I push start and watch the display count down from 2:00. 1:59. 1:58, 1:57. With my eyes fixed on the numbers, I realize that Jude, my internal voice, or whatever it is, might be right.

I go to the credenza by the front door; I know I have a notebook in one of these drawers. I find it; bottom drawer on the left. I go back to the kitchen and find the pen for grocery lists in our junk drawer.

I lean over the counter and touch the tip of the pen to paper just as the microwave goes off. I open the microwave door and feel the hot mug between my hands. On the edge of pain, I turn the mug until the handle is in my hand. I look out over the breakfast bar, beyond the pillars to the living room, over the leather couch and the flat-panel tv, past this big, cavernous space out onto the Cherry and Spoon Bridge and I can't seem to find one thing to land on. So I close my eyes and pull the mug to my lips. The warmth rises into my nostrils and down into the emptiness in my chest and I momentarily feel at peace.

I look down at the page in front of me and it comes easily. I put down the mug and begin to write.

Jude held the bent wheel in her hand, giving up on putting things right. She stood up. "You take the cart, I'll take the bumper." The cart whined and clunked out a rhythm with its damaged wheels. Squeak squeak ka-thunk squeak squeak ka-thunk squeak squeak ka-thunk. Jude and I walked in silence to the front of the store. She put the bumper down and glanced into the store at my coworker, Beth, who was watching us.

"Later," Jude said and walked across the parking lot, through puddles of light. She disappeared into the darkness behind the gas station.

"Thanks!" I yelled, my voice so loud it startled me. I watched the darkness, hopeful, for just a minute. I waited, but the shadows were still.

My hand cramps up already. Geez, in college I could write like this for hours without stopping. Now, I'm rubbing my hand as if I just slammed it in a car door.

I look at the microwave. It flashes 4:19.

I should go to sleep, but now I don't want to stop. The stories keep coming to me and it feels like I'll never rest if I don't write them down; if I don't put them on paper.

So I write.

I write about Emma sitting in her car, a bottle of mouthwash in her hand, her odd paper bags, and her humming hearing aid.

I write about Jude and the day she came into the grocery store, her job application, her wet hair, and how she held my hand.

I write about Alison Bouchard of the Garden District, in the first person and in the third person, and about the great house she lived in, the visit with Dr. King, and my mother's visit with Jackie Kennedy.

I write and write until my hand cramps, then I rub out the kinks and write some more.

I move to the couch and look out at the Cherry and Spoon Bridge for awhile. I write about Elizabeth and Jacqueline, dancing.

I flick my fingernail on the piping of the couch. I write about Jude and our nights behind the Harmony Opera House, sitting in the cold darkness, giggling and—

"What are you doing?" Eli is suddenly behind me.

I drop my pen and close my journal abruptly. I didn't even hear him wake. "What…" I clear my throat, "What time is it?"

"Ten."

He leans over the back of the couch and rubs my shoulders. He's still in his pjs. "What are you doing?" His voice is soft and caring. Good. It seems like the night triggered a reset button and we're going to start on the right foot today.

"Writing."

He gives a little tug on my journal as if he's going to take it. My grip on it tightens, but I try to laugh so that it doesn't seem so mean. "Hey!"

"Writing?" His voice is deep and craggy. He shuffles off to the kitchen. "Back to poetry?"

I haven't written poems for years. I tried to get some of them published once and only got rejections. I stopped writing. I'm not sure why.

"No, not this time." I'm hoping he didn't see Jude's name all over the page when he snuck up behind me.

"Then what?" His voice gets clogged, so he clears his throat. He scoops teaspoons of coffee into the maker, but his eyes don't leave me as he waits for an answer.

"Stories, just things."

He smiles. "Things, huh?"

I don't respond. I put the cap back on the pen and put my journal, facedown, on the coffee table. Somehow facedown makes it feel more secure. I go to the kitchen and ponder breakfast, but I'm not really hungry.

"How long have you been up?"

Does he mean out of bed? Or awake and writing? Instead of either answer, I go for what sounds reasonable. "Around seven thirty." I look at the three cereal boxes in our cupboard.

"Seven thirty?!? Geez. What's gotten into you?"

Haven't heard that question for awhile. I just shrug.

"Does it have to do with that friend of yours?"

"Jude!" I slam the cereal box on the counter. Why does everyone refer to her as "that" something? That girl. That friend. "Her name is Jude. Was Jude."

He sits down at the kitchen counter and waits for the coffee to brew. "So tell me about her."

Tell him about her? That jars me. I've just spent the last two hours so lost inside myself.

"Come on, Ally, how'd you meet? At school?"

"No. At the grocery store I worked at."

"Was she a good friend of yours?"

"She was my best friend." The words come out soft and shaky.

"How come you never mentioned her before?"

"I don't know, I guess she never came up." I try to get my voice under control. "Have you told me about every friend you had in high school?"

He thinks on that for a moment. "Yeah. Pretty much."

"Really?"

He thinks again. "Yeah."

That can't be true. We haven't had that many discussions about high school. But I let it slide. I think about my notebook and where I left off… with Jude watching, waiting.

"So what are you writing?"

"Eli!"

"Come on, you used to share your poetry with me."

"I know, but this isn't poetry. I'm just journaling. Like writing a diary." Not exactly.

"You're writing about Jude, huh?"

I don't say anything.

"She killed herself right?"

I just nod. I don't want to have this conversation.

"Do you remember the last time you saw her?"

"No," I lie, "I don't." He looks puzzled, so I quickly say, "It was so long ago."

"Yeah, but, you have to remember when she wasn't around. You had to wonder about it."

"Eli, I was in college then," another lie, "I'd left Harmony. She killed herself after I left Harmony."

"Oh. Sorry."

"It's okay." I fight back the tears I don't know why they're coming. Because I just lied to Eli and this is the state of our relationship, or because of Jude.

"Hey, I'm sorry." He wraps his arms around me and I let loose. Crying into his pjs that smell like sleeping human with a touch of his cologne. After the sobbing stops he softly says, "Why did this girl mean so much to you?"

I feel embarrassment rise up from my feet, into my thighs, stomach, chest, neck, and face. I gently pull away from him. "I don't know."

He looks at me for a minute as if I may come up with an answer, then gives up, I guess, and tries to get lost in the newspaper on the counter. He pours himself some coffee. When he settles in a bit, I go to the couch and open up the journal.

"A diary, huh?" He says behind me. "If you ever want to share anything…"

"Yeah," I say softly. "I'm going to take a shower," I try to hide the fact that I'm holding the journal tight to my chest.

"So early?"

"I have an appointment."

"Oh." Eli feels uncomfortable about my appointments.

When I get to the bedroom, I find myself looking for a hiding spot for the notebook.

Not under the mattress, he'd look there. Not tucked behind books on the bookcase; he'd look at the bookcase. Not in my closet or the laundry basket, or in one of my drawers.

I put it in my messenger bag because that will go with me.

As Eli shuffles the paper in the kitchen, I bring the messenger bag into the bathroom with me and cry as quietly as I can.

I sit in the lobby of the therapist's office. The walls are dark blue and there are no windows. Why would she and her partners choose this wall color? Is it meant to be soothing? My cell phone rings. It's Eli. I know I should answer it, but I can't bring myself to do it. I swallow hard and flip the phone closed. I'll tell him I was already in seeing the doctor, that my appointment started early. It'll just be one more lie that I don't understand why I tell.

The door opens and one of the other therapists comes out with a client. Thank god it's not Dr. Vonda. I'm not ready for her yet. The shrink and client say good-bye. I watch the client walk out then look back at the shrink. She's still there, smiling at me. I shift in my chair as I politely smile back. She turns and walks down the hall, back to her office.

I suppose I'll have to tell Dr. Vonda about my little encounter with Eli last night and this morning. I'll have to tell her about the notebook safely tucked away in my messenger bag. And I suppose she'll take his side. She always does.

I lean my head back on the wall. My eyelids are so heavy they just close automatically.

Jude is riding her skateboard. It's nighttime and she's riding down 16th street, just a block away from the store. Funny how images come to mind. At that time of night, she probably went down the street where streetlights lit every corner. She rode all the way downtown; a mile, a mile and a half maybe. She'd jump off the skateboard around 5th and Main, just before the police station. Just in case. She walked back to the alley. The opera house was just a few blocks away from the police station, so she kept an eye out for the "fuzz."

As the metal scraped the cement, she would pry open the door and duck into the dark space.

I open my eyes and check my cell phone. Ten minutes until my appointment. I take the notebook out of my messenger bag and start writing:

> There was a pop then a flare as Jude struck the match on the "Phil's Tavern" matchbook. She lit her cigarette first, then the lantern she stole from Emma's barn.
>
> The lantern provided little warmth, so she zipped up her jacket and put her free hand in her coat; the other hand was helping her finish off a cigarette. "Just my luck," she thought, "coldest fucking September in fifty years." She pulled the newspaper with that headline close to her and read the news once again. "Fuck!" She thought it was ridiculous that was what was on the front page. All the fucking tragedies that happen to people everyday and that's the fucking headline.
>
> She wadded up the paper, then stuffed it into the ten-pound potato bag she dug out of the trash at the back of the store. She wadded up the next page of the paper and the next and the next and shoved each wad into that plastic bag. One, two, three newspapers went in, then she closed up the bag and squished it down.
>
> "Shit!" she said. She'd need one, or two more newspapers before this would be right. Good enough for now.
>
> She threw the newspaper-filled bag on top of the pile of clothes she had gathered over the course of several weeks. Clothes she dug out of the drop box in front of Goodwill. It was like a garbage can, this drop box, a brown metal container. "After-Hour Donations," it read on the front. Jude watched one Sunday afternoon, when this robust, older woman pulled bags and bags of clothes out of the trunk of her car. The clothes of her dead husband maybe? The woman couldn't lift the clothes into the dumpster, so she just left them outside.
>
> Jude watched. And waited. After the woman left, Jude grabbed one bag, not too heavy, then another. She dragged these through downtown alleys, about four blocks, back to the incinerator. She dumped the clothes out into piles, sorted through them in case there were any she wanted (there rarely

were); she picked out a few men's shirts and a pair of men's slacks that hung off her body awkwardly then laid the rest of the clothes in a neat pile against one wall of the incinerator.

Jude plopped down on the pile of clothes, holding the cigarette close to her face. It provided little warmth. She pushed the toe of her boot against a sticker on the cement wall to the side of her new makeshift bed. She couldn't tell what it said, but the red sticker had the word "family," and "s," and "en." She rubbed the sticker with the toe of her boot and tried to imagine what it originally said. It looked to be about twenty years old, so that would put it in the 1950s.

"Family" was the second word; "en" was somewhere in the middle; the "s" was at the end.

"Our Family is Often the Worst," Jude said aloud, then laughed to herself, thinking of *Leave it to Beaver*, and *Father Knows Best*, and all that crap.

She moved her foot and worked on taking out "family" first. "Father fucking knows best," she said as she kicked at the "y."

A shiver ran through her. She pulled her jacket up tighter and lay down on the pile of clothes. "Alison Bullshit," she said to herself. What was it really? Jude smiled as she thought of the girl at the store. "Alison Boo…" Jude really tried to remember now. "Boo…shhhhh…." She stamped her cigarette out on the wall, mindlessly making a circle with the ash. "Boo…shhhh….ittttt!"

It surprises me that I remember this is how she whispered my name—the name she gave me in the dark. Her breath in my ear, the "shhhhhhh" long and soft, the "t" at the end always tickled.

I suddenly feel a tingle up my thighs so I shift my thoughts. I relax back into the chair and stare at my notebook while I think of the metal… the metal rattling around Jude—Jude listened to the rhythm of it shaking around her. One piece of rusting metal clanked, clanked, clanked against another piece of rusting metal. It was somewhere above her. I start writing again.

Jude shifted her body to avoid a lump of clothes digging into her side. Then she felt cold cement on her hand, so she shifted again. There was a musty old shirt under her neck. She tried to ignore it, but the smell itched in her nose. Jude sat up. "Shit!" She was suddenly so tired. Too tired to deal with this.

Dr. Vonda puts her hand on my shoulder and says my name. I practically jump out of my chair. Dr. Vonda smiles at me as I look at her. "Ready?" she asks with a smile—the same smile the other therapist gave me. What, do they learn this in school? I follow her down a narrow hallway with all the doors shut. I dread the appointments. Jude would think this ridiculous.

"A shrink, Ally?" she'd say.

"Sit down," Dr. Vonda instructs. She looks down at my hands and says, "I see you have a journal with you. What are you writing about?"

Not her too?

Before I know it, I launch into telling her about Jude's death, and Jude would have hated that. "Waa, waa, waa, I have a problem. Boo fucking hoo," she'd say.

I readjust the pillow behind my back as I sit on the couch facing Dr. V and then she asks the same question Eli asked this morning, looking over her glasses at me, "Why does this girl's death mean so much to you?"

How does she know it means so much to me? I haven't shed one tear. Can she see that my hands are shaking? "I don't know, she was my friend."

"But she's been out of your life for awhile now."

She holds her pen in her hand, waiting for some gem to come out of my mouth. Just once, I'd love to see her notes.

"Well she…she just disappeared one day. Left our friendship behind…" Lies, lies, lies. "I always wondered what happened to her. I thought she ran away, but now she's dead."

"How do you feel about the fact that she killed herself?"

"I don't know," I stare at an assorted collection of rocks in a little Zen garden thing on a shelf. "I guess I feel…bad."

"Why?"

"Because, maybe I could've done more."

Then Dr. Vonda goes into this whole thing about how I'm responsible for myself and Jude was responsible for herself and there are things that people carry around that we never know about and we can't save everyone and besides I was only eighteen-years-old and blah blah blah. And I know she's right, but I'm not telling her the whole story either. I don't want to tell her the whole story. I'm not telling her what really happened between us. I'm not telling her about how I left Jude that one night, and how badly I treated her.

"She must have had amazing survival skills."

"Who? Jude?" My mouth is so dry. I swallow twice to try to take the burn out of my throat. "Yeah, she knew how to take care of herself, for sure." I get a glimpse of Jude. Standing like James Dean as she smoked a cigarette and leaned against a brick building, one leg bent so that her foot could rest on the building.

"How did she take care of herself?"

I know how she did it. Jude told me the stories about the lady at Goodwill who helped her.

"Ally?" Dr. Vonda moves her head and tries to put herself in my sight. "How did she take care of herself?"

I swallow again. Why is it so dry in here? Why doesn't she have any water here? "She just did. She lived in the incinerator."

"What incinerator?"

"The one at the back of the opera house in Harmony. Well, it used to be an opera house, then there was this grocery store that was there for like, twenty-five years, but they closed down when I was little. I guess that's why there was an incinerator." I can't seem to stop talking.

Dr. Vonda looks a little shocked, and she keeps nodding. "She was very resourceful."

Isn't this session over yet? I can't believe how scattered my thoughts are. "Yeah, she was."

"So you know it's not your fault?"

"Yeah." I look at the clock.

"You don't sound too convinced."

I take a deep breath. "No, I know it wasn't my fault."

"Well, we're out of time for today."

Thank god.

"Is she who you're writing about?"

I nod.

"Well, why don't you spend some more time writing and thinking about this and we can talk about it more next week if you need to."

Won't be too hard to think about it. I didn't even tell her about Matt and Bobby, or Ben, or whatever his name is. My impending interview. I rip a check out of my checkbook. "Okay, see you next week." Forced cheerfulness. Can Dr. Vonda tell that I just want to gather my things and get the hell out of here as soon as I can?

"When's closing night?"

"Oh, um, Sunday." I back my way toward the door. Dr. Vonda stands confidently with her hands folded in front of her. I fumble with my jacket, trying to find the arm hole.

"I've got tickets tomorrow. I've heard it's good." Why does she look so tall right now?

"Well, Tennessee Williams," found the arm hole! "How can you go wrong?" I've got my jacket on and now we can say our good-byes and I'm free. Out into the fresh air of a fall day in Minneapolis.

My heart is pounding as I leave the building. I pull my collar up against the wind and head toward the coffee shop. My latest ritual after a session with Dr. Vonda. But I don't feel like I can sit down right now. My hands are still shaking and I don't even know why. So I step across the street and into the park. Leaves are falling from the trees, drifting down to the ground, leaving piles of reds and oranges across the grass. The wind is cool so I shove my hands into my pockets and hunker up my shoulders. But I have to walk. I need to shake off some of this excess energy.

When I realize how fast I'm walking, I slow my pace. Geez, Loring Park isn't that big; the way I'm walking I'll get around it in five minutes. So I slow my pace and take time to pay attention to the gold and red leaves blowing across the sidewalk in front of me.

A homeless man is in the fetal position on a bench next to the pond. He's dressed in black and has his back to me. His hand rests on his shoulder as if he's hugging himself.

I look away from him quickly and stop on the bridge over the pond, looking at the building I just left. Then I look back at the man and swallow the lump in my throat. I search his face for something familiar. It's habit. All these years I've spent looking for Jude in the faces of homeless people, men or women.

I look down at my hands and wonder why I didn't think she pulled herself out of a life on the streets. I hoped she would, and I looked for her. I really, honestly, thought she would end up in New Orleans. Or in San Francisco. But, we talked about New Orleans so often on those nights we'd huddle together.

"Tell me a story, Ally." Bodies close, arms interlocked, breath mixing together. It was so cold. That's why we did it. Just because it was so freakin' cold. My throat aches.

My cell phone rings and I almost hope it's Eli. And dread that too. I frantically dig the phone out of my coat pocket. It's Mom again. Calling from work this time.

"Hi Mom." I try to sound cheerful. She can always detect sadness in my voice.

"Ally? It's Mom."

She doesn't quite understand caller ID. "Hi Mom." Not as cheerful this time.

"What's wrong, honey?"

"Nothing."

"I've got Ben and Matt here."

I wait for a minute, but she doesn't say anything more.

"Yeah…?"

"They want to talk to you."

Again another long pause, I'm thinking she's handing the phone to them.

"Hello?"

"Ally?" It's still Mom.

"So am I talking to them now?"

"Yeah, just a minute."

A man's deep voice comes on the line and he introduces himself as Detective Sampson, Harmony Police Department. I didn't even know they had detectives in Harmony. And he sounds so official for a guy who hangs out at a truck stop. "We're trying to track down any living relatives for Miss Jude Jenkins," his official-sounding voice declares.

"I don't know any," I say quickly, maybe too quickly as I try masking my lie. The last thing Jude would have wanted was her father to control the end of her life.

But I don't have to worry about that. Matt, or Ben, this Sampson guy told me they found Jude's dad and that he died in 1989.

Bastard, I think. Serves him right.

"There are no other relatives you know of?" He has a monotone voice reminiscent of *Dragnet* and I work to suppress a laugh rising up my esophagus.

I clear my throat instead. "No," another little tickle suppressed by a cough, "I don't know of—" but then I remember. The story Jude told me one of those nights we spent together. There was a woman, a relative of Jude's mother. "Wait, there is someone."

"Ma'am?"

I try to push this *Dragnet* guy out of my immediate thoughts and think back on what Jude told me, but, "I can't really remember right now…"

Then this Detective Sampson starts rambling on about how Emma was going to be buried in a public grave and as he's talking with that dry, monotone voice of his, my mind wanders.

Jude once told me about her Aunt Betty's house—she didn't live in Harmony, she lived in… in…Columbus, I think. Jude and her dad visited Aunt Betty when Jude was ten years old. She said she remembered the smell of fresh-baked cookies following her aunt out of the kitchen. Her aunt held the plate in front of Jude and said, "Go on, take one." Aunt Betty's voice was soft and sweet. She even had a little southern accent. Jude looked at her father, who nodded his approval. So Jude took one and let it melt on her tongue. Her cousins sat quietly enjoying the cookies. One cousin was older than Jude by a year, and one was younger by a year. The other two were much younger. And even though there were four of them, they fell in line, as if Aunt Betty had trained them for this very moment.

Jude looked out the big picture window at her uncle's semi (he was a trucker); the semi was parked by an old maple tree—its trunk wider than any tree Jude had ever seen. Her uncle went on week-long trips across the country and Aunt Betty told Jude's father that maybe someday the kids could go with him, one by one.

"I thought she meant me too," Jude told me. "I was so stupid, you know? I cried for two days when my dad told me she only meant their own kids. But I kept thinking, maybe if they got to know me better, he'd take me in the semi too. But we never saw them again after that trip."

Her aunt went back into the kitchen, calling the oldest daughter with her. Jude stared at the clock on the wall. Her youngest cousin said, "A little bird comes out on the 6 and the 12." Jude watched the clock hopefully.

"I thought they were so rich. Jesus, they had a clock with a bird! And Aunt Betty wore an apron! But they weren't. Hell, Highway 30 was just beyond their backyard. They only acted rich."

"So what happened?" I asked Jude.

"I never saw them again. Dad said they were too high-falutin' for us. It made him feel stupid." (That's when I saw her kicking that family sticker with the toe of her boot.) "Even though I begged him to go back there; I kept thinking that's the only way I'd get to know my mom. Aunt Betty looked so much like her, I mean, from what I saw in the pictures. Did I show you a picture of my mom?" Jude pulled a picture from under her Salvation Army pillow. It was a small black-and-white with crumpled corners. She blew on it, rubbed it with the sleeve of her coat, then handed it to me. Her mom looked so much like Jude, only older.

"She's pretty."

"Yeah," Jude took the picture back and looked at it. "Aunt Betty is pretty too. But Dad didn't want to have anything to do with her, so we never went to visit again. Even when Aunt Betty called and asked us to."

"Maybe your Aunt Betty can help you now." I said stupidly, hopefully.

Jude just looked at me, a scenario turning behind her eyes. Then she looked away, "Nah. She'd take one look at me and wonder what kind of cat dragged me in. She'd just call my dad and send me home."

Jude put the photo back under her pillow.

"But I had that one trip and it seemed like I knew my mom better after it. My aunt, she called me over to sit on her lap, you know, just like a mom. And she held me like she really cared. I remember how good she smelled. Like cookies and some kind of fancy perfume. A little bit of hairspray too. She smelled nice.

"I always dreamed of living with her. Especially when Dad…" she looked down at her hands. "I always thought it'd be cool to live with her and my uncle. But my dad always said, 'those…'"

I try to remember now, what the name of the family was. Jude said it right then and there… Wait! It was a street in the French Quarter of New Orleans. So I run through the streets I know so well, from Canal Street into the district—Iberville, Bienville…Bienville? No. Conti, St. Louis, no, Toulouse, definitely not, St. Peter, Orleans, St. Ann, Dumaine. Dumaine! That's it! Jude said, "Those Dumaines have too many mouths to feed. They don't need me."

Now I suddenly realize there is silence on the other end of the phone. "Officer…?"

"Detective," the guy's voice is forceful, then softens, "Sampson."

"Detective Sampson," I correct myself, "Jude's relative—her name is Betty Dumaine. She lives in Columbus, Nebraska, well, at least she did in the 80s. Her husband is a trucker."

"Do you know the husband's name?"

I try to think over the story quickly again; trying to figure out if Jude mentioned her uncle's name. Besides, how many Dumaines can there be in Columbus? "No, sorry," I say. As the detective thanks me, I realize I don't know what's about to happen to Jude. "Officer, I mean, Detective Sampson…? What happens if you can't find her Aunt Betty?"

"Well, ma'am as I told you, Ms. Jenkins's remains will go to the University for medical study."

"What? Why wouldn't Jude be buried too?" And please, not next to her father.

"Well, as I told you," he has become irritated with me now. Like I become irritated with my mother when she doesn't listen, "Because Ms. Jenkins's skeleton is fit for medical study."

"But Emma was buried…"

He takes a deep breath, I can tell I daydreamed through this part too. "Yes, Emma's body was not in a state for cadaver use. It was too decomposed."

Jesus. Nice bedside manner. "Well, if you can't find Jude's aunt, can I pay for her burial?" I know Eli would lecture me about this, but it just doesn't seem right that Jude isn't buried somewhere.

"No ma'am. We need a relative to claim the remains."

"Why?"

"That's the law ma'am. The body is the property of the state until a relative claims it."

Property? Geez. And then I hear my mother's laughter rising in the background. She's close to the phone so I know I'll be passed off any minute.

"How long before I know if you find Jude's aunt?"

"We'll call around in the next few days. No hurry since the remains are skeletal. I'll let your mother know if we find out anything."

"May I call you in a few days myself?" I ask quickly.

"Yes, ma'am. You can reach me at the station: Detective Sampson. Thank you for your help."

"Thank—"

"Ally?" Mom's back on the phone again. "I've gotta go, but we'll talk later." More laughter in the background. It's a regular party over there at the Harmony truck stop. Truck stop! "Mom, do you know…?" The phone goes dead. "Mom?"

A wind snaps at the back of my neck and I turn sideways to cut it. I'm again looking at the homeless man sleeping on the bench and I walk toward him. My hands are freezing. The man looks up at me as I pass by, he has hope for just a minute as I approach, then it disappears. What was that flash of hope? That I'd give him money? That I would say hello? Treat him as human?

Now that I'm past him I wish I would've said hello. But how stupid. What? Is he going to say hello back?

Fuck. It's time for that coffee now. I walk faster than ever as the adrenaline kicks in. Maybe I can find Jude's aunt myself. Maybe I can help Jude now. Maybe I can do something to make things right.

* * * * * * *

I blow on the coffee as I sit down at the computer in the coffee shop. The screen glows in front of me. I swipe my credit card and immediately wrap my hands around the mug. My fingertips kind of burn as they warm up. I click on the internet and it's so simple. There's only one listing for Dumaine in Columbus. Charles Dumaine. Some detective I am!

I call the number immediately and a man picks up. "Hel—" his voice cracks. He clears his throat, "Excuse me, hello?"

Even though I have an extra moment to prepare, I almost forget what I'm doing. Who it is that I'm calling. "Is, is...Betty there?"

"Just a minute. I'll get her for you."

Thank god he didn't ask who was calling. What would I say? How would I describe myself? I guess I still have to.

"Hello?" A cheery voice with a slight Southern accent answers. I suddenly imagine an aproned woman holding a wooden spoon benignly in her hand, or perhaps she's wearing an oven mitt.

"Mrs. Dumaine?"

"Yes."

Jesus, I sound like a telemarketer. I swallow hard. Speak fast! I should've thought this through. What the hell am I doing? I left this mess behind me. Years ago—so far behind. Now, here I am in the middle of it again.

"You don't know me," I say quickly, worried she'll hang up, "but I'm... I was a friend of your niece, Jude."

There's silence on the line and I panic for a moment. "Jude Jenkins, your sister's daughter."

"Yes, of course, I just haven't seen her in years." Betty's voice is soft and I'm glad for that.

"Yeah, I know. I..." Why didn't I call the detective and let him do this? Why was I so impulsive? I take a deep breath. *Just do it, Ally.* "My name's Alison Bouchard." (With a hard "r" and a hard "d.") "Your niece and I used to hang out when we were in high school."

"And you're looking for her? I haven't seen Judy in years."

Judy? I never thought of her as a "Judy." "Yes, I understand," I don't want her to hang up abruptly, so I talk faster. "I have some bad news... about Judy—Jude."

"Yes?" She sounds concerned now.

"They found her. In the back of her Aunt Emma's barn. She kill—" Oh fuck. Why am I delivering this news? "—she's dead. She, it was suicide, I mean, she did it a long time ago, when we were kids, teenagers." Another deep breath. "Jude died."

"Oh no," her aunt says, "I'm so sorry to hear that." I can't tell if her voice is quivering or not. I can't tell if she's sad enough to cry. I want to hang up. "I felt so bad for that little girl. She was too quiet, too... Well, I only saw her a few times, but, after my sister died, that little girl was... withdrawn. She wasn't quite right. I hated to see her go off alone with that father of hers."

I feel my shoulders relax. Relieved Jude won't be rejected again by her family. And now I want to tell Aunt Betty how her instincts were right. I want to get it off my chest after all these years, but Jude vowed me to secrecy.

I will never forget what she told me, or when she told me, or where. Rain dripped in from some rusted spot on the top of the incinerator. It pattered hard on the metal above us. Jude was shivering. I remember her shivering, sucking on her cigarette, her hands shaking. It was so cold. Now I remember it was a late rain, just before Thanksgiving. Then she said, exhaling smoke through her nose, "You can't tell anyone, Alison."

I nodded my head, but that wasn't enough.

She grabbed my shoulders. "Promise me, Ally." She looked in my eyes and I saw her tears welling up, one broke free and rolled down her cheek like a betrayal. "Promise me." She whispered her plea.

"Yeah, of course. I won't tell anyone."

"I don't want to live in that life anymore. No more. Just like I said."

No more. No need to tell anyone now anyway. And Jude definitely wouldn't have wanted Betty to know any of this. I wasn't going to break that promise—not even now.

"She—you always meant a lot to her," I say to Betty. "I don't know if you know that, but she talked about you and how kind you were to her."

"Oh, well, I barely ever saw her. Course, I saw her a lot when my sister was alive, but after that, I only saw her once or twice."

"Well, you made an impression on her."

"Ooooh, that's very sweet of you to say."

"No, it's true," I wait a moment for a response and get another "ooooh" from her, so I go on, "Anyway, here's the problem. She...her body, her skeleton, is at the medical examiner's office in Lincoln. They won't release the body to anyone but a relative." Quick, Ally, say this quickly, "And if they don't find a relative, then they'll give the body, the skeleton, to the university for study. I'd like to have Jude buried next to her mother. She would've wanted that. I can pay for the funeral, but I can't claim the body."

I was expecting resistance. I was expecting a "don't get me involved in this mess" attitude. But I didn't get that at all, instead she asked where the remains were.

"The medical examiner's in Lincoln."

"Who do I call?"

I gave her the detective's name and number in Harmony.

"I'll check with my husband. We might be able to help with those expenses. No sense in you paying for it all, but it's very generous of you."

"I don't mind, really." If she saw where I lived, she wouldn't hesitate to let me pay. "In fact, I insist," I say timidly. When did I become this rich bitch?

"And I'll check into the plot next to my sister. They buried that no-good husband of hers next to her on one side, though—I'm sorry, I know he was Judy's father, but I didn't like him."

I want to say I'm glad his sorry ass is dead, but I don't want her asking questions. I wonder if his undertaker found any scars, any deformities, from his encounter with Jude. "Well, if you could check into the burial plot that would be nice."

I give her my cell phone number and my home phone number, "but my cell phone is the best number to call." I don't tell her it's because I don't want Eli to know what's going on.

"612? Where's that?"

"Minneapolis."

"Minneapolis! Well, isn't that something?"

"So, may I call you later to see what you find out?"

"Oh, sure, dear. I really am sorry to hear about this. I always wondered what happened to that girl." (Emphasis on "that" different from my mother's.) "I prayed for her so many nights."

I don't say anything about the praying. Jude didn't really believe in God. She thought that God wouldn't let so many people suffer so much. I just say good-bye to Betty and thank her for helping.

"Of course. Anything for family," she says.

That image of Jude kicking the red "Family" sticker comes into my head once again. "My Family Softens the Blows." But she keeps kicking the word, intent on erasing "family" completely.

Chapter Four

"Eli?" I open the door cautiously, as if I don't want him to hear me come in. It's three o'clock in the afternoon and I've been out all day, just wandering around downtown. "Baby?" I force the word out. That's what couples call each other isn't it? Baby, sweetie, honey.

He isn't home and I feel relieved. Why? This is ridiculous. I love him. I've loved him since the first time I saw him back in Williamstown twenty years ago.

The message light is blinking. Two messages. I try to ignore it and sort through the mail, but I can't. I hit the button.

"Ally? It's Mom. Say, you won't believe this, but they found that relative of Jude's already. Those fellas down at the station are something else aren't they?"

I shuffle the mail over and over, not really paying attention to what's there.

"She had an aunt in Columbus. She's going to have Jude buried. Isn't that great?"

Keys jiggle in the door.

"Okay. I'll talk to you later." Mom fumbled with the phone and now there are sounds of clunking and a dropped phone on my answering machine until finally the machine stops. Just in time.

"Honey?" Eli drops his keys on the table by the entrance.

"Yeah." I shout back to him and my voice echoes off the high ceilings.

"Hey baby," Eli rounds the corner, then kisses me on the cheek.

"Hey," I continue sifting through the mail.

"Where were you all day?"

I don't know why I almost want to cry as Eli reaches down and pets the cat.

"Just walking around downtown. Early Christmas shopping."

"Christmas shopping?" Eli smiles at me, "Since when do you go Christmas shopping in October? Or shopping at all, for that matter?"

He quickly pushes the flashing message button on the answering machine and I jump to try to stop him, but it's too late.

"Alison?" More scuffling sounds on the phone. "This is Betty Dumaine of Columbus, Nebraska."

"Who?" Eli says.

Well, I can't stop the machine now, so I just shush Eli. "I got in touch with the medical examiner's office and I am able to claim Jude's remains. So why don't we talk about funeral arrangements? I appreciate you…well…" there's an uncomfortable laugh, "…offering to help on that. You know, Bob and I, we're both retired, so it would be a stretch for us. Anyway, please call me at 555-2229." There's a long pause, then her voice comes back on, "that's area code 402. Bye."

"Sounds like you've been busy," Eli is opening the electric bill, hiding a smile.

"I was Christmas shopping too," I say, trying to convince myself of… something.

"So you're helping on the costs of the funeral?"

"Only because they don't have anything, Eli. It's not like there's anything to it. I just, I just want my friend to be buried, that's all." And I suddenly realize that I don't even know how much something like this costs. Just a simple burial. No need to prepare the body, maybe we'll have her cremated. Well, I'll pay for it anyway. No matter what.

"Hey, it's your money," Eli's voice is soft, but I feel needles go into the back of my neck. That's his way of ending arguments about money. He wants the big, nice condo, so we get the big, nice condo. He wants a brand new car, so we get the brand new car. I want a scooter, or a new computer, or an ipod, or a new cell phone; then he reminds me about how he had to pay for this trip or that trip, or for the entire mortgage, or for the whole car, and then he says, "but hey, it's your money."

He continues, "So, when are you going to tell me about her? Am I going to have to call your mom to get the inside scoop?"

Out of Harmony

"No!"

Eli jumps at my abrupt snap.

"No," I force a laugh and grab his arm. "Mom hardly knows anything about her, anyway."

"So? Are you gonna tell me?"

"It's not that big of a deal. I mean, we were friends about a hundred years ago, that's all."

"A friend from a hundred years ago, and you're paying for her burial?"

I look at my watch. "We'll talk later, honey, okay? I've got to get ready for work." I leave him there and walk back to the bathroom and shut the door. Turn on the faucet; make it sound like I'm doing something. Then I panic. What if he does call Mom?

But really, she didn't know—she doesn't know. She only knows that she didn't like Jude. She doesn't really know anything about her, or me for that matter. She was so wrapped up in her own sorrow back then—wallowing in her misery—that she barely paid attention to us. She was absent on... everything: parenthood, her marriage, her house. Her crappy job at the truck stop was the only thing she put any energy into.

By the time we came home from school, she had been home from work for an hour or two. She'd watched *General Hospital* and would be at the end of *Ryan's Hope* when we came in the door. She wouldn't engage in conversation, really. She'd just say, "Hi kids, how was your day," then she'd go upstairs and lie down while we watched tv.

Sometime around five, the front door opened and closed. Dad's bloody boots dropped with a thud onto the plastic tray just inside the door. Mom came downstairs like a ghost and went into the kitchen, just like she was on autopilot. She'd bang a kitchen cabinet and rattle a pan. Another pan rattled. Dad's footsteps sounded on the stairs. The pipes in the kitchen moaned when Mom turned the water on. Dad cleared his throat from the bedroom. The fan over the stove clicked on to the one speed that still worked. The shower came on in the bathroom. The water turned off in the kitchen. The tiny window in the bathroom opened. Something crackled in the frypan in the kitchen. Dad coughed. Mom opened the back door.

There were no "how was your days" or "welcome homes" or even "what a crappy day I had." That was just a given. They'd shared so many crappy days they didn't even like to talk about it anymore. Dad knew that men had pinched Mom and flirted with her and Mom knew that Dad had been ankle deep in blood all day. Her only question could have been—"what was it today, Eric? Cow or pig?" But she didn't want to know; he didn't want to tell.

Dishes rattled. The shower turned off. Silverware clanged. Dad cleared his throat again. Pretty soon, all five of us would be sitting around the table and Mom and Dad would be asking their children, "how was school today?" They wouldn't look at each other, only at us. And they would listen only to avoid each other. And before Dad had finished his hamburger (he could eat only the stuff that was not easily recognizable), Mom was up, washing the dishes. And when he was done, Dad would take his plate to the sink and say "that was good"—not to my Mom, but to the air over her head, and Mom would just give a slight nod, but she would focus on the plate or fork or knife or spoon in her hand.

And this was how it was done. This was how twenty years of marriage looked on people who didn't want to care anymore. All they wanted was some time at the end of the day to watch tv.

Now, as I look through my closet trying to figure out which black outfit to wear to the theatre tonight—I have four—I start to think about the fantasy life I created for my parents, the one in New Orleans. And it wasn't out of disrespect that I imagined my parents different. When I tried to reinvent myself—I had to reinvent them too. They deserved that much.

In our home in the Garden District, we had a cook, and a maid, and a gardener. At the end of the day, Mom would open all of the windows and a breeze would gently blow the curtains into the room. Air moved through the house like a whisper. Mom would sit in the living room, with its twelve-foot-high ceilings and dark wood, reading a book in the afternoon light. She sat in her favorite chair. When she heard my father's footsteps on the front porch, she took her eyes away from her book and smiled as he came in the door. He loosened his tie and said, "Good afternoon sweetie. How was your day?" And mother would excitedly tell him about how her women's group sent a letter to a senator or congressman, or about how they helped a person without means with some unfairness—some major injustice in the world. And Dad sat, relaxed with his shoes off and tie loosened, on the couch across from Mom's favorite chair, and listened, and smiled.

Mom put a bookmark between chapters and set her book aside then asked, "How was your day, dear?" And she listened too, willingly, smiling. And they talked together about racism and the south and what could be done. And the cook (African American, of course) came out of the kitchen and told them it was time for dinner and they rounded up their children and went to the kitchen, relaxed and happy. (And in my youth, I didn't realize how racist this scene was in the first place.)

This is what I dreamed at the kitchen table as I watched my parents move through their world of clanging dishes and cracked linoleum. Of dried sow blood and greasy-smelling uniforms. Maybe this is the story I should be writing down.

"Hey," Eli wraps his arms around my waist and I jump. "Sorry," he laughs softly, resting his chin on my shoulder. "Hey, baby," his voice is a whisper in my ear. He kisses my neck, then turns me around, "Whenever this burial is, of your friend, I think you should go." He looks at me with his blue eyes. A Jew with blue eyes, that's my Eli. That's what I used to say to him when we'd lay in bed and I'd twist his black curls around my finger.

"Well, yeah, I mean, I guess I was kind of planning on it."

He wraps his arm around my waist and pulls me close. I feel myself resist, but then I remember what Dr. Vonda said this morning, "Step into your relationship, Ally."

"I'll pay for your flight home."

I don't say anything as he kisses my earlobe. I could pay for my own flight.

He cups my face between his soft piano-playing hands. "This girl—"

"Jude!" God, I sound like a twelve-year-old. I try to relax into his arms.

"Yeah, yeah, Jude. Well, your show's going to close in a few days, right? So, I was thinking that you should fly home and say good-bye. You can see your mom and catch up, you know. Take a few days and relax."

"Yeah." I swallow a lump that aches in my throat.

"And, then, when you're ready, maybe you can tell me the story about this girl, about Jude."

Eli pulls me close again and I rest my chin on his shoulder. "You can tell me why her friendship was so important to you." He whispers in my ear.

I look out our fifth-floor window. "It's raining," I say, my hands clutching the back of his sweater.

He turns and looks out the window, then moves behind me again. "Remember Portland?" Eli whispers in my ear as his hand follows the curve of my hip.

"The window in the office isn't open, is it?" I pull away from him and run to the den and look at the closed window. I push on it and check the lock, as if some great disaster might happen. Of course it wasn't open. It was too cold out today. "I didn't want rain coming in," I yell out to Eli. The room is getting dark and Eli turns on a light in the living room. I can see my reflection in the glass in front of me.

Eli doesn't say a word. I see his reflection move past the door. After a moment I hear a cupboard open and close. Dishes rattle as he takes them from the dish drainer to the cupboards. I move into the bathroom and turn on the water. In the kitchen, silverware clangs, a pan rattles. I turn off the water and look at myself in the mirror, then quickly look away. There is silence in the kitchen. And more silence. And more. I flush the toilet just to make the silence go away.

Chapter Five

When I get home from work that night, I heat up the other pot pie, the one I got for Eli last night. There's a message on the answering machine. "Hi baby, I'm going out with the guys again for a bite to eat. See you at home in about an hour."

As I shove the pot pie in its measly little container into the oven, I think that the guys seem to be getting a lot of attention lately. I look at my cell phone and see there's no message. Why didn't he call my cell phone? Who are "the guys" anyway?

I fight back the feelings of jealousy, and the thoughts that Eli has a lover.

Mozart meows at me and stretches her paw up onto my leg. I reach down to pet her and look across the room where a shadow moves across the wall from a passing car at the top of the hill. Squares of light cross over the piano.

"Someday I'm gonna learn to play," Jude said to me once, "Piano, drums, guitar, bass—everything."

I take the journal out of my messenger bag. The timer on the oven counts down from forty minutes.

"Chapter Two," I scribble at the top of the page.

Who am I kidding? There is no chapter two. There's not even a chapter one. Just writings…stories…remembrances.

Okay. I write the heading, "Jude." I tap, tap, tap the pen on the page. I could write about the music, but the words I've resisted come out instead. I scratch "Jude's Relationship with Father" across the top of the page. The ink sinks deep into the paper.

The first words come out. I write "No more," and stare at those two words.

This isn't what I want to write. Not at all. I don't want to sit in Jude's darkness. But there are some secrets I carry for her that weigh me down. There are some memories that won't go away no matter how hard I try.

Fuck it! I don't have to write this.

I scratch the words out, one by one, until a block of ink sits over each word. My jaw is clenched so tight that my teeth ache. I try to move on but those blocks of ink stain the part of my hand that rests on the page and I bring the stain with me to the blank lines below.

I rip out the page, crumple it up, and throw it on the ground where Mozart bats it around.

I rub the ink off the heel of my hand, from knuckle to wrist, and stare at the page. Then I just start writing.

>Jude immersed her hand in the water up to her wrist. She watched it move, suspended between the sand and the top; pulsing gently with the rhythm of the water.
>
>"Hey," she said, "what's your favorite, all-time band?"
>
>"I don't know," I said quickly, not thinking about it at all. Sweat rolled down my face; it was hot that day. Summer was closing in on us. We were sitting on a sand bar in the middle of the Platte River.
>
>"Mine's—Heart. Well, that's my new favorite band. My old favorite band is the Steve Miller Band."
>
>I watched her hand suspended in the shallow water, the surface crossing her wrist. She could sit like that for hours. I'd seen her do it. But not this time. She stood up, brushed the sand off her butt, and moved toward the shore.
>
>"Come on, Ally."
>
>She waded toward the bank on the other side of the river.
>
>I was always afraid there'd be a sudden drop-off somewhere in the river, a place where the water would suck me in and never give me back.
>
>But not Jude, she forged ahead, fearlessly. The river didn't scare her. She had a relationship with it.

There was a shady spot on the bank, a place tucked away from land traffic. She sat down and I sat next to her.

"Where are you gonna go, Ally?" She whispered it like it was a secret between us.

"I told you, Kearney."

"No, I don't mean school." She seemed mad all of the sudden.

"What do you mean?"

"What are you going to do?"

"Study theatre."

"And then?"

"I don't know, find a job, move away from here. L.A. or New York."

"What about New Orleans? You always talk about it."

"They don't have a lot of theatre in New Orleans. I mean, my options are limited."

Jude snuggled up next to me and took my arm. "You know what I think we should do?"

"What?"

"Forget about college. Forget about New York and L.A." Her voice was almost a whisper. She pointed her rough hand up toward the bluff. "We should jump in your car and go to New Orleans. Right now. Today. Just drive away and never come back."

"Yeah, but, what will we do?" My throat was dry and I felt my arm quiver in the strength of her hands.

"Who cares? We'll find something, anything. We'll fill our lives with music. We'll just go and see what happens."

Even though she was whispering, her voice was strong, and joyful. I'd never heard that kind of lilt in her voice before.

"I don't know…"

"Come on, Ally!" She tugged at my arm. "Let's get out of this town. We could be sitting by the Mississippi River tomorrow."

"But I graduate in two weeks."

Her voice went back to normal. "So? You think a few more weeks are going to make you smarter?"

"No, but I think a high school diploma will at least help me get a better job. Plus, I've got my family—"

"How old are you?"

I swallowed hard. I knew what she was getting at. "Eighteen."

"And?"

"And I can't just leave my family." I stood up, pulling my arm away from her. "And I will graduate."

"Okay, fine," she stood up and grabbed my shoulders so we were eye to eye. "Then after you graduate. Let's go."

"Jude—"

"Okay, whatever." She left me there on the shore and waded back into the river. Her rolled-up pants were getting soaked because she seemed to be sinking deeper.

The oven beeps at me. I leave Jude in the river as I put oven mitts on my hands. I flip the pot pie out of its tin and onto my plate. I poke one hole in the top and watch the steam pour out into the air in front of my face.

I like to hold my face over the steam whenever I have a cold and try to breathe in the moisture to relieve the pressure. But the steam can't take away the weight in my head right now.

I blow on my first bite and tap my pen on the page. I'm reluctant to write what's next. I blow on the bite of pot pie again and again. I'm tempted to leave Jude there, wading away from me, but as I take the first bite of pot pie, I flip my pen over and write:

"Jude!" I stood up and followed her into the river. She moved faster than I did, so I couldn't quite keep up. "Jude! Wait!"

She stopped and looked into the water beneath her—it was up to her knees—then she just dropped. She fell back into the river as if she could float on that little bit of water; her butt sank down to the bottom.

I looked down on her sunlit face; her long hair was dipped back into the water.

"I'll go to New Orleans with you."

She squinted one eye up at me. "Alison Bullshit."

"No, really, after I graduate. Fuck college."

Jude looked at me hopefully, with a rare smile crossing her face.

"Another pot pie?" Eli kisses my neck and I practically throw my writing hand into his face.

"Eli! You scared the shit out of me."

He laughs.

"Seriously!" I say, trying to laugh it off with him. I pull the journal to my chest.

Eli kisses the other side of my neck.

"You smell like alcohol," I say as I quickly pull away.

"One beer." He sits on the stool next to me, his foot on the rung of my stool. "Come here often?"

"What time is it?" I try to look behind me at the microwave clock.

He glances over. "1:22."

"You closed the bar?"

"They're open 'til three these days, Ally. Where've you been?"

"At home, eating pot pies." I wave my fork in the air, then smack it down on the counter.

"Geez. What's with you?"

"Nothing," I try to soften my tone, "I'm tired."

"Hey," he grabs my hands and pulls me into the living room. "Let's dance."

"What?!?"

He runs over to the receiver and pushes the power button. Classical music fills the room so he starts looking through the cds. "Let's dance. We haven't danced in a long time."

"Eli. It's one thirty in the morning. I'm not dancing now." I head toward the bedroom, the journal clutched to my chest.

"Come on! What happened to the old Ally that used to dance at midnight with me?"

I try to bite the words into my tongue, but they come out anyway. "You mean the same one who used to eat dinner with you at eleven thirty? That Ally?"

Eli's animation disappears; his arms fall to his side. "What's that supposed to mean?"

It seems clear to me. I keep walking.

"Ally!" My name echoes across the cavernous room. "You have something to say, so say it!"

"I hate eating dinner alone, that's all!" I yell back like a fifteen-year-old and I hate the way my voice reverberates. Even the piano next to me hums from my voice.

"Well, then why don't you come out with me?" He keeps yelling across the room. He just stands there in the same place, not taking one step toward me.

"I've never been invited." I yell back. I think that's true. Isn't it?

"I've asked…!" Then he turns his back to me and shuts off the cd player. "Whatever!" He doesn't look at me; he just dismisses me with a wave of his hand.

I stare at his back as he walks away from me. I don't know who's being unreasonable here, so I go to the bedroom and plop, stomach-down, on the bed with the journal in front of me.

The tv mumbles on the other side of the door.

I try to block it out. Is he mad at me? I think about going out there to apologize. But do I have anything to apologize for? Except for blurting things out? Why doesn't he apologize to me for once? My pen is tapping rapidly on the closed journal in front of me.

I open the journal to where I left off. I read over my words on the page, over and over again, trying to forget what just happened with Eli.

I start to trace over the words, "I'll go to New Orleans with you." I make the o's bigger, rounder. I triple-cross the t's. I stare at the words on the page. Was it really a promise?

I feel this empty space that used to be filled with guilt. It's just hollow now, as if guilt carved out a hole in the walls of my chest and then abandoned it. But the hole remains. Every now and then, this tingle washes over my chest like when you stand too close to the edge of a large drop off. It's inside, this tingle, bristling my ribs.

The floor creaks next to the bed and I look to see if Eli is trying to sneak up on me again, but no one's there. "Mozart," I whisper, but Mozart isn't there either. The floor creaks again.

Tell me a story, Ally. Goose bumps rise on my skin.

"Tell me a story," Jude's voice was soft whenever she asked.

I know what story she wants. The same one I told her a thousand times. It used to distract her from what her father did to her; now it distracts me from what I did to her. So I start writing:

"They danced."

I tap my pen on the page again, thinking of how stupid this story is—how adolescently romantic. *Tell me a story.* The voice is insistent now.

> They danced like they were at a great ball, thrown by King Louis-Philippe at the palace in Versailles. Elizabeth and Jacqueline held each other and danced around the room—

Jacqueline wearing her most expensive gown with long white gloves. Elizabeth, her hair pulled back away from her face, her thumb resting on the back of Jacqueline's left hand; Elizabeth's left arm strong, bearing the weight of Jacqueline's right arm. They danced in circles—Elizabeth guiding Jacqueline around the room, strong but gentle. Elizabeth's left hand splayed across Jacqueline's petite right shoulder, they turned around and around, giggling at times—waltzing, ballroom dancing, close but not too close.

"Don't go to America," Jacqueline whispered, her lips brushing Elizabeth's ear.

Elizabeth didn't reply; she spun Jacqueline around and gently released Jacqueline's weight down across her knee. Elizabeth looked down into Jacqueline's deep brown eyes. She held her like that, feeling how Jacqueline relinquished into the movement. Elizabeth pulled Jacqueline back up slowly. She pulled Jacqueline toward her body and her lips landed on Jacqueline's. Softly. They broke apart before Elizabeth was even sure that she followed through with the kiss.

Jacqueline smiled. Then pulled Elizabeth toward her and kissed her in a way that Elizabeth could never forget. Teeth clicking, tongues tied, full-lipped. Soft.

Elizabeth gave in, her gloved hands running along the sides of Jacqueline's breasts…"

"Writing again?" Eli's voice comes from the doorway.
I shut my journal. Quick. "Yes."
Elizabeth went to America in the end anyway.
"Come on. What are you writing?" He climbs into bed next to me.
"Eli, you'll wrinkle your tux."
Jacqueline was left behind.
"Come on, Ally. Share it with me."
I feel pulled by everything around me. I used to share my poems with Eli, but I don't want to share this.
"Eli. Would you stop? It's personal, what I'm writing."
"Personal? I thought you were writing stories."
"Well, yeah, but—"
"At least tell me what kind of stories you're writing."
"Fiction."

He laughs. Just a short, brief little outburst of a laugh, but laughing nonetheless.

I feel shame wash over my face. I've always wanted to write stories. I wanted to write like Flannery O'Connor or Eudora Welty—one of those great Southern writers. Or Tennessee Williams. My kin.

Maybe that's just stupid.

I roll over, hug my journal, and close my eyes. "Eli," I try to muster the strength.

"Yeah baby?" His voice is almost a whisper. I can still smell the alcohol on his breath.

Then I say something unexpected—for both of us. "What if I take the next couple of shows off?"

"You want to take the next show and the one after that off?" We'd talked about me taking the next show off already. "That's the rest of the season, right?"

I nod. "I'd like to take some writing classes and…" I open my eyes to see Eli listening intently. "…and I'm just tired of theatre. I need to figure out if there's something else I want to do."

He smiles slightly. "Sure, baby. Take all the time you need."

"I've got money in savings; I'll still be able to pay my share of the bills."

"Don't worry about it sweetie. I'll take care of you. I make enough money for the both of us."

I feel heat rise into my head. "I know, but, I want to keep up my end of the bargain." Oh god, my voice sounds timid and shy. Like the voice of a woman who tells her man she's scared of something. I'm not scared.

He just laughs again and says "Ally." Almost as if he's embarrassed. Then he crawls off the bed and goes to the bathroom.

As I replay this whole awful thing between us tonight, the toilet flushes.

I can feel the bed shake with every beat of my heart.

I close my eyes again. I don't feel satisfied. I don't even feel happy to get some time off.

Maybe I'll never be happy.

Chapter Six

I'm in the greenroom all by myself. Sleep was on and off all night and I wish I could take a nap—just plop down on one of the greenroom sofas and fall asleep. I decide to call Mom instead, to see what's new with Matt and Ben. But the conversation with Mom is as satisfying as my sleep last night.

"I tried to tell them what it is you do at the theatre, but I don't understand it very well."

"I'm a stage manager, Mom."

"Well, I know you're a stage manager, but that doesn't mean much to me."

"Mom, I've told you—I make sure the actors are onstage when they're suppose to be—"

"Well, they're adults. Seems like they should know when to be onstage."

"Mom—they don't hang out in the wings when they're not onstage. They're back in the greenroom or in the dressing room. Or sometimes they have to make a quick change and it's my job to tell them how much time they have left."

"Well, I don't understand it very well."

I sigh, but try again. I know she can get this. "Or all the light cues and sound cues—I make sure they all happen when they're supposed to. It's like

I'm a conducter—like Eli. You've seen him work," And she did once. "It's like that—I pull all the pieces together."

"I don't understand what Eli does either. It doesn't even seem like those musicians look at him. It seems like he just dances around and looks silly and they all ignore him."

"Well, Mom, why do Matt and Ben even need to know what I do for a living?"

"Well, because I'm proud of you; even if I don't understand very well what it is you do."

I don't think I'll ever get my mother to understand—so I finally give up. And I'll try to explain it again the next time she asks.

"Oh, by the way," she says just before I'm about ready to hang up, "I talked to Betty and she said—"

"Betty?"

"Jude's aunt. You know, you talked to her a few days ago."

"You talked to her?"

"And she told me that they're going to bury Jude next week. I told her that should be okay for you because your show shuts on Saturday—"

"It closes on Saturday," I correct her.

"Well, shuts, closes, whatever. But the burial is on Thursday. So are you coming home for it?"

Why didn't Betty call me? Of course, Mom probably called Betty first, getting the phone number from Matt and Ben, and she said, "Oh, don't you worry, I'll tell Ally when the burial is—"

"What time Thursday?"

"Oh, I don't know." And she never gets all the facts. "I'm sure you can call the funeral home and find out."

"What funeral home?"

Silence.

"Mom?"

"Well, I'll ask around and find out for you."

"Thanks. Mom, I've gotta go back to work. I'll talk to you later."

Exasperated, I click my cell phone shut as I plop down on a chair in the greenroom.

"Trouble at home?" Softie pour herself a cup of coffee. I didn't even see her come in.

"Oh…ah…no." I wave my cell phone. "My Mom."

Softie laughs. "Oh yeah. Moms."

"Yeah…" I feel awkward. I never seem to know how to talk to the crew.

Tom comes in. He's a big guy—tall and broad. He's the sound guy. They call him "Bulldozer."

I wonder why they don't have a nickname for me. Ally. That's it. Sometimes Al—just like at home.

Tom starts to bullshit with Softie and she bullshits back.

Alison Bullshit. If only they knew that was once my nickname.

Then I say something. Just the first thing that comes to mind. "Did it hurt to get that tattoo?"

Softie and Tom look at me in shocked silence. They look at each other like, "she speaks?" They weren't even talking about tattoos.

"That one, on your wrist, did it hurt?"

Softie looks down at her right wrist where a dragon wraps its tail. The tattoo starts by her elbow and ends on the back of her hand. It's a pretty green, kind of an emerald.

"No, not really." Softie examines her wrist.

That's what people with lots of tattoos always say.

"I was thinking of getting one—on my shoulder blade, but it seems like it would hurt."

Yeah. Right. I gave up on that tattoo idea about five years ago.

Softie stands up from her position on the arm of the couch and walks toward me.

"It's not that bad, really. People always think it hurts more than it does. I take it you're a virgin?"

My face rises in temperature.

Softie laughs. "A tattoo virgin."

"Oh, yeah, I guess."

"You want to touch it?" She says in a low voice. Then she kneels down and extends her arm to me.

I catch my breath. "Oh, shit, look what time it is—" I swallow hard. "I need to get back to work." I quickly stand up and brush past her. "Excuse me."

When I get out into the hallway, I listen for Tom and Softie to laugh, but they don't. They just continue their conversation. I hope I don't become one of their jokes. Jesus. See—that's why I don't talk to the crew. They're just so much younger than I am.

I take my messenger bag and my coat and go through the wings. It's an hour before curtain so there's no one back here yet; I have just a few minutes before the crew comes in, though. They'll need to check props and costumes. For now, I turn on the light at my desk stage left, throw my headset around my neck, and open up my journal.

But I can't write. I'm only thinking about the funeral. What do they do at a funeral when there's only a skeleton? And who's going to cry for Jude now? Her Aunt Betty?

I bite my bottom lip to keep it from quivering.

Then I start to write down numbers. If I use my next paycheck for the funeral, I'll have to take some money out of savings to cover the rest. Maybe I should have taken Eli's offer of help. I suppose I could grovel and ask him to cover the utilities this month. I hate the fact that I feel financially capable because of Eli's money.

But anyway, is it my fault our utility bills are so high because of a 3,000-something square-foot condo? I would have been perfectly content in something smaller.

One of the crew members is clunking around on stage right, then leaves.

I close my eyes and push my fingers into my temples. It feels good to close my eyes; I'm so freaking tired. I listen to the heat kick on in the theatre and suddenly I notice how cold it is in here. A shiver runs down my back.

An image jumps into my head. I pick up my pen.

> Jude shivered in the rain. Her hair was plastered to her face and she peeled the hair off like tape and pushed it back over her ears as rain dripped over her long eyelashes. She inhaled water.
>
> As she walked through downtown, she opened dumpster lids, checking if they were clean enough for her to climb inside. But they smelled of rotting trash and thick, wet crud. She didn't belong with the trash, no matter what her dad told her. So she kept looking.
>
> She pulled on doors to stairwells; she hung out in the 7-Eleven until the clerk told her to get out; she stood under the eaves of the Goodwill and shivered some more. Then she remembered the abandoned Opera House. She knew the stories of ghosts, but she didn't believe them. She spit into the rain and walked toward the west side of downtown.
>
> The building loomed over her. It was one of the tallest buildings in Harmony. The tallest was five stories; this was three. She pulled on chain-locked doors, she peered into boarded-up windows; she looked up to the second story, trying to figure out how to climb up.

She walked around to the back of the building, all the time looking up. She even got on top of the incinerator and tried to reach a window. When she jumped off the incinerator, the door swung open. She crawled down and looked inside.

No mice or rats. No rank-smelling crud. It was actually pretty clean. She jumped inside. Rain leaked in through a few corners and cracks in the cement, but otherwise, it was pretty dry.

She took off her wet army jacket. A tattoo of a dragon wound its way up her forearm.

The house manager's voice comes over my headset. "Ready to open?"

I put on my headset, set my watch next to the script, and announce to anyone who's listening, "Five minutes to doors."

I just remembered that Dr. Vonda will be at the show tonight. Why does that make me suddenly nervous?

"Christ, she's just a person, Ally." Jude's voice is clear as a bell in my head.

"I know," I whisper to the voice, "but—"

Jesus, I think I am losing it.

The voices on the other side of the curtain fill the theatre. This hollow space is alive with voices now.

Softie takes her place in the wings at the prop table. Of course it's on my side of the stage. She smiles at me and waves like a little kid; not like someone who has dreads and sports tattoos. I hope she didn't hear me whispering to myself. I feel myself blush again as I awkwardly wave back.

"Actors, places please," I speak into the microphone. Softie and Tom are talking into the headsets off-speaker so the actors can't hear.

"She's sleeping with some Hollywood guy," Tom's voice is soft in the headset. I know he's talking about one of the actresses because I've heard this rumor kicked around too.

"Like someone famous?" Softie whispers back.

"Yeah, not Brad Pitt, but someone like him."

"Jake Gyllenhall?"

"No."

"Josh Hartnet?"

"No."

"Gabe Kaplan."

I try not to laugh out loud. I wouldn't think Softie would even know who Gabe Kaplan is. "Hey guys," I hate to ruin their fun, but we've got a job to do, "let's focus on the show."

"Later," Softie whispers, I assume to Tom.

The houselights go down. The voices in the audience become quiet.

"Warning lights one, two, three. Warning sound one."

Everything is quiet in the headsets as the actors stand in the wings. Jessie, who plays Maxine, stands next to me waiting to go on. She gives me a slow-motion wave of her fingertips as she tiptoes past. She doesn't smile because she's in character already. "Standby lights one, two, three. Standby sound one."

Softie lights a cigarette for Jessie/Maxine. Softie cups her hand as if there's a breeze and holds the flame up to Jessie/Maxine's face. Softie whispers something in Jessie/Maxine's ear and Jessie/Maxine blows smoke into the air as she smiles.

"Ally?" Jeff, the lighting guy, whispers into the headset. The house is quiet. Everything is dark. Shit! *Focus Ally.*

"Uh," I clear my throat. "Go lights one, two, three. Go sound one."

Jessie/Maxine steps onto the stage to meet Daniel, who plays Shannon. I glance at Softie who stands next to me and she watches Jessie/Maxine move onstage. Is something going on between them? Jessie is a good thirty years older than Softie. God, couldn't be. Softie looks at me for a second and smiles.

I look back to my script. Where are they? Geez.

I get myself back into it just in time. "Warning lights four through seven." *Gotta focus Ally. Gotta stay focused.*

Softie moves back to the prop table. She wears the black outfit of a stagehand: black low-rider jeans which fit her twenty-something body perfectly, and a black t-shirt.

"Ready lights four through seven." Jeff again.

God! "Go lights four through seven. Thanks Jeff."

"Something wrong?" Jeff whispers as his light cues synch perfectly with what's going on onstage. He saved my ass that time.

"Nothing." I whisper back and try to focus on the script in front of me.

"Good show guys," I say as I walk past Softie and the other techies who are standing outside the stage door smoking. A cold rain is spitting down and they seem unfazed. I throw my hood up over my head. No walking home for me tonight.

"Hey Ally," Softie suddenly walks next to me. "I was sorry to hear about your friend."

"What?" I stop in my tracks.

"That friend of yours who died—"

"Jude."

"Yeah, I'm sorry about that. It seems to be bothering you."

I feel slightly embarrassed that people have noticed. "How did you hear…?"

"My girlfriend runs lights at the orchestra. She knows Eli." Softie seems excited to tell me this news, but I feel exposed. Naked.

"Oh."

"She said he's a nice guy." I look up at the sky and feel little hits of ice on my face. I turn my body to extract myself from this slowly. "Yeah. He is a nice guy."

Softie stares into my eyes for an uncomfortable amount of time. She's wearing a thin jacket and it seems to be enough for her.

I'm shivering. "Well," I keep turning my body slightly.

"Yeah, sorry," she releases me from the conversation.

"See you tomorrow. I've got a bus to catch."

"Yeah, see you."

I don't look back. I take off running for the bus stop as if I'm going to miss it. But the bus is nowhere in sight.

I don't know; I just feel like running.

Sleep doesn't come easily again tonight. Why would it? Eli's not home. It's one thirty. And even worse, I'm not really thinking about him.

"My girlfriend works with Eli," Softie's voice comes into my head. There was something so casual, so familiar about her words. As if we were old friends.

And her girlfriend and Eli talked about Jude. And me. And Jude.

What the hell?

How much does everyone know?

Jude killed herself. Okay. We were friends. Okay.

Jude would've hated everyone talking about her. "It's our secret, Ally."

She would probably even hate it that everyone knows her name. Everything was our secret. That she was abused was our secret. That she lived in an incinerator was our secret. That we…

But that was my secret. "Don't tell anyone, Jude." I pulled the Salvation Army blanket up over my breasts.

"What do you mean?" Jude sat there topless, her nipples firm in the cold air. The cold air didn't even seem to bother her. I didn't get her; sometimes she seemed so shy, but other times… "You don't want your mommy and daddy to know we're in love?" She giggled as she pulled out a cigarette.

"I was sorry to hear about your friend." Softie's voice comes back to me.

I feel mad at myself for saying her name, "Jude." It felt like I had no right to say it that way. It felt like I had no right to be familiar with it after all these years.

"Jude."

Thank god Softie didn't say it back to me.

I turn on my side and pull the covers up over my ears. Maybe the thoughts will stop spilling out.

Where the fuck is Eli?

Maybe out with Softie's girlfriend. Maybe Softie is out with them having a drink. Maybe Eli's having a threesome right now.

This is ridiculous. Softie and her girlfriend would never have a threesome with Eli. And Eli? Not really a threesome guy.

Geez! Maybe I should just call Eli.

But I don't want to. I don't really want him to come home right now. I want time to fall asleep first.

"Hey, Ally," Softie's words today, but Jude's words at the store so many years ago. She approached me while I was stocking butter.

"Hey," I said back to Jude, but I didn't look at her.

I didn't want Jude there. I wanted her to go away.

I felt the same way then that I feel about Eli now.

Okay, not the same thing. I was young then. I didn't understand things.

I sit up in bed. Angry. I want to scream. I'm so fucking tired and I'm tired of this.

Just as I'm about to get out of bed, I hear the key in the door. Crap.

I lie back down and pull the covers up to my chin. Turn over.

Eli will be in any second to kiss me on the cheek. I'll close my eyes when he does.

Jude used to kiss me like that too. Kiss me on my shoulder, thinking I was sleeping. But I wasn't.

I close my eyes. I wait for Eli to come in.

The tv comes on.

He usually comes in the bedroom first. Takes off his dress shirt, puts on a t-shirt. One that smells musky and sweaty.

But he doesn't come in. The channels change every three seconds or so. He's plopped himself down on the couch.

There are no kisses for me tonight.

Chapter Seven

Elizabeth Perrier walks in front of me. I'm in New Orleans, leaving an event. Some kind of concert or show in a venue by the Mississippi, just off of Jackson Square. I'm walking down some steps, lots and lots of steps and I'm in the middle of a crowd of people. I don't know what the event is, but it's done.

I see Elizabeth so clearly and she's dressed in the clothing that Jacqueline would have made for her. She looks strangely out of place, but no one else seems to react to her. She's a few steps ahead of me and coming to a landing. I call out her name, but she doesn't hear. So I call it out again, louder, and include her last name too. "Elizabeth Perrier!"

A woman right in front of me turns around and looks annoyed. Elizabeth stops and looks back up at me. I don't even know what I'm going to say to her.

"Elizabeth! Hold on!" She's waiting at the landing for me to catch up. I step toward her one step, two steps, and then I step right through her. She's gone.

I look down the stairs and up the stairs, but she's nowhere in sight.

I feel suddenly alone. There's nothing to do now but follow the crowd to this parking lot at river level. I don't know where I'm going, but I know I have to get to my car. So now I stand at what looks like the Ferry Building in San Francisco. The Mississippi has turned into the Bay.

I've got to find my car, but I have no idea where I parked it. The crowd moves around me and I start to move with them. Some people move one way, others another way, and others just disappear back into the city.

My instincts tell me to follow the crowd moving toward Fisherman's Wharf.

There's a parking garage that several people go into and I see Softie up ahead. *Softie!* I yell, but like Elizabeth, she can't hear me. She's got to know where she's going, so I follow her. She goes down these stairs that look like they belong to a subway. She's far ahead of me, but I see her turn a corner. I try to run, but too many people are in front of me and I can't get around them.

I finally make it. I turn the corner and everyone else goes the other way. I can't see Softie up ahead and no one else is in this hallway. But I have a feeling, so I go down the hallway. It ends at a ladder going up to another level of the parking garage. Softie must've gone here, there's nowhere else to go. I grab onto the rungs and start to climb up. The space is tight and cement surrounds me, but I keep climbing.

I come to a small landing and crawl into the space. Cement walls surround me on three sides; on the fourth wall is an opening to the street, but it's blocked by bars. The space is only big enough for me to sit up; there is no way to stand.

"Softie!" I yell out again. My breath is shallow, but I try to slow it down, take deep breaths. I'm not going to cry. I look out through the bars and onto the street. The St. Charles Streetcar clamors past. Now I'm in New Orleans again.

I realize I'm dreaming. *Wake up, Ally.* But I can't. I can't seem to wake up.

"Ally." A voice echoes. I turn around and there's Jude.

"We can't get out." She says as she sits in a corner, a shotgun at her side. Holy shit.

"No, Jude, that can't be, there's got to be a way out, I just came in."

"No," she positions the shotgun so it's aimed at her head.

"Jude! No, I just came up that—" but the ladder is gone. The floor is solid. The only way out is through these bars. "Don't do anything Jude. We can get out, I know it!"

I start pulling on each bar, but they don't give. They don't even wobble. I reach my arms out through the bars. How will we get food? I'm really thirsty too. I can't even swallow the dryness in my throat anymore.

"Hey!" I yell out to the street. "Help!"

"No one can hear you, Ally." I don't want to look at Jude. I can't; I can't see what she's doing. "I've tried. No one can hear me."

"Help! Softie!!" I wave my hands wildly outside through the bars. "Help!"

I jump so high my head hits the cement ceiling. A shotgun blast. One single blast.

My heart is racing. My back is wet. *Wake up now, Ally. Wake up.* I start to cry. I can't turn around; I won't. I won't.

"Ally, Ally, Ally. Ally!"

Eli finally wakes me up.

"It's just a dream."

My crying makes Eli pull me toward him. My heart is pounding. Sweat makes my t-shirt stick to my skin.

"Shhhhh, shhhhh." Eli holds me.

This is ridiculous. Why is he rocking me like a baby? I pull away from him.

"Are you okay?"

"Yeah," I say and try to swallow, "Yeah. Could you get me a glass of water?"

He leaves and it gives me a second to recover alone.

I shiver at the thought of me and Jude trapped in that cement box. And why didn't I do anything to stop Jude in that dream? I just reached my hands out through those bars and yelled for help, cried for help, yelled out for—

Eli comes back with a glass of water. The outside of the glass is wet and water drops onto my bare thighs.

Eli looks concerned. "What kind of dream did you have? First you were screaming and then you started to cry, and I mean you were sobbing."

"I don't even remember," I lie. "What was I screaming?"

"You were just screaming for help."

So why didn't you wake me up sooner? I want to ask.

"Ally, I really think you should go to the doctor. You're just not sleeping well and you're tired all the time. Maybe they can prescribe something."

"Eli, I don't want to take sleeping pills. I've told you that before."

"Well, then talk to Dr. Vonda or something, because this can't go on like this. They've been getting worse since you found out about Jude."

I hate how he says her name, like she's so familiar to him. "I know. I see Dr. Vonda every week. We're talking about this stuff." I sound calm, but I feel myself get angry inside. "I'm sorry I keep you up."

"It's not me I'm worried about."

"Don't worry about me. I can take care of myself." I put my water on the bedside table and lie back down.

He doesn't move and I try not to feel uncomfortable that he's just staring at me. I keep my eyes closed. He exhales deeply then lies down.

Good. This is over for the night.

I get to the theatre at six o'clock. A little earlier than usual, but what am I going to do at the condo? Look at the rectangles? Instead, I sit in the empty theatre and look at the set. It's a good set. A solid set. Tomorrow it will be gone.

Tomorrow I will be free. I'll have at least eight months of freedom from the theatre life. Maybe then I can figure all this shit out.

I hope that's the right thing to do. I just have to figure out why I feel so rotten inside. Why there's this space inside of my gut that seems to hate me so much.

Softie moves onto the stage to set props. She's here early too.

I sink down into the seat. But she can't see me anyway; the house is dark. I hold my breath for fear that she'll discover me here.

I think about last night's dream. How I reached through those bars and cried out for help, cried out for Softie, of all things. Begged her to come save me.

Jesus. *Okay, don't freak out Ally.* There's just something about Softie that reminds me of Jude. That's all.

Softie starts to sing. Her voice is pretty good, but she's being all animated and goofy. All by herself. She turns to the house and sings as if there's an audience. I feel heat rise into my face as her eyes wash over me. I recognize the song from the radio; at least I'm not so much out of touch.

She's so young. She performs as if she's a rapper. She grabs her crotch and pumps her other fist up in the air as she sings.

I smile and sink down in the seat. I shouldn't be watching this private moment of hers. I should've made my presence known. Now she turns her back to me. She's still singing, but her voice is softer, like she's singing to herself. I quietly release my breath in one long, slow exhale.

Once Softie moves off the stage, I quietly get up and leave the theatre.

"Hey Al," Softie's voice startles me while I pour coffee.

I do a quick look over my shoulder and give her a meek "hi" back.

"How's it going?" She's standing next to me, getting a cup, waiting for me to be done with the coffee.

"Good," I hope she can't see that my hand is shaking as I pour. I stop and put the pot down.

"Is that all you're having?"

I look into my cup and it's not filled. "Oh, yeah, I'm trying to cut back." Crap! Well, I can always come back for more. I put a sugar packet in it, stir, and take a sip. Now it's too sweet. "Well, maybe I'll take a bit more," I say and wait for her to finish.

She pours more coffee in my cup. I notice she smells like patchouli. "Say when," she says.

I don't usually like the smell of patchouli, but it smells good on her. Kind of subtle.

I don't say anything and when the cup is filled to the very top, Softie stops pouring and laughs. "So much for cutting back!" She's looking at me in a way that is exciting and unnerving all at once. "You didn't say 'when'."

I feel myself blush and give a nervous kind of gutteral laugh. It sounds fake. "I guess old habits die hard." What an idiot.

I try to figure out where she might go next so I can go somewhere else. Will she stay in the greenroom? Will she go backstage? Will she go to the sound booth?

"Is something wrong?" She asks and I realize I'm just standing there looking into my cup of coffee.

"No, no, it's great. Thanks," I carefully hold up the brimming cup as if I'm saying cheers.

She holds her styrofoam cup up to mimic me. "You're welcome."

Please get me out of this. "Thanks."

"You're welcome." She laughs and I sit down in the greenroom. I don't really know where to go. I pick up a magazine and start reading something about Brittney Spears. I don't really care about Brittney Spears.

I'm not sure, but I think Softie is watching me. I sip my coffee and it's too freaking hot. I feel it burn my tongue and there's nothing I can do about it. I just hold it there, the pain coating my mouth.

"Are you going to George's party tonight?"

"What?" I didn't know George, the director of the show, was having a party. I guess I just don't pay attention.

"Closing-night party. It's tradition."

"Oh, yeah," I've always skipped the closing-night parties, the opening-night parties, the mid-run parties—I don't know. I'm freaking 40-something. Isn't it time to stop going?

"Yeah? Great. See you there." Softie moves slowly around me and is heading out of the greenroom.

Wait. Did I just say "yeah"?

I swallow the burning coffee and watch her walk away.

I did it. I got on a bus and went to George's house. I don't know why. I guess to get out. Or maybe because of Softie. I don't know.

George's house is just off Lake of the Isles, so it was an easy bus ride, and Eli's out late as usual, so, here I am. George's "wife" (I thought he was gay) opens the door and welcomes me in. I walk into a freaking atrium, just about as big as the apartment Eli and I lived in when we first moved here. I swear.

The house seems to be inspired by Frank Lloyd Wright; the windows look like the leaded glass I've seen in bona fide Wright homes. Oh hell, what do I know?

There's a fire blazing in the fireplace that is between two sunken living rooms, or it splits one huge sunken living room. A lot of people are milling around the food and drink table. I see lots of wine bottles and start to make my way over.

"Hey, you made it."

I feel a touch on my shoulder and turn to face Softie. I feel a deer-in-the-headlights look cross my face. My heart is pounding in my chest. "Oh, yeah. Eli's got tech rehearsal tonight, so I—"

"Yeah. I know."

"You do?"

"Jane does too," she says it kind of like "duh, Ally," but she has a smile on her face.

"Oh yeah."

"Yeah," she nods her head and keeps her eyes on my face, even though I look away.

I don't know what to say.

After a few awkward moments, she asks, "Want me to get you something to drink?"

I feel a rush go up my thighs. "Oh, no, you don't have to…I can…"

"You look like a wine girl. White or red?" She takes a step toward the table, and moves her hand as if she's weighing the options. She's got kind of an Idgie-from-*Fried Green Tomatoes* look. With dreads.

I try to remain cool and calm. "Um, white, yeah, thanks."

She goes to the table and pours me a glass. She changed from her black stagehand attire. Now she's wearing low-rider jeans and some kind of boots, like biker boots.

I try not to stare at her, so instead I look around this huge room. The crew is sitting on one side of the fireplace and the cast is sitting on the other. Funny how we all break off into our own groups.

"Here you go." She hands the glass to me with her dragon-wrapped wrist.

"Oh, thanks." I take a sip. Savagnion Blanc. How did she know?

"How'd you get here?"

"Oh, uh, I took the bus."

"Don't you drive?"

"Yeah, I drive, but I don't like to drive to the theatre when we live so close, you know." Why didn't I stop and get my car to come here? That was dumb. Now I've got to take the bus to get home and it's already midnight. The buses come every half hour after midnight. I did not think this through.

"That's very environmental of you."

"Yeah." I kind of laugh and take another drink.

"Come here," she grabs my hand and pulls me toward the techie group. Her hand is soft and warm. I take another drink on the way over. It swishes up to my nose.

"Hey, guys, look who decided to join the riff raff!"

Lots of "hey Ally's" rise up to the ceiling and I wipe the wine off the bottom of my nose and upper lip.

"Sit here," Softie pulls me down beside her on the couch. I'm kind of half-sitting on a stagehand's lap. "Beastie, man, move down," Softie tells the stagehand, aka Beastie, "make some room." My left butt cheek is now aligned with the right, but I'm not so comfortable. I take another drink and suddenly realize my glass is empty.

"Hey Beastie, get Ally another drink while you're over there. The white wine."

"Oh, yeah," I give Beastie my glass, but I shouldn't really drink anymore. I'm such a lightweight.

"So Ally, what's your story?" Softie's soft patchouli scent fills my nostrils. It's nice.

"My story?"

"Yeah. You're always kind of on the edge of things. No one knows much about you except me, and I hear that from Jane."

"Jane?" I ask, wondering how Jane knows anything about me.

"Yeah, my girlfriend."

"Yeah, I know who Jane is, but—"

"She and Eli are pretty tight."

They are? "Oh, yeah."

"So?"

Beastie hands me another glass of wine.

"So…" I take a sip.

"Okay," she seems to be searching her mind. I feel like my lips are permanently stuck on the wine glass. "So, your friend was found dead?"

My throat makes a loud gulping sound as I swallow a big swish of wine. I hate that Eli talked to Jane about Jude.

"Yeah, she was."

"This friend was from college?"

"High school."

"Right, high school."

I readjust myself to try to feel more comfortable. Maybe I should take the focus off of me. Yeah, that would be good. "How do you like working at the theatre?" I ask awkwardly.

"It's a good gig. I'm not the Manhattan type, you know? Never liked it."

"Oh…have you…did you…have you lived there? In Manhattan?"

"Hell's Kitchen baby," I blush when she calls me baby, "I wanted to live in Chelsea, but you know."

"Oh. And you worked in theatre there?"

"Yeah, I got an internship at Lincoln Center, then did some summer stock stuff, then did a few Broadway tours, but that sucked. I hated the road. Then I found the job here and well…" She raises her wine glass with her dragon-wrapped arm and that gesture exposes more of the tattoo.

"Cool," I take a drink with her.

Cool? Do they even say that anymore? I find myself looking at her tattoo. I want to touch it so badly. I don't know why. The colors are so vibrant and the lines so intricate. Softie pulls up her sleeve a bit to expose even more of the dragon. I look at her face and she smiles at me. I take another drink.

"What about you?"

"Me?"

"Yeah, how did you get into this theatre life."

"Well, I graduated from the University of Nebraska—"

"Nebraska? They have theatre degrees there?"

I take another swig of wine.

"Just kidding," she says. She touches the back of my wrist and the wine burns me from inside. "Hey," she smiles, "you're blushing."

"I…" I gulp hard. "Must be the wine."

"Yeah, must be." She gets up and moves away from me, but gives me a look, a flirty look, over her shoulder.

I want her to come back. I want her to…

I want…

I look at my cell phone. It's 1:15 and Eli hasn't called. I should call him, but instead I turn off my cell phone. I stand up, and go to the table to get more wine. As I start pouring, Softie puts her hand over mine and whispers, "meet me in the bathroom."

I start to shake.

I watch her walk away, looking over her shoulder at me once as if to say, "It's all yours if you want it."

I gulp down the entire glass of wine and put down my wine glass.

I should go.

I look around the room, planning my escape.

But then I follow her.

The room is kind of spinning around me. I can't get the shower tiles in focus. Then I feel her lips on my neck, her hands going up under my shirt.

I feel like I should say stop.

But I don't want to.

Her lips taste like red wine, bitter and fruity. I suck on her bottom lip and she lets out a moan. My knees start to quiver. I should stop.

"Let's get out of here," she whispers as she bites my earlobe.

I don't want to stop here and now because I don't want to think about what I'm doing, but I say "okay."

She grabs my hand and leads me out of the bathroom and back into the living room. No one seems to notice that we're holding hands, but I pull my hand away anyway. She doesn't stop to say good-bye to anyone. She unapologetically grabs our coats out of the closet, hands me my coat, and pulls me out the front door.

Her scooter is parked on the sidewalk just outside. It's too freaking cold for a scooter ride, isn't it? She hands me a helmet. "We're only going to the other side of Lyndale," she says, as if she knows what I'm thinking.

I don't say anything. I just climb on the back of this tiny scooter as if all reason has left me. I don't know why I'm doing this. But I am.

I wrap my arms around Softie's waist. Her abs are solid and tight. I press my breasts into her back as the scooter starts.

"Ready?" Her warm breath kisses my cheek.

"Yeah." I squeeze tighter as the scooter moves down the driveway.

Chapter Eight

My neck feels strained cradled in her shoulder; my breasts are pushed into her ribcage. Her hair now smells like musty patchouli and cigarette smoke. Another tattoo winds its way up her stomach; this one of a thorn bush with roses.

I drank too much. Why did I even go to the cast party? I never go to these things.

And now here I am, lying in Softie's bed, this tightening in my spleen, my head spinning, my body sinking to the bottom of the ocean with bricks tied to my feet.

"I should really go."

"Eli?" Softie stretches, releasing me from the position lovers take after it's all said and done.

"No, not Eli..." Well, yes, Eli.

She laughs again.

"What about your girlfriend?" I ask.

"We have an open relationship." She lights a cigarette. Her fingernails are painted black, but have chips in them, as if she's been picking the polish off.

"An open...?" I put my shirt back on, then pick up my bra. Crap. I take my shirt off and struggle with the bra straps, holding my arms close to my body, covering my nipples. I'm so glad I don't have to see Softie tomorrow.

Softie blows smoke up into the air. "She does her thing, I do my thing, but we still have our thing together."

"So this isn't a problem?" I mean, Christ, I just slept in the bed Softie shares with her girlfriend. Do they live together? Is the girlfriend coming in any minute?

"Nah. She's out with someone tonight herself."

I don't like the glint in her eye. Eli? Do I ask? Before I can decide, saliva rises in my throat, a burning kind of sensation, the sides of my tongue tingle. I run into the bathroom just as my stomach churns out the wine from the party and the two shots of tequila I drank when I got here.

I spit into the toilet one last time, wipe my mouth with toilet paper, then flush. As I'm rinsing my mouth with water to try to get that burning sensation out of my throat, Softie says, "Hey, are you okay?"

"No, no, I've got to go home." I won't cry. I refuse to cry about this.

"I'll get dressed and give you a ride."

"No! No, that's okay. I...I can make it home on my own."

"Are you sure? You're like two bus rides away."

"I'm fine. I'm going to walk anyway."

"Ally, you can't walk through this neighborhood at night, this ain't the Sculpture Garden."

She's right, but I don't care. I just want away from everyone right now. I want to go home, but I don't know where that is. I wish it was our old apartment. Our old lives.

"I'll be fine. I'm a big girl." And about two decades older than you, I want to say, but it doesn't seem the time to be a bitch.

"You know, it's hard for people to be monogamous."

And what is *that* suppose to mean? Does she want me to feel better for what I did? Or is Eli sleeping with her girlfriend? And how can that be okay with her?

This is FUCKED UP Ally! Jude's voice says to me.

"I gotta go." I am not going to cry, period. I grab my jacket and my shoes and just leave Softie standing there.

I don't care. I did fuck up. If Eli fucked up, too, well, that's on him. But I fucked up. Me. I sit down on the stairs in this crappy old building (Softie's salary isn't that bad) and put my shoes on. It smells like old, wet carpet here, but my butt isn't wet.

A door opens down the hall. I throw on my jacket and fly down the stairs, just in case Softie is following me with her scooter keys in hand.

Drugs are being exchanged between two guys on the front stoop of the apartment building. I just need to walk three or five blocks west to get out of this neighborhood. It'll be fine, I'm just going to walk fast, and I'll wear Jude's attitude.

I can't really pull that off, though, but I'll try. Anything to get away from this.

Why did I drink so much? Christ, I never hang out with the crew. I've always had such good boundaries. But I thought, hey, I won't be doing the next few shows; I can take a break from those boundaries.

Meet me in the bathroom, that's what started all this.

Even as I think about it now, I feel…attractive…alive…

The sad thing is, I almost hope Eli is out with Softie's girlfriend tonight. That would make this all feel better. I wouldn't feel like I've betrayed him.

But the truth is, while Softie removed her shirt, while she stripped off my underwear, Eli wasn't the one I felt like I was betraying.

The one I felt like I was betraying was Jude.

Cold light spills onto our bed. Neither one of us shut the blinds before bed last night. Eli is sound asleep, his back turned to me. He was asleep when I got home last night—I mean this morning.

My eyes don't stay open willingly. I fight to keep them open as I look at him. I snuggle up to the back of his head and breathe in, smelling for any traces of patchouli. I smell it, but then realize it's on me.

It's only seven a.m. and I just got home a few hours ago, but I want to take a shower; I need to take a shower.

I carefully roll out of bed and drag myself to the bathroom. Mozart jumps out of bed too, but not as cautiously. Eli stirs and I stand completely still until I'm sure he's still asleep. Then I tiptoe to the bathroom.

After I step into the shower, I realize that my body feels foreign to me. I run soapy hands over my breasts, stomach, pubic hair, but my body feels numb.

Eli comes in the bathroom while I'm showering. Crap. I thought he was deep asleep.

"What are you doing?" He clears his voice while he pees; his eyes are squinted closed.

"Everyone was smoking last night. I feel gross."

He clears his throat again, but still talks with a frog, "What time did you get home?"

"Four thirty."

"Geez. You hit the town." He opens the shower door and puckers his lips. His eyes are still closed.

I give him a quick kiss. I haven't brushed my teeth—what if he senses something on my breath…

"I'm going back to bed." He wipes water off his face from where the shower splashed him, his eyes still closed, he stumbles out of the bathroom and back to bed.

I put my face into the stream of the shower and let it wash over me. Then I start to cry.

I can't go back to bed, even though I'm exhausted. I lie on the couch instead. Mozart jumps up next to me, then onto my stomach. She starts kneading with her paws as she purrs. I close my eyes and wish she would keep doing this, but she stops and lies down on my chest and stomach, still purring.

It's only minutes before I drift back to sleep.

Blinding white light. My head feels full of sand. My mouth feels like I've been chewing the same sand.

"Ally," Eli softly shakes my shoulder.

"Hey."

There's heaviness everywhere in my body. My neck aches.

"It's three o'clock."

Three o'clock? In the morning?

I open my eyes and quickly close them again. The sun is pouring into the condo.

"Three o'clock?" My voice sounds broken. I try to clear my throat and swallow.

Eli gives a soft laugh. "You've been sleeping all day. Sorry baby, I've got to practice."

"Oh yeah, opening night." I don't want to talk. I want to go back to sleep.

"I brought you some water." I feel a cool glass on my arm.

Oh fuck. Now I'm awake enough to understand the heaviness that's living at the core of my body. Softie.

"Sit up." Eli gently tugs on my pajamas. He cradles the back of my head. "Drink this. You'll feel better." He's not laughing at me anymore. He's being…well, he's being Eli.

I drink the water he holds to my lips. It feels so good.

"Thanks." I take it from him and drink the whole glass.

"Want some more?" He half-whispers.

I nod my head, but saying yes would have felt better. I lie back down and put my arm over my eyes. That feels better.

"Don't fall asleep again," Eli says as I hear the click of the water dispenser on the refrigerator.

"No," I clear my throat and muster the energy to say it louder, "No."

God, what did I do?

Eli returns with the water. I sit up slowly. He doesn't have to cradle me this time, but I fall into his shoulder.

He gives a soft laugh again. "What is it, baby?"

I want last night to go away. "I miss you."

He lets me drink the second glass of water, then opens his arms and motions for me to fall into him. And I do.

"You don't have to miss me." He strokes my hair.

"Where?" I clear my throat again. "Where do you go after rehearsal?"

"I go out with the some of the guys."

"And no women?"

"Well, there are a couple of women," he says matter-of-factly. "Is that what the past few weeks have been about?"

"Who?" I ask gently.

"Who what?"

"Who are the women?"

"Jane from the crew and Michelle, one of the violinists."

Jane. Softie's girlfriend. And Michelle? I don't know Michelle.

"Are you jealous?" He speaks softly as he moves hair off my forehead with his index finger.

"I'm lonely." And then a flood hits and I start to cry. Unexpectedly, unashamedly.

"Hey," Eli pulls me closer into him. He's dressed and ready for the day—jeans, black t-shirt. His muscles aren't as firm as they used to be. He's kind of soft these days. I squeeze my arms around him.

"I'm sorry," I manage to say.

"It's okay."

He thinks I'm apologizing about crying, so I don't say any more.

And we sit like that for a long time.

Me crying.

Him holding me like someone in love.

Chapter Nine

Eli always reserves the best seat in the house for me on his opening night. And, unless I have a show, I come to every opening night. I still feel hungover from last night. My head aches, my mouth is dry, and I'm a big fat cheater.

I open the program and find myself looking for the names of his female "friends." Part of me hopes Eli is cheating too. It would make me feel… less guilty. Jane. Michelle. There's a picture of Michelle. I hate to say it, but now I'm not so worried. She looks to be in her late forties or early fifties, she's got a shock of salt and pepper hair in a Roseanne Rosannadanna style.

Only Jane's name is listed, there's no picture. But that's okay, because Jane reminds me of Softie and Softie reminds me of being a shit.

I take a deep breath, trying to put goodness back into my body.

I leave for Harmony tomorrow. Maybe a few days away will do me good. Although going for Jude's burial isn't exactly a getaway.

A woman behind me is talking about Eli. "…saw him conduct the Christmas show last year. Oh, he was so good." I hear her say. "He's a treasure." I almost want to turn around and say, "That's my Eli," but the words don't come and the lights go down.

The buzz of the audience quickly fades. There is controlled applause as the members of the orchestra walk onstage and take their places. I see

Michelle and now I know for sure that she is not Eli's type. Then I scan their faces for someone who might be his type. Maybe he just used Michelle's name, but he's sleeping with someone else.

God, Ally, you're the cheater.

The lights onstage come up and Eli steps into the light. He always did look handsome in his tux. He's the youngest conductor of the Minneapolis Orchestra and seeing him now makes me wish I felt more fortunate.

Eli bows and his dimples are visible from here. He turns his back to us and then raises his arms up over his head. I can tell he's mouthing something to the orchestra and some of them laugh, most of them smile. His arms come down with a great whoosh and off the music goes. His entire body moves with the rhythm as his arms swing all around his torso.

Eli made the headlines once when he came down into the audience at the end of a show and did a magic trick for a nine-year-old boy in the front row. Something simple, like pulling a coin from behind the boy's ear. But that one act landed him in the newspaper. And that one article spurred a line of parents with their children to come to the orchestra.

Now he goes into the audience after every show. Performing magic for children and senior citizens. They call him the "Magic Conductor."

The music starts with Eli's original composition. This is the first time I've heard a full orchestra play it and it reminds me how brilliant Eli is.

I close my eyes and listen to the rhythms that I've only heard from a piano. The violins twirl. The bass thump, thump, thumps. Something whirls. An oboe? I try not to distinguish it. I try to just listen to the sounds spinning over my head into the back of the auditorium.

Then a cymbal splashes inside the music, and something else plays with it to make a shhhhh…tik…shhhhh…tik…shhhhhh…tik tik sound.

I've heard this sound before.

Shhhhh…tik…shhhhh…tik…shhhhhh…tik tik.

Shhhhh…tik…shhhhh…tik…shhhhhh…tik tik. And then I realize it's the same sound Jude described of how her skateboard sounded on pavement. Shhhhh…tik…shhhhh…tik…shhhhhh…tik tik. Jude loved sounds, different sounds, unusual sounds. She said that sound, of the wheels of her skateboard bouncing over each crack in the pavement, comforted her.

Suddenly I feel peaceful—happy that Jude can take me away from what a shit I am. As long as I don't think about what a shit I was to her. Sshhhhh…tik…shhhhh…tik…shhhhhh…tik tik. There it is again in the music, just like the soft sound of wheels on smooth pavement followed by a hiccup of jumping of wheels. Shhhhh…tik…shhhhh…tik…shhhhhh… tik tik. I remember Jude telling me this, her index finger, cracked and dry, extended out and bouncing up and down as she went "shhhhh…tik…shhhhh…tik…shhhhhh…tik tik."

Sometimes Jude liked to look down at the concrete below the wheels and anticipate each tik. Sometimes she just looked forward and watched the streetlights and utility poles pass by.

She maintained her speed by setting her left foot to the ground and pushing off four or five times in a row. Shhhhh…tik…push, push…shhhhh… tik…push, push… shhhhhh… tik… push.

She thought about nothing in particular because this was her time not to think. It was her time to just be.

Shhhhh…tik…shhhhh…tik…shhhhhh…tik tik.

And this is where I want to be. Away from here, lost in a story.

Shhhhh…tik…shhhhh…tik…shhhhhh…tik tik.

So she rode down the crowded Main Street of Harmony, past the sporting goods store, the appliance repair, the shoe store, the bank. She navigated around a woman carrying a package into the post office.

Shhhhh…tik tik…shhhhhh.

She didn't even glance at the newspaper office, the shoe store, the furniture store, the other shoe store, or the theatre.

Shhhhhh…tik tik…shhhhhhhh.

No, she didn't stop until she was right in front of the music store. It was there that she stared at the row of guitars hanging from the ceiling. She saw them through the window. She looked past the clarinets and saxophones, the flutes and the violas—all the way to the back of the store—where one drum set stood alone. It was fire engine red and had three cymbals. She stared at it through the plate glass window. She wanted it so badly.

Shhhhhh…tik tik…shhhhhhhh.

I open my eyes to see Eli bouncing his foot to the music he is creating. I can feel the movement of the audience.

Shhhhhh…tik tik…shhhhhhhh.

I close my eyes and see myself standing with Jude at the front of the Harmony Music Store. She was pining for that drum set.

She stared through the window and told me the story about how, when she was twelve years old, there was this girl in her class who played the drums. She watched her carry a snare drum to school every Tuesday and Thursday. One Tuesday afternoon, Jude stood behind the girl as they were getting on the bus. The girl sat down and put her snare in the seat next to her. Jude walked past and glanced at the girl, then took her usual place in a seat at the back. Jude always sat alone.

She watched the girl. The girl talked to one or two other kids, but she didn't really look like she had any friends on the bus. Jude ignored the draw she had to the girl and looked out the window of the bus as the school flashed past.

My eyes open at a strong sound in the orchestra; a tuba, I think. Eli's starting to break a sweat, his hair is wet at the temples and neckline. I close my eyes and hear it again, shhhhh…tik…shhhhh…tik…shhhhhh…tik tik. I wish I had a pen and paper.

Jude finally got up the courage to talk to the girl. The next Thursday, the girl sat down, and put her snare beside her. Jude sat across the aisle from the girl. "Hey," she said.

The girl looked unsure and shy. She nodded at Jude.

"How long you been playin'?" Jude asked.

"A year," the girl said proudly.

Jude looked to the front of the bus and didn't speak until the bus pulled away from the school. She leaned across the aisle and said, "I'm Jude."

"I'm Andrea," the girl said and smiled.

"Are you a seventh grader?"

"Yeah. You?"

"Yeah." Jude never knew how to start a conversation. She felt awkward and blurted out, "I'd like to play the drums."

The girl smiled at Jude, and kind of laughed, then gave an affirming, "Oh."

Jude again looked out the window, feeling lost on how to connect anymore with this Andrea girl.

Shhhhh…tik…shhhhh…tik…shhhhhh…tik tik. I don't want to open my eyes so I keep remembering, trying to hear Jude's voice tell me this story.

Every day for a week it was like this—Jude got on the bus and sat across from Andrea. They had a stilted conversation. Andrea got off the bus. Until one day when Jude finally said it. "Can you show me how to play drums?"

Andrea was shocked for a moment and Jude said that embarrassed her, so Jude quickly said, "I went and asked the stupid band teacher about playing drums and he told me they had too many drummers already and that I should play the clarinet." Jude tugged on a tattered edge on the bottom of her jeans. "I don't want to play the fucking clarinet. You know?"

Andrea laughed, loosened the grip on her drum. "That's stupid. I mean that Mr. Jared would think the clarinet would be a substitute for the drums."

"Yeah." Jude finally felt like she was connecting to Andrea, "Yeah, that's what I thought. So I thought if I could go in there and show him that I was meant to play the drums, then he'd let me do it."

Andrea thought this over for a minute. "Well, what are you doing tonight? I could show you how to do a roll."

"Really?"

"Yeah. My mom could give you a ride home later. Where do you live?"

Jude panicked, as if Andrea's mom might just see Jude's house and know her secret. And she hadn't even told her dad yet about her secret desire to play the drums. What would he say? It depended on whether he was drunk or not.

"Um," Jude said, "tonight won't work. How about tomorrow? And I can walk home, no prob."

Andrea agreed.

Shhhhh…tik…shhhhh…tik…shhhhhh…tik tik. There it is again. In the music Eli created. I should be listening more closely.

Jude imagined having this new friend. Hanging out at Andrea's house after school, learning how to "roll," just goofing around. She'd have a real friend for once. And then she imagined the questions. "Have you ever kissed a boy?" "Who do you think is cute?" "Would you ever go to second base?" "Hey, what's that bruise?"

All the questions Jude couldn't answer. Not really. All the questions that left a sickening feeling in her stomach. "Yes, I've kissed a boy." She would want to say, just to get it out.

"Who? Who?!?"

"My father."

"That doesn't count!" And Andrea would laugh as if Jude were ridiculous.

"I've already gone to second base."

"With who?"

"My dad." Jude would want to say as she looked in another direction.

Andrea wouldn't understand that. She'd think Jude was sick. And Jude felt sick too.

"Come on, really…" Andrea would say.

And Jude wouldn't have fun with this game. Not at all. She would always feel like a pervert.

"What about you?" Jude imagined changing the conversation. And she would guess that Andrea had some insignificant little kiss with a boy in the sixth grade. A kiss that would make Andrea giggle. And Jude would half roll her eyes at this, and half wish she knew what it was like to feel normal like that.

But it was all about the drums, Jude thought to herself. She imagined the power of sitting behind a full set and playing them. She wouldn't have to talk to anyone; it would just be her and the drums. Really playing them. Hitting them with force and precision. Making people clap to the sound, the beat, the music. She would bang on the cymbals like a true rock star. And maybe she would be good enough to join a band and make lots of money and move away from home. And even if she couldn't move away, she imagined herself telling her father, "I have to practice." And it would consume her, take over her life, and her father wouldn't want to disrupt her so he would leave her alone. She would be safe behind the drums. He couldn't sit next to her and stroke her hair while she played. He would have to give her the space required to play as her arms flew around her.

So that's why she had to go to Andrea's. She could handle the questions. No problem. Anytime girls asked her those questions and she said "no" to all of them, they could tell she was lying anyway. And they'd tease her, "Oh yeah. Right!" And they would create the fantasy life of Jude and never know the real, awful truth.

The next day, on the bus, Andrea was all excited that Jude was coming over to her house.

But Jude felt that sickening feeling again in her stomach and was afraid that she couldn't pretend. That she couldn't seem normal like Andrea. "I can't come over tonight." Jude said.

"Why?" Andrea asked.

Jude shrugged and suddenly felt exposed. "My dad needs me to come home right after school."

"Why?"

"That's just the way he is." She wasn't going to cry. She promised herself.

That was the first time Jude showed me her vulnerability, in that detached way she had. She stood there like a stone, looking into the glass at the Harmony Music Store, holding her skateboard underneath her arm, gazing at the drum set. "I see Andrea in the hallways sometimes at school, but she doesn't really talk to me." Jude's voice cracked. And I didn't know what to do except that I reached out for her hand and held it. I held it tightly, the way girls in Nebraska shouldn't dare touch each other. I felt her pulse on my thumb as it grazed her wrist. I softly stroked the back of her hand with my index finger.

Jude let go of my hand and dropped her skateboard to the cement. "It doesn't matter anyway," she said, "it wasn't like I was going to be a rock star or anything."

Now the audience applauds wildly. Some yell "Bravo" as Eli bows. I fumble with my program and feel lost. What will I say when Eli asks me how I liked the bridge in the third movement or the crescendo at the end? What will I say if he asks me if I was thinking about "that girl" again?

Do I tell him I was only thinking about her to escape the guilt of cheating on him?—*with a woman*? What should I say?

The violins rise at the beginning of the next piece. They rise to a pitch and linger there, trilling with excitement. Eli's baton is suspended in the air, pulsing with the violins, then it swoops down and the entire orchestra joins the violins in a burst of energy.

I begin to think about what will happen when we get home tonight. How Eli's hands will fall on my shoulders as he turns me around to face him. His hot breath will warm my neck. He always wants to make love on opening night. He once told me that it brings him back to the ground after all the bravado. So now I have to pretend. Pretend I am faithful to him; pretend I think he's faithful to me; pretend Jude isn't lurking in the back of my mind; pretend I'm sure he's the person I want to be with.

I should feel lucky. Feel proud of him. Feel how fortunate I am to be with the "Magic Conductor."

And now as the lead violin rests into a lulling rhythm, I try to relax. I try to think of how his hair smells woodsy and clean. He will cup my face in his soft hands and look at me with those blue eyes and ask, "Did you like your song, baby?"

And I'll say *yes*. But I didn't really hear the song; I was lost in thought about Jude and I'll try not to feel guilty about that or the fact that I cheated on him.

The music swells again and breaks into a feverish pace. And I can see Eli pulling me toward the bed and I'll land on top of him. At first I'll break away from his kiss and rest my chin on his shoulder, my face an inch from the duvet. His breath will be hot on my neck and he'll lay tiny kisses there and on my ear. His body will be a flood of affection and his conductor hands will drift over my spine and shoulders. My heart beats with the wild rhythm of the orchestra, the frantic pitch of the violins and somehow later tonight the music will rise above me again and my thoughts will be suspended long enough to make love with him. Long enough to feel how much he loves me.

The smooth rhythm will pulse in my ears as Eli moans, and I will grab his face in my hands and kiss him. And love him.

The music slows again, then rises, then slows and I disappear into the moment that Eli and I first met in Williamstown. Backstage at the small theatre. He asked me out for a drink and promised me a magic trick. As the music shifts again I remember Eli held my hand and dabbed an ash on my palm for his great magic trick and he laughed at how I couldn't figure out how he got the ash to move from one palm to another. And I remember standing beneath the stars as he pointed up to the Big Dipper and I felt as happy as I feel in this moment with the music that Eli creates rising over me and I'll want to hold Eli tightly as he moans and I'll cry out myself. And I will enjoy that one moment of feeling totally free from everything inside me.

And I'll be completely in love for that one moment and will have taken care of my relationship for awhile. I will stop the questions for awhile.

The music slows and I can see Eli rolling off of me. My heart thumps in my chest and I know I will want to pull the covers over my exposed body. The music stops and the audience again applauds. It's a rambunctious group. They whistle and yell and Eli bows again and for some reason I feel like I'm going to cry. I try to suppress it, but a moan comes out of my throat and I look away from Eli. Look to the rafters, the ceiling, to the people around me with broad smiles on their faces. Showing their appreciation for him. I glance back to the stage as the house lights come up and I see him looking at me, winking at me, but then his face turns somber. And I know he sees me crying, but the house lights dim again. He stares out toward my seat, but I know he can't see me as I wipe the tears from my cheek. The audience quiets. His eyes linger on the darkness too long and I'm uncomfortable with the concern he shows. I can almost feel his "I love you" being whispered in my ear. I gulp and think, "I love you too," but I want to cry from the guilt of it.

And I think this is just a phase I will get through. "It's not always going to be equal, Ally." That's what Dr. Vonda said. Feelings of love aren't always equal.

But what about feelings of guilt? Is Eli guilty too?

Chapter Ten

It's eleven thirty when we get home. Eli drops the keys in a ceramic dish we got when we went to Venezuela in '95. The heavy clink reverberates in the hallway. I discreetly try to walk away before Eli grabs me, but I don't move fast enough. His hand behind my head, he plants a hard, passionate kiss on my lips.

I try to fall into it. Maybe I just feel guilty about Softie. Crap. I don't want to think about her, so I try to think about Jude. I try to get excited to be with Eli by thinking about Jude.

Jesus Ally, get a grip. How about thinking about Eli? Remembering how it used to be. Now Eli is kissing me, soft and tenderly, and I try to take myself back to those feelings I had in the beginning. On those lonely nights of summer stock; we spent every moment of our free time together—we went to the drive-in, the horse races, the small towns that surrounded Williamstown, the museum, and movie after movie after movie. And I started to forget how it was with Jude. *Criminey, there she is again.*

Eli's hand runs down my side and rests on my butt.

Okay now, think about Eli. After I met him, I finally believed it was possible for me to feel normal. To fall in love with a man.

I remember the time we were lying in a field behind the theatre in Williamstown, looking up at the stars. Cheesy, but true. It was just after his show closed. In fact, now I remember, it was his last night in Williamstown; I still had a few weeks left. And he asked, "What are you doing after the summer?" Just like that. His voice was soft, almost whispery. Now, after twenty years of being with him, I know that's his timid and unsure voice.

I didn't get it. I just said, matter-of-factly, "I guess go back to Nebraska." I couldn't really think of any other options.

"Why don't you come to New York with me, Ally?" His eyes lit up when he asked, but his voice shook. He was so cute.

New York? My heart raced at the thought. "What? I mean—what?"

He positioned himself above my face. "I know it seems fast, but, I don't want this to end. I have a small apartment in Brooklyn and I'm sure we can find you a job in the city somewhere. Or you can just live with me for awhile, see how things go, you know?"

"Eli—what?" Eli was the first man I'd ever had sex with and I was trying so hard not to fall in love with him for that reason. I was trying not to get my heart broken.

"Ally, I don't want to lose you."

Two weeks later, he came back to get me and I was in his car, going to New York City. It was a dream come true. He loved me. And I loved him too. Maybe not as passionately, but I did love him. I do love him.

And so I fall into this kiss, and another and another. He guides me toward the bedroom and we giggle together as I walk backward and he walks forward, entangled in passion. His passion.

He drops me on the bed, just as I knew he would. He gives a soft moan. And I think this is a person I could never hurt. I could never leave Eli. How could I? As we get older, we'll have less sex. It'll all be okay. If it weren't for the sex, I'd be perfectly happy with him.

Eli straddles my leg as he sits up to take off his tie and jacket and shirt and I feel a tingle run up my thigh and butt. I feel like I can muster up enough excitement to do this. To make love with him tonight. Jesus, what's wrong with me?

Maybe I should look up female impotence on the internet. Maybe that's what I have. Or fear of commitment. But, heck, we've been together for twenty years, if that's not commitment then…?

I'm out of the moment and Eli must sense it. "Ally?" He looks at me, concern on his face.

I grab him and kiss him again. I'm bisexual. That's it. This Softie thing was just the other side of me coming out. I've been with Eli for twenty years and I love him. I do love him.

I strongly roll him over so that I'm on top, straddling him. And I feel how ready he is to be inside me. So I let him. And my thoughts run wild as I slowly move my hips on top of him. The music that washes over me is a waltz and I imagine Elizabeth Perrier dancing with Jacqueline Montalban, there in a dark room in Paris, with clothes flung all around. Jacqueline stripped Elizabeth down to her underwear and pulled her close. And they danced, naked hands touching, fingers interlaced. Jude created this version of the story…as she kissed my stomach. She whispered it to me in the darkness and we kissed.

This thought is what makes me explode on top of Eli, and my reaction makes Eli explode inside of me. I suddenly panic, wondering if I took my birth control pill this morning. Eli pulls me down so that I'm looking at him, face-to-face. And he kisses me. And I remember that I did take my birth control pill this morning. And now guilt washes over me, guilt from Softie or from Jude, and I roll off of Eli and go to the bathroom. I close the door. Eli moves on the other side of it. He's humming, so I know he didn't get suspicious. I mean, he didn't notice anything unusual about my behavior. I'm okay. We're okay.

I spend a long time in the bathroom, looking at the walls. On the wall opposite the toilet, I hung the photo of Mt. Rainier that Eli took, and next to it hangs the photo I took of El Reloj in Puerta del Sol in Madrid. The clock's hands are stuck on 8:45 in the picture. Such an unattractive place for the hands to be frozen. I should have waited to take the picture until 9:10 or something. But the light of sunset is perfect.

"Ally? Are you okay in there? What are you doing?"

I'm sitting on the toilet, but I'm not doing anything, really.

"I'll be there in a minute," I call out and my eyes rest again on El Reloj.

I haven't wanted to escape my life this much since my growing-up years, trying to rearrange my history. I just did it differently then, that's all, standing at the library card catalogue, looking for some way to escape my parents, the slaughterhouses, and trucks full of pigs and cows.

I pulled out the little drawer of the index file and fingered through the cards, one by one. I started looking under "ghosts" first, and randomly looked through the F-G-H file. Fingering my way through the F's, I saw France. French. French Quarter New Orleans.

I looked at the card. "French Quarter New Orleans. History and establishment of the French Quarter of New Orleans." Somehow, in my mind, the fact that I was French connected me to this place and time.

And so it was, early one Saturday morning, that thirteen-year-old Alison Bouchard picked out that thick, heavy book on the French Quarter in

New Orleans. There were current pictures of it and pictures as it was some 130 years before.

This was after the fire of 1788, when the town burned down on Ash Wednesday. This was the French Quarter built by the Spanish. With two-story buildings and iron railings with intricate patterns. This was the French Quarter with the Cabildo and the armistad where Jackson Square still stands. And along the streets, planters hung down from the second stories of these homes inhabited by the bourgeois and criminals. By slave owners and prostitutes.

And in that photo, I transported myself—but it wasn't really me. It was an embodiment of me as Elizabeth Perrier, who left France to escape the nagging plea from her parents to marry and have a family.

Like me, Elizabeth wanted to escape the normal expectations that parents have of their daughters. Even my parents had these visions. "You'll see what happens when you get married and have kids of your own," my mother always warned.

And so I escaped with Elizabeth to New Orleans. She found a flat in the French Quarter and, being a socialite, she quickly found friends. Her life was one of parties and sleeping late, of fancy dinners and the finest clothing. Elizabeth was footloose and fancy free.

But I wanted her to be normal too. I wanted her to find love someday.

Enter Walden Bouchard, who looked like a young John Travolta, but had a name right out of Thoreau's writings. Walden was an esquire in New Orleans, and top at his job. He was soon to take the position of barrister (a term I'd heard on an episode of *Bewitched*) in the Province of New Orleans. Walden was enchanted by Elizabeth and quickly began to woo her. But he knew that she was a reluctant wife and he was very strategic in his courtship. He placed himself in her life as a man of mystery: elusive and dark. He showed up at parties and watched her from afar. When she looked his way, he'd take a drink from his glass, peering over the brim, and holding eye contact with her. After six or seven parties, she began to ask about him, the man with the dark hair and brooding eyes. One day, he appeared next to her, holding a bouquet of fresh flowers, simple but elegant. He kissed her hand and introduced himself as Walden Jaques Bouchard.

Elizabeth was beside herself. Her knees went weak when his lips touched her hand. From that moment on, Elizabeth Perrier knew she would fulfill her parents' wishes.

Walden built a mansion for Elizabeth in the Garden District. They would pass the mansion down through the generations until it eventually landed in the hands of my father, Eric Bouchard, who wouldn't work at a slaughterhouse, but who would be a judge.

And I became all this I constructed just to make myself feel whole, normal. I would want the same things girls my age wanted. And I would be more than my slaughterhouse father and my truck stop mother. I would be Alison Bouchard. An artist. A rich bohemian. Someone who would be taken care of by fate and live in a career others could only dream of.

I was going to be Alison Bouchard of the Garden District of New Orleans. I was going to tell myself a new story, one with a happy ending.

I turn off the bathroom light and carefully step through the dark toward the bed. I try not to wake Eli as I crawl in bed. Once I settle, I listen. Eli softly snores beside me. I turn onto my side and run my hand across his shoulder, his soft shoulder. And I realize how lucky I should feel to have him here with me.

I touch his hair that has little curls around his perfect musician ears. I try to curl up next to him but I feel awkward, like my legs and arms shouldn't even be attached to my body. I move back to my side of the bed and through all this he still purrs a soft snore. I stroke his hair one more time.

"Please let me love him." I whisper into the air of the quiet room.

My eyelids are heavy and I easily drift off to sleep.

I wake up knowing I didn't sleep well. I don't know what I dreamed, but I feel the residue of dreams in my body.

Eli's finger touches my nose. I focus my eyes on him. He's smiling at me.

"What time is it?"

"Eleven thirty," he says and kisses me. "I guess we wore ourselves out last night."

I don't say anything. I'm leaving for Harmony today. I make a move to roll out of bed, but Eli pulls me back and drapes his arm and leg over me.

"I've got to get going." I don't really have any time limits, but I feel a need to get on the road.

"Just stay a few more minutes," he whispers. "I've been meaning to talk to you about something."

My heart sinks. I've been waiting for this conversation—the "you've been acting weird lately, don't you love me?" talk. The "you've been distant lately, this is all your fault our relationship is in trouble" talk.

"Ally?"

"Yeah?" What I wouldn't give to just be able to fall asleep on the spot.

"Ally, I've been thinking."

I wait, and the more he pauses, the more I want to jump out of bed and get on the road to Harmony.

"I think we should have a baby."

He just says it. Just like that. Out of nowhere.

"A baby?" My voice echoes off the ceiling.

"Yeah. Remember when we met and we talked about how we'd like to have kids someday?"

Is he nuts? Did we talk about that? Maybe once or twice like a million years ago. When we were young.

"We're not getting any younger Ally. And we're doing okay now. We've got this big place and two extra bedrooms."

I never once considered he bought this condo with a family in mind. It's so modern, so, so the lifestyle of a couple without kids.

"And now you're taking some time off. I can see the theatre life is hard on you."

And having a baby would be easier?!?

"I'll have to think about it, Eli." That's what I say. Think about it?!? I don't really know what to say and now he looks so disappointed like I should've seen this coming. Like it didn't come out of the blue. I—it just doesn't feel right to me. Not now.

"You've never thought about it before now?"

"No. We've never talked about it Eli."

"I know we've never talked about it out loud. But, you love kids. You're always saying, 'oh, look at that baby.'"

"Eli, yeah, I love kids, but…" Where do I begin? "I'm 42 years old. You're 42 years old."

"So? Lots of people like us have their babies this late in life." He thinks fast, "Brad Pitt!"

Brad Pitt?

"Okay, um, Jeff and Cindy!"

Some of our friends in New Orleans.

"Cindy was 42 when she had Michael."

Spelled Michael, but pronounced Me-cale.

"They love that kid. You love that kid."

"Yeah, but I get to leave that kid."

"Come on, Ally. Just think of it. You can quit your job, stay at home, write."

And why do I have to have a baby to stay at home and write? I don't want a baby. "I don't—" and then I look at his face. His eyes are big and hopeful. So I say, "Let me think about it."

And then I know that was the wrong thing to say because now he's happy. Now he thinks there's a way. Now my days will be filled with "look at that baby"; "have you decided yet?"; and "come on, we're running out of time."

"I've got to go." I jump out of bed quickly.

"Hey, wait a minute." Eli grabs my wrist. "You can at least give me a hug."

I turn my hand to get free, but Eli's grip is too tight. It burns where I try to resist him. I pull back a little, but Eli doesn't let go. So I give into it. What else can I do?

"It feels good to hold you, Ally."

I stare at the window across the room. It seems so far away. Why is Eli's body so hot? I feel like I'm sweating around my hairline. His grip won't loosen.

"I should get on the road so I don't have to drive in the dark."

He kisses my forehead, "Good idea." Then he lets go.

I'm sweating. My t-shirt feels damp. I can't seem to move fast enough to get out on the road.

Chapter Eleven

I'm driving on I-35, south toward Des Moines and road kill makes me think of Eli. A dead freaking deer on the side of the road, its belly torn open, makes me think of my boyfriend.

I think we should have a baby. I still can't believe he said it. How did he get that idea? Because we're not getting any younger? Because I wanted a change in my life?

How did my wanting a change become me having a baby?

Well, I'm not going to have a baby. I don't want to have a baby.

Now I just have to tell Eli.

I look in my rearview mirror and see the figure of the dead deer lying at the side of the road.

I don't want to think about the baby thing anymore. It's a beautiful day. The sun is shining; it's kind of warm out and I'm alone at last.

I got out of the condo pretty fast. I just packed all of my stuff in a small suitcase. Toiletries, a few changes of underwear, an extra pair of jeans besides what I have on, a couple of long-sleeved shirts, and black pants and a black button-down shirt for the burial. Nothing fancy. Jude wouldn't have wanted that.

And I brought a notebook and paper. I put the notebook and pen in the passenger seat but I don't know why since I obviously can't write while driving. But it somehow comforts me.

In the next seven hours, I have no one to answer to and only stories to roll around in my head. I have the windows rolled down because I love the wind whirring around the car, stereo on so loud the bass shakes the speakers, and my hair "blown to bits" as my mother would say.

Mom is so excited that I'm going back to Harmony, even though it's for Jude's burial. "We haven't seen you for ages," she exclaimed. "Karen and John are excited to see you."

That's Mom's take on things. My siblings and I haven't jelled for a really long time. Karen always has this weird attitude toward me, like it's somehow my fault that she works at the cardboard-box company and her husband is unemployed. I suspect I won't even see my brother John when I'm there; he's always too busy doing this or that. I haven't seen either of them for a couple of years now. Maybe I should make a point of it. My nieces and nephew have to be so big now. Candy must be 13, which makes Schylur 11, and Kira 4.

I can just see Mom giving them enough hugs and kisses for all of us. Even though she wasn't the best of mothers, Mary Bouchard is definitely grandmother material. She gets to swoop in whenever she wants, make the kids happy by smothering them with attention, then go home and do what she wants. She'd be so excited if she knew Eli was talking about having babies.

That feeling of dread sneaks back into me and I don't want it. I don't want to feel this dread for having to deal with a partner asking me to be a baby machine.

Mom would probably think that would fix everything between me and Eli. She'd probably want me to be just like her and make a family to replace the broken one from childhood.

Mom sometimes mentioned how her alcoholic mother beat the crap out of her. Or how her mother would leave her and her sister for days; she'd just disappear and leave them to fend for themselves. I think this is what made her disappear in our lives sometimes. Not physically, but mentally. I think she had to kind of shut down in order to give us a life different from what she knew.

I know she had dreams once. She talks about how she always dreamed of being a teacher, but then she dropped out of school at age seventeen. She claimed her teachers were no good and caused her failure. She let it slip once that she was failing every subject. Months before dropping out, she met Eric Bouchard. He became her world and was her escape route from bad grades and a dead-end life.

Dr. Vonda thinks maybe Mom has dyslexia or some such learning disability because I told Dr. Vonda once about how my mom was a legend in Harmony. While language is not her strength, math is definitely Mom's thing. At the truck stop, Mary Bouchard has always prided herself on being able to total up her tickets without a calculator or a cash register. She told me it was a game she played with herself to keep her job interesting. "Nine, carry the one, two, carry the five…"

One day many years ago, her boss questioned her method, but Mom challenged him. "You add a column of numbers on your calculator and I'll add a column by hand. We'll see who's faster." Even as she said this, she had all the confidence in the world that she would win, and she would be correct in her calculations.

Sure enough, her boss accepted the challenge. Now I know this story because it is a legend in Harmony. Folks started to hear about the challenge and took time off work to be there. I know this from my classmates' parents. I know it from my teachers. The mayor was even at the event.

So there was Mary Bouchard, sitting at the counter, a pen in her hand, a crisp page of notebook paper, without one grease stain, in front of her. And across the counter from her, her boss stood looking for an extension cord to plug in the calculator. All of the waitresses gathered around; folks, with unbussed plates still sitting on their tables, sat in the booths. The mayor of Harmony sat at the end of the counter. He was to be the test giver, and the final judge.

Mr. Connors, my mother's boss, finally settled into a spot on the counter, his calculator ready. It was one of those old calculators, with a little lever on the side. Mary wet the tip of her pen with her tongue. The Mayor sipped on his coffee, making a loud slurping sound in the quiet restaurant.

Lois, one of the waitresses, handed them each a sheet with numbers on it—a predetermined quiz the mayor had thought up. Lois popped her gum and then counted off—"okay, one…two…three…(pop)…GO!"

Mr. Connors's arm flew, punching in numbers, pulling the lever, punching in more. Punch, punch, pull. Punch, punch, pull. A bead of sweat formed on his brow, daring to roll onto the bridge of his nose.

Mary delicately looked over the columns of numbers. She had no need to use her fingers to count. (Punch, punch, pull.) She simply added the numbers in her brain, quickly and thoughtfully. (Punch, punch, pull.) It seemed to everyone in attendance that she even paused to take a sip of coffee herself. Some even say she lifted her cup and clicked it with the mayor's. (Punch, punch, pull.) Finally, she put down her pen and announced, "Three hundred twenty-eight thousand, two hundred twenty-nine."

Mr. Connors stopped. He looked at his finely printed row of numbers with the dropped "3s." He wasn't even halfway done. The waitresses looked at the answer sheet in front of them, the one the mayor had prepared. The waitresses all screamed together.

The mayor patted Mr. Connors on the back and finished his coffee. He left the place cajoling. "Beaten down by a woman," he said, "what a laugh!"

I knew this story was true because every day I began a new math class, my teacher looked at me with anticipation. "Well," he/she would say as they looked down at the roster, "Alison Bouchard," (always the midwestern pronunciation, with a hard "ard"), "are you the daughter of Mary Bouchard?"

"Yes," I'd say, feeling shy because I knew what question was next.

"The Mary Bouchard who works at the truck stop?" And I'd feel my face blush in embarrassment. Thank god they didn't announce the career path of my father as well.

"Yes."

"Well, Alison, I expect big things from you!"

It only took the teacher a few weeks to realize math was not my best subject. That I, Alison Bouchard, took after my slaughterhouse father and not my calculative waitress mother who dropped out of school at age 17.

My mom's other strength, which I did not inherit, is her connection to practically everyone in Harmony. She knows people in the Mayor's office, in the feed and seed business, in the slaughterhouse. She knows businessmen and farmers; she visits with out-of-town guests and regulars.

So it doesn't surprise me that Mary Bouchard got involved with this whole investigation around Jude in the first place. Of course she talked to Matt and Ben as soon as possible after she saw the article about a body found in Emma's barn. Of course she gossiped her way through pouring coffee, telling Matt and Ben god-knows-what about those months Jude and I hung out together. "Didn't like her," I could hear my mother say, "she had a trashy mouth and looked like an orphan."

I pull up to a gas pump at the Mason City exit. The wind across the Iowa plains is always strong here. It's just down the road, in Cedar Lake, where Buddy Holly's plane went down. Every time I stop, I understand how that plane crashed. Paper napkins float across the parking lot like tumbleweed and a constant wind rattles the metal cigarette advertisement over my head. A gust every few minutes shakes my standing car. It's a warm fall day. I'm grateful for that.

I walk into the convenience store where rubbery hot dogs spin on a warming machine inside the front door.

"Pump number four," I say to the man behind the counter. He wears

Out of Harmony

an Iowa Seed baseball cap and a checkered shirt with snap buttons down the front.

"Fifteen twenty," he says. He hands me back four crumpled ones. Coins fall out of the cash register and into a little metal cup at the side. It looks like something from the game Mousetrap.

I always appreciate the drive back to Harmony. It gives me a chance to move from my life as the girlfriend of a conductor at the Minneapolis Orchestra to the simplicity of Harmony. To the language of hard R's and "bucks" and "I'n it?" As in "i'n it sump'tin?" or as in "that's five bucks," or as in "Neb-Rrraaaska."

I'm back in the car and looking through my ipod. I could listen to one of Eli's recordings and I feel like I should listen to it, but I search for Cyndi Lauper instead. How can I go wrong with Cyndi Lauper? I plug the ipod into my car stereo, put the car in gear, and get onto the I-35 ramp headed for Des Moines.

"Why don't you fly, Ally?" Eli had urged me for the past week.

"I want to drive. I like it."

"I don't get it," Eli was half-teasing, half-serious. I could tell by his tone. "An hour to fly there, I'll even pay your way, I told you. It's so much safer."

"I like having the time to think."

"Geez. Seven hours of thinking?" He patted my leg and laughed.

I didn't think it was funny.

"Oh come on. Where's your sense of humor?"

He squeezed my knee hard and I pulled away from him quickly.

"God, Eli!" I stormed out of the room and shut the bathroom door a little too strongly.

"Ally," he knocked on the door, "come on, I was just kidding."

I didn't answer because I didn't want to say what I was thinking. I didn't want to say "you're always kidding. Everything seems to be a fucking joke to you."

"Baby, you can drive if you want. I don't care. I just want you to be safe."

When I came out of the bathroom, he gave me a hug. I didn't hug back. "You've got to work through this, Ally."

I ignored the deeper conversation he was bringing up and said, "I'm driving to Nebraska, Eli." I broke from his hug. I didn't want to be the irrational one anymore. The one whose friend just died. The one who wouldn't commit. The one who had an affair.

Shame rises in me as I pass a makeshift billboard in the form of a semi-trailer that announces a tractor/livestock show outside of Latimer, Iowa. It happened in early August, nearly two months ago. I wish I could go back two months in time—when Jude was alive to me and I wasn't an adulterer.

How do I know that Eli hasn't cheated too? How do I know that Jane is just "one of the guys" to him? Softie made it sound like something had happened between him and her girlfriend. Softie and Jane, with their stupid open relationship.

Another wave of shame. So powerful I want to cry, but nothing comes. It's easier to blame them. They somehow seem to have it all worked out.

"True Colors" comes from the ipod and I turn up the volume. This song always reminded me of Jude. Not for any particular reason. I was in college when it came out, so it was a few years after Jude and I ran around together. A few years after she disappeared.

I laugh at myself now. Why would I ever think she would have gotten out of Harmony? How could I have so much hope that it was the town, not her self, she needed to get away from?

Come to think of it, Jude probably would've hated this song. She would've thought it too sappy. She would've gotten much more into REM or the Violent Femmes, or better yet… Ani DiFranco. She would've really gotten into Ani.

Jude's music was a lot like Ani's. Well, I guess I only heard that one song. She sang it to me once. Her eyes drifting from my eyes to the ground, as if she was embarrassed. But she was disarming. Her voice was rough but appealing.

"It's set to kind of a mix of carnival and funeral music, like this," then she hummed the tune. It made bumps rise on my skin. "It'll be like an organ in a church." She kept humming it and it did have kind of an eerie joy to it.

Then she sang in a low voice with a quick rhythm, but her voice was soft. "Give me my pride, give me open eyes, give me every last word when we say goodbye."

My eyes rest on the license plate of the car in front of me; a car that's going about ten miles below the speed limit. Other cars are zooming past us. I look in the rearview mirror and pass the car myself. Then I turn off the stereo and try to think of the rest of the words that Jude sang to me so long ago. We went to the river all the time that spring and early summer, before she disappeared; before I went to college.

She sang the song that day, two weeks before I graduated. Now I remember that I didn't promise to go to New Orleans with Jude then. It's not like I wrote.

No. She walked away, all defeated, and dropped down on a sand bar.

I caught up with her as she sat with her knees pulled to her chest. She watched her foot leave an impression in the sand; she'd push her foot into the sand, then pull it away. There were five tiny dots on top of two pads—her heel and the bridge of her foot. The water ran up over the sand bar and washed it away. She did it again.

"Hey Ally," she said without looking at me.

"Yeah?" I started pushing my feet in the sand to see if I could do the same thing.

"I wrote a song. Wanna hear it?"

I nodded.

Then she did that creepy music and started singing in a low voice. Weeks later, we wrote down the lyrics together. I probably still have them in that box of stuff Mom wants me to go through in Harmony. But I remember snippets of the song and I can still hear her voice singing it, "This is the sound of my mind gone blank and the noise that I hear when I'm trying not to think; I gotta bend my ears when I wanna hear, just a little bit of anything to block the fear."

Then she stopped and looked at her hand under the water. She said, "I wrote it for you, Alison."

I didn't know what to say, so after an awkward silence she started singing again. "Every time I wake I gotta prove to myself that the world ain't fake; It surprises me I'm allowed to live but then maybe I'm dead I ain't positive; Because it seems to me no one knows what's real; The only certainty in life is to do what you feel."

Then she hummed that eerie music again that made me want to leave right there and then.

I remember now how I hung onto myself, hugging my arms around my stomach, like something bad was going to happen. Like I should have seen it coming. Like I should have known she was never going to run away again.

I didn't know what to do so we sat in silence for what seemed like an eternity. Then I came up with something. Something stupid.

"They say that out in Kearney there are sandhill cranes," I said. "I heard about it from this lady at the store. They fly in by the hundreds and cover the Platte River Valley from Grand Island to Kearney. That would be cool to see."

Jude kept pushing her foot in the sand, watching it leave an impression and then disappear. As if she had never been there. As if she didn't exist.

"Maybe we should go." I said. Now I know I was just throwing her a bone.

Jude stood up. The seat of her men's shorts were soaked. "Let's try to get to that sandbar." She pointed to the other side of the Harmony bridge. She made it sound dangerous, but the Platte was running so low you could walk anywhere across it and barely get your ankles wet.

"Would you want to go to Kearney with me?"

"What for?" Jude asked.

"Well," I suddenly felt stupid, "you know, to…to see the cranes."

Jude laughed, but then stopped when she saw I was serious. She looked down at her feet, now submerged in the Platte River. "The sandhill cranes?"

"Yeah." I gulped down hard.

"How far is Kearney?" I don't think she really cared.

"Like, three hours. A lady I work with at the store said it was so worth it."

"Three hours to see some stupid birds? I don't think so."

"But, we could go look at the college too." I thought I'd figured out a way to tell her how much I liked her song.

"College? For me?"

"You could get into the music program…"

"Right." Jude laughed in a way that told me she was insulted. "I'm Jude Jenkins—not Alison 'Booooochar.'"

I don't know what got into me. Guilt? I stood up and faced her. I spoke strongly, "Your music is good, Jude. Geez, it's great." I was one step away from nifty.

Jude turned her back to me and looked down into the water.

"Come on," I pulled Jude's arm, trying to take her back to shore.

"Why?!?"

"We're getting in the car right now and we're driving to Kearney to see the fucking sandhill cranes."

"No!" Jude pulled her arm from my grip. "I told you, I'm not going anywhere. Not now! Not ever! Christ, let it go, Ally."

"What?"

"I'm not going anywhere," tears formed in Jude's eyes as she looked away, down to the bend of the river. "I'm a nobody."

After that song? She thought she was a nobody? "Don't say that."

Jude walked away then, looking down at her feet as she stepped onto the next sandbar. She looked peaceful as she watched her impression wash away with each movement of the river.

She looked like she was thinking of New Orleans.

Now I look out across the plains from my front windsheild and wish

I could drive forever. I wish I could drive to Louisiana, or Kearney even. I wish I could go somewhere to bring Jude back.

Ames is just a few miles ahead of me. I'm a little over halfway home and I'm just not ready for it yet. A truck whizzes past me and another and another. Must be a convoy. Breaker, Breaker—haven't heard that song in a long time.

I think about playing the alphabet game, where each letter of the alphabet is picked out on billboards and road signs. Trucks are off-limits. But that game is better on I-80; there's a lot more road signs to choose from. There's not much out here.

The wind blows across the interstate and I fight my car to keep it in line. I see the trailer of the semi in front of me swaying. The semi has a bumper sticker on the back that reads "Welcome to America. Now speak English."

Great. Where the fuck am I?

I smile at myself. For this fucking language. I picked it up from Jude, just as my mother feared. "Fucking redneck," that's what Jude would say about the bumper sticker, but then she'd say something like, "Too bad I'm one too."

I never thought of her as a redneck—maybe she thought she inherited that from her father. Or maybe she thought of herself as a member in the redneck club because she lived in an incinerator. Because she tore the red "family" sticker off the incinerator wall.

Or maybe she thought it because of the way people looked at her.

"I can't come in here by myself," Jude told me once as we stood in front of the vast magazine assortment at Harmony Travel and News. She glanced at the woman behind the counter.

"What do you mean?" That lady was always nice to me, but she definitely looked at Jude differently.

Jude made a nod toward the clerk. "She doesn't like me coming in here. She thinks I'm gonna steal something."

I moved between Jude and the clerk. The clerk got out of her chair and repositioned herself to have a good view of Jude.

"That's crap." I whispered. Jude kind of laughed.

"Better be careful. You're starting to sound like me."

That was right after we met. It was the day she shared her first secret with me. Jude put the *Rolling Stone* back on the shelf and whispered, "Let me show you something, Ally." She seemed slightly playful. Relaxed.

"Sure." I put my *People* magazine back on the shelf.

We stepped out to the street and I started walking toward my car.

"Leave it there," she said, her hands in her jacket pockets. She nodded for me to follow her around the corner.

We walked a couple of blocks in silence. I had somehow learned to let Jude tell me things in her own time. She stood at the end of an alley and looked both ways, I guess for anyone who might have been watching. Then she grabbed my sleeve and said, "C'mon."

"Where are we going?" I followed her down the alley.

She didn't respond; she just jumped up on a ramp behind the abandoned Harmony Opera House.

"This place gives me the creeps," I looked up at the three-story structure.

Jude looked up to the top of the opera house then back at me. "Why?"

I shrugged. "I don't know it's…spooky."

She laughed, then held out her hand, begging me to join her. "I like it. Remember that old grocery store that used to be here?"

"There was a grocery store here?" She helped me climb up onto a concrete platform.

"Yeah, my mom brought me here once. I just barely remember it, but I remember this old guy was real nice to me."

A few pigeons flew out of a window on the top floor.

"I can trust you, right?" Jude's voice sounded young all of the sudden. This was one, two months after we started hanging out. Let's see, it was October. Right before Halloween, which amplified the creepiness of the abandoned Opera House.

"Yeah, you can trust me," my breath rolled out in a puff in the air. I blew on my hands.

"Cuz it's real important. You can't tell anyone." Jude seemed to be having second thoughts about showing me her home. "I live here."

I looked back up to the top of the Opera House. "What?"

"Here." She pointed to the concrete and brick structure at the end of the platform we were standing on.

"What?" I didn't believe her at first, but I wasn't sure I should tell her I thought she was kidding.

"C'mon." She lifted up a metal bar and pulled open the rusted metal door. She jumped into the structure and looked back up at me, her legs were out of sight.

"What…what is this?"

"It's where I live," Jude whispered. "C'mon." She wiggled her fingers at me.

I had a sudden moment of thinking perhaps she was some kind of serial killer. There was always something a bit edgy about Jude. Then I poked my head inside the door and saw a small mattress, a camp stove, some candles, cardboard on the floor and walls, and a few pictures—two that looked like they were right out of a motel.

"What is this?" I said as I jumped down into the structure. It was a little warmer inside, but not by much. Kind of like being in a garage.

"I think it was part of the grocery store. Don't shut the door all the way," she warned.

The ceiling was only a few feet above our heads, probably about seven feet tall. It was about as long, but not quite as wide, maybe only six feet wide. It didn't really smell like anything but dirt in there. Jude sat down on the mattress. "Here, sit." She moved some old clothes out of the way. I sat on the thin mattress, copying the way Jude sat with her knees pulled to her chest.

"This is where I live." She said in a proud way.

"Don't you get cold?" I was of course not thinking in survival mode, as Jude had to.

"Oh yeah, that's why I got this," she rapped on the metal camp stove. "It's not much, but it helps a little. And see?" She patted on the mattress beneath us. "I have a sleeping bag. It's not so bad."

At first I felt kind of like the place was too dirty. A used sleeping bag from Goodwill; a mattress on the floor; the occasional bug crawling across the mattress.

But really, it wasn't so bad. We'd hang out there at night. Fire up the camp stove, pull the sleeping bag up over us, sit shoulder-to-shoulder. We'd have some candles lit. Sometimes we sipped on hot chocolate I bought at McDonalds. Other times, we sipped on black coffee that Jude somehow got for free from the 7-Eleven that was a block away (where Jude and I also used the bathroom).

When the cops came through the alley on their nightly drive-through, we quickly turned down the camp stove and blew out the candles. We could hear them coming when they turned the corner, their tires picking up gravel. It was like a game—hiding out in the incinerator. Well, a game to me. To Jude it was something more.

"You can't ever tell anyone about this place, Ally." She said to me that day she showed me her home.

"I won't."

"Seriously." Jude's voice changed when she talked like this. It was like she could turn off the being-a-kid button and turn on this other, serious button.

"Yeah. I know."

She rested her chin on her knees and clasped her hands around her ankles, then said softly, "I can't go back, Ally."

"Maybe someday you can." God, I was so naïve. I really thought Jude just had some argument with her dad. I thought that she'd eventually go home. That they'd patch things up.

"No, you don't know…you can't ever know…" It scared me the way she was almost crying.

I didn't say anything because there didn't seem to be anything to say.

I move into Des Moines where I never know if I should go the speed limit or 20 miles faster like everyone else. I move into the right lane and opt for the speed limit. I'm in no hurry anyway.

And I feel tired. Tired of all this freaking thinking. I laugh at myself. I wish I could stay overnight at a motel. I could just call Mom and Eli and tell them I had some car trouble; I could spend the whole night writing. Writing the stories that work through the thoughts in my head. But this car-trouble story is not without problems—Eli will say "I told you to fly" or even worse, he'll come down to rescue me. And Mom—geez, Mom will go tell everyone in Harmony about how her daughter got stranded in Des Moines and "Isn't that just her luck?" and make it some fantastic story. "She had to walk all the way to some seedy motel. She could have been raped!"

So onward I drive. Even though I know I shouldn't, I pick up my ipod and try to find something new. I look up, look down, look up, look down. Finally, I just hit shuffle and let the ipod determine my music. Eli's rich music comes in through the speaker. Oh well, it's a relief to get Jude's music out of my head. The sound of the rough and edgy organ. The beat of her lyrics, like a drum boom boom booming.

Jude loved the sound of the drums. It makes sense that she made her lyrics drumlike. She liked to rap tap tap on everything. Pop cans, empty bottles, dumpsters, alley walls, the floor, the air, some paper, her skateboard, the wall. Rat a tat tat, she drummed with her fingers, broken chopsticks (found in the dumpster), slightly bent forks (from Goodwill), pens, pencils, even the ends of shoelaces. Tap, tap, tap.

It was as if she couldn't stop herself. She drummed mindlessly while she talked, while she listened, sitting in class, at the grocery store, eating from a can—rat a tat tat on the side.

That's why I finally decided to buy her a pair of drumsticks, because of all the tapping. So it was a day in December, I guess a few weeks after she told me about her dad, that I stepped into Harmony Music Store.

"What kind of drumsticks do you want? Mallets, brushes, or just drumsticks?" The clerk was older than my dad and about two feet taller than me. His graying hair somehow intimidated me.

"I want drumsticks," I said loudly, "you know, like for a drum."

The man gave a kind of half smile. "Well, do you want Truelines, Zildjian's, Vic Firth's, Promarks?"

I gave him a blank look.

"Do you want hickory or maple or nylon?"

I said nothing.

"5A's or 7A's?"

"Uh, whatever's least expensive," I said, embarrassed. The man gave me an annoyed look. "Well," I felt nervous, "what do they cost?"

"Depends on what kind you want—a pair could cost ya three bucks. Or it could cost ya ten bucks."

"Okay, um," I looked unwittingly at the rows of sheet music to my left, "I'll take a pair of the three dollar ones."

"Wood or nylon. For three bucks, you can't get more than hickory with the wood ones."

I really just wanted to get out of the store with freaking drumsticks in hand. "Wood is fine." Wood was all I'd ever seen. Who played with nylon drumsticks? What did they even look like?

"We've got some nice Zildjians for three bucks."

"Okay," I followed the man to the back of the store. He picked up the drumsticks and started telling me all of the features of these particular sticks. My mind glazed over. I just wanted to have the damned sticks.

He thumped the pair of sticks in his big hands a couple of times, waiting for my final approval.

"Uh, yeah, they seem fine."

He gave me another half smile. I felt about four feet shorter than he at that moment. I paid for the drumsticks and left the store as quickly as I could. Just as I opened the door, a brisk fall wind kicked up and the door practically knocked me backwards. I stumbled over the threshold as I pushed my way out of the store.

I quickly jumped into my Pinto and drove home. I tucked the

drumsticks under my jacket and went inside. Mom was in the kitchen, just my luck. I tried to avoid her attention as I dug in the cupboard for the foil.

"What are you doing with that?" my mom asked.

"What?" Again, I felt myself blush.

"The foil."

"Oh, uh, a school project." I said and quickly went to my room. She never asked about my school projects, so I knew that would be the end of the conversation. Besides, she was used to the creative flare I brought to my projects. Once, I had to make a map. Most kids sat down with a sheet of paper and drew. I constructed a two-dimensional chart—with latitude and longitude—of Venezuela. I papier-mâchéd the landscape—hills and valleys—and painted the ocean with juice from various canned veggies and fruits that we had in the kitchen. Cranberry juice, olive juice, pickle juice, and beet juice. The combination of these juices made the best ocean stain a young girl could find. Mom brought some tea bags from work because she heard that they stain nicely too, so I was able to paint the beaches with the tea. I got an A and Mom never questioned my tactics again.

So off to my bedroom I went with my piece of foil and the drumsticks tucked under my jacket. Thinking these drumsticks would somehow make things better for Jude. That they would somehow give her hope or some such thing. And by the time I got to the bedroom, I looked out the window and saw that it was beginning to snow.

Now, a strong gust of wind tries to push my car off to the shoulder. My pen rolls back and forth on the notebook in the passenger seat. I take the next exit in West Des Moines and pull into the parking lot of a gas station. It's a busy place; people are lined up at the pump, truckers are parked out back, people go in and out of the Quick Mart.

At first I feel awkward; hoping no one asks me any questions. Then I think, who cares about some woman writing in her car? I park in a spot at the edge of the parking lot, trying to be inconspicuous. I open my sun roof, lock my doors (my mother's warnings of being raped and murdered at the side of the road still play in my head), shut off my car, and pick up my pen and notebook. I put myself back in my bedroom, looking out the window at the snow coming down while I held Jude's drumsticks in my hand. I imagined Jude out there, alone on the streets, shivering in the incinerator. And I knew those drumsticks wouldn't change a thing.

> Jude felt the first snowflake drop on her forehead and burn into a droplet that rolled down her face. When it crossed the bridge of her nose, she wiped it away like a tear. As the flakes

dropped around her like confetti, she pulled up her collar and shuddered. The snow accumulated fast. She watched it stick to passing cars that, at first, ground the snow into the pavement where it melted into water, but the faster the snow came down, the less it melted. It began to stick to the road, to the cars, to the trees, to Jude's eyebrows, to her hair, to her shoulders, to the wheels of her skateboard. The wheels became sluggish and Jude pushed off so hard that she felt a muscle tighten and ache in her right thigh. The snow crunched and moaned and she strained to push her way through it.

"Fuck!" she said as she finally picked up the wet board, its wheels frozen, and shook the snow off of her wet hair.

So she stomped through the covered ground—the snow crunching under her work boots, soaking into the fabric as it piled on top of the toe, then fell at the end of her step. She kicked it every now and then, as if this would make it go away. As if this would change the winter ahead.

"And she imagined her father, drinking his bottle of gin, the burn rising inside his belly, up into his chest, his arms, his throat. Sitting in front of the tv—warm in his chair, drinking drinking drinking. If she were there, he would tell her to come over to him. She wouldn't want to, afraid of what would happen if she got too close. But he would hold the bottle up to her face and swish the liquid inside. "Go ahead, drink up." Jude would shake her head no because she hated the taste of alcohol. She hated it because he would hold the back of her head and force the bottle into her mouth. She would get so much in her mouth at once that she would want to spit it out. A trickle would go down the side of her face. All she could do was to swallow it. And he probably laughed as he watched his daughter wipe the alcohol off her face.

And that night winter began, Jude knew going back was not an option. Going back would be like dying. So she let the cold go deep inside her. Her hair was soaked, her jacket, her shoes, her shirt—everything, soaked and cold. She shivered.

She walked toward the grocery store, a good mile away from her hideout. She stood with her arm draped around the lightpost, looking into the glass front of the store.

Out of Harmony

I look out the car window. Cars are pulling in and out of the parking lot, constant movement is going on around me as guilt rises in my chest.

Why do I still feel guilty that I wasn't at the store that night? I told her once that she could come to the house, just to warm up, or to stay one night. I bet she imagined herself—going to my house, ringing the bell, knocking on the door—whatever it was to make herself known. And I would have opened the door to see Jude with snow blanketing her shoulders, her hair wet, her board locked.

Looking back, I'm glad Jude didn't come over. Because what would I have done? to open the door to find Jude, cold and wet at my door, with my mother lost in the kitchen, banging cupboards while my father sat in his bedroom, looking hopelessly at the snow falling outside, knowing he'd have to watch the blood of the animals soak into that crisp whiteness. Knowing he'd actually see the blood as it drained from their bodies.

I would have done exactly what Jude had been doing. I would have tried to hide my family from anyone I came in contact with. I would have quickly rushed her past my mother in the kitchen, who would take mental notes to gossip about the next day. I would have rushed her past my father in the bedroom so she couldn't see the blank stare in his eyes. I would have pulled her into my bedroom and kicked out my two younger siblings, even as they poked a broomstick at the ceiling, trying to get the rats to scurry overhead. And while I was trying to hide my life away from Jude, she would think I was trying to hide her away from them.

And it was this reason that kept Jude from coming over to my place. No, she had been through it before. She had gone over to two different girls' houses in 7th and 9th grades. She went over to their houses and even said hello to their parents. And after each occasion, her friends told her they couldn't hang out with her anymore. "My mom thinks you're a bad influence," her one friend said as she rolled her eyes. "She called you 'white trash'—can you believe it?"

And Jude had managed a little laugh—she had tossed her bangs back out of her eyes as if words didn't matter. As if words didn't penetrate her psyche like gin. She had just laughed—her tough laugh—her "I don't give a shit" laugh—and she had walked away. She walked away as if the words didn't hurt her deep inside. As if she were all these things the parents thought she was—as if she invited her father's advances. As if she was the shit that would rub off on their precious daughters.

For this reason, Jude never knocked on my door, or stayed at my house.

I take a deep breath to fill my chest with something other than sadness and turn back to the page.

Jude walked through the snow. One mile, from the grocery store to the alley where she lived. The snow grew higher and higher on her boots. It soaked deeper into her hair; it stuck to her clothing. When she finally got to the incinerator, she immediately lit the camp stove as she peeled off layers of wet clothes. Her skin was clammy and goose bumps rose over her body as she stripped each layer off. She rubbed the dampness out of her skin with the Goodwill blanket. The blanket was rough and scratchy. She quickly pulled on her dry clothes. She rubbed her hand over the small flame on the camp stove. Every now and then, she'd push out the door of the incinerator to make sure that snow didn't lock her in. She lay down on the bed roll and pulled the slightly damp sleeping bag over herself. She lay there quietly, trying to keep herself from thinking about her father. Trying to keep herself from thinking about rubbing off on me. Trying to think about how to keep people from knowing that she was there. Trying to figure out how to disappear.

The wind blows hard over the Iowa plains and my car sways, even sitting still. A swirl of dirt rises like a tornado over the field next to the gas station. I put the pen and notebook back on the passenger seat and watch the dust churn across the field until it breaks up and settles on the horizon.

I close the notebook. I turn on the car. I put the car in drive. I sit at a light at the freeway entrance and see signs to Kansas City, to Omaha, to Minneapolis. I consider straying for a moment, then turn onto the freeway toward Harmony.

My mind is blank for awhile. As if my brain needs to shut down and just watch the landscape roll past. I'm in the part of Iowa where hills roll out in front of me and around me.

A faint scent of cigarette smoke rises in my car. I wonder where it comes from. A passing car maybe?

My eyes stray off the road and onto the water tower in Adair; it's painted yellow with a big smiley face in black.

"What's that fuckin' thing?" Jude's voice rings.

Suddenly I get an image of her, on that day in November when the snow came down, drawing a smiley face in the snow with the toe of her boot. She studied it for a moment, then kicked it away.

As I remember what we were doing out in the snow, shame, regret, and embarrassment rise up inside me.

It was that day after the snow fell, I woke up at nine a.m.—on a Saturday morning, no less. Mom and Dad were both off at work. Dad had picked up an extra shift and Mom always worked on Saturday mornings. Karen was still asleep and John was downstairs watching Saturday morning cartoons. I could hear the tv through the floorboards. *Bugs Bunny.*

I went downstairs to watch tv with John, my mind in a half-daze. My hair pushed up on one side of my head, lines from the pillow marked my face. Outside the living room window, I saw the blanket of deep snow on the ground. Overnight, the snow had covered the tree branches, weighing them down. It had piled on top of cars and houses. It had buried bushes and grasses. Dad had already shoveled the sidewalk—before the landlord could get on his case about it. I had heard the sound of metal scraping cement when it was still dark out. There were crisp cuts in the snow where the sidewalk met the grass. The space where Dad's old chevy was parked left a blank spot in the street. An empty space.

Cartoon voices and sounds came from the tv and I looked at John, sitting cross-legged on the old brown couch.

I looked out the window at the snow piled high on curbs and lawns and rooftops and suddenly panic washed over me. Jude had been out in the snowstorm; I wondered if she was safe inside the incinerator.

"John, I'm going out," I said as I grabbed my keys.

"In your pajamas?!?" John laughed.

I felt like yelling back "Yes, in my pajamas!" but then I felt ridiculous. "NO!" I yelled as I ran up the stairs, two at a time, to my bedroom. I felt a sense of urgency as I threw off my pj's and pulled on some jeans. I wondered how warm Jude's sleeping bag really was.

And I bought her freaking drumsticks for Christmas! Drumsticks when I should've bought her a warm blanket. I looked at the glistening foil-wrapped package and thought about taking them back to the jerk at the music store.

But then I imagined hauling over a blanket to her. "What the fuck is this?" she'd say. "I don't need your fucking charity."

So I left the drumsticks behind and threw on my old winter coat—it was my dad's old army jacket, but it was warm enough. It went down to my knees.

I brushed the piles of snow off my car and got down to the ice below. "Fuck!" I said my new favorite word.

Dad got me a free scraper from the hardware store. It was crap, but it was better than nothing. I started the old Pinto right away. I was relieved that it wasn't really that cold outside—it was more damp, and dry, all at the same time. Still, I had this fear of finding Jude's cold, hard body frozen inside her little concrete house. Or maybe her body burned to a crisp inside that old incinerator—the camp stove having somehow overturned and catching her sleeping bag bed on fire.

My body began to sweat under all my clothes as I scraped the hatchback window.

I drove my Pinto over mounds of snow. I plowed through the unshoveled city streets, passing snow plows going the other way. I got stuck once and rocked the car back and forth, forward and reverse, forward and reverse, until I got myself out. I kept myself from crying by biting on my tongue, by holding my breath.

I trudged through the snow in the dirty alley, which also hadn't been plowed yet.

As I approached the incinerator, my heart began to pound inside my coat. This was the first time I'd ever come to Jude's hideout uninvited. This was long before we slept together.

I saw the snow pattern in front of Jude's door. Like a snow angel, there was a wing that fanned away from the entrance. The snow had been brushed back, piled in a neat tower where the door stopped.

I pounded on the metal. "Jude!" I yelled and it echoed off the alley walls. There was no answer, so I pounded harder. "Jude!"

On the third time, when I got no answer, I reluctantly pulled open the door. A small amount of warmth welcomed me. Jude's bed was neatly made. Kerosene laced the air.

I didn't know whether to be relieved or to continue to panic. Where could she go on a morning like this?

I suddenly felt mad at her. Why did she have to live like this? Why was she so stubborn? I wanted to gather her things together and load them in my car. I wanted to tell her enough was enough, she was coming home to live with my family. I wanted to...

"What the fuck!?!" I heard her voice echo in the alley. I jumped. "Who the...?" Jude had her protective voice on—her "don't fuck with me" voice. But then she saw me. "Hey! What the... why are you here?!?"

"I was worried about you. The snow, I..." I suddenly felt like I was five years old and got caught playing with matches.

Jude squeezed past me and went to her camp stove. "Yeah, well, don't worry the fuck about me."

I felt a sudden flash of embarrassment.

"And close the fucking door."

I gulped. "Do you want me to leave?"

"No," her voice softened, "Just close the fucking door."

I pulled the door shut and sat on the bedroll. I felt somehow uncomfortable, as if I couldn't sit still. Jude was messing around with the camp stove.

"What are you doing?" I felt less comfortable with the silence than with getting into her business.

"I got more kerosene."

"Where?"

"I blew the guy at the gas station, okay?!?"

I kept quiet after that. I knew she was kidding—she wouldn't blow the guy at the gas station. At least I hoped she wouldn't.

It was quiet for a long time as she fiddled with the camp stove. I felt like an obedient child. I was actually too hot, but I didn't want to take my jacket off. I didn't know if Jude wanted me to stay or to go.

As she tinkered in silence, I tried to figure out what to say. There was a click click click from the camp stove, but no flame. "Fuck!" Jude said softly as she wiped dripping snot from her nose.

I felt my heart pound as I tried to open my mouth—my words caught in my throat. I swallowed down the dryness.

Click click click.

"Fuck."

"I should…" I managed to say.

Click click click.

"I should get back to my sister and brother."

Jude didn't say anything.

"They're home alone."

"Aren't they old enough to take care of themselves?" She finally spoke. Her voice was normal again.

"Well, yeah, but…"

"The nice thing about snow," she finally got a flame in the stove, "is that it doesn't get so cold out. You know?"

"Yeah. I was thinking that on the way over."

"Nice hair, by the way."

I blushed as I touched the mound of hair on the left side of my head.

"I hear it's the new thing."

I laughed. "Yeah, well, I was worr—" I rechose my words. "I thought you might like some company."

"Did you see how I kept the snow away from the door?"

"Yeah. It looks like a snow angel."

"A what?"

"Snow angel. You know…?" I flapped my arms up and down like an idiot.

She looked blankly at me.

I relaxed my arms at my sides. "Didn't you make snow angels when you were a kid?"

She shrugged and looked away. It was the same look I got from her everytime I said something like that. "Didn't you ever play 'Operation'?"; "Didn't you watch *Bugs Bunny*?"; "Didn't you love going to the pool when you were a kid?"

You'd think I would've learned to stop asking these kinds of questions.

"Hey," I said quickly, "let's go out to the river." By that time, going to the river was something we did together about once a week. Just to hang out. Jude always seemed calmer by the river.

"You want to go to the river?" she looked at me incredulously.

I took a knit hat out of my pocket and pulled it down over my hair. "Yeah, come on!"

She looked reluctant, but she pulled her Goodwill gloves on and shut off the camp stove. "Okay," she said willingly, "let's go."

Jude sat quietly in the passenger seat as I drove out to the Platte. Luckily, the highway had been plowed; still, I drove slowly, just in case there were slick spots. Jude slouched down in her seat, letting the heat inside the car blow into her face. Once when I looked over, her eyes were closed, her face had softened so that she looked like a little girl—peaceful and innocent. Then she woke up and asked if I had any cigarettes in the glove compartment.

I got to the road where I would've turned into the state park, but the roads were, of course, not cleared. I couldn't even tell where the road ended and the grass began. But I really wanted to show Jude this one thing. I needed to.

Jude snickered, "Hah. You're screwed."

I sat on the lonely highway, keeping watch in my rearview mirror and glancing back into the park. I knew my way around. Even before I met Jude, I would go to the river just to sit high on a bluff, hang my feet over the side, and pretend it was the Mississippi—flowing southward to New Orleans.

I knew this road led to a little bridge on the other side of the trees. So I gunned the car, onto where I thought the road was. I gunned it fast so we fishtailed around on snow and, hopefully road. Jude didn't say a word, she just held onto the bar above the passenger window. I turned the corner and saw the bridge, but the car kept turning, spinning uncontrollably, in a perfect 360 degrees until we stopped facing the direction we came. My car jerked because I didn't give it enough gas for the clutch. But once it stopped, I pretended that I meant for it to do so. I turned off the ignition and said, "Okay, here we are."

"Jesus," Jude just looked at me with, I wanted to think awe, but I think it was more surprise. It felt good. Like I had just proven something. Like for once I wasn't "good ol' Ally." Like I was a bad ass. Just for a second. And I kept it to myself that I was worried we wouldn't be able to get out of the snow as easily.

"C'mon," I said to Jude. She reluctantly followed me.

We stepped into mid-calf-deep snow. Jude didn't say a word. She simply followed.

"Watch," I said, making her stop where she was as I moved a few feet from her.

"You find a nice, even patch of snow," I set my feet in the snow, keeping my stance open. I put on my hood and spread my arms, "then you just fall back."

I landed with a thud, but the snow perfectly broke my fall. I raised my head slightly to look at Jude, who looked unimpressed. "then you do this." I swished my arms and legs—spreading my legs, then bringing them together; raising my arms above my head, then bringing them to my sides. Swish, swish, swish.

"The trick is getting out of this so that you don't ruin it—like this." I sat up, twisted to place my hand outside the angel, then pushed myself up. It was easier when I was a little kid, but I still managed. I left footprints at the bottom of my angel.

"There!" It wasn't half bad. It wasn't the best angel either, but I thought maybe Jude would have better luck. "Now you try."

"Nah." Jude said as she looked at the angel.

"Yeah. Come on." I pulled her sweatshirt hood over her head. I felt like I wanted to kiss her. Even then. But I didn't. "Try it. It's fun."

Jude pulled the hood down. "No. Don't want to."

"Why not? Try something new. C'mon." I was almost pleading. Jude turned and walked toward the car. "Just do this one thing. It'll make you feel better."

"I don't need to feel better." Jude opened the car door.

I grabbed hold of her arm before she closed the door. "C'mon. Please? Do it just once." All I wanted was for her, for once, to have some fun. I guess there was some part of me that wanted her to have some of her childhood back.

She ripped her arm from my grip. "No!"

The strength of her voice was like a slap across the face. "Gawd. Okay, then," I said as Jude slammed the car door. If it weren't my car, I would've just fucking walked back to town.

She sat there, with her face turned to the front windshield, her jaw clenched. She didn't move.

"Jesus," I said, brushing the snow off my shoulders. I quietly got back into the car and my tires spun. I put it in reverse, then in first, reverse, first, reverse, first. I rocked back and forth, spinning tires, snow and dirt flying up behind the car, Reverse, first, reverse, first. Jude sat quietly. Reverse, first. Finally, I spun forward, fishtailing but moving. I gunned it and got back to the highway.

There was complete silence in the car as we drove the seven miles back to town. I was so mad, my fingertips burned from gripping the steering wheel.

I stopped the car in the alley. Jude didn't get out; she just sat there. "I'll see you later." I said without looking at her. I found out later why she didn't just get out of the car.

"Yeah." Her voice was soft, but I didn't care; I was too angry. When she finally got out, I drove away. When I got to the end of the alley, I glanced in my rearview mirror. She was still standing there, looking at my car as it turned out of sight.

Eli's music suddenly fills my car in a crescendo and I turn down the stereo. I grip the wheel as I think of what came next. But the full orchestra makes me think of how Eli wrote this piece when we went on vacation to Spain. He was inspired by La Sagrada de la Familia in Barcelona. He said he thought of this music when he looked up into the towers of the cathedral-in-progress and felt emptiness that needed to be filled. And so he heard this music with trumpets and french horns, violins and oboes. It rose to the top of the tower and swirled around until it burst out like a bird from its entrapment in a cathedral prison.

Right now it's bursting and I turn off the music.

"Are you in love with him, Ally?" Jude's voice rings in my head.

If Jude were here, she'd press me for an answer. She wouldn't speak any words, she'd just stare me down. And I'd say, "I care deeply for him. I would never hurt him." And there would just be silence for another long, uncomfortable moment. And then she'd say "Ally and Eli" in a singsong voice that would be followed by "first comes love, then comes marriage, then comes baby in a baby carriage." Then every time I would talk to her about my relationship she'd say "Ally and Eli." As if to say, "But you aren't in love with him," or "you don't want to have a baby."

I pick up my ipod to find different music. My hands are shaking, but I want to take control of my music situation. I search through artists, trying to find something I'm in the mood for; something that gets my mind off Eli. My tires shake because I've drifted to the shoulder and have run over those pavement variations in place that warn about leaving the road.

Geez. I take the Shelby exit and drive into the parking lot of a small diner. I don't turn off the car, but I take my foot off the clutch. The car jerks forward and stalls. What's wrong with me?

I'm facing the interstate. I grip the steering wheel to stop the shaking in my hands.

"But you don't want to have a baby." Jude's voice again.

"Ehhhh, shut up!" I say it out loud because then maybe that voice will go away.

"Are you okay, honey?" A woman is peeking in through the passenger side of my car. She's got to be about seventy years old; her hair is tied back. She's looks like a farmer's wife.

"Yeah. Fine."

The woman stands a few inches away from the car as if she's slightly scared of me. "Maybe you should take a break from the road, dear. Get a bite to eat."

"No, really, I'm fine," my voice shakes and I can't stop it.

"They have good cinnamon rolls here. You should get your blood sugar back up." The woman's husband backs his beat-up pickup truck next to her. "You take care now; there's other people on the road with you."

Okay, now she's pissing me off. "I'm fine." I manage not to say "leave me the fuck alone" and I grip the steering wheel so she can't see my hands shaking.

The woman looks at me one last time before the truck pulls away.

"Ally and Eli," Jude's singsong rings in my head again.

Shut the fuck up! I think. *If you hadn't left, I wouldn't be with Eli now.*

"You're the one who left," Jude sounds hurt this time.

Okay, maybe a cup of coffee would do me some good.

I get out of my car and the wind seems to want to blow me away. I'm above the interstate, watching cars zip past. There are a few buildings on the other side of the overpass, but other than that, this diner, and one old-fashioned gas station, Shelby isn't much to write home about.

Turns out, the diner and gas station are connected. There's a place to eat at the counter and some Formica booths along the glass window. A few farmers sit at the booths; they had a perfect view of me sitting in the car all this time.

"Coffee to go, please." I say to the woman behind the counter.

"Honey, we don't have it to go here. You'll have to sit down and drink it." She sloshes a small glass of ice water in front of me and taps the counter for me to sit.

No "to go"? How can that be possible?

"I'll be right back," I say to her. The woman looks perplexed.

Her confusion doesn't change when I return with my notebook and pen, plop down on the stool, and open the notebook.

The woman sets the ivory mug of hot coffee in front of me. It's pitch black and steam rises off the top of it. "Can I have cream and sugar please?"

She looks at me as if to say "oh, one of those."

As she gives me sugar packets and a container of cream, she asks, "Whatcha writing?"

Her question shocks me. No one in the cities would ever ask someone what they're writing. "Um, a story. About my friend. She died."

"Oh, I'm sorry to hear that, hon."

She stands looking at me for a minute, as if asking for me to say more. I take a sip of coffee.

"Tell you what, coffee is on the house," she taps her finger on the counter.

"Oh no, you don't have to—"

"Shoot, honey, when someone offers you a free cup of coffee, you just take it; unless it's coming from an old farmer who wants to sleep with you," she winks at me and laughs with a smoker's cough.

She makes me smile, "Well, thanks."

She waves me off then goes to the tables with a hot pot of coffee.

I rest my chin on my palm and stare down at the page.

The waitress is laughing and coughing with some of the farmers. They're talking about a church social, it sounds like, and I suddenly get an image of the farmers in polyester suits.

I've been doodling mindlessly and suddenly realize that I've drawn a snow angel on the page, my pen swooping back and forth like the arms and legs of a child.

I stop, turn the page, and look around to make sure no one has seen my weird angel-doodle.

I write "Two Weeks After Snow Angel," on the top of my page and underline it. I didn't see Jude for two weeks after that incident. I wonder what she did all that time?

I blow across the top of my coffee and take a sip. Then I write.

> Just before Christmas break, everything warmed up for a day and it began to rain. And the rain turned to ice as the sun went down and the ice covered the snow with a thin crisp crust.
>
> And at eleven thirty that night, Jude reappeared at the grocery store. Her hair was frozen into chunks of long strands. Even her eyebrows were covered in ice. "Alison?" she said to me softly, her eyes to the floor. "I need your help."
>
> Jude had waited out the last half hour of my shift. She sat on the ledge by the storefront windows, her knees tight to her chest. She pulled at the skin on her fingers—scratching them with her bitten-to-the-nub fingernails, biting them—tugging the nearly dead skin off.
>
> I wondered what frostbite looked like.
>
> She pulled enough skin off in some places for blood to come to the surface of the skin. She picked and scratched, bit and nibbled, until the skin was raw and more rough edges were exposed for her to scratch and pick, nibble and bite.
>
> After my shift, I called my dad to let him know I'd be home late. Even though it was midnight, I didn't think he'd worry about me. He knew I often came home at one in the morning after working a late shift. He knew it because he loved to stay up late at night—even after I came home and went to bed—watching war movies. He was infatuated with war movies. Anything that had to do with World War II. He wouldn't talk about his time in the war, but he would watch those same old movies over and over again.
>
> "Dad?" Jude was a few feet away from me and I turned my back so she couldn't hear me say, "I have to go over to a friend's to help her out."
>
> "Okay," he said. I heard the sound of explosions and gunfire in the background. I wondered how Mom could sleep with all that racket. But I guess maybe she found it as

comforting as I did. Listening to my Dad, late at night, in a private world we weren't allowed to enter. "Drive safely," he said just before he hung up.

Jude's hair was still wet, but had thawed out during her time waiting in the store. I wished she would have put her hood up as we walked outside, but she never put her hood up. She was trying to play it cool, but I could see how nervous she was. A sheet of ice lay beneath the layer of snow. I could feel it when we walked out to my car—every now and then I'd hit an icy patch.

"I couldn't do it by myself," she said softly, ashamed.

"It's okay," I knew that all was forgiven between us about the snow angels.

When we got to the incinerator, I could see Jude's problem. A sheet of ice covered the side of the building. Her crypt was sealed.

Her bloody fingers made sense now. One corner of the door of the incinerator had been painstakingly clawed at—there were little chips in the façade of the ice.

"I don't know what to do," Jude said. And then the inconceivable happened. Jude began to cry.

Feeling uncomfortable, I looked away from her. Then, I went to my hatchback and pulled out the hardware-store ice scraper. I walked past Jude and started chipping away at the corner of the door.

Jude wiped her tears with the palm of her hand. She rubbed away the snot with the sleeve of her jacket. I heard her sniffle a few times as I worked on the ice.

Chips of ice flew up around me as I worked with determination. After I chipped away the top and part of the side, I handed the scraper to Jude. She just squeezed her fingers into the top of the door and pulled, but the door was too frozen everywhere to budge any bit.

She chipped away at the sides for awhile. The tears had stopped flowing. When she got to the bottom of the door, she handed the scraper to me.

The water had seemingly puddled at the bottom of the door and the result was a chunk of ice about four inches thick.

I pounded away on the ice but it wouldn't budge. I chipped and chipped and chipped until there was a snap! of plastic.

"Fuck!" we both yelled simultaneously.

I threw the broken scraper to the ground; it bounced and slid under my car.

"Do you have a shovel at your house?" Jude asked, and all I could think of was it was fucking one in the morning and I didn't really want to be messing with this until three. My hands were getting numb.

"Why don't you just stay overnight at my house?" I asked.

Loud voices came from the bar at the other end of the alley. Some guy stumbled into the alley unaware, and unzipped his pants to pee.

"You don't fucking get it, do you?" Jude ignored the pissing man.

"What's the big deal? My dad won't care and my mom's asleep. They won't even ask questions."

Jude said nothing, but the scream that came out of her throat as she violently kicked the door to the incinerator was enough for me to know. There was something more to this than her fear of my parents asking questions.

"Hey!" The pissing man was zipping up his pants as he zig-zagged toward us. "What's going on there?"

"Fuck," I said quietly. So Jude didn't want people to know about her hideout and here she'd just invited some drunken creep to discover it.

Jude quickly called out to the guy, "Do you have a shovel or something? I think my cat's in here."

"Shit, no way," the guy said. He wore cowboy boots, a red baseball cap with a dirty ring around the brim, tight jeans with a heavy belt buckle with a bucking bronco on it.

"Yeah," Jude said, "I've been looking for her since the ice storm and I can hear her in there when I call for her." Jude pulled on the guy's jacket and made him come closer to the tin wall. "Buttons!" Jude called out and the guy leaned closer to the incinerator. Jude acted excited, "Uh! There!" She pointed her finger into the guy's arm. "Did you hear her?"

"Yeah, I sure did!" The guy stumbled back a bit with his skinny chicken legs. "Shit!"

Out of Harmony

I tried not to burst out laughing.

"Yeah, so, we almost managed to get her out, but there's all this ice at the bottom of the door and I'm so close and Buttons is so scared. I know she is." Jude's voice had a little-girl lilt.

"No waaaaay." The guy sounded like a stoner. A laugh exploded from my throat and I quickly turned it into a cough. The guy didn't seem to catch on. "Yeah, my truck's just around the corner. I've got a shovel in the back. Stay right here, and don't cry, okay?"

"Okay," Jude nodded her head innocently and my eyes started to well up with all the laughter I was holding inside.

The guy said to me. "Don't cry, it'll be okay." Then he zig-zagged back down the alley, slipping on the ice once and catching himself. When he was around the corner, Jude and I broke out laughing.

"Oh my gawd," I said, "You're so lucky he's drunk."

"Yeah, well, I know how to work drunk guys, believe me."

Headlights appeared around the corner and a big old blue Ford pickup came rolling down the alley. He stopped right behind my car.

"Why don't you two get in your car and warm up. I'll take care of the ice."

"No, no, that's okay," said Jude, but I was really thinking of how much I would've liked getting in my car to warm up. "I'm sure it'll take you no time at all to get Boots out."

"I thought your cat's name was Buttons," the guy said.

"Oh yeah, I'm sorry, Boots is at home. I always say the wrong name."

"I just thought..." the guy started chipping away at the ice with a shovel that appeared to be for shoveling shit. There was dung and hay stuck to the bottom of it. "...that was the name because my mom's cat is named Buttons."

Ice flew up in all directions as he chipped and chipped away at it. He cleared it out pretty fast and even cleared the path away from the door so that it could be opened. "Buttons!" He called out and I thought I would pee my pants.

"Buttons!" Jude called and it was all I could take, I burst out laughing. The guy looked at me and I pretended like I was crying.

Jude just looked at me and smiled. She once again called out, "Buttons!"

While the guy was looking at me, Jude squeezed her way into the incinerator. "Hey, do you have a flashlight?" Her voice was hollow and echoed inside her metal shelter.

"Oh, shit, yeah," the guy ran to his truck and brought out a flashlight. I couldn't take anymore, so I got into my car to keep warm.

I turned on my car and the heat was slow to rise around me. I watched as Jude squeezed out of the incinerator. She pretended like she was crying. The guy patted her shoulder, grabbed his shovel, and left her holding the flashlight.

She jumped in the passenger seat of my car, laughing. "Look, I got a flashlight out of the deal!"

"How...?"

"He felt so bad that I was still looking for my cat he told me to keep it." She clicked it on and off. "It's a nice one too."

"Oh my gawd!"

She put the flashlight under her chin and it lit up her face. I never noticed how beautiful her skin was before. "Hey, do you have to go home now?"

"Jesus, it's like one thirty, yeah."

"Why don't you stay over at my house?" She clicked off the flashlight.

Staying a night in that freezing cold concrete box didn't appeal to me, but I didn't want to say that to Jude. "Nah, my dad is expecting me." I didn't really know if this was true. I didn't really know if my dad would notice that I hadn't come home, and I knew my mom wouldn't notice that I was missing in the morning. She'd just leave for work at six and not check to see if I was in my bed.

"Oh, yeah." Jude looked deflated. "Yeah."

My cell phone rings. I quickly drop my pen and search for the cell in my jacket pocket. A new waitress looks at me, my coffee is gone, the farmers are gone. Jesus, how long have I been here?

"Hello?"

"Ally, it's Mom."

"Yeah?"

"Where are you? You should be here by now."

I look at a white-face clock with black lettering above the counter. "Shit, sorry Mom. I…I stopped for coffee and lost track of time."

"You stopped for coffee?!?"

She knows me well enough to know that I hardly ever stop on the drive to Harmony, unless it's for gas.

"Uh, yeah, I…I'll get back in the car right now."

"Where are you?"

"In Iowa, past Des Moines, Shelby. I'm like, an hour and a half away." Geez, I feel like I'm in trouble.

"Okay, well, I can't wait to see you. Drive safe."

"I will."

I look down at my pen and paper. I didn't even get to the snow angel part of the story. I rub my hand and consider asking for a refill on my coffee. Instead, I just look at the waitress and say thanks. Then I get back in the car and drive toward Harmony.

Chapter Twelve

Seventy miles outside of Omaha and my anxiety continues to rise. A semi passes me and I can see that it's full of pigs. Pigs crammed so tightly that one has its snout poking out of the metal frame of the trailer. I want to scream "animal cruelty!" I want them to be released and treated humanely. But I know it'll all be over soon. I try not to look at any of their confused and terrified eyes.

I take my foot off the accelerator for a minute to let the semi get ahead of me, as far as he can before I impede with the flow of traffic. I don't want to follow him all the way to Harmony. All the way back to the slaughterhouse where my father killed pigs.

"I saw your dad kill a pig," Jude told me once for no other reason than to be mean. She got in those moods sometimes. "Shot it right here." She put her index finger between her eyes at the top of her nose. "Poor bastard didn't have a chance."

I didn't say anything. I tried not to engage in her moods. But I wanted to tell her that wasn't my father; that was his job. It's hard to imagine my father killing anything. Eric Bouchard was a gentle man—and it's hard for me to imagine that he steadied a shotgun with his shoulder, squinting one eye as he looked through the crosshair with the other. Dead Shot Bouchard. Ninety-eight percent of the time, he got them in one shot—it put both of them out of their misery. He and the creature.

"My dad, he was in the war." That's what I'd say to Jude when she wanted to be cruel about Dad's job. And it usually shut her up. It was as if it somehow connected her to his life. "World War II," I always added because her dad fought in Korea. "Drafted at eighteen, came out at twenty-five. He fought at Omaha beach." Maybe it was my tone that stopped Jude from digging into my Dad anymore. The tone of a daughter with a shell-shocked father.

He wouldn't talk about it, but my grandma once told me about how he came back changed. How he sat in the corner for days just staring into space. He didn't talk. He didn't eat. He barely moved. He just sat in the corner, staring. What was he doing? Watching the same scenes play over and over and over again?

It's hard to imagine Dad fighting on the front lines, although I can imagine him being an obedient soldier—standing shoulders back, spine straight, pushing himself so upright he was probably a clean six feet tall.

By the time I knew him, his shoulders slumped, his spine arched, his head drooped. He still managed his "yessirs" and "nosirs"; I heard it whenever the landlord stopped by for a "visit."

"Your kids are messin' up this yard. There's worn spots all over it."

"Yessir."

"You're going to have to put new seed down in the spring and keep those kids off it when it's time to grow."

"Yessir."

"Paint's peelin' on the house too. Didya notice that?"

"Nosir."

"You'll have to take care of that soon too."

"Yessir."

And every Saturday and Sunday after that, my father dutifully scraped the old paint off of the house that wasn't ours. He worked overtime one night a week to save money for house paint and trim paint, paint brushes, trim brushes, sandpaper, rollers, and paint trays.

He never asked us to join him in martyrdom. He simply worked every weekend day of the summer—sanding, scraping, painting. We played in the yard around him, further trampling down the grass.

I watched my father, stripped and sunburned, demoralized as the landlord stopped by to see his progress. "It's going slow," he'd criticize.

"Yessir," was all Dad said. "Yessir, it's slow going."

And with all his "yessirs," Dad knew what I did not. He knew that by showing the landlord he was willing to put his heart and soul into another man's house, he was forgiven those months he fell behind on the rent. He proved to the landlord there was no other tenant in Harmony who could possibly take care of this man's property like Eric Bouchard. It was sweat equity, but he would never own this house. It just bought him a different kind of security. And he would die for that security—he was pushing a lawn mower over the lush lawn he was able to provide the landlord once us kids were grown, when he had a sudden heart attack. My mom heard thumps on the wall from inside the house. Three loud thumps. We guessed he was trying to tell her he was in trouble. It wasn't until a neighbor called to say Dad was laying in the yard that my mom found him. His heart had already stopped, his face was blue, his eyes were fixed on the clear blue sky, clouds reflecting their movement over his pupils.

A car honks as it passes me on the freeway. I look down at my speedometer and see I'm only going forty miles an hour.

"I didn't really see him kill a pig," Jude offered up after she realized she went too far.

"Yeah, I know," I said quietly. But I didn't know at all. I didn't know if she ever did or did not see my father with a shotgun and see the animal fall to the ground with a thud. Maybe she even knew that he would come home, beaten down and sad, and that Mom would start in on him right after he got in the door. Do this, do that, don't do that, why would you do that? She was relentless and he just sat back and took it. Did Jude know all of that too?

No, get a grip Ally.

The semi full of pigs is long gone, so I hit the gas and bring my speed back up to seventy, but my foot seems to resist. I turn onto to Highway 680 and feel my heart tighten as I get closer to Harmony. Dread consumes me.

The thought of staying with my mother makes me feel this dread every time I return to Harmony. I clench my teeth every time I think about how much happier she's been since Dad died. It's like her whole personality changed. She wasn't that beaten down, crabby, nagging woman anymore. She moved out of the crappy house years ago and seems to have nothing but space and freedom in her new life in an apartment.

But I remember her standing at the casket, holding onto the edge of it as if she were never going to let go.

And me? Stupid me. Unbelievably, I was freaking thinking of Jude right then. I kept watching the door, hoping that maybe she would walk in at any moment. Walk in to say how sorry she was for my father's death. Then I looked back at my inconsolable mother, feeling angry for her tears.

Then I looked back toward the door. Watching. Hoping. But then again, after how things ended between me and Jude, I wasn't sure I could handle seeing her again. So I turned back to my inconsolable mother.

My cell phone rings with the tone Eli set up for me: "Flight of the Bumblebee." "Now you'll know it's me," he said. Now the tune whirls. No, I can't. I know he knows I'm driving. I should just pick up the phone, but I can't. He'll ask where I am, how I am. Why is it taking me so long to get there? Am I excited to go home? And he knows the answer to that already. It seems to ring forever before it finally goes into voice mail.

Now the seconds seem to take forever while I know Eli is leaving me a message. I wonder what he's saying, how he's feeling? Is he pissed off? Is he hurt? Is he oblivious? What a shit I am. He's my boyfriend, my partner, and this is how I treat him? My phone makes a trilling sound, letting me know that Eli has left me a voice mail. I'm afraid to pick it up. Whatever it is, it will need some kind of response.

I take a deep breath and let it out. Okay, play some music. No shuffling again since I am not in the mood for Eli's music. Bette Midler. That's what I need. I've always played Bette Midler to shake me out of my moods. *Live at Last*; there's nothing like it.

Bette's voice comes out of my speakers. She's making fun of her own song; the audience laughs. And then she breaks out with "Friends."

I used to play this all the time after Jude left—well, died. But I thought she left. I had always imagined that she went off to New Orleans or San Francisco or LA. I envisioned her hitchhiking across the country with the money she threatened to steal from Emma. And I would even drive past Emma's farm, hoping to see her. I had no idea that her body was resting in Emma's barn.

"Do you think I'm crazy like her?" Jude asked me once.

"No!" I said emphatically. "No one can be as crazy as her."

Jude didn't say anything to that. Somehow I don't think it made her feel better. She felt some connection to Emma, that's for sure. Maybe it was a romantic notion that she could go live with her. I don't know.

But Jude told me she had given up on Emma that night of the ice storm. When Emma walked from Perkins with her stomach full.

I'm sure Emma had her usual (Mom knew this): two eggs, overeasy; bacon (two strips); toast; and a piece of apple pie with the crust cut off. The waitresses at Perkins (and the truck stop) knew to cut the crust off and they also knew to remove the jam selection from Emma's table. She liked to dip her toast in her eggs (because her mother never let her do so) and she didn't like the jam on the table (because it reminded her of her mother—who made her eat toast with jam).

So on the night of that ice storm, Emma had her overeasy eggs, two strips of bacon, two pieces of toast (no jam), and crustless pie, and was heading back to her bumperless car.

I can clearly see her pulling up the collar of her black wool coat that she never buttoned. The belt of it hung freely off her waist (as always); one side of the belt hung much lower than the other side and was dangerously close to dragging on the ground beneath Emma's feet.

She walked carefully because a layer of ice lay beneath the packed snow and every now and then there was a slippery spot.

It had snowed once again while she was in the restaurant and, even though it was just a dusting, she knew it was enough for her to have to clear it from her windshield. (She cleared the side windows and back windshield only as much as she thought necessary, which really wasn't enough at all.) She dreaded the task.

She clupped, clupped, crunched through the snow with her regular dress shoes (her shoes never quite fit right). The shoes she should have worn to church (but she didn't attend), the shoes she should have only worn during good weather.

Clup, clup, crunch. Clup, clup, crunch.

She didn't look up as she walked, so she didn't see that her windows had already been cleared as she approached the car, nor did she see Jude, who was leaning on the front left wheel well.

Clup, clup, crunch.

Emma had her keys out; she had the habit of jiggling them as she got closer to the car.

Jude blew smoke out of her lungs—it mixed with the vapor her warm breath caused in the cold air.

Clup, clup, crunch.

Emma was at the driver's side door, putting the key in the lock.

Jude stood upright and watched Emma.

Emma fumbled with the lock; she dropped the keys into the snow. They dropped with a "chink."

Jude dropped the cigarette to the ground and stomped it out with the toe of her worn work boots.

Emma came back up. She rose with dizziness and steadied herself against the car. The dry taste of eggs was in her mouth; she swallowed hard. She needed a good swig of Listerine to get the taste out.

Jude stood still, watching Emma.

Emma fumbled with the keys once again. She tried one key, but it didn't fit. She sorted through the keys and found the one that looked like it belonged to the car. It slipped easily into the slot. She opened her car door, then looked once again at the snow-free windows, wondering how they got so clean.

She saw movement from the corner of her eye and jumped. For a moment, she thought maybe the ghost of her dead mother had come back to haunt her. She let out a small yelp.

"Emma?" Jude said too softly for Emma to hear.

"You!" Emma said suddenly, "leave me alone!" She didn't know who this girl was, but she looked like a hoodlum. She wore a heavy army coat, worn denim jeans, wet old work boots, and her hair was long and slightly damp. Her wet bangs stuck to her forehead.

Jude spoke louder, "Emma it's me. Judy—your niece."

"Who?!?" Emma's hand trembled as she reached into her pocket and held tightly to her bulging pocketbook.

"Judy. Your brother Bill's granddaughter."

Emma noticed her last name on the girl's army jacket. "Jenkins" was clearly visible over the girl's left breast. "Did you do this?" Emma loosened the grip on her pocketbook and motioned to the cleared windshield.

"Yes," Jude said. She played with the snow with the tip of her right foot.

"Why?" Emma was suspicious of the girl and returned her hand to her coat pocket. "You want to be paid or something? Because I…"

"No, I…" Jude stepped closer to Emma and Emma took a step back. Jude yelled louder. "I was wondering if maybe I could stay with you a few nights. Just until things thaw out a bit."

"Stay with me?!?" Emma was shocked at this stranger's gall.

"Yeah. Out on the farm. Remember, my dad and I came out there that one time to change your tire."

"My tire's not flat!" Emma yelled back. She wasn't quite sure what this girl was talking about. She turned up her hearing aid.

"No, we were there to fix your tire. A few years ago."

Emma fussed with her hearing aid.

"I just need a place to stay—for one or two nights, that's all. You won't even know I'm around." Jude nervously turned her lighter around in her hand, rolling it end over end.

"Stay with me?" Emma still couldn't believe what this girl was asking. She was beginning to look familiar though. She kind of resembled Emma's mother. Emma shuddered. "Go on home, young lady." Emma stepped into the car and eased herself down into the driver's seat. She wanted the little beast to go away.

"Please, Emma," Jude was right up next to Emma now, blocking the door from closing. "I don't have anywhere else to go."

"No!" Emma spit out quickly, appalled that this girl was practically accosting her. "Shoo! Now go away! Go on home!" Emma pushed gently on Jude and Jude backed up.

"But, Emma—"

Emma slammed the door shut. She locked the door with the click of a button and motioned for the girl to go away.

Jude stepped away from the car.

Emma turned on the car and pulled forward to a different parking space just to get away from the girl. She put the car in park and leaned down and felt under her seat. The bottle of Listerine was heavy, but she managed to pull it up. She opened the cap and lifted the bottle with both hands, to her lips. She took a swig and let it sit in her mouth—she swished it around and felt the bubbles build. Then she swallowed and let out a long "aaaahhhh" as the liquid burned in her throat. She took another swig and another and another.

She didn't pay attention to Jude standing outside her car—wiping tears from her eyes.

This is the Jude I imagined confronting me at my dad's funeral. As the mortician closed the lid on my dad's casket, I imagined Jude showing up and standing before me the same way she did with Emma that night.

I saw her as clearly—walking in the door of the funeral home, her oversized army coat hanging off her shoulders. Her hair with droplets of water glistening in the bright white light. Her frayed bell bottoms dragging on the floor. Her lighter in her hand, twirling end over end.

I saw that look on her face—of hope and fear and anger—she could carry all three with amazing capability. Jude always managed to look vulnerable and untouchable at the same time. And as she approached me, I would stand there, frozen.

And of course, I know now that Jude was already dead by the time we buried my father.

Now with the Iowa countryside rushing past me, I inhale a deep breath of fresh air, to let all these stale feelings rush out through my nose and mouth. But I can't inhale deeply enough.

The signs for Interstate 29 creep up on me. North or south? North or south? I have to think quickly. It's been awhile since I've been back home. I mean since I've been back to Harmony. My siblings take care of my mom, so no one needs me. Not really. At least that's what I tell myself to feel better.

Of course, it's north! It's a trick. I have to go north to Missouri Valley, and then go through Blair. Harmony is south of Blair, but this is a shorter route than going through Omaha.

Geez, what's it been? Two years since I took this road? Two years. Eli is a great excuse not to go back. "He's got the Christmas show at the orchestra." "His family is visiting over Easter." (Forget that he's Jewish—Mom doesn't understand "that religion" anyway.) Well, my job has been a good excuse too. "I've got a show opening that weekend." It's the easiest excuse there is. I don't think I'll tell them that I won't be working for another six months or so.

I'm sure there's something wrong with a daughter not seeing her mother for two years and not wanting to see her mother, but that's all I can do to keep my sanity. And now I'm so close to Harmony, there's no turning back. And I still can't inhale deeply enough.

I turn up the music to make it all go away.

Part Two:

Harmony

Chapter Thirteen

"Well it's about time!" My mom opens the door and the smells of pepper and soup stock hit me immediately. "I thought you'd never get here."

"Good to see you, too, Mom," I say almost in a whisper. She laughs and then sputters out some coughs. She pulls away from me and I notice how much older she's gotten. Her skin sags on her neck and tiny wrinkles are like cracks around her eyes. She's wearing a red sweatshirt appliquéd with potted plants and a small cat rubbing up against a pot. Her polyester pants look like they came from the back of a magazine.

Her place is organized, but slightly cluttered. Mom has taken up collecting dolls in the last ten years. That combined with the Home Shopping Network has left her living room an Ebayer's paradise. There are dolls of every size and shape. Every weirdness and freakiness, scattered everywhere in the room. Three-foot-tall dolls in the corners, miniature movable-parts dolls on shelves above the couch, hard plastic dolls with porcelain faces and those freakish marble eyes on end tables and in baskets. One doll propped in a small high chair in the dining room. All of the dolls have a fine layer of dust covering their clothing and coarse hair.

"Let's get this thing in your bedroom," she grabs the suitcase from my hand and leads me down the hallway. Her pink slippers swish swish swish on the wood floor and, I don't know, it seems like she's kind of stooped over. Her hair is short and simple, and thinning, but she still dyes it.

The bedroom smells like lemon furniture polish and looks the same since my last visit: white walls, a single bed with a dip in the middle, and one small window that looks down onto the parking lot. In this bedroom, Mom has hung the third-grade class photos of all three of us kids. "I like that all of you are missing teeth," she told me once.

I see my mom in the mirror over the dresser and notice how her lips droop, her eyes droop, and she now has jowls that she didn't have before. And her face is so thin. "How was the driving?" she asks like I'm one of the truckers that stop in at her job.

"Fine. Good. No problems."

"I've got some dinner on for you. Turkey casserole with them noodles you buy at the store." She indicates some kind of package with her tiny hands and I nod as if I know what she's talking about. "You hungry, sweetie?"

"Sure, yeah," I say but I haven't really been hungry since Mom told me about Jude's death.

I follow Mom back down the hallway and into the dining room where the freaky doll in the high chair sits. I hope she doesn't pull that thing up to the table while we eat and then I begin to wonder if maybe she doesn't pull it up when she eats; when no one is with her.

"I saved that article from the paper about that girl."

"Her name is Jude, Mom," I say, then I mumble, "She's not Marlo Thomas, you know." The doll's eyes stare at me.

"What honey?"

"Nothing." How did I go back to being seventeen again? "You changed your hairstyle."

"Oh, yeah," she touches the sides of her head, flattening a phantom imperfection." Well, I changed it about a year ago."

Ouch.

"Oh! Did you see this?" She walks behind the doll in the highchair and picks up a plastic doll with a bonnet from a rickety little stand in the corner where three dolls are huddled. This doll has a swirly ink stain that serves as a permanent tattoo on its left arm. "I got this for one twenty-five. They had it marked for two-fifty, but I told the lady 'if you think anyone's gonna pay two fifty for this!?! Well, you've got another thing coming.'"

"Another 'think' coming," I correct her.

"What?"

"It's another 'think' coming, not 'thing.'" I try not to sound like a smartass; I should have let that one go.

"Another think? That can't be right."

"It is."

Mom stares at me, her lips turned down, the corners of her mouth pinched. "Well, anyway," she says, "it was a good deal—a very good deal."

"I guess I should unpack," I say now as I look at my mother's soft face.

"The top two drawers are for you. You don't need more than that do you? I have some of my sewing things in the bottom drawers."

Sewing things? I've never seen Mom sew. "No, Mom. I'm only staying for two days."

"Do you want to eat now, Ally?" Before I have a chance to answer, Mom disappears into the kitchen.

I open my suitcase and put the clothes for my two-day stay in the drawers. I hear Mom clanging pots and pans in the kitchen.

I drop my cell phone on the bed and I know I should call Eli. Tell him I made it safe and sound. I see the message envelope on my phone, but choose to ignore it. I just don't want to listen to Eli's message right now.

I sit on the bed and speed-dial home. It's three o'clock. Eli should be getting ready to go to work. The phone rings and rings until our machine picks up. Eli's professional voice comes through and when I hear the tone, I talk quickly, hoping he won't pick up. "Eli, I made it to Mom's. Have a good show!" I try to sound as cheery and loving as I can muster and hang up quickly.

"Al-ly?" Mom calls in a singsong voice from the kitchen.

"Yeah Mom?" I yell back.

"Al-ly?"

I yell louder, "Yeah?"

"Ally!" She yells louder.

"Mom!" I'm sure the neighbors can hear both of us yelling back and forth. Maybe Mom's hearing is starting to go? I head toward the kitchen. "What Mom?"

"What do you want to drink with your casserole? Milk?"

"No, just water." I sit in the little dining room with the creepy doll in the high chair.

"Just water?"

She seems shocked, but I just shake my head and say, "Water's fine, Mom." There's a long pause as I hear her moving around the kitchen. I stare at the doll, thinking about how this is going to be a long two days.

"You know, that Emma was a crazy old bird," she says out of the blue.

I take my eyes off the doll and turn around in my chair. "Oh yeah?" I yell toward the kitchen.

She pops her head around the corner, she seems happy to have found something I'm interested in. "You knew who she was, didn't you?"

"Yeah, she shopped at the store all the time."

"You know she used to come to the truck stop a lot. At least before the Perkins went up. She'd sit at the table for hours, and she'd fall asleep in her food. I saw it myself."

"You knew her when she was younger?"

She brings a hot pad and the casserole dish out to the table. "Well, I guess. I suppose she was in her late fifties when she came into the truck stop. Oh, she was a little bitty thing. And shy…" Mom's voice rises on the last word as her hand raises into the air as if she were God's witness.

"Really? Was she weird then too?"

"She was different, that's for sure. Her mother did a job on her, I tell you."

"Yeah?"

"Oh, yeah. You think I'm bad…"

She disappears into the kitchen again and I feel ashamed for a moment.

"Her mother was a mean old bitty." She returns with her milk and my water.

"How do you know?"

"Criminey, the whole town knew back then. That poor Emma didn't stand a chance." She sits across from me, and next to the weird doll, at her four-seat table.

"Well, like, how did the town know?"

"I don't know. But one story that went around was about her and that shotgun—the one they found in Jude's hands."

I never even considered where Jude got the gun. I wait for Mom to elaborate, but she's too busy dishing out casserole. This is another frustration I have with her. She drops a stunning sentence on the table, and I have to drag the rest of it out of her.

"So, what was the story, Mom?"

"What story?"

"The story about Emma and the shotgun."

"Oh it wasn't Emma's shotgun. She hated that thing. It was her mother's."

I give her a moment to finish scooping, then she begins eating. "Oh, this is good, isn't it?"

"Mom! What's the story?"

"Well, I made this turkey last week and invited your brother and sister over. I froze whatever was left and made a stock out of the carcass so you could eat when you got home. I still have enough to make a soup too."

"No, Mom. I don't care about the casserole. I want the story on the shotgun and Emma's mother."

"Oh that. Well, let's see, how did it go?" She takes another bite of food. "Well, you know Emma's father died when she was twenty and after that, the farm really wasn't much of a farm. It was just a house and a barn sitting on twenty acres of overgrown weeds. Jim Larson's dad, you know the Larsons that own that land outside of town?" I didn't know, but Mom was on a roll, so I just nodded, "Well, Jim Larson's dad wanted to buy some of the land. He went over there, walked up the driveway with weeds up to his knees, but before he could get past the Buick, Mrs. Jenkins appeared on the front porch holding a shotgun. She told him to get off her property. He tried to talk to her, but didn't get three words out his mouth before she let a shot fly over his head. He never tried to do that again, I can tell you. Scared him shitless." She stirs her food and says, "Eat up honey, your casserole is getting cold."

I pick up my fork and stir the turkey mixture on my plate. "But how do we know Mrs. Jenkins was mean? Maybe she was just afraid of someone taking her land, or raping her or something." I take my first bite of casserole.

"My God, look at what she did to poor Emma."

"This is good, Mom." I say it quickly because I don't want to loose track of this conversation. Mom nods appreciatively. "But maybe Emma was just a little off, you know. How do we know her mother had anything to do with it?"

"After her father died, Emma's mother made her a slave to the farm. For years and years, poor Emma had to take care of her mother, and god knows what abuse she had to put up with. I know she hated that old shotgun. Her mother carried it around night and day and threatened Emma with it a few times. If you ever noticed the back of Emma's left leg, there was this long thin scar. Emma told me once that a bullet grazed her there. When I asked how did that happen, Emma said 'Momma was trying to teach me a lesson.'" Mom lets out a rattling cough and I'm not sure, but I believe that damned doll in the highchair has turned its head toward Mom.

"Emma considered having the gun buried with her mother, but then she would have had to take it to the funeral home and that was too far for her to carry the damned thing. She told me the first time she ever touched the gun was when she found her mother dead in the bedroom. She picked it up off the floor, holding it as far away from her as possible, and placed it beneath her mother's left arm. She wanted the mortician to take it with her mother's body, but she didn't mention it when she called the mortician. She was in town when they picked up the body, and when Emma returned home, she found her mother gone, but the gun still lying on the bed.

"She didn't know what to do with it, so she took it out to the barn and laid it in a corner. I guess that's where Jude found it."

"Jesus. How do you know all this, Mom?"

"Ally, don't take the Lord's name in vain," she scolds and I wonder (A) when she became so religious and (B) how she turns this mother thing on and off.

"Sorry," I say and she scoops another serving of casserole on my plate. "That's enough, Mom." I put my hands over my plate. "So, how do you know all of this about Emma?"

"Well, Emma told me," she puts the spoon back into the casserole dish. "You'd be surprised. When she was younger, she talked to the people she knew. Told them things you couldn't imagine."

"So she'd come into the truck stop and just talk to you? Like a normal person?" It was hard to imagine that she was ever normal.

"Oh sure. She wasn't always that frail old woman. But she aged fast. I guess it was from all that drinking or something. And she got stranger the older she got. More drawn in, you know?"

"Well, what kind of stories did she tell you?"

"Oh all sorts of things. She told me she used to love to ride on the tractor with her father when she was a little girl. Every summer, she got up early in the morning to go out with him so she could ride up and down the rows of the field. She could only ride with him until breakfast, then she had to help her mother clean the house.

"See, that was the thing about Emma. She'd tell you a story like that and you'd think she was normal, then she'd tell you, in the same tone, about how she and her mother cleaned the house everyday. They scrubbed floors, washed walls and windows, cleaned out cupboards, swept and washed down the front porch. And all the while her mother said things like, 'Why did I ever agree to marry a dirty old farmer?' But during the school year, Emma's only chore was to wash the dinner dishes. Her mother inspected her work before Emma had a chance to dry and put the dishes away. Mrs. Jenkins once found a dish with a bit of food still stuck on it; she got so angry, she threw it just over Emma's head, smashing it against the wall. Then she'd say, 'What's wrong with you?!? Why are you just standing there! Clean that mess up now!'

"I don't think Emma knew that wasn't normal. I think she thought everyone lived like that."

"Really?"

"Well, sure. Do you think your life isn't normal?"

I think about that for a moment and decide to pass on the answer I want to give. "So do you know anything else about her?"

"Well, you know a lot of people thought she was rich because she carried around all that money with her. But she was living on her small inheritance and made shortcuts wherever she could. She paid the electric bill so she could stay warm in the winter, but she tried not to use the lights or the electric stove. She paid the water bill so she could take an occasional sponge bath and flush the toilet. I know for a fact that she stopped paying her garbage bill years and years ago. Suzie Myerson, she works for the garbage company, she told me. If Emma had any garbage, she would put it in a small paper bag and bring it to town with her. She'd throw it in the garbage cans at the store, or behind the mall, wherever she ended up going. She lived on a very tight budget, you know."

"But how did she buy that new car, then, back when I was in high school?"

"Oh yeah. I remember that car. She loved that thing. Well, she ended up selling off some of the land. She figured she wasn't going to use it. In the end, she owned the acre that the farm and the barn were on and that's it."

I sit quietly eating my casserole. Actually, Mom is a really good cook.

Mom continues, "Oh, but there was a mess over there. Did I tell you?"

"No, you didn't."

"Well, when they went into Emma's house, they found newspapers and junk mail stacked in the living room. Cans of cat food and empty bottles of Listerine were stacked in the kitchen. The toilet was backed up. The kitchen floor was rotting. And in the barn were about 20 cats that she had been feeding and watering. So they figure she must've known about Jude, because she went out to the barn frequently to feed the cats. It wasn't like Jude was hidden away. She was right there, in the corner, in plain sight."

In plain sight? I see Emma, slowing down, looking at the body of her niece in the corner, head blown off. A shudder runs through me and I sip some water to try to shut the image down. Mom clangs her fork on her plate as she kind of stirs around her casserole, then takes a bite. She makes an "mmmmm" sound. And now that image of Jude is in my mind and I can't shake it so I try to concentrate on the last moments before she died instead. As if that's better…Jude sitting with the shotgun between her legs. Holding the barrel to her forehead, her thumb gripping the trigger. And

I wonder, did she cry? Or did she finally feel relieved that it was all about to be over.

"More casserole honey?"

I shake my head no. I put my fork down.

"Aren't you going to finish what's on your plate?" She looks at me with her eyebrows arched up.

"No, I'm done."

She stops chewing what's in her mouth and stares at me.

"It's good, Mom. I just don't feel like eating anymore."

"You should have some milk then," Mom mumbles and I act as if I didn't hear her.

I stare back at the doll whose glassy eyes are fixed on me.

The phone rings at nine. "Al-ly!" There's that singsong voice from Mom again. I put down my book and go out to the kitchen. Mom hands me the phone.

"Hey baby." Eli. He's calling me at intermission? That's new.

"Hi." My heart pounds in my chest.

"How are things going?" I look out at Mom sitting in front of the tv. She's watching the Weather Channel of all things. I guess she's on a break from the Home Shopping Network. I turn my back and face the refrigerator.

"Fine. Everything's fine." I mindlessly push down on the corner of a photo of my nieces and nephew. At least I think it's them; I haven't seen them for a few years. How sad.

"So, did you talk to Jude's aunt?"

It doesn't sound right when he says her name. He didn't know her and he sounds as if he did. And why is he spending his intermission asking about this anyway? "I just got here, like, three hours ago." I turn my back on the photo.

My annoyance shows, but he lets it slide. "I know, but you seemed pretty anxious about it."

"Yeah. I know. But I don't even know her aunt." I let that last part slip. I've been trying to keep everything about Jude from Eli.

"You don't?" He's silent for a minute, then his voice sounds sad, "I guess I just assumed you knew her."

"Yeah, because she's from Nebraska and don't we all know each other?"

More silence.

"Sorry." I lower my voice, "I guess being back home is kind of getting to me." Way to change the subject, Ally.

"That's okay," but I can tell it's not by the tone of his voice. "Well, I should get back. But Ally…?"

"Yeah?"

"Did you get my voice mail?"

Uh-oh. "Did you leave a voice mail?"

"I was thinking that maybe we should take a trip to New Orleans. We haven't been in a long time and I think it would be good for us."

Well, this is out of the blue. Knowing Eli, he just thought this up—probably wondering how to get things back to normal. How to fix things between us. If he only knew. "When?"

"How about the week after next? I don't have any performances or rehearsals that week. And now that you're not working…"

I take a deep sigh and look back toward Mom watching the Weather Channel. "Yeah. New Orleans sounds great." No family sounds even better.

"Great. Let's do it! Love you, baby."

Baby. I forgot about the baby thing. Crap. "Yeah, me too," I manage to say. I hang up the phone and know that Eli will take care of every trip detail: the tickets, the hotel, transportation from the airport. The only thing I'll have to do is show up.

I return to the living room. Mom is still watching the Weather Channel, but I think she's been listening to me and Eli. I try to cut out Eli's part of the conversation to figure out if there's anything she heard that I don't want her to know.

"How is Eli, honey?" She doesn't turn away from the television.

"He's good." I sit down next to her, but can't stop shaking my foot. She gently reaches over and squeezes my knee as if to say, "please stop."

I flick my fingernail on my bottom tooth. The guy on tv is showing the nationwide forecast. What does Mom get out of watching this?

"Mom?" I take another shot at connecting with her.

"Yeah?" She doesn't take her eyes away from the rotating radar.

"Do you like your job at the truckstop?"

"Oh I don't know. It pays the bills." Her eyes are still on the tv. "Look at that. It's going to rain in Minneapolis tomorrow."

I take a deep sigh.

"Do you…?" I want to say "know anything about Jude. Know her father? Her mother?" But I don't. I don't finish my sentence.

She doesn't even notice. "Look, it's 20 degrees warmer here than in

Minneapolis." That's her way of saying, "you never should have moved *there*."

I tap my feet on the floor and pick at a hangnail on my left index finger.

The weather station goes to commercial, but Mom's eyes stay on the tv. "Look at that dog. Isn't it cute?" She doesn't really want an answer. It's like the tv has put her into a trance and she's in her own world that I'm not part of.

"I'm gonna take a drive," I say and get up from the couch.

"Haven't you outgrown that, Ally?" Mom doesn't take her eyes from the tv set.

I feel embarrassment rise up from my knees. I didn't know Mom ever realized my penchant for getting in the car and driving around town, just to escape for awhile.

I choose not to answer her question. I just grab my jacket and the spare keys Mom gave me to the apartment.

Just when I get to the door, Mom says, "They found your drumsticks next to her."

I turn and look at Mom. Her back is to me; she's still staring at the tv, as if she didn't just drop this bomb on me. "What?"

"Those drumsticks you gave her; they were next to her body."

Suddenly, I'm looking at the guy on the tv, washing his arms across a map of the United States, following high-pressure systems.

"I remember that Christmas day you took them to her, wrapped in foil. And you took her some food too."

Something with big red splotches appears to be churning over the Gulf of Mexico.

"You told me some cock-a-mamie story about how her dad was out of town."

There's dark green over Kentucky.

"I worried about you, Ally, going out there with that girl. She stole things, you know. People talked about it all the time, how they'd have to watch her when she went into places."

I want to say, "because she was hungry and alone and scared and homeless," but I don't say anything. I just watch the dark green move from Kentucky to Pennsylvania, then jump and start back at Kentucky.

Finally, I say, "Don't wait up for me."

"Remember you're meeting Jude's aunt tomorrow at the funeral home," she yells after me like I'm 12 and it's a school night and she hasn't just said the most incredible things to me.

"See you in the morning," I say as I shut the door.

The air already feels lighter than the dark green and big red splotches. It's brisk outside and I wish I'd brought my gloves with me on the trip. I pull the sleeves of my jacket over my hands as I hold the cold steering wheel.

My hands are shaking. I can picture the drumsticks lying next to Jude's nearly headless body. As if she just dropped them to pick up the gun.

What the fuck is this?

That's what Jude said to me that Christmas day as she took all things wrapped in foil from me. She sounded surprised more than angry.

"I snuck some food for you," but now I feel bad that I didn't give Mom credit for her generosity. She piled the food on, even if she didn't like Jude.

"But Ally, I couldn't..." Jude said. But her eyes widened when she opened all the wrapped food. "It's still warm," she looked at me hopefully.

I almost wanted to cry at how happy she looked.

"And I got you this," I presented her with the long thin package of foil-wrapped drumsticks.

"No, Ally," she started to hand the wrapped drumsticks back to me, but I stopped her before she could finish her sentence.

"I don't need anything in return. It's not that big a deal anyway. Just open it."

The foil crinkled as she stripped it off of each drumstick. "Cool," she said, not too excitedly. She held the drumsticks in her hands and started rat-tat-tatting on her camp stove, the foil-wrapped food, a can of soup sitting close by, the cardboard on the floor, the blankets hanging on the walls—anything she thought would make noise.

If Mom could've only seen how happy Jude was at that moment. If Mom only knew the whole story.

I worried about you Ally. That's the first time I've ever heard Mom say that. I didn't really think she ever paid attention.

Does she worry about me now? It embarrasses me that she might be paying attention. If she only knew what kind of trouble I was getting into now. If she only knew the mess I've made of my life with Eli.

I find myself staring at the building Mom lives in, the window of her living room, and the light that's on inside. Tv images make the light in her apartment change color. I feel jealous of her. I feel jealous of the simplicity of her life.

I drive out of her blacktopped parking lot and onto 23rd street. Is that right? There're only 23 streets between here and downtown? I never thought of it that way before. Anyway, I decide to go the long way, to stay on the dark side of town a little while.

I pass the cemetery where my dad is buried. It's just two blocks away from Mom's apartment. I wonder if that was one of the highlights of that apartment complex for her? "I'll be close to your father," I can hear her say to Karen.

And Karen probably rolled her eyes like I would, but at least she's here and has a right to roll her eyes.

I think of that picture of the kids on the refrigerator. What kind of aunt doesn't even know what her nieces and nephew look like? There's Kira and Candy and Schylur, or is it Schyler? Well, they call him Sky. Where did Karen come up with those names?

Kira was born right after Eli and I moved to Minneapolis, and I thought I would come home often to see her. But then Karen and I started fighting and it was just easier to stay away.

Blah blah blah. You're full of excuses, Ally. Jude's voice comes through loud and clear.

"Me?" I say to her. "You taught me how to make excuses."

Bullshit.

"Okay, case in point," I say to the voice in my head. I think about that night, after the ice storm, when Jude got the drunk guy to get her poor lost cat out of the incinerator. "You begged me to stay with you that night."

I never begged.

I called my dad and made up some excuse about losing track of time and staying the night at a friend's house.

It was your idea.

I think about that for a second.

It was.

I pull into the parking lot of a seed company, wishing I had my notebook and pen. I rummage around in my glove box and come up with a pen and the owner's manual to my car. Not enough free space to write. So I just sit back and close my eyes for a minute, trying to remember that night.

I remember holding a hot chocolate from the convenience store as I leaned back against the cold wall of the incinerator. Jude had covered all the walls with cardboard so it wasn't as cold as just exposed concrete, but still. Jude struck a match and lit the small camp stove. She rubbed her hands over the tiny flame. "It'll get warm in no time," she said. And I soon found out that everything is relative.

"Just sit close to me," said Jude.

See? It seems like this was all her idea. Why would I want to spend a night in that cold incinerator?

I scooted closer. She pulled the opened sleeping bag up around her shoulder while I held my end of it around my shoulder. Jude rested her head on my shoulder. "Tell me a story, Ally," she said as she sipped on hot chocolate. Her hair had thawed out and she seemed relaxed for the first time that crazy evening.

"What do you want to hear?"

"Tell me about New Orleans."

"You want to hear more about Elizabeth?"

"No, tell me about your life in New Orleans."

"Oh, that." I felt silly about my stories. Jude grabbed my hand; her hand was cold and dry. It was rough to the touch where tiny scabs had formed over the bleeding skin. "You know," I said, "I've never actually been to New Orleans."

She didn't say anything. She lightly squeezed my hand. "Tell me about Alison Bouchard's life in New Orleans. Where is it that she lives?" Jude readjusted her head on my shoulder, as if getting even more comfortable.

"She lives in the Garden District." I felt slightly uncomfortable, like I needed to move away. But I didn't.

"Oh yeah, in the Garden District. What is Alison's house like?" Jude finished the final sip of her hot chocolate and then she readjusted herself. She laid her head in my lap and closed her eyes.

Her hair had been recently washed, I could tell. Somehow, she got the woman at the Y to let her use the showers several times a week. Her hair looked so soft that my hand impulsively began to stroke it.

"Tell me a story," she said slowly, as if falling into sleep.

"Every Sunday morning, my dad, my mom, my brother and sister all walk three blocks to St. Charles Avenue. It's got this grassy median and that's where we stand and wait for the streetcar.

"My brother likes to hang his head out the window on a sunny day and my dad always yells at him. We go around Lee Circle, and my brother always shoots at the statue of Robert E. Lee. Then we head on over to the French Quarter. We get off the streetcar and cross Canal Street, and more tracks for other streetcars, then we walk down Bourbon Street."

Jude gave a small, half-asleep laugh and mumbled, "Bourbon Street."

"Yeah. There's all these places on Bourbon Street where musicians perform—jazz, blues, cajun—it's one big party on Bourbon Street and it's alive with music."

"What's cajun music?" Jude asked.

"Well, the cajuns are these people that settled in Louisiana from Nova Scotia. They were like, refugees or something, and they farmed in Louisiana.

They talk kind of funny and they have this music that's like, accordions and those washboard things, you know?"

Jude shook her head no.

"Well, I took a record album out of the library once and it sounds kind of like country music with accordions. Sort of. I don't know. You kind of have to hear it."

"How do you know so much?" Her voice sounded sleepy.

"I used to go to the library and look at books and stuff. I don't know."

"Did you have to do a paper or something?"

"No," I laughed uncomfortably. "I just did it for fun. Kinda weird, huh?"

I leaned my head back on the cold wall and realized how ridiculous my fantasy life of Alison Bouchard really was. I looked at the camp stove, quietly hissing heat into Jude's little home.

All the walls were covered with cardboard. Big boxes of cardboard that were shoved from wall to wall almost perfectly. I didn't know how Jude managed to find such large pieces of cardboard until my sister started working at the box manufacturer outside of town. So she somehow got these boxes, ripped them apart, then shoved them up against the wall. The dirt floor had cardboard on it, too, a couple of layers of cardboard.

I'd never noticed the small picture of a woman—I assumed it was Jude's mother—propped in a corner of the room. Next to the photo were all of Jude's belongings—the clothes she wasn't wearing. A t-shirt, a sweatshirt, and another pair of jeans.

The hissing camp stove barely kept the place warm. My fingers were once again numb, and my toes were starting to ache.

"I don't think it's weird," Jude said quietly. "I think it's kind of cute."

Now, even though my eyes are closed and my head is back, my heart flutters inside my chest, just as it did then.

"Do you wanna lie down?" Jude's voice was drifting in and out of a mumble.

I didn't even consider what might crawl over my head in the middle of the night. "Yeah," I said.

Jude moved so I could lay down. The bedroll was made for one person, but we squeezed in tight and pulled the sleeping bag over us and around us as best we could.

Jude lay behind me, her knees tucked in the crook of my knees, her chin resting on the base of my neck.

Warmth rose in every place our bodies connected. My body wanted to fall asleep, but my heart was racing. Jude softly groaned into sleep and I felt my body relax into hers. She put her arm around me and held my hand. Her breath warmed the back of my neck.

It was an impulse to pull Jude's hand up under my chin. Maybe it was an impulse for her to caress my chin with her index finger. "You have soft skin." She whispered, half asleep.

Warmth rose up inside of me, like drinking hot chocolate in reverse.

I felt a little kiss behind my ear.

"Good night, Ally," she whispered and I felt her hand soften as she drifted off to sleep.

I closed my eyes. I was surprised at how comfortable it felt inside the incinerator, in Jude's arms.

Now, I'm startled by the butt of a flashlight rapping on my window. "Hey!" a male voice says.

The flashlight is blinding me. Being a good city girl, I don't roll down the window. I just say, "Yes?"

A police officer's face appears behind the flashlight. "Roll it down."

I roll down the window halfway. "Yes, officer?" My voice is shaking.

"What are you doing here?" He's leaning down to look me in the face. He's well over six-feet tall.

"Just—thinking, writing, sort of."

Excuses.

Shut up, I think to the voice, *it's not excuses*.

He runs his flashlight over the passenger seat, over the abandoned pen and owner's manual from my car.

"You having car trouble?"

"No, no, I was trying to find paper. I'm…I write. I was just thinking."

"Just thinking all the way from Minnesota?"

"Well, I…I'm from here. My mom lives here. I'm visiting." Then I try something new, "Do you know Matt and Ben?"

He looks at me blankly.

"They're detectives from the Harmony Police Department?" I sound like I'm trying to get out of something—like I'm guilty of something more than just thinking. "I…they…I'm here for a funeral, of a friend…they found dead…in a barn."

He leans his elbow on the hood of my car. "Oh, that Jenkins girl?"

"Yeah! Yeah, Jude Jenkins."

"Ol' crazy Emma's niece?"

"Yeah." Ol' crazy Emma's niece.

"She was your friend?" He sounds suspicious as he flashes the light into my backseat.

"Yeah."

He flashes the light onto my face again, then puts it down at his side. "Well, you best move along. You can't just sit here and think." He looks away from me and down the street in front of my car.

"Really?" I thought it was a free country.

"Yeah. Really," he flashes the flashlight in my face again. "It's not like it used to be here. We've got Mexicans here now. Drugs. You get me?"

You're racist?

"Yeah. Sorry, officer." There's no one else around tonight. I've passed maybe two or three cars on the road.

"They feed on girls like you, so you best move along."

And you're sexist?

"Sure." I roll up my window, put my car in first, and drive off. The officer follows me for a few blocks, then turns. I'm sure he's headed to the "Mexican" side of town.

Close call, Jude says.

"Close call," Jude said the next morning when we awakened to the sound of thudding on the outside of the incinerator. Jude held her hand over my mouth and the footsteps crunched around us. Her hand smelled like hot chocolate. A tiny crack of sunlight landed across the bridge of Jude's nose. She raised her index finger to her lips, asking me to be quiet. Then the footsteps walked away.

Jude got up and looked outside. "Cop," she whispered. "That was a close call."

My heart was thumping in my chest and I was actually too hot.

"He's gone. You can relax." She was already laying down on the bedroll again; I was still sitting up. She tugged on my shirt.

I laid back down next to her and pulled her hand up to tuck it under my chin. She was spooning me.

She softly said, "Ally?"

"Yeah?" My face was freezing cold and I wished the camp stove was on again. But the rest of me was fairly warm.

"That day with the snow angels?"

"Yeah," my tone changed slightly; that day was still a sore point for me.

"I didn't do it because—"

"It's okay, Jude. It doesn't matter." I tried not to sound annoyed.

"No. It does matter, cuz, I know I hurt your feelings."

I just laid there as she told me the story about the snow angel—how she stood above it and looked down on its perfect wings. She said she wished she could just plop down and become an angel, too, but she couldn't.

She couldn't do it because what she was wearing that day were the only dry clothes she had. Her other pants and shirt were drying over the small table she found in the trash the week before. She laid the wet clothes over it strategically so that the wobbly leg of the table didn't support the whole mass of wet, heavy clothing.

I turned over to look at her as she continued the story, her head resting in the palm of her hand. "Christ, you don't know how bad I wanted to make that angel, Ally. I remember, I mean I'm sure I remember, my mom once, making a snow angel. I swear I remember her showing me how to, just like you did. Getting on the ground and flapping her arms and legs. And I did it too. I lay down in the snow and swished my arms and legs as wide as I could. And Mom told me I was doing a great job. And then she reached down and pulled me up by my coat. I think it was a pink coat, even." She squeezed me tighter and gave a little laugh as if to say, "yeah a pink coat." "And when I looked down, there was the most perfect snow angel I'd ever seen. Better than yours even. But then, I think, how could that be—I mean, I was three years old when she died. So, how could I remember that?

"And when you kept insisting that I do it, I just wanted to say 'Fuck you,' but I didn't. I didn't want to hurt your feelings any more than I already had because, well, you're my friend. So, I just had to get out of there as fast as I could. I just had to leave."

Fuck! That's all I could think. How could I have been so stupid? Her face nestled into the side of my face and I wondered if my tears had dripped down onto her hand.

"Sorry," she whispered close to my ear.

I turned my head to look at her. She was smiling. I hardly ever saw her smile. And then, I kissed her. It was a brief kiss, that first one. But her lips were surprisingly soft and, well, willing, I guess. And so I kissed her again. And she kissed me back. A long, steady kiss. And another, and another.

Suddenly, the Harmony Opera House is sitting right in front of me. I wipe a tear from under my eye as I look up at its stone façade. A sign across the front of the building says it's available for weddings and parties. Where its windows used to be boarded up, they've now put in new glass. The stone-carved letters that say "Harmony Opera House" are underlit. The place is on the National Register of Historic Places.

I drive around to the alley, preparing myself to see Jude's home. My headlights illuminate the back of the Opera House and I think the shadows are playing tricks on me. Things don't look the same. I stop at the end of the alley and close my eyes for a minute. I'm tired. I've been driving all day.

When I open my eyes, the scene is the same. There's the platform that led to the incinerator, but the incinerator, Jude's home, is gone. There's just an empty space covered by cement.

Shit!

I get out of my car and stand in the very spot where the incinerator was. I rub my arms for warmth. I hope that police officer doesn't find me here. What would he say then? He'd probably have me committed. So I crouch down below the platform—never mind that my car is running and the headlights are on. But at least no one can see me, standing in this empty space in the dark, trying to…

Hell, I don't even know why I'm here. I blow into my ice-cold hands. *Jesus, get back in the car, Ally.* It was easier to be cold then, I don't know why. I'm spoiled, I guess. I imagine Jude walking into the life I lead now.

"Nice digs, Ally," she'd say sarcastically as she'd look around the condo I share with Eli. She'd see the high ceilings, the expensive furniture, the fantastic view of downtown, the nice stereo system. "Damn, you're Miss high-and-mighty aren't you?"

And I wish I could give Jude a little of what I have now. I have too much and it makes me feel sick.

I'm so cold now that I get back into my car where the heater is still running. I turn it up even more and it makes me feel guilty—for all this warmth.

I stare at the space where the incinerator was at the back of the Opera House, my hands gripping the cold steering wheel, and I take a deep breath. I wish I could go back and fix so many of the things that went wrong after that kiss. But I can't. I can't change anything for Jude now.

I told you it was you, the voice says.

I gulp down the pain in my throat and throw my car into first gear, then second, then third. My tires spin on gravel at the end of the alley. I cross the viaduct and head toward the river. Into fourth, then fifth. I'm going fifty, sixty, seventy and in no time I'm crossing the river. It's dark, so I can't see a thing except the highway in front of me.

And I want to go, just keep driving and driving, throw the cell phone out the window.

But I don't.

I turn around at the golf course at the top of the hill.

I cross the river. I slow down to sixty, fifty, forty, thirty. I cross the viaduct. I pass the Opera House.

I wipe my eyes and nose with the sleeve of my hoodie.

Mom's window is dark.

When I get inside, I tiptoe through her living room. The lights are off except for a night light in the bathroom. I tiptoe down the hallway, past the open door to Mom's bedroom.

"Ally?" she whispers, just like she asks on the phone.

"Yeah, Mom, sorry. I didn't mean to wake you."

"What time is it?" I don't know why she's whispering in her own house.

"Uh," another sniffle as I check my watch, "11:45."

"Go to sleep honey, it's late."

"Yeah," and already Mom is lightly snoring. Part of me wants to crawl into bed with her, where it's safe and innocent and simple.

Instead, I go into the room Mom has set up for me, with the single bed. I turn on the little light next to the bed, something she obviously got at a garage sale, with a dingy beige shade and little beads around the trim. A warm glow circles the bed.

I strip down to my t-shirt and climb into bed; no brushing of teeth, no washing of face. I just want to cocoon myself in the scratchy cheap sheets and old, thin blanket. I shiver as I turn off the light. It takes awhile for the sheets to warm up from my body heat.

I curl up on my side, pull my knees to my chest, and hope sleep will come easily.

Chapter Fourteen

A block of sunlight rests over my eyes. My body feels heavy; the cold sheets have me shivering. I try to open my eyes to see the clock. Birds are twittering around outside the bedroom window.

I rub my eyes and listen for Mom. Then I hear Jude's voice again. She says "baby." Not like a term of endearment, more like a reminder of what Eli wants from me.

Just flat like that, "baby"; almost like it's one syllable. Like a taunt.

I roll over and pull the sheets and thin blanket up under my chin.

Baby.

Then I yank on the covers and blanket and pull them over my head.

Stick to your own fucked-up life, I think to the voice.

I can hear Mom in the bathroom, doing the half-whistle thing she does; she blows out and in to keep this constant, quiet whistle going. Then she starts banging things around; it sounds intentional.

And then, I don't know, I must fall asleep or something because next thing I know, Mom is standing over my bed. She's quiet and I can't seem to open my eyes, but I know it's her. I feel her pull the covers down off my face and she gently lays a kiss on my cheek. Just a soft little kiss. For a minute, I think she's trying to wake me, but then she gently puts the covers back over my face and steps softly out of the room. I hear the soft click of the door behind her.

Out of Harmony

Warmth washes between me and the cold sheets. Mom's never done that before. I can't even remember the last time she kissed me.

Now I hear her in the kitchen, clanging some pans about. I close my eyes and wish for sleep to come again. I must get my wish because the room is brighter now and I wake up to a rustling beside my bed. I see a sudden movement that appears and then is gone. My eyelids are heavy; I close them again before I can focus on anything. Maybe the movement I saw was the drapes. But it seemed like what I saw was black and shadowy. I try to open my eyes again, but the weight is too much.

"Ally," Jude says and I see her standing outside the incinerator, where there's now a big empty hole. "Ally," she says again as she takes a drag on a cigarette. The smell fills my nostrils.

"Ally," the voice is clearer this time as smoke seems to make her image stronger—like a genie from a bottle.

"Allison!" the voice is more insistent and suddenly I'm shaken awake.

"Ally!" Mom is standing over me. "Ally. It's getting late. You have to be at the funeral home at eleven. Get up!"

I roll onto my side, away from Mom, and hope to catch another glimpse of Jude before I'm fully awake.

"I'm coming back in five minutes," Mom says.

Five minutes go by fast when you're half-asleep, because it seems like no time when Mom is standing over me again, her voice strong, "You have to get going. It's eight. You should call Eli before you leave." Then she shuts the door so strongly that I'm sure the neighbors can hear.

Geez. I want to yell out, "I'm a grown woman!" but I don't.

And why does she care whether or not I call Eli?

I pretty much just shower and get out the door before Mom can mention calling Eli again. "Aren't you even going to have any breakfast? You don't want to pass out at the funeral."

"No, Mom, I'm not hungry," I'm starving. "I want to make sure I'm not late."

"It's nine. The funeral home is only five minutes away. What's your rush?"

I don't say anything, I just grab my jacket, my notebook and pen, and turn the knob on the door to escape to the hallway.

Mom is watching me go, which makes me feel uneasy. "Karen's coming over later with the kids to see you, so you've got to be back by two."

I open the door and start to close it behind me when she says, "And don't forget to call Eli!"

Okay, number one, why would she invite Karen over when she knows I have this funeral today? Number two, why this obsession with Eli right now?

I look down at my cell phone as I walk to my car. It's turned off. I wipe some fingerprints off the front of it, then put it in my pocket without turning it on.

Okay, so there's got to be a coffee shop in Harmony in this day and age, doesn't there? I drive toward downtown; it seems like a logical place for a coffee shop. I could go to Perkins or the truckstop, for that matter, but I don't. And why isn't Mom working at the truckstop this morning anyway? Day off?

As I drive down Main Street and past the library, I think about my dad. He was the person who first took me to the library. I remember when he got me a library card and I thought it was the most important day of my life up to that moment. There seemed to be so much responsibility around having a library card. You could get FINED if you didn't bring a book back in time. There were penalties. And the books were like gold that you got to hold in your hands and take home with you for awhile.

If Dad only knew the kind of fantasy life I created because of our trips to the library. If he only knew about Elizabeth and Jacqueline. If he only knew about me and Jude.

"What're ya looking at there anyway? All these mornings?" Dad asked once on our drive to the library. He used to take me there every Saturday morning, before I could drive.

"Stuff on New Orleans." I said plainly. I think I was even leaning forward on the passenger seat, before the days of required seat belt use, as if I could get there faster. At least that's what I remember.

"New Orleans?" There was a lilt in his voice, as if he was trying not to laugh.

And I suddenly remember while I searched around for stuff on New Orleans, Dad stayed at the library with me. He went and read newspapers and magazines. "I'll be right over. Come get me when you're ready to go."

But that first time, I spent fifteen minutes or so looking up stuff in the card catalogue, then I felt like Dad had been waiting too long, so I went and got him. After we left, he asked, "You didn't find any books?"

"I just looked at the card catalogue," I told him.

The next time we went out there he told me to take my time. "I'm in no rush," he said and he squeezed my shoulder.

On the way home, I would tell him what I found. I was holding a large book on New Orleans history on my lap. "Back in 1888, when the Spanish took over New Orleans, there was this big fire where some guy knocked over a candle and his house caught went up in flames," I looked at Dad to make sure he was listening. He was. "And so they had this thing they did where they ran to the Cathedral when there was a fire to tell the priest to ring the bells. That told everyone there was a fire. But this guy, whose candle set his house on fire, he ran to tell the priest and the priest told him that it was Ash Wednesday and they didn't ring the bells on Ash Wednesday. So the whole French Quarter burned down, well, almost all of it."

"Really?" Dad said. He seemed impressed.

"Yeah, so then the Spanish built the French Quarter back up and that's why it has all those balconies and stuff. So it's not really French anymore."

"So why do they call it the French Quarter?" Dad asked. I just shrugged my shoulders. I didn't know the answer to that.

So I started making up stories about the French Quarter and the Garden District, and as I grew older, the story of Elizabeth and Jacqueline evolved. By the time it evolved into something Dad would have blushed at, I was able to drive and went to the library on my own.

Well, that's not my life anymore, so Dad wouldn't have anything to be embarrassed about. He wouldn't need to know about Softie: a drunk happening. So all he would know is what Mom knows, which is that I'm with Eli. There's nothing to be embarrassed about.

And now I wonder just how much Mom knows. How much she knew about Jude.

I suddenly feel the need to make that call to Eli, but I'm still driving around because there's not a single freaking coffee shop in Harmony. I guess I was silly to think there might be.

I drive back over to the library instead; I don't really know why. It's close to downtown, I guess. I park in the tiny parking lot and, as my cell phone powers on, I look in my rearview mirror at the stone façade of the Harmony Public Library. It looks just the same now as it did back then.

The phone is ringing.

"Hello?" Eli's voice is all craggly.

"I'm sorry. I woke you up."

He clears his throat. "What time is it?"

I look at my watch and suddenly feel stupid for calling him this early. "God, I'm sorry. It's almost nine thirty."

Another throat clearing, "That's okay. What's up?"

I fight the urge to ask, "Are you alone?" He would think that ridiculous and no matter what, he'd say "Of course I am."

"I just wanted to hear your voice."

"Oh yeah?" his tone turns all low and sexy. "Why's that?"

I'm not in the mood for low and sexy. I'm in the mood for comforting. "Jude's funeral is in a few hours."

His tone changes. "Oh. Yeah."

"Eli?"

"Yeah?"

Everything feels wrong. That's what I want to say. Everything feels freaking wrong. I'm turned upside down. I don't know what the fuck I'm doing. "I miss you." That seems easiest.

"I miss you too, baby. What are your plans today, I mean after the funeral."

"Ugh. Mom asked Karen to come over this afternoon. So now I have to see her."

"Oh yeah, your mom told me. That should be good for you, though."

Mom told him? What the fuck? "Good for me? How's that?"

"Well you haven't seen her in forever. It's about time don't you think? Family is important."

Family's im...? Whatever.

"Ally, come on, you need to be open to this; she's your sister," Eli says to my silence.

"Yeah. So, I'm at the library now. I think I'll go write for awhile."

"At the library? Since when have you gone to the library?"

"Eli, this is Harmony. There are absolutely *no* coffee shops. Where else am I going to go?"

He laughs softly in a kind of half-asleep way. It makes me feel warm to him. It makes me say my automatic "I love you" before I hang up the phone.

I feel good at the slight satisfaction I have in making that phone call. Now I won't have Mom nagging me about calling; she'll be happy.

The wind practically pushes me back into the car as I open the door. I rush to the glass doors of the library to get out of the biting wind as quickly as possible. Even the inside of the library looks exactly the same as it did when I used to come here. A copy machine and an urn of hot coffee greet me as I come in. For my 25-cent donation into a Styrofoam cup, I get to fill another Styrofoam cup with black steaming coffee.

I take my first sip of cheap coffee as I scan the main level. It's one giant room with rows and rows of books on shelves in a "U" shape around the card catalog and tables in the middle of the room. The stairs to the upper level winds around just to my left.

I go up the grand staircase that looks like something out of *Mame* to get to the second level. Here's where I used to spend most of my time; in the row directly to the left at the top of the stairs. And I'd take the big, heavy history books to the tables in the center of the second floor.

Now I take a seat at one of those white-topped tables. Of course some initials are carved into the tops, some in pencil or pen, and some more permanently with a sharp metal edge. "JH was here," (scratched); "Lily and Tom," with a big heart drawn around the names (pen); a timid "Cathy" (pencil).

I open my notebook and return to the place I always go to feel normal. Back to Elizabeth Perrier and Walden Bouchard. To the day they met. And I write and scratch and write and scratch. I make up a whole new story about how Elizabeth and Walden carved their names into a tree with a big heart around it, but then I scratch away that story too. Everything I write feels empty and frivolous.

I look at the big white-faced clock with black numbers that sits by the microfiche rooms. It's only 10:05. What kind of writer can I be when I'm bored with my own writing time?

I turn the page, take a sip of my now-cool coffee, and stare at the blank page. I pick a little white fleck off of my black sweater.

And then I realize that I haven't heard Jude's voice since that groggy moment when Mom was trying to wake me. The day of her burial and Jude's not speaking to me?

Okay, wait a minute. Now I have lost it. Jude doesn't talk to me. She can't. It's just me, imagining things.

I relax into the straight-backed wooden library chair, take another sip of coffee, and listen for Jude's voice. At least if only to guide me into a story to write.

Something.

Anything.

Nothing.

I take another sip of coffee and then I write "Jude Can't Wait" at the top of the page. I don't know why I write it, but I do. I tap my pen on the page.

> Jude stands outside the store, her back against the tiny gas station at the end of the parking lot. Every now and then, she paces. She wonders if she should go through with it.

I take another look at the clock on the wall. It's only 10:10. I don't know that I can write this story. My hand shakes as it returns to the page.

> Jude takes a final drag on her cigarette, then smashes it beneath the toe of her work boot. "Fuck it," she says to herself as she crosses the vast parking lot.
> It's about one hundred degrees outside. She passes a few cars, a giant bin of watermelons at the front door, then goes inside, her heart pounding inside her chest.
> A blast of cold air hits her when she gets inside.
> She looks around for me.

I look at the clock on the wall. 10:15.
"She looks around for me," I write again.
I scratch that out. "Jude looks for Alison."
"Jude just wants to ask why. That's all. She just wants to know."

Again, I scratch each word out. I wish I could take it all back. I grit my teeth as I work, scratching each word so that it becomes a little block on the page. The pressure of my pen on the page stops my hand from shaking. I take time over each word so that an indentation is left on the pages following this one. I'm deliberate and slow, and mad. And I want to stop.

I want to stop feeling this way about myself.

It's 10:30. Fuck. It. I'm leaving here. I can't write this. I won't write this. Fuck. It.

I grab my jacket off the back of the chair, throw my stupid non-enviro-friendly Styrofoam cup away and leave.

I get in my car and decide that I don't want to go to this fucking burial/funeral thing, whatever it is. I hate this. I hate that Jude did this. I hate everything about this fucking day and this fucking stupid life.

I throw my cell phone, notebook, and pen on the passenger seat, put the car and gear, and drive.

I'm staring at the funeral home as my hands rest on the steering wheel. My eyes are locked on the door and I'm so tired I want to close my eyes, but I can't even blink right now.

I don't want Jude to be dead. I want to have that little bit of hope, mixed with fear, that I will see her somewhere in New Orleans or L.A. Someplace warm, just like she always dreamed. That would make my life so much simpler right now.

A woman taps on my window and waves. "Are you Ally?" she yells through the glass.

I nod to her.

"I'm Betty Dumaine." As she steps away from the car, I take a deep breath. Here we go.

She waits for me at the entrance of the funeral home. A cold gust of wind greets me when I get out of the car. I run toward Jude's Aunt Betty and we quickly go inside the funeral home.

"Whoo!" she says as she rubs her arms. "It's a cold one today."

Jude would have laughed at us. "Fuck. This ain't nothin'," she would have said.

"I'm Ally," I hold my hand out to Jude's relative. She takes it delicately, like a Nebraska-taught lady; her hand simply rests in mine and she doesn't grip. Aunt Betty looks different than I imagined. She's rounder, but maybe that's because of age. And shorter, she's about five-foot nothing. She kind of looks like an aging Betty Rubble. Black hair (dyed I'm sure) that's flipped up in a kind of a housewife wave. Her face is warm, just like Jude described it, but she has too much rouge on. I half-expected her to be wearing some kind of appliquéd sweater like Mom's, as is common in Harmony, but she's dressed in a floral-print blouse and a tan skirt that almost hides her stocky legs.

"Thank you so much for tracking us down," she says and I notice that her bottom teeth are crooked, just like Jude's. We stand there for an uncomfortable moment. Then Betty says, "So, did you know Judy from school?" She walks toward the mortician's parlor, looking back at me while she talks and I follow.

"I knew her from Super Valu. That's where I worked, but, yeah, I'd seen her around school."

"And, did she come into the Super Valu with her Aunt Emma?"

"No," Betty really didn't have a clue. "No, she came in alone."

"Well, how did she get into Harmony? Did she borrow her dad's car or something?"

I try to figure out how much to tell Betty. How much would Jude want her to know? "She..." How much do I want to give away? "She had friends, you know, that had cars."

"Hello, Mrs. Dumaine," the mortician extends his hand toward Jude's aunt.

"Oh," Betty manages to look away from me and quickly extends her hand to the mortician.

He leads us back to a room where an urn sits on some weird pedestal. Jude on a pedestal.

Next to the urn is a drawing. A rough sketch. "What's that?" I ask Betty.

"I was hoping you could tell me," Betty smiles at me. "They found it in Jude's pocket."

It takes me a moment, but I know what it is.

"Hey Ally," Jude's voice was soft that last night we saw each other. She was happy. She seemed so happy. I opened my eyes and saw her smiling above me.

"Yeah?"

"Let's go see the sandhill cranes."

She took me by surprise. She seemed to have softened so much that she was a whole new person. She wasn't the "fuck this, fuck that" Jude. Maybe because she started to trust me.

"Ally?" Betty's hand rests on my shoulder, but I can't speak. The drawing is rustic, not perfect in any sense. Kind of abstract. Some lines are clean, others are a little jagged, but the wings are unmistakable.

"Sandhill cranes," I manage to get the words out, but my voice shakes.

Betty picks up the sketch and examines it closer. She lifts her glasses above her eyes and holds it close to her face. "Oh yes, I see it." My knees buckle and the mortician grabs me before I fall. He leads me to a chair. And the stupid thought crosses my mind that he must be trained in falling patrons. "Thanks," I try to wave him off as I gain control. And I don't know where Betty is at this moment, but somehow the sketch is in my hands and my eyes are following each line and I see Jude clearly as she sketches it. She's angry, she's crying, she's lost.

She's there in the incinerator all alone while I work at the Super Valu, trying to escape. But I was scared. I was just so scared.

"Ready to go?" The mortician has his hand on my shoulder and holds the urn like a football with his other hand. He and Betty both look at me.

"Uh, yeah. Yeah, of course." My legs are still shaky, but I take a deep breath. I follow them to a black car sitting outside the door where the hearse usually pulls up. I know it's the family car. I've done this before.

"Here," I hand the sketch to Betty after we settle in the backseat.

"Oh no, dear. It obviously means a lot to you. You keep it."

"But…" I can't argue because the words are too shaky. How can I tell Betty this isn't a happy memory for me now? I put the sketch upside down next to me on the seat, resting my hand on top of it, and I swallow down the ache in my throat.

We drive out to the cemetery. I turn my head toward the window to hide the tears. Betty must have sensed it though, because she grabs my hand that's resting on top of Jude's sketch. She squeezes it, but I keep my head turned to the glass, trying to hold it together.

"She'll be with her mother now," Betty says softly as she lets go of my hand.

I was glad when Betty told me that was where they were going to place Jude. I contemplated telling Betty I wanted to toss her ashes out over the Platte, but I didn't think that was right either. That was more my favorite place than hers. And since I was the one who practically pulled the trigger…

"Is Jude's dad out here too?" I manage to ask as we pull into the cemetery.

"I'm afraid he bought the plot when Sandra died." I note a bit of tightness in her voice.

"Did you have a problem with Jude's dad?" I examine her face, to see if there's anything else that looks like Jude.

Betty's face looks pinched. "I never liked him. Not from the day we met. There was something about him. Anyway, Judy will be laid at her mother's side." Then she looks at me with fear, "Do you think I'm horrible, talking about Judy's dad this way?"

"No," I fight not to tell her why.

"You do, don't you? I suppose it is unfair, since Judy knew her father. I suppose she was much closer to him."

"No, really," I can't tell her. Jude wouldn't have wanted her to know. "Jude and her father didn't get along very well."

"Really? But when they visited that one time they seemed so close. I mean, she seemed like a Daddy's girl. Oh, I didn't think this through at all. I just had my own selfish needs in mind."

The limo pulls up alongside a tree. The markers are all flat on the ground in this cemetery, but I can see where a hole has been dug, about twenty feet from this curving road.

"She was not a Daddy's girl, believe me." Just the thought makes my stomach turn.

The mortician opens the car door for us and we step out into the cold, gusty wind. As the door slams behind us and we follow the mortician, who is carrying Jude's ashes, I suddenly realize I haven't prepared for this moment. I should've written some words to say, or something.

"Hello, Betty!" A friendly voice calls from behind us.

As Betty walks toward the man, I see the bible in his hand. *A fucking minister*, I hear Jude's voice in my head and I almost laugh. But I think Jude would've done anything to make her Aunt Betty happy. I just hope he doesn't do any talk about the damned.

Betty introduces me to Reverend Mike. He seems like a nice enough man. About fifty years old, wearing some kind of polyester-blend suit. "We're Baptists," Betty tells me as she links her arm with mine, "Judy's father was a Methodist, but I hope you think this is okay."

I want to tell her it really doesn't matter, but I don't want to be rude. "I don't think Jude had decided on a religion yet."

"Oh," Betty looks surprised.

"She was a teenager," I say quickly, trying to ease her mind, "She—she was still trying to figure things out."

"That's something else I want to ask you about—"

The wind takes my breath as it slaps my face with another cold gust.

"Shall we begin?" The minister asks.

Since we're all shivering, there are no objections.

I try to tune him out as he talks about heaven and hell, and forgiveness of our sins.

Then Softie pops into my head. Well, not Softie really, but what I did with Softie. What I did to Eli, and Jude. Eli for the betrayal and Jude for… for wasting her life on my stupidity. On my fear.

Betty squeezes my hand and smiles at me. I take in a big breath of air and the tightness in my chest fights it. Betty hugs me.

If only she knew. If only she knew.

Then this feeling rises up into my chest and I try to push it down like I have so many times before, but Dr. Vonda would tell me to pay attention to the feeling, to not fight it. So I close my eyes and feel the shame.

"Ashes to ashes. Dust to dust," the minister is calling out and I see myself waking up next to Jude. It was a damp morning in the spring—the air was humid and stuck between warm and cold. I lay there next to Jude, her arm draped over me. The incinerator smelled of wet gravel and mildewed cement.

I pushed Jude's scratchy army blanket off of my arms. Jude was breathing on my neck. I usually welcomed this, but not that morning. I didn't know why.

Jude's voice rumbled into a loud purr, a soft snore. Her face was so relaxed I could see her youth—it was a rare moment when her face wasn't tensed into hardness. And I watched her.

I watched her eyebrow twitch and a slight smile rise around her lips.

Then her mouth relaxed again. Her face was so beautiful—full lips, high cheekbones, a perfectly formed nose.

I drew my finger down the bridge of Jude's nose and she opened her eyes for a second, smiled, then closed her eyes again and softly snored.

Her hand twitched in mine.

But as I drew my finger across her dark perfectly shaped eyebrow and the garbage truck roared through the alley, the shame suddenly took hold.

It was at that moment Jude's arm around my waist became heavy and seemed to tighten around me. Jude's breath kissed my face and I felt the shame rise in my body. The shame washed over me as quickly as my father pulled the trigger. A shock ran through me.

Jude moved and put her forehead close to my chin. Her breath warmed my collarbone. And suddenly it was too hot. My legs burned next to hers. My skin under the army blanket broke out in a sweat. My palms were wet. The damp air seemed to lay on top of me, too, like another blanket.

It was at this moment in time, with warm and cold battling into a damp fog outside, that I decided to run.

I didn't even look at Jude's face. I just rolled out from under her arm. She stirred, then turned over. I was naked from the waist up so I put my hands over my breasts while I found my shirt and bra.

And I thought about my teacher at school who told me to be careful about hanging out with Jude, saying she could be a bad influence. So in that moment, I believed that teacher. I convinced myself Jude was a bad influence. That I would never have slept with a girl if it weren't for Jude and her manipulation.

I convinced myself that I wanted to get married and have kids, like everyone else. This was not who I was. This was not who my parents raised me to be.

Now as Jude's urn is being lowered down into the grave, I suppress an uncomfortable laugh that wants to come out of my esophagus. How stupid can I be? I wanted to want to get married. I have Eli, but I've been fighting marriage for so many years. "Why do we want to ruin this with marriage?" I always said until he stopped asking.

I wanted to want to have kids. *Ha!* Look at me now. Running from Eli. Just like I ran from Jude way back then when I grabbed my coat and pushed the door of the incinerator open. It made a loud squeal and the bottom of the door scraped against the swelling cement. I was sure it woke up Jude.

I didn't look to find out. I just jumped in my car and drove. I drove out onto the country roads, through the light fog. I didn't go home, couldn't go home. I just drove as the sun burned off the fog and melted the little mounds of snow that sill clung to the side of the road and the black-soiled fields. I drove in circles, along the stream toward the highway, up a hill, around a curve, to the south, around the horse farm, past the dealership and around again—stream, highway, hill, curve, south, horse farm, dealership, stream, highway, hill, curve, south, horse farm…

And I cried. Part of me felt so lost and I wanted so badly to talk to Jude, but at the same time, she was the last person I wanted to see. And then I felt guilty. Stream, highway, hill, curve, south, horse farm, dealership, stream…

And I couldn't stop.

I didn't want to go home. I didn't want to see my parents. I didn't want my sister asking—accusing—"you stayed overnight with Jude again??" Her intonation on "Jude" insinuating something. Something I wanted to deny.

I thought I just needed to stay away from Jude's bad influence for awhile. So I could get back to being myself again.

I filled my car with gas, grabbed a package of twinkies and a coke, put the car in gear and headed for the edge of town. Stream, highway, hill, curve, south, horse farm, dealership, stream, highway, hill…

"And as we throw this dirt on her grave…" the minister's voice has reached a fevered pitch.

I wipe the tears from my eyes.

"…we remember that which Jesus taught us…"

Betty squeezes my hand tighter. I feel uncomfortable and fight the urge to wrest my hand away from her. If she only knew.

"Our Father who art in heaven," the minister throws a handful of dirt down onto the urn in the grave.

"Hallowed be thy name, Thy kingdom come," and I move my lips along with Betty, but the words won't come out.

"On Earth as it is in Heaven."

I'm Eli's girlfriend.

"Give us this day our daily bread."

And Jude is gone.

"And forgive us our sins."

Jude is dead.

Amen.

Chapter Fifteen

I don't know how I got here. The last half hour is a fog. But now I'm sitting with Betty at the Perkins on Highway 30 drinking coffee and eating a piece of apple pie.

"How long did you know Judy?" Betty asks.

"A year, I guess, maybe a little longer."

"Well you must have been close."

I look down at my pie, flicking flakes of crust with the tines of my fork.

She continues, "I mean, you took so much interest in getting her buried, even after all these years. Twenty-some years, isn't that something? Only a close friend would go through all this."

I manage a little smile toward Betty, but I hope she can't see my embarrassment. "Well, I don't know. I mean, she didn't have anyone, you know. I mean, there was you, but my mom, she works at the truck stop, so she heard about Jude and I just wanted to help." I talk quickly because I feel myself rambling.

"But you came all this way from Minneapolis for the burial. That's a true friend."

I shift in my chair and put down my fork.

"Don't you like your pie, dear?" Betty takes a sip of her coffee.

"Yeah, I'm just taking a break." I look beyond her head out the window and to the highway that passes through town.

"Alison?" Betty puts down her cup of coffee and leans in as if she's going to ask me something so important it will unnerve me. "Was Jude a troubled girl?"

"Troubled?" I have to think about that for a second. "Well, she was… she had troubles."

"What kind of troubles?"

"Oh," I wonder how much Jude would've wanted her Aunt Betty to know. "She and her dad didn't get along."

"Did he touch her?"

At this I must look totally shocked because Betty says, "I'm sorry. That was a horrible thing to say. It's a horrible thing to think. Forget I ever asked it. Just forget those crazy thoughts are in my head."

I pick up my coffee mug and see that my hand is visibly shaking. I hope Betty doesn't notice.

But she does. When my mug hits the saucer, Betty puts her hand on the wrist of my shaking hand, which is still wrapped on the handle of the coffee mug. "Please, just forget I said it."

I want to cry, but I'm not going to. I should say "yes, he did. He did horrible things to her," but I don't want to say it.

"Tell me your happiest memory of Judy."

That takes me by surprise too. My happiest memory. The day we met? Wading in the river? Something like that would have been good to say, but instead I say, "The day we made snow angels. We just plopped down in the snow and looked at the sky and we made snow angels. When we stood up to look at them, Jude told me about how her mom taught her to make snow angels when she was a little girl. It was the one memory she had of her mom, and so every time there was a big snowfall, she would make a snow angel."

Betty wipes some tears from her eyes with a neatly folded napkin.

I don't know why I said it. I don't know why I changed that story to fit into a box that Betty could open.

"Oh, that's just so sweet. Thank you." I don't know if Betty is crying for Jude, or for her long-dead sister. "So, she did have happy times."

"Yeah. She did." I think. I don't know for sure.

"Why do you think she did it?"

I put my hands on my lap so Betty can't see that they're quivering.

"I mean, why did she have that drawing in her pocket?" she asks. "Why does that mean so much to you?"

"I…" I can't think of words to say. I can't think of how to explain it.

"I'm sorry. I've upset you. But I just want to know."

"We were supposed to go see the sandhill cranes out by Kearney. But then she disappeared and I couldn't find her."

"You know, I do not understand why her father didn't report her missing to the police. They said they had no record of a missing person. Did you talk to her father after she went missing? You must've asked him where she was."

My heart is pounding in my chest. "No, I didn't really know her dad."

"You didn't?"

I shake my head no.

"But you knew where she lived. You never knocked on the door?"

"No, I didn't know where her dad—where she lived."

"Well, then you knew the phone number; you must've called…"

At that, I just lose it, but I try to stay in control. "Um, you know, I didn't have anything to do with this. We were just friends. That's all. I didn't kill her or anything." I grab my thighs to stop my knees from quaking.

"Oh no, honey, I'm not saying you were a part of it. I just want to understand…"

"Okay, you want to understand?" I throw my napkin down on the table. "You abandoned her too. You could've asked her to come be with you; you could've protected her, but you didn't. You didn't do anything to help her."

Betty starts to cry into her napkin.

People are looking our way now. I feel half-embarrassed and half-ashamed for lashing out at her. I take a deep breath. "I'm sorry. I…that was out of line, but I feel like you're telling me I could have done more too."

Betty doesn't stop crying. The waitress brings us more napkins.

Finally, I give in. "Her dad didn't report it because he didn't know. Jude didn't live with him." I have to give her something.

Betty's crying turns into sniffling. She wipes her eyes as she says, "What?"

"Jude didn't live with him. She lived on her own."

"What do you mean?"

"She ran away from home right before I met her. When she disappeared, I thought she just ran away again. I didn't know." I turn to Dr. Vonda's words, "I was only a kid then myself."

She dabs her eyes again and looks at the streaks of mascara on the napkin. She picks up the new napkin and tries to wipe away the Alice Cooper look to her eyes.

"She wouldn't have wanted me to call the police, I know that for a fact."

"But you could've called them anyway." She sniffles.

"She took care of herself. I thought she went to New Orleans or San Francisco or New York, just like she dreamed of."

"But, maybe a pimp would have grabbed her off the bus to make her a prostitute, didn't you worry about that?"

"You didn't know her. She wouldn't have—she wasn't vulnerable like that. I told you, she took care of herself."

Betty sits back in her chair, somewhat exasperated, somewhat defeated.

"I didn't know her, you're right." Her voice is shaking, but her words are now controlled. "I had my own family to raise and I couldn't take on one more child whose father was a troublemaker. I didn't want trouble."

Her hands are splayed out on the table as if she's about to push herself up. "I failed her. That's all. I failed her." She looks ashamed. She looks defeated.

"It's okay. She liked you. She talked about you a lot."

"I should go. It was nice to meet you, Alison."

"Wait." I put my hand on hers. "She—" I shouldn't tell her any more, I should let Jude rest in peace, but I can't let Betty suffer like this. "She didn't want you to find her either. She didn't want you to know how bad her father was to her. It—"

Betty has relaxed back into her chair.

"It embarrassed her, the things her father did. It made her feel like trash. She didn't want you to know her that way. She wanted you to think of her as your sister's daughter."

Betty is crying uncontrollably again. So I sit with her for awhile longer, telling her. Telling her about what Jude did to her father to end what he had done to her.

I think she feels better by the time we leave the restaurant.

But I never do tell her why I think Jude killed herself.

I get back to Mom's house twenty minutes late. Of course, for the first time in history, Karen was on time.

"Well, it's about time!" Mom jumps off the couch as I open the door.

Every time I see Karen I feel my gut tighten, preparing for whatever verbal assault may come my way.

"Haven't seen you in awhile." That's Karen's greeting as she half-hugs me—her torso a foot away, turned slightly to the left; she pats me on the back.

"How are you?" I ask rhetorically. My niece Kira, Karen's youngest, hangs on Karen's right hand and looks sheepishly around Karen's arm.

"Just great." Karen answers sarcastically. I know there's more to come.

"Hi Kira," I lean down and touch under my blond-haired niece's chin. She got the locks from Dad. She tucks her chin down and giggles, then pouts and nestles further behind Karen's arm.

"Karen!" Saved by Mom. "I have to show you this quilt I started working on."

Quilt? Since when did Mom work on quilts?

"Mom's new thing," Karen says and rolls her eyes. "Let me catch up with Alison first, Mom. I mean, we did wait for her and everything."

"Come on, Kira," Mom grabs Kira's little hand and Kira willingly goes with Mom.

"Just came back from a funeral," I say to Karen, but she seems to ignore me.

As Mom and Kira leave the room, Mom says, "The funeral was at eleven, it couldn't have taken all this time!"

I yell back to her as she disappears into the bedroom, "I went out to lunch with Betty!"

I don't know if Mom heard me, so I look back toward Karen. She's gained a lot of weight since I last saw her. She's got to be close to 220 pounds—and she's even shorter than I am, so she doesn't carry it well. She's got on navy blue sweat pants and a well-worn "Go Big Red" sweater.

"How are the Cornhuskers doing this year?"

Karen grins at me. "Like you care."

"You're the one wearing the sweatshirt." I smile back at her.

She backs down. "How're things going?" She sinks down into the couch and slides one leg comfortably under herself.

"Good." I sit down at the other end of the couch and feel strain on my torso as I turn toward her.

"Heard you moved."

"Yeah. Condo."

"Mom showed me the pictures you sent."

Uh-oh. Here we go.

"How are things for you?" I ask, trying to take the focus off of me.

"Oh great. Just great. Kevin is unemployed—" she mimics a lady getting her nails done, splaying her hand out as she talks, like she's a prissy woman, "you know, he got laid off in the spring. Oh, and you know, I pick up double shifts here and there so that we can pay the bills. And I think Candy is having sex at the age of thirteen, so things just couldn't be better."

She tucks her chin back into her rolly face and looks me directly in the eyes, unashamed.

I want to be a sarcastic ass and say, "Well, you did name your daughter Candy..." but I fight trying not to match her attitude. I fight reverting back to a teenager.

It seems like forever before I finally pull myself back into who I am. "Yeah, Mom keeps me informed. I'm sorry things are so hard for you."

"Yeah, me too." Sarcasm, with a little nod of the head. She just stares at me. I lean back into the couch, but I can't get comfortable. I look at a picture on Mom's wall, above the tv. A pastoral scene with three ducks flying over a lake. A lot of browns and blacks and grays in the picture.

"Sorry to hear about Jude." Karen's demeanor has changed. I feel like she's almost gleeful something bad has happened in my life.

I clear my throat. "Yeah. Thanks."

"She was that girl that used to hang out in downtown, wasn't she? Brown shoulder-length hair? Army jacket? Dressed like a guy?"

"Yeah." I find myself staring at the ducks again—their wings extended.

"There were some boys at school that used to torment the heck out of her."

I feel my stomach drop.

"What?"

"Yeah, some jocks. I saw them once—they drove past her in a car and started throwing rocks. Like, big rocks—the size of a fist. I know one hit her right here," she puts her hand on her right shoulder. "Man, it must've hurt. But she didn't yell or anything. She just stood there and took it."

"When did you see this?" I still want to protect Jude—I want to find those guys and say, "Look. Look what you did. She's dead."

"Crimeny, I don't know Ally—it was like, three kids ago."

I feel my heart pounding and I try to calm down. I try to hide how much that story pisses me off. "She had a tough life."

"Yeah, well, we all do. Except maybe you."

"What's that supposed to mean?" Oh god, did I really just open that door?

Karen just glares at me for a minute, her body tense. And then she sits up. "Um. Let's see. Fancy job in Minneapolis." She counts off using her fingers, "Successful handsome boyfriend—and I don't know why you don't just marry him—nice new car, nice clothes, eating out at places that would take one of my paychecks, huge god-knows-how-much-it-costs condo in downtown—"

"It's not in downtown." My voice is almost as loud as hers.

"You have everything you could possibly need; and then you come in here and make fun of my sweater—"

"I wasn't making fun! I was making conversation!" Now I stand up, ready to walk away from this stupidity.

Karen is standing now too. "Face it Ally, you're a stuck-up high-class bitch who swoops in here once every two years and expects to fit in with our family. Well, you know what? You're not like the rest of us and it's time you accept that."

I can feel my chin quiver, but I'm not going to cry. Not over Karen's stupid rants.

"You girls keep your voices down! The neighbors will hear!" Mom is walking briskly down her short hallway with Kira in tow. "What are you two fighting about now, for God's sake?"

"Nothing." Karen says. "We're leaving."

She grabs Kira's hand from Mom's grip and pulls Kira toward the door.

"And just so you know," she looks at me from the doorway. "This is my best Cornhusker sweatshirt, so you can go fuck yourself."

"Karen Marie!" Mom claps her hands together.

Karen just turns and shuts the door forcefully behind her.

"What was that all about?" Mom puts her hands on her hips and looks at me, waiting for an answer.

"We were just talking—I don't know."

"Why did she make that comment about her sweater?"

"Mom, I just asked her how the Cornhuskers were doing and then she went off telling me that I was too high class for this family—"

"Ally, can't you just try to get along with your sister for once."

"Mom! I didn't do anything!" Here I go again, slipping back to adolescence. I stop myself. Pull myself together. "I'm going for a drive."

"Ally, come on. We only have a few days together."

"I know Mom, but I need to get out of here." I grab my jacket and just leave Mom standing there hoping I'll come back in.

I get in my car and see Mom looking out the window of her apartment at me. I look away, put the car in reverse, and speed out of the parking lot. I need some space, some time away from everyone who wants something from me. Some kind of explanation.

I drive—just like I did twenty-five years ago. Past the Opera House, out to the Platte River, across the tracks, past the lake, the drive-in, the putt-putt golf course, back into downtown, past the Opera House, down Main Street, past the old music store, down Broad, out to the church where there used to be only gravel roads, past the tennis courts, past the new housing development.

I don't even know where to go anymore. I don't know how to escape.

I drive around and around as if I'm stuck in some crazy pattern, like this river cat I saw at a zoo once. It was in a tiny enclosure and it circled around and around and around again as if it couldn't stop. Someone once told me it was stir crazy.

My thoughts spin in the same direction. I churn the conversations today over and over in my head until I feel battered by them. Beaten down and stir crazy inside my head.

Now I drive onto a gravel road that looks somewhat familiar, and all I want to do is go home. I want to go back to Minneapolis and sit on my couch and look at the skyline. I want to go back to where I feel normal and safe. I want to go back…to feeling like Eli is home. I want to feel in love with Eli again.

The gravel kicks up and bites the bottom of my car. A trail of dust rises behind me. And then I stop. No one behind me. No one in front of me. But the driveway to the right of me leads to the little farmhouse. And the barn.

Emma's place.

Jesus. How did I end up here?

I look in my rearview mirror and down the road in front of me. No one seems to be around for miles. So I turn into the driveway. Part of me is saying I shouldn't. Part of me can't help but go.

The road is dry and rutty. My car bounces all over the place, the steering wheel fights my hands. Everything is overgrown and spilling out of the broken and rotting fence. Tall grasses surround me. The closest neighbor is—I try to look around, but my car is bouncing too much on this narrow road. I keep my eyes on my destination.

Emma's farmhouse sits quietly at the end of the drive. I put the car in park and stare up at the two-story frame. I can almost hear Emma clunking around in those shoes, the floorboards creaking beneath her 97 pounds. The paint is cracked and peeling. Some of the wood is naked and aged. The screen door at the front hangs by one hinge, waiting to fall. Its screen is ripped and hangs limp; it waves in the steady wind.

I almost expect to smell Listerine, and death, but all I smell is the cold Nebraska dirt.

I step closer to the house. One step, two, three. Cautiously. I look around, but there's no one within a mile. Still, I move cautiously, as if the house will rise up and scream down at me. Begging me to leave it be.

I see something on the door. A note of some sort. Curious, I inch closer to the house.

"CONDEMNED." Clear as day. I don't even need to go up the steps to see it.

But I do go up the steps. Each one creaks under my weight. It sounds so loud, even though I'm out here all alone. I stand on the porch, this big, beautiful porch that must have been where the farmer and his wife sat on hot summer days. In rocking chairs, sipping iced tea or lemonade, looking over their crops. But now, it's falling apart; floorboards missing, the rail rotting, the roof appears that it's about to crumble to the ground. I step carefully and try to peer between boards on the picture window at the front. Nothing. All I can see is dark glass between the boards.

Grasses rustle with a strong gust and I'm pelted by dirt and sand or something. It stings. Then the knocking starts. A creak and then a knock. A creepy feeling crawls up my spine and I practically run off the porch. I look at the house from the driveway, if you can call it that. It looks lonely, and old, and ruined. A gutter hangs off the roof and is swaying in the wind, hitting the house with each gust.

I pull my collar up around my neck, then put my hands in my armpits. Even with gloves, they're cold. And then I look at the barn. Criminey. The barn.

My heart pounds inside my chest. I swallow hard. Do I dare walk over there? Do I dare…?

The dirt and gravel crunch beneath my feet.

A strong wind hits my back, almost pushing me forward. I resist, but still move toward the barn where police tape flaps in the wind. As if that would keep anyone out, way out here. But the police tape is just a remnant now. Just a reminder that something happened a long, long time ago.

My hand is on the door of the barn. The door moves with the wind, back and forth, begging, retreating, begging. I raise up the handle; it clunks, I pull.

I want to cry for how scared I am.

Another gust of wind and the huge barn door is pulled out of my hands and forced open. I wait for it to come back and hit me, but it doesn't.

And then I look. I see this big open space. A loft above, dirt below. I expected to see hay. Isn't there always hay in the movies? But, no, this is just big and open, like a garage. Did the police clean it out? Is that what happened? Surely Emma would have kept something in here. I expected to find old rusted farm equipment, moldy hay, hundreds of plates for the cats, a million mice, age-old blood splattered on the wall; brain matter—something. But this is just empty and hollow and dark. The wind makes it sound like I'm inside a glass bottle. An empty glass bottle.

There's nothing here. There's nothing to see.

Nothing is frozen in time. This space has moved on, cleared out old thoughts and memories. It's just me. I suddenly realize it's just me.

I'm the one.

I'm the one stuck in all of these pockets of time.

Chapter Sixteen

I sit in my car staring at Mom's apartment building. It takes me ten, fifteen minutes to muster the strength to go inside. To face the barrage of questions.

I open the door to a crispy, soupy smell. Some kind of casserole dish, I'm sure.

"Ally?" Mom's voice sings from the kitchen. She clangs some pots, then appears from the kitchen. "Where did you go?" she asks sternly, like a mother.

"I told you. For a drive."

"I know. But where? Where do you go Ally?" She has her hands on her hips, a dish towel dangling from her right hand.

Her question takes me by surprise. She's never asked before, in all these years. "I ended up at the farm."

"The farm?"

"Emma's farm."

She drops her hands and starts wiping them on the towel, "Oh, Ally."

I walk past her, toward the bedroom, because I don't want to cry in front of her.

"Karen called," she blurts out to my back.

That stops me in my tracks.

"She wanted to apologize. She said she was out of line."

Wow. Karen apologized?

"You should call her back."

Another "should," just what I need. I keep moving toward the bedroom.

"Dinner's ready."

"I'll be right there."

I close the bedroom door and sit down for a minute. I take the folded piece of paper out of my jacket pocket, unfold it, and look down at the sandhill cranes.

I toss the paper onto the bed. It lands at an angle, trying to fold itself back up. I take off my jacket, take a deep breath, and go out to the dining room.

An iceberg lettuce salad with slightly green tomatoes sits in a salad bowl I've never seen in the middle of the table. Mom even has the salad utensils that go with it. She has two warming pads sitting expectantly on either side of the salad bowl. And there are folded purple cotton napkins sitting next to our plates. Wal-Mart has served Mom well.

"How was the funeral?" Mom asks from the kitchen, just like she'd ask "how's the weather?"; "how was your day?"; "what's new?"

"Fine." What am I supposed to say?

Mom comes out of the kitchen and sets two water glasses down at each setting. "How was her aunt?"

I sit down at the table, next to the freaky high chair doll again (who, thankfully, does not have a place mat and settings in front of it). "She was…fine."

Mom just looks at me, waiting for more. I take a drink from the water glass, glancing over the rim at her. She's still waiting.

"It was windy today," I set the glass down and put my hands in my lap. I can tell she's disappointed.

She pulls out her chair and sits. "Well…" Oh god, she's not going to let this go. She unfolds her napkin and puts it on her lap, "so you went out to lunch with Betty. How was that?"

I mimic her movements. She hands me the salad bowl. "It was okay," but what I'm really thinking is that I wish I would've gone back to Minneapolis right after the burial, then I would have avoided the lunch with Betty altogether, and this conversation. I hand Mom the salad bowl.

"What did you two talk about?"

"Nothing, really." I take my first bite of the crispy, tasteless salad that has Dorothy Lynch salad dressing on it as I try to think of the perfect diversion.

"You spent two hours with the woman and you didn't speak about anything?"

"Not really," I say. "Hey, did Eli call?"

"Oh!" Mom suddenly looks flustered and darts off to the kitchen. She holds a piece of paper in her hand when she rounds the corner. "Something…" She looks as if she's trying to discern her shorthand. She places her index finger under her bottom lip. "He booked a trip—to New Orleans…" Her voice goes up and she looks at me, seemingly hopeful that I can finish the sentence.

Mom waves off the blank look I must be giving her and says, "Oh, just call him back."

I take another bite of salad. I should feel excited about going to New Orleans, but I just feel indifferent.

"How is Eli doing?"

"Fine." Somehow, I've led us from one subject I don't want to talk about to another.

"How's his work?" Mom never quite understands what it is that Eli does.

"It's fine, Mom. He's still conducting."

"And how's your new place?" She disappears off into the kitchen again, this time bringing back a tuna casserole thing.

"It's good. It's beautiful, but it's really Eli's place, you know. I mean, he's the one who bought it."

Mom looks at me with confusion. "Eli's place?" She seems to be mulling this over as she puts the napkin back onto her lap. "Why you two don't get married is beyond me."

I ignore her and spoon out the soup-and-tater-tot mixture onto my plate. I have to admit that sometimes this crap really hits the spot.

"And your work? How's that Ally?"

"Good," I take a deep breath. Maybe I should ask about her life instead.

"What is it you do again? I never know how to explain that to the gals at work."

"I'm a stage manager, Mom. I kind of help the show run. I help get all the technical stuff ready, I make sure the actors are in their places, I call the sound and light cues." I can tell I've lost her. "Stuff like that."

"And you work at some fancy theater, too, don't you?" I always want to correct the way she says thē-ate-er, but I don't.

"Yeah, Mom, one of the biggest regionals in the country."

She looks at me blankly.

"It's a well-known theater," I add.

She nods and dishes out some of the casserole. As she takes her first bite, she opens her mouth to cool it off. She always does that, takes a steaming hot bite without blowing on it first. When she finally gets the first bite down, she makes an "mmmmmm" sound.

"It's good Mom," I say. I should've said it before, but better late than never. I take another bite and wonder what she was going to put on the other warming pad.

"So you and Eli are going to New Orleans?"

"Yeah."

"Why do you two like that place so much?"

"Well, Eli loves the music. There's jazz and blues and cajun and zydeco." With a bite of casserole perched on my fork, I can tell I lost her on zydeco.

"What about that hurricane? Didn't it take everything? Is it even safe to go there? I hear those people are killing and raping each other and selling drugs—"

I won't even get into her "those people" comment. "No, Mom, the city is coming back. We'll be in the French Quarter, it's all fine."

"Well, be careful. Do you think Eli's cds will ever sell well enough so he can quit his job?"

"What? Mom, he—the cds aren't like top-40 kind of things. I mean, they're more like classical music—and even if they did, he loves his job. I mean, he wouldn't quit."

"Really?"

The phone rings and breaks up the conversation.

Mom begins talking to a friend, it seems, and I realize I didn't even know she has friends. I've only heard her talk about co-workers. God, we don't know anything about each other.

"Ally's here right now," she says to the phone, "Yep. Leaves tomorrow." She nods at me and holds up her index finger, then turns her back to me.

I keep eating slowly, feeling watched by the stupid high chair doll the entire time. Mom has her back to me, but I can hear her talking. She's gossiping about some people in the building. Some couple that broke up. I wonder if someone cheated on someone else. Like me.

I put down my fork and toss my napkin on the table. I could clear the table, but Mom has the kitchen entrance blocked with her long phone cord. I really should get her a cordless phone. I make a mental note.

She just keeps talking and talking about some broken relationship and how this woman goes to the bars now looking for men to sleep with and the high chair doll keeps staring at me and Mom's plate isn't cleared so I don't know if I should stack dishes or not and I feel like I should wait for her to get off the phone, but then I finally get up and go back to the bedroom.

The sandhill crane drawing has managed to fold itself back into a little square and flip over so it's lying flat on the bed. I tuck it in my notebook and lie down on the bed. The ceiling fan churns above my head.

I stare at the dolls lined up on a shelf on the wall across from the bed. One has a freaky shiny face and her long-lashed eyes seem to stare at me. The fan whirs whirs whirs above me and I feel weird. I feel—like when I lived in New York City. Millions of people around me, but I had no friends. Except for Eli. At the end of the day, there was always Eli.

I can hear Mom's voice rumble through the closed bedroom door.

I pick up my cell phone.

"Hey," Eli picks up. His voice is soft and I feel almost normal again.

"Hey," I say back.

"Did you get my message?" He sounds excited.

"Sort of. You got tickets for New Orleans."

"We're going for a week. How's that sound?"

"Good. Great." I try to muster up enough enthusiasm to meet his.

"I booked a room at the Savoy on Canal Street."

"Oh, Eli. That's so expensive." I don't know why I care. Eli always pays for our trips.

"I know. I want us to have a special trip. You know?" His voice is soft and, well, romantic.

I swallow hard. "Yeah."

"Maybe we could…" He doesn't finish his sentence.

I don't finish it for him. I just wait through the long awkward silence. The ceiling fan spins, spins, spins above me and the dolls stare at me with their marble-cold eyes.

"…maybe we could try."

"Try?"

"To make a baby."

That old song, "You're Having My Baby," plays in my head. Yuk. "Oh," is all I manage to say.

The ceiling fan seems to be whirring faster. Mom laughs hysterically through the door. She's actually snorting. I've never heard her laugh so hard.

"I should go. Mom's waiting for me." I close my eyes to keep them from following the ceiling fan blades.

"Ally?"

"Yeah."

"I love you."

"I know."

He sighs deeply, but doesn't say anything.

"So, I'll see you tomorrow." Can he hear my voice shaking?

"Yeah. I'll see you tomorrow."

"Bye." It's almost as if he doesn't want to hang up, but I do right away after my good-bye. Before he can say any more.

I open my eyes and stare at the light in the middle of the ceiling fan. Gold trimmed and old fashioned.

You can't run away anymore, Jude's whisper comes from the swish of the ceiling fan.

I put my arm across my eyes.

"Ally?" Mom calls from the kitchen. "You haven't finished your dinner!"

Now she wants to be a mom. I'm over forty years old and now she wants to be a mom.

Her head pops into my doorway, uninvited. "Ally!" She scolds. "Come back and eat dinner. I made it special for you."

After she leaves the room, I have a little, short outburst of a cry. It's just a spurt of crying, like a sneeze. It lasts for just a second before I pull myself together and roll off the bed.

When I get to the small dining room, Mom's sitting at the table, head resting on clasped hands, and she's staring at that weird doll. I sit down in silence.

She breaks herself out of her daydream and puts her hands in her lap. "Everything okay with Eli?"

"Yeah, fine." I stare down at the few bites of tater-tot casserole left on my plate.

"Aren't you going to finish?" Her mood has changed since she got off the phone. She's not so happy-go-lucky anymore. She seems almost…sad.

"I—" The stuff is cold now, and sticky. "It's good, Mom, I'm just not that hungry."

She looks at me blankly.

"I'm still sad, you know, the memorial service and all."

"You never could finish your whole dinner. You always left a few bites on the plate, even with all those starving children in China." She gives me a soft, warm smile. It makes me feel better for a moment. "What time are you leaving tomorrow?"

"I don't know. In the morning. Ten, eleven."

She nods her head. "Well, I'll miss you, Ally."

She actually sounds sincere. I look at her face and see delicate lines around her eyes and lips, and along her forehead. Her expression is soft, not pinched like usual.

"I'll miss you too, Mom." I'm not going to cry. Despite the ache in my throat, I will not cry.

"I'd like to talk to you more often." Still sincere, and calm. I've never seen her so calm before.

"Yeah, I'd like that too." And I mean it. It surprises me, but I do mean it.

She takes a deep breath and puts her napkin on the table. "Well, are you going out tonight?"

I think about that for a minute. "I suppose I should stop by and see John." He's a good excuse to get out, besides I haven't seen him in so long; I kind of miss my little brother.

"Well, you know John. He's probably at the casino tonight. But you can try to stop by."

I look back at the light fixture on the ceiling. I wouldn't feel like I had any family if it weren't for Eli.

I take a deep breath and Mom just sits there, looking at me.

Then she shyly says, "Well, we could play some cards if you want."

Mom's eyes are so sad. Have they always been like that? She looks so vulnerable right now, I just want her to be happy. "Sure, we can play some cards."

"Really? You'll play cards with me?" She practically jumps up and starts clearing the table. Why haven't I ever seen this side of her before?

I help her stack up the dishes and forks and serving plates. As I start rinsing dishes and loading the dishwasher, Mom says, "Oh just leave them. Let's have some fun and worry about these later."

She opens a small drawer in the kitchen and pulls out two decks of cards. "Canasta?" she asks. My dad loved canasta; he taught me and Karen and John how to play. We spent so many Sunday afternoons playing while Mom made dinner. I didn't even know she knew how to play.

"Yeah, canasta is great."

"Your dad and I used to play it all the time before we had you. It was a cheap form of entertainment, you know." She shuffles the cards like she's done this a million times. She looks happy. In this moment, actually happy.

She tosses the cards—to me, to her, to me, to her—while she whistles. Her half-whistle. In this moment, I find it kind of comforting. "Your draw," she says.

This is what my New Orleans mother would have done—the Mary

Bouchard who was an interior decorator in the Garden District. She would have played canasta with her grown-up daughter. And she would have whistled. An endearing half-whistle, sucking in her breath instead of blowing it out.

"Are you sure you want to throw that?" she teases. Then she picks up the stack and starts throwing cards down like a master. She throws down kings and jacks; she makes a natural out of eights, and starts throwing down some wild cards so I think she might go out. I almost break a sweat looking at the two jokers in my hand.

She laughs and says, "See, your Mom's not so dumb after all."

And I wonder if she really feels I think she's dumb, but I don't say anything. She discards and I pick up two more cards from the stack. I see how pleased she is with herself, and for the first time I can remember, I feel pleased with her too.

It's midnight when Mom finally goes to bed. "I had fun Ally." She kisses me on the head as I put the cards back in the box. She smells like a cheap sweet perfume, but for once, it doesn't bother me.

"I had fun too, Mom."

And I actually did.

After she shuts the door to her room, I think about going for one last drive past the Opera House. Past all the places Jude used to roam. But I decide to try something different, so I go into my room. I can still hear Mom moving around her bedroom as I dig out the notepad and pen from my already-packed suitcase.

I lie on my stomach and tap the pen on the page.

"You should be a writer, Ally," Jude whispered to me once. She was leaning back against the wall of the incinerator. My head was on her stomach. Sometimes I heard her stomach growl and gurgle.

And I remember feeling like I'd really like to be a writer. But I was afraid.

"What's to be afraid of?" she asked. She was stroking my hair.

"I don't know. Maybe I'm not a writer at all."

She laughed. "That's not right, Ally. You're something else, you know?"

"What do you mean?"

"You're a writer."

It feels like those words she said give me permission now to write her story. I want to go back. Back before Eli. So I can change things.

My pen makes a rat-a-tat-tat on the paper that would make Jude smile. She'd want to copy me. I write:

The New Orleans Opera House.

I underline it. There is no New Orleans Opera House, but I want to change Jude's story. I want her to be happy. I want us to be happy.

But happiness isn't what comes out. Instead, I write, "In the dark incinerator, the young girl lights a match."

I roll over on my back and look up at the ceiling fan. I haven't adjusted the speed, but it seems like it moves slower now. Like a slow afternoon on a hot New Orleans day.

I'll be in New Orleans this weekend. Maybe I can find someplace to sit and write.

Eli will want to stay out late; go to the jazz clubs, see his friends, make a baby.

Now that dread creeps into my body again; the peacefulness is gone.

I turn over on my stomach again and look at the page.

In the dark incinerator, the young girl lights a match.

Maybe I don't have to go to the clubs with Eli. And by the time he gets back I'll be fast asleep.

In the dark incinerator, the young girl lights a match.

I tap, tap, tap on the notebook again.

I don't want to make a baby. I don't even want Eli to say the words "make a baby." Hell, I don't even want to go home to Eli. I just want to stay here with Mom and play canasta every night and write after she goes to bed.

In the dark incinerator, the young girl lights a match, Jude's voice whispers to me insistently.

I ignore her because for once I'm thinking about Eli. I mean, Eli is my best friend. Up until a few months ago, I told him everything I was feeling and thinking. We've been so perfect together. Other than the baby thing, we've had no real problems.

The baby thing is what's wrong with me now. Isn't it?

In the dark incinerator, the young girl lights a match, I can almost hear Jude's finger tapping on the page.

But the baby thing doesn't explain Softie—or Jude.

The tapping stops.

That doesn't explain the unhappiness that's creeped into our lives in the past few months.

I've just got to settle back into our relationship. And I've got to tell Eli that I don't want to have a baby. I've just got to get through this.

I have another appointment with Dr. Vonda this week and then maybe I can figure out how to tell him. Then it's off to New Orleans. That's good. Then we can work on things without baby-making involvement. We can work on the relationship in a place we have memories. In a place we both love.

I stare at the words on the page, *In the dark incinerator, the young girl lights a match.*

I have to tell Eli that I don't want to have a baby.

I have to tell him.

As much as I dread it, it's time to go home.

It's time to go home to Eli.

Chapter Seventeen

Mom's coughing wakes me up. She's in the bathroom next to my bedroom. It's seven a.m. I easily close my eyes again.

She starts coughing again. It rattles in her lungs. I hear the water turn on and off, on and off. Another long, rattling cough. Then another that trails behind her down the hallway. Now she's in the kitchen, rattling dishes.

The clock next to me reads 7:05. Shit, it's early, but now I don't feel like I can get back to sleep.

"Hey Mom," I say as I enter the kitchen.

"Oh, did I wake you?" She coughs again.

"Are you okay?"

Another cough. "Oh yes, yes." She waves me away with her hand. "I've just got this constant tickle in my throat. It's all those years working around cigarette smoke, you know."

She pours her coffee. "Besides, when you're as old as I am, your body starts to do things it didn't do before."

"You're not that old, Mom."

"Sixty-six in January." She puts a box of cereal and the milk in front of me.

"You're not that old."

"You want coffee, Ally?"

"Sure."

"When are you two going to New Orleans?"

"Monday."

"Monday?!? You're just getting home and then you're turning around and leaving again?"

"Yep." I pour milk on my shredded wheat.

"Well," she finally sits down, "no grass grows under your feet, does it?" Then she says, "It's a good thing you don't have kids. Or is that 'a good think'?" She smiles at me.

I smile back and say, "It's thing. And yes, it is a good thing."

She gives a soft laugh. "It's been good to have you here, Ally." She doesn't look at me when she says it—she looks past me, kind of—she looks toward her dolls.

"It's been good to be here too, Mom."

She coughs again and starts clearing the dishes before I'm done. Because this is what she does. This is the life of Mary Bouchard of Harmony, Nebraska.

And I actually think I'm going to miss her.

I can't seem to settle in my car as I drive out of Harmony. I fidget with the cd player, my water bottle rolls around on the floor because it didn't fit into the drink holder and I tried to put it in the little side pocket built into my door but it fell out when I took a turn, and my cell phone beeps at me because there's some message, I'm sure from Eli.

I just want to turn the car back around and crawl into the bed at Mom's house and just lie there. I want to play canasta and laugh with Mom tonight. I want to write down Jude's story and not be worried about Eli and babies.

I want to throw my cell phone into the river, and forget about everything.

I want to go back to sitting with Jude on the riverbank and dreaming of how big life could be.

Well, geez, I got everything I wanted, didn't I? This big career in theatre, meeting celebrities, working steadily; how many people in theatre can say that? Now I live in this fancy place in a big city and have this great guy in my life who makes me feel, well, like I have a normal life.

But still, I want to turn around and go to Harmony. Back to where things are simple.

Heck, I could get a job somewhere in town—the movie theatre. How much money do you need to make to live in Harmony anyway?

My cell phone rings. I blow air out of my mouth so my lips rumble.

"Hello." I try not to sound bitchy.

"Baby, where are you? You didn't call me."

"Was I supposed to call you?" Bitchy. How else could that question come out except bitchy.

"Didn't you get my message? Besides, you always used to call me before you hit the road." He sounds a bit on edge.

"I'm sorry," I try not to say it out of obligation, but that's how it comes out, "I'm only about fifteen minutes outside Harmony anyway."

"You just left?"

"Yeah. Mom and I stayed up late playing cards."

The phone beeps, then goes dead. "Lost signal" flashes on my screen. I throw the phone on the passenger seat.

Both of my hands are on the wheel and I look out over the road ahead. Dead cornfields sit on either side of the highway. Migrating birds dip and swoop around the shoulder and suddenly, my chin starts to quiver. It feels like a wall of floodwater hits me. It's like this strong force comes out of nowhere and takes me over. I start to cry. Sobbing crying.

I clutch the steering wheel harder and focus on the road through the tears. It's like trying to see through a driving rain. No one is on the highway except for me, but I pull over to a gravel driveway leading to a farm.

Tissue. I need tissue desperately. I look through the glove compartment and find some fast-food napkins.

I can't stop crying. I want to go back to Mom. I don't know why. Or back to—someone. Not Eli. I don't want to go home to Eli.

Stop this, Ally. God, stop this now.

Why can't I control this?

I start to laugh through the tears because I don't know what else to do. This is ridiculous. I have a great life and Eli is a great guy. He cares about me. I could hear it in his voice.

And now I'm crying even harder. *Jesus, Ally, get a grip.*

God, I miss Jude. I wonder what she'd say. I instinctively look in my rearview mirror—as if I'll see her there. In the backseat, walking behind my car, back in Harmony.

I cry so hard I use up my four fast-food napkins and now I have to resort to wiping my nose on the sleeve of my shirt.

I have to stop. I have to stop!

But I can't seem to gain control. I feel desperate, panicky. I need to talk to someone.

I pick up my cell phone. There's a signal now. I search through the names in my directory. Eli is first. I keep scanning. What's wrong with me? Dr. Vonda, but I would just get her voice mail. I can't leave a voice mail now—colleague, colleague, coworker…Mom. I keep going. Colleague, coworker, colleague, colleague. Geez, I don't have any friends. At least not any true friends—no one outside of work. Coworker, colleague…work—and then I find it. A number to call. I swallow hard, try to contain myself. I shouldn't do it, but something compels me to hit "send."

It rings and rings and rings. I almost hang up, but then… "Ally?"

I think I'm going to come off as the normal Ally, but my voice quivers. "Yeah, it's me…" And then I can't talk anymore.

"Hey, what's wrong?"

"Softie…" I can't even manage to get out any other words.

"Where are you? Ally?"

And then I hang up. I turn off my cell phone.

I sit on the side of the road and cry for ten minutes, twenty minutes, I don't know. And then I start driving. Back to Eli. Back to my life with Eli.

Chapter Eighteen

I feel ready for bed when I get home at six thirty; I'm just wiped out. Eli is usually gone by now, but he waited for me to get home. He meets me at the door and takes my bag as he asks, "So, when did you and Softie become friends?"

I feel myself blush. "What?"

"Jane's partner, Softie—when did you become friends?"

"What are you talking about?" I'm so tired from the drive I can barely get the words out.

"She left a message for you."

I can't speak. I lean down to pet Mozart so that it takes Eli's attention away from my shock. It didn't even occur to me that Softie might have my home phone number. Or that she would call it. And leave a message.

Mozart runs away when the wind makes the windows creak. I stand up. My diversion didn't work because Eli asks, "So you and Softie?"

I don't know what to say.

He laughs, "Why are you blushing?"

I can feel a little bit of sweat forming under my hairline. "Eli…" I sound whiney. *The lady doth protest too much methinks.* "I can have friends, too, you know." I walk past him and grab my bag from his hand.

"I know, I know. Geez. Why are you getting so upset?" He follows me toward the bedroom. "Hey," he grabs me around the waist and turns me toward him. "Don't I get a kiss?"

I give him a peck on the lips then move away.

"I missed you too," he says in a disappointed tone.

I act like I didn't hear and take my bag into the bedroom.

How long can we live like this?

"Hey," he appears at the door. "I just didn't know you two were friends, that's all. When did you start hanging out?"

Hanging out? If he only knew. I throw the bag on the bed. "Closing night." At least it's not a lie.

"Oh—that night you stayed out late."

I slowly unzip the bag and try to discern the tone of his voice. He sounds innocent enough.

I wish I were innocent. "Yeah."

"Funny she hasn't said anything to me."

Said anything? What's he talking about? "What do you mean?" I slowly open the flap of the suitcase to expose my laundry.

"Well, I've had drinks with her and Jane a few times over the past few weeks, and she never asked about you."

What the hell? "Why are you hanging out with them?" My voice comes out irritated and I can't stop it. "That's who you've been going out with after work? They're 'the guys'?"

"Ooooo," he grabs me around the waist again, "Is someone jealous?" Now he's acting all turned on and that pisses me off.

I pull away from him and grab the toiletries to take to the bathroom. "Don't you have to go to work?"

"Come on, sweetie," he follows me to the bathroom, "we're just hanging out, having drinks."

I put the mini-shampoo and mini-conditioner back in the medicine cabinet. I slam it shut, but I don't mean to.

"Hey, hey, hey," he turns me toward him and tries to get me to look into his eyes. I resist, so he moves my chin with his index finger. His voice is soft and sweet, "Why don't you and I go out for drinks tonight after the show?"

Something about the way he says this makes me warm inside. "Really?" I sound like a teenage girl being picked first for basketball. "Yeah, okay."

"Great. Let's meet at Stage Left at eleven."

I suddenly feel my energy drop. Eleven? What did I just get myself into? I'm tired. I'm middle-aged. I want to stay home.

Why doesn't he want to stay home?

"Is that okay?" Eli asks and I feel myself melting a little bit for him.

"Yeah. Sure. I'll see you there." Eleven. I need a nap.

"Okay, baby, see you later." He kisses me again, with hope.

Mozart lies beside me on the couch. I turn on a sitcom and rest my head on a pillow. Mozart rubs her head up under my chin. My eyelids feel like weights, so I close them and listen to the actors onscreen talking to each other while canned laughter rises in the background. Their voices get thinner and thinner as I drift off to sleep.

But sleep isn't restful.

Eli grips my shoulders tightly. He demands an answer—about Softie—about Jude. "You never tell me anything." He yells and squeezes tighter.

"Eli, let go." I'm crying.

Then Jude appears behind him. She's smoking; her eyes are glistening and alive.

She walks right through Eli, right through me—and makes us both disappear.

I turn and see her walking into Harmony, on the south side where there are train tracks—she's following the tracks. She can't see me.

I follow her, though. I watch her walk on the rails, her arms spread out like a highwire performer. And then she falls and I want to run to help her, but the ground catches her first. She stumbles, regains her balance, then jumps back onto the track, arms spread out.

I try to jump onto the track, too, to follow in her footsteps, but the track turns to water and I find my feet in mud.

As I look down at my feet, I lose sight of Jude.

Grain mill. Depot. Slaughterhouse.

Those are the buildings ahead of me. She must have gone into one of them.

I try the grain mill first. It's dark and dusty. A tower rises above me and I look up into deeper darkness. "Hello?" I cry out and my voice echoes back to me, "'lo…'lo…'lo." At least I know I'm real. I think.

Jude doesn't answer.

I don't want her to kill herself again. I feel desperate to find her.

"Hello?" I call out to the longer part of the mill. "'lo…'lo" comes back.

"Jude?" What comes back sounds like "dude."

No answer.

I run outside and over the rocks of the tracks to the depot. I look down the tracks in both directions, but I don't see Jude, so I go inside.

The building is cold. Two dim light bulbs hang from the ceiling, spilling barely enough light out for me to see my feet. This is just one single room, barely bigger than our condo. It's gray-stoned walls seem to close me in.

"Jude?" No echo. No answer.

The air is dense and still.

"Jude?" I try again, but I can barely breathe.

The lights flicker and go out.

I gasp for air. I can't seem to breathe…in…enough…

Sweat drops down my face. I gasp. I cough.

I fall.

When I hit…

The solid…

Cold floor…

I wake up.

My lungs shudder as I take a deep breath. Mozart jumps off my chest and I sit up.

I'm shaking.

The condo is dark except for the glow of the tv. I fumble with the remote and mute the sound.

I'm not quite awake as I hear my voice call out. "Jude?"

"Jude" comes back to me.

I shiver. It's so cold in here that if the lights were on I believe I could see my breath.

I put my shaky legs on the ground and try to get my bearings. But I feel eyes on me. I feel like someone is standing in a corner of darkness.

I make my way to the kitchen and try to stay focused on the light switch. I feel an urgent need to turn on the lights. I just walk straight ahead and don't look around. My heart is thumping as the lights come on. Jesus, I half-expect to see Jude standing there; I expect to hear her say, "Surprise! You didn't really think I would kill myself?"

I look out across the expanse of Eli's condo. It's just me, I'm alone.

Okay…*god, Alison, eat some food, take a shower, then go meet Eli.*

I wish I could just crawl into bed and hide. I'm still shaking as I make my way into the dark bedroom. The darkness makes the hair stand up on my arms again, but Mozart runs in ahead of me. I hear her jump up on the bed. That makes me feel better. Mozart is a big scardy cat; if anything was in that room, she certainly wouldn't run in unless it was to hide under the bed. I turn on the light and everything looks normal. Except for that damned drawing of Jude's. It's sitting in the middle of the bed like some origami creation, perched and ready to fly.

Did I leave it there?

I must have.

I pick it up but don't open it. I just tuck it under the black underwear in my underwear drawer. Thank god Eli didn't come home to find it.

Well, what if he did? "What's this?" he'd ask. And I'd tell him "something Jude drew." But then he'd launch into all sorts of questions about Jude. Uncomfortable questions.

Things he just doesn't need to know.

As I open the door of Stage Left, I feel like going out is the right thing to do for our relationship. I'd rather be home, getting ready for bed—but this is what I should be doing.

I didn't dress up, but I'm dressed nicely. Jeans, my Euro-looking flat black shoes (I don't wear heels), and the most feminine blouse I have—an orange-and-brown three-quarter-length sleeved, form-fitting blouse. I definitely look better than I did a few hours ago, and I think I've settled down a bit since that dream. I'm less shaky.

The door of the bar closes behind me and I immediately see Eli waving me over. I feel a rush of energy—maybe even some happiness. But as I walk closer, I see the two women Eli is sitting with.

Oh, shit.

I feel stunned as Eli helps me off with my jacket.

"Hey Sweetie," a kiss on the cheek, his hand on my arm, he pulls me closer to the table, "look who decided to join us."

Is this some kind of joke? Are they in cahoots?

"Hey, Ally," Softie stands up and kisses me on the cheek. Right in front of Eli.

I feel my face burn red. "Hey."

"Ally, have you met Jane?" Eli asks as he motions to her.

"No, hi Jane." She's petite with short black hair. She doesn't have any tattoos or piercings—that I can see anyway.

"I've heard a lot about you, Ally, from both Eli and Softie." She's just short of winking at me with her big brown eyes.

"Oh, yeah. You too." I know I'm supposed to say, "Well, I hope it's all good. Hahahaha." But I don't want to say anything. I want to disappear.

"Are you cold? You're shivering." Eli puts my jacket back over my shoulders, like it's a shawl for old ladies. I sit down on the high stool and Eli rubs my back before he sits on the stool next to me. My shirt rides up in back, so I reach under the jacket and tug it down, then my sleeve feels twisted, so I tug it here and there.

"So how've you been?" Softie asks. I read, "what the hell was that phone call about?" into her tone.

"Good. You?"

Eli starts talking to Jane, pointing out someone at the bar.

"Good." She leans into me and whispers, "Why did you call?"

"Bad moment—that's all. I'm fine now. Thanks." I'm still fumbling with my shirt. "Sorry I bothered you."

"You worried me. That's all. You were crying."

"I know, I—"

"Hey, Ally," saved by Eli. "Isn't that the guy who donated like two million to Theatre Cairn? O'Flannagan? O'Falley?"

"O'Malley," I say, "Yeah. I think it is."

"Ladies—I have some work to do." Eli straightens his collar and walks away—leaving me there alone with Jane and Softie.

I watch his hands move up and down as he talks to Mr. O'Malley, and his eyes are bright and entertaining. He's working his magic. He wants to bring an Irish band to America for a special engagement with the orchestra and needs to raise some money to do it.

"Ally," Jane grabs my hand and holds it—to my discomfort. "I know what happened between you and Softie and it's really no prob—you know?"

I don't know. I don't understand any of this. Any of what I got myself into.

"We're polyamorous."

Poly…?

"And I haven't told Eli anything. That's really between you two."

She caresses my hand and I feel a tingle go up my spine.

"Okay?" She squeezes my hand.

"Yeah. Okay." I suddenly feel sick. "Excuse me." I go to the bathroom and I can feel their eyes following me as I walk, but I won't look back. I open the bathroom door. There's an empty stall in the middle. I sit down. And cry.

I'm too loud, but I can't hide it. The flushing in the next stall drowns me out for a minute.

My mouth fills with saliva. I feel as if I'm going to throw up. I stand and hang over the toilet, my tears dropping into the water. I spit. Nothing else comes out. I swallow, then sit down again.

I don't know how long I sit there crying—maybe ten minutes, maybe twenty. Women come and go and I start to worry that if I stay here too long, Softie or Jane will come to find me.

I use toilet paper to wipe my eyes and blow my nose. I wait for the bathroom to empty, hoping no one new comes in, then I come out of the stall and look at myself in the mirror.

Oh god. My eyes are puffy. My nose is red.

I splash some cold water on my face before I realize there are no towels in the bathroom—only hand dryers. Okay.

What am I going to do? Squat down under a hand dryer? So that's what I do. How ridiculous. Hot air blows on my face and I manage to give myself a pitiful little laugh.

Now that's a picture.

I don't know if I just heard Jude's voice or my mother's voice in my head—but it's good to feel like I can share this face-drying moment with someone.

I look in the mirror and my eyes are still a little puffy. I take a deep breath and go back into the bar. It's dark, but I see Eli, still talking to Mr. O'Malley. They're laughing.

I tug on Eli's jacket sleeve, "Eli."

He treats me like a mosquito at first, kind of privately shooing me away.

"Eli," I'm insistent. "I'm not feeling well—I'm going home."

"What?" He turns back to Mr. O'Malley, "Excuse me a minute, Daniel." He pulls me away. "Baby, this is important here."

"I know, I'm sorry," my voice quivers. I swallow to try to control it. "I'm leaving. I don't feel well."

"Okay. Okay. I'll see you at home." He's too engaged with Mr. O'Malley to argue like he wants to.

Now I look toward the table where Softie and Jane sit. Damn that I didn't bring my jacket with me to the bathroom.

"Hey guys, I'm going home. I don't feel well."

"What?" Softie says pleadingly and holds my hand. "Are you sure?"

I pull my hand away and look in Eli's direction. What's with these two? "Yeah, I just don't feel well. I'm tired. I've been driving all day."

"Is it because of what I said?" Jane sounds apologetic.

"No, no," I lie, "I just really don't feel well." I almost put my hand on my stomach, but then choose my forehead. "I have a bad headache and I'm really tired, you know?"

"Are you sure?" Softie asks again.

"Yeah, really, I'll talk to you guys some other time." A lie. I have no intention of doing this to myself again.

"Well, it was good to finally meet you." Jane stands up and throws her arms out to hug me.

Oh, god, okay, I'll hug you.

"Bye, Ally," Softie gives me another kiss on the cheek and I again blush red.

I try not to pause long enough to feel anything about this. I just grab my jacket and go.

Outside, the cold air slaps me and it actually feels good. Goose bumps rise on my skin. For a moment, I wonder if this is all a sign. Jude's death, my good time with Mom, my seemingly conservative values. Maybe I should move back to Harmony.

"One more day until we go to New Orleans," Eli whispers to me the next morning. He wakes up before I do. I don't know how he does it. He must've gotten home around three a.m.

I clear my throat and shield my eyes against a sliver of sun peeking through the blinds.

"Are you excited, baby?"

"Yeah. Yeah, of course." And actually I am; I love New Orleans. I feel at home there.

"Are you feeling better?" He pats me on the hip.

"Yeah, I guess." I have a killer headache.

"What happened last night?"

"I felt nauseous. Must've been something I ate."

"I think I convinced Daniel O'Malley to give us some money for the Irish Green Band." He throws the covers off himself and climbs out of bed.

"Good," but all I can think is that I can't believe he doesn't show any more concern than that for my well-being. "I think I'll go to the coffee shop and write this morning."

"What?" comes his voice from the bathroom.

"I think I'll go to the coffee shop to write." I yell louder.

"Oh yeah, okay. Will you check us in for the flight after one?"

Mozart jumps on the bed with me. I start to pet her.

"Honey?"

"Yeah."

"Are you listening to me?" Eli appears at the bathroom door.

"Yeah, I'll check us in."

"You should've stayed last night. We had a lot of fun."

I sit up in bed as the faucet comes on. My eyes are still heavy. My whole body feels like it's filled with sand. But now my brain is clicking off scenarios and replaying scenes faster than a Wall Street ticker.

What would've happened had I stayed? Why do Softie and Jane have such a weird relationship? How did I end up in bed with Softie? How would Eli react if he found out? Why am I so judgemental? Why does part of me wish I had slept with Jane instead of Softie?

Eli moves from the bathroom to the kitchen. "Ready to have breakfast?" he pauses at the door.

I'm petting Mozart as she purrs out a symphony. I shiver. "I'll be there in a minute," I say.

Eli goes to the kitchen as I climb out of bed and throw on some warmer clothes. The wood floor is cold beneath my feet so I throw on some warm socks too. I open the blinds to let cold sunshine fill the room.

I can hear cupboards opening and closing, but I peek out into the hallway anyway to make sure Eli isn't close. I open my underwear drawer and pull out the drawing. I open it and look again at the progression of a sandhill crane moving into flight.

"Ally!" Eli calls from the kitchen.

"Yeah!" I call back as if I'm heading toward the kitchen, but I suddenly feel inspired.

I throw on some jeans, brush my teeth, wash up a bit, fix the parts of my hair that stick up, grab my notebook, pen, and Jude's drawing, and rush past Eli in the kitchen.

"I'm going to the coffee shop," I say it matter-of-factly, as if I do it everyday. As if I'm a real writer.

"You're not having breakfast first?" His spoon pauses in midair, milk dripping from it.

"No. I'll grab a banana or a scone or something there."

That's it. I'm out the door. No time for good-byes.

The coffee shop is filled with that slightly burnt roasting smell of coffee. I wrap cold fingers around the green coffee mug and hold the pen in my other hand. It's easy to launch into a story today.

> Jude walked to the river. Five miles to the river, along the highway, tears rolling down her cheeks. She didn't like to cry. She didn't like the way it made her head hurt.

Out of Harmony

But she walked. And cried. The sun was starting to warm the cement so she stripped off her jacket.

Once, she even stopped to sit down at the side of the highway. She embraced her knees and raised the toe of her boots to let her calves stretch. Trucks whizzed past her, throwing debris around her head.

The cappuccino machine buzzes behind the counter. A man in a beret sifts through some coins. I look out the window to Loring Park and wonder where Jude really drew those cranes. I unfold the tattered page. Then I see the dirty thumbprint on the back of the paper. It's got to be Jude's. Doesn't it? I put my thumb over the print. It's about the same size.

As I trace my fingertip along the intricate, circular lines of that thumbprint, I feel a kind of buzzing in my hands. I quickly turn the page over to the drawings. It's a rough sketch, but it's easy to see the crane take flight.

I pick up my pen again.

Jude sits alone at a table for four in the Harmony library. She took a discarded piece of paper from the copy machine and found a book about the Sandhill Cranes. She has the thick book open to a photographic layout in the center.

She sketches the first crane. Its legs straight, its wings at rest. Her pencil, from the library desk, scratches across the page. She doesn't like the wing; she erases it and tries again.

She rounds the wing more this time, and scratches in some feathers. She draws out the droopy feathers at the rear. That's pretty good, she thinks as she looks back and forth between the book and her sketch.

She starts on the second figure, its legs slightly bent, ready to take flight. Wings out, head forward. Now she's figured out the wings, the feet, the long legs, regal beak. It takes her only a minute, maybe two, to draw this bird, perched for flight.

Her eyes stray to the book from time to time, but it is the paper in front of her that she's focused on. It is the paper that seems to mean everything in this moment.

The third bird lifts off the ground, its body transformed into a long, thin, perfectly balanced rocket; wings raised, legs dropped below its body at a 90-degree angle. She draws each figure rapidly, intently. The wings on each bird in various stages of flight—one bird, wings down, next bird, wings

> perfectly aligned with the body, third bird, wings up—it flies off the page until only it's feet are showing, right at the edge of the page.

I look out the window toward the park. Then back to Jude's drawing. I thought the thumbprint was made by dirt first, but now I think it's a pencil print.

> Jude drops her pencil on the table, closes the book, and picks up the page. She stares at the cranes.

When I write about Jude, and think about that time with Jude, I feel alive again. I feel like the Ally I was supposed to be. But Jude was so miserable. I know she was. I look back at the page.

> Jude crinkles the page into a tight ball and throws it toward the reference files. "Fuck this," she says under her breath.

But, at the end of things with her, I was miserable too.

> The librarian at the reference desk glares at her. Jude pushes her chair away from the table, letting it make a loud, rough noise on the linoleum floor. She leaves the book sitting there and sticks the pencil in the jacket of her coat.
>
> She feels the librarian's eyes following her, but she doesn't care. On her way out, she grabs a clean sheet of paper out of the copy machine and steps out into the fresh air of late spring.

Into the fresh air of late spring?

That's stupid, I think. Into the fresh air of late spring. Jesus, what drivel.

"Fuck this," I say to myself. I slam my journal shut to the surprise of a woman sitting at a neighboring table. "Sorry," I say to her.

She doesn't say anything back; she just returns to her studies. College student.

I feel stuck. I feel like I can't write the truth about Jude. Partly because I don't know it—partly because I want it to be different.

I want me to be different.

Part Three:

N.O.

Chapter Nineteen

Eli paces as he waits for boarding the plane. He always paces.

I sit reading a magazine. Well, not really reading, more like flipping pages.

A woman sits next to me with a toddler on her lap. The boy is very fidgety—he throws his bottle on the floor, she picks it up, he throws it again, she picks it up, he grabs for a box of animal crackers and tears the box top off—then throws it on the floor. She doesn't pick it up. He throws the bottle on the floor.

Eli is still pacing, oblivious to the woman, or to me for that matter. He starts to talk to some businessman standing next to a pole.

The boy throws his hand on my arm and makes a "baa!" sound. I jump and he giggles. His hand has left a sticky imprint on my arm.

"Sorry," the woman says, but she's laughing. "You're a silly boy."

Brat. *Encourage him why don't you?*

Eli is still talking to the businessman.

"Eli!" I kind of whisper/shout to him.

He doesn't hear.

"Eli!" I'm saddled with both of our carry-on's, so I'm pretty much stuck.

"Husbands," the woman says. "Mine's getting coffee for himself." The boy drops the bottle; the mother picks it up.

Don't get me wrong—I like kids, I really do. I just seem to be more aware than ever of how much energy they take.

"Eli!" A little more force this time, same result.

The lady smiles at me. "He seems to have selective hearing."

"Yeah," I try not to sound too snotty. I just don't want to engage in a comparison of how men treat us. "Eli!" I almost shout it this time, and Eli's face turns deep red as some eyes turn toward him.

He walks over to me and the carry-ons. "Yeah?"

The woman next to me laughs in that womanly all-knowing way as she again picks up the bottle from the floor.

"I've got to go to the bathroom." Now I sound annoyed, but I can't help myself. "Will you watch the bags?"

"What's wrong?!?"

Now he sounds mad? Are you kidding me?

"Nothing," I try to whisper, but the woman with the kid is still listening. "I was trying to get your attention for awhile, that's all."

"I didn't hear you," he gives me attitude right back.

I sigh and leave him with the bags, the kid, and the woman.

When I come back, Eli has an audience of two. He's totally entertaining the kid with the bottle. The woman has, in fact, handed her baby over to Eli.

The boy holds his bottle in his mouth with one hand while the other hand tries to take the coin from Eli's hand. Before the boy can grab it, the coin has disappeared. The woman squeals, "Where did it go? Where did it go?"

None of the three notice me as I stand next to the trio. The woman and boy are engaged with Eli and he's engaged with them.

Now the coin seemingly comes from the bottom of the kid's bottle and the little boy's eyes become giant saucers of wonder. Eli is laughing with the mom as he launches into another trick.

I feel my stomach clench as I watch Eli with the boy. He would be a good father. I feel like I'm going to cry—my throat tightens, my eyes start to water. I step away from the scene to go back to the bathroom before Eli sees, but he's so engaged with the little boy, he didn't even know I was standing there.

I glance back to the gate and see Eli, the woman, and the boy playing together.

And I feel empty. I feel like a failure.

* * * * * * * * *

Our flight lands in New Orleans at 10:28 p.m. Every five years we try to get here, but this time, there seems to be more at stake. I've decided to make the most of this trip.

Eli grabs my hand as we sit in the cab. "It's like a second honeymoon, baby," he whispers in my ear. Not that we ever had a first honeymoon. But I have to change my attitude. If Eli is going to treat this as a way to mend our relationship, so am I. I guess that means I should be honest about not wanting to have a baby. That's it. When we get to the hotel, I'm going to tell him.

I look out the window as we drive down Canal Street. It looks a little battered after Katrina, but it's coming back. New palm trees have been planted and are now anchored by steel wires. The trollies run up and down the street. Some businesses are open, some are rebuilding. Construction is everywhere.

New Orleans is humming—a little quieter than before, but it's still breathing.

New Orleans will be good for both of us. I can tell. Eli will get to sit in on a set and play some jazz, even the new tune he's been working on. And I'll write. I'm going to walk all the paths I imagined Elizabeth Perrier walking. I'll go back to the first stories I've ever created. Back to basics. Maybe I'll get back some of my spirit through the process.

Eli tips the bellman and I immediately set up the luggage rack so I can begin unpacking.

"Hey, hey, hey," he turns me around to face him and kisses my neck. "That can wait." His hand threads through my hair.

"But," I try to come up with some excuse, but there is none. Except that I don't feel like making love. That I never feel like making love. Eli's lips fall on mine to stop any more words, any more excuses from escaping. He leads me to the bed and plops me down.

His tongue licks the back of my teeth and I try not to think about how my hand is uncomfortably trapped between his chest and mine. No, I want to fall into this. I want to fall back into the way things used to be.

"Hey," he pulls his lips from mine quickly. "Let me get a picture of you." He scurries off the bed like a little boy and digs into his suitcase.

"Eli…" I whine. He always wants to take a picture of me on our first day in New Orleans. He's done it since 1989, the first year we came here.

"No, no, this is tradition," he says as he plays with the back of the digital camera. This is his tradition, not mine.

I feel awkward, lying here on the bed. I start to get up.

"Come on, Ally," Eli jumps on the bed and aims the camera down at me. "Give me a sexy pose this year."

"Eli!" I throw my hands up over my face. "No!"

He crouches down and tries to pry my hands away. "Come on, Ally," his voice is soft. "It's just for our scrapbook. No one else will see it."

I let down my guard and look at his hopeful face, but the inside of me wants to run, out the door, down the hall, into the elevator, through the lobby, out into the street, and away, away, away. "Eli, no, please?" I'm almost crying. *Geez. Control yourself Ally.*

Eli has a disappointed, sad look on his face. "Okay, okay," he releases his grip on my wrist and sits on the bed, looking down at the camera, thinking.

"How about one of the two of us together?" It's always been me in these photos. Me alone. Smiling, happy, Ally. Looking at the love of her life. The one who has it all.

I don't react fast enough, enthusiastically enough for him.

"Maybe we should just forget it," he turns off the camera and it makes a sad, whirring, good-bye kind of sound.

"No, Eli, please," now I'm begging. I put my lips to his ear and entwine my hand into his armpit. "Please, let's take one of the both of us."

"Nah. It's silly, this whole picture-taking thing." He stands and puts the camera into its case.

"Okay," *time to compromise*, I think. "How about one of me over here by the window?"

"Ally, it's okay." Eli's voice is a little perturbed. "Maybe we should order some dinner."

He's digital camera free now. Unencumbered by that discomfort.

"Eli…" I go over to him with a pouty look on my face. Am I one of those women now? I lick his ear and whisper my "I'm sorry."

"Really?" he whispers back and leans his head into my kisses.

"Yeah."

"How sorry are you?"

I lick his earlobe again. "Really, really sorry." I pull him toward the bed and fall on top of him. I kiss his neck; he smells a little bit like man-sweat. I try to ignore it.

That's when he says it. He says it like it's something sexy to say. "Let's make a baby."

I ignore it. I'm not even sure I heard right. But then he repeats it. "Let's make a baby."

I want to say "no," but I don't say anything. I plant my lips on his to stop him from saying it.

But he breaks away, "Let's make a baby." He drops tiny kisses on my forehead and on the bridge of my nose. He rolls us so I'm beneath him. "Let's make a baby."

All I can think about now is whether or not I remembered to pack my birth control pills...

He moves on top of me.

I did pack birth control. I did.

"Let's make…"

…Because I don't want this.

"Let's…"

I don't.

The next morning we begin our routine. We're out the door by nine a.m. and it feels good to be moving.

We go to Royal Blend Coffee Shop and sit in the courtyard. It's mid-November and there's a chill in the air this morning, but we just tug our jackets up around our necks and sip our coffee.

I still haven't told Eli that I don't want to have a baby, but I want to enjoy my first day in New Orleans. I want to put that aside, just for today.

Eli works on music. He can play it in his head. Every now and then, he stops and plucks out notes on the metal table; the table shakes on the uneven ground and I quickly pick up my coffee to prevent it from spilling. He finishes plucking, then looks at me apologetically. "Sorry," he says and his eyes have this little-boy glint in them that always wipes away any agitation I feel.

I smile and return to the nearly empty pages of the journal. I don't want to write about Jude while Eli sits here next to me, so I've decided to write about Elizabeth. Just Elizabeth—in New Orleans, before she meets Walden Bouchard. Although, right now, my writings seem to belong to some cheesy romance novel than to a piece of real literature.

My attention is diverted by a guy with a bicycle who comes into the courtyard. I watch him lift his bike over his shoulder and take it upstairs to the balcony. He goes into some room there and I wonder if those are apartments or businesses, or some storage space for the coffee shop.

Eli pounds on the table as if he were playing a piano. In that moment, I feel like we belong together. Two people living the artist's life. Him with music, me with writing.

I look back to the balcony and try to picture Elizabeth standing there, looking over this courtyard. Someone must've held residence here long before it became a coffee shop.

Perhaps it was in this very courtyard that Elizabeth met Walden Bouchard. Perhaps this is where he got down on his knee and proposed to her.

Perhaps this is where Elizabeth forgot her relationship with Ms. Jacquelin Mantalban and began the life her father always wanted for her. Perhaps this is where Elizabeth learned to live an acceptable life.

"Let's go to Preservation Hall tonight." Eli has his intense musician face on—eyes slightly dazed, hopeful and excited.

"Got something new?" I ask.

He folds the sheet music into a little rectangle as if I'm somehow going to steal his idea (I can't even read sheet music), and stuffs it in his zippered coat pocket.

"I think so," his voice sounds excited, anxious. His knee rapidly bounces up and down.

"Yeah, okay," I say. How can I deny him the chance to sit in with the guys at Preservation Hall? Even though Eli conducts the Minneapolis Orchestra, jazz is his great musical passion.

"Ready?" he says.

"Can I finish my coffee?" I try not to sound annoyed.

"Oh yeah. Sorry." His voice is soft and I know his mind is on the music.

I return to the page in front of me, hoping Eli is still lost in music so that he won't talk to me. I look at the words, over and over, but I can't concentrate with Eli's jitteriness. I want his attention to go back to his music; I want him to stop looking around, to stop bouncing his leg. I want my attention to be on my writing. I want us to go back to that happy moment we shared just minutes ago. That moment where we were lost in our own worlds. Lost in our separate lives.

This afternoon, Eli is hanging out with his musician buddy, Dave. Musicians hanging out with musicians—an instant club with their own language. Eli met Dave years ago in college. Dave is a bit more gritty than Eli, a little more suitable for the musician's life here in New Orleans. He also has a wife and two kids; and Eli won't let me forget that.

But I have this afternoon to myself and now I am on the bank of the Mississippi, sitting atop the levee, drinking a café au laite from Café du Monde. Watching the seagulls and pigeons. The seagulls swoop down over my head to pick up crumbs from Café du Monde. Their wings thump on the air. I suddenly have an image of Jude, leaning back on her hands, watching Sandhill Cranes fly overhead.

I turn to the back of my journal, as if this is some secret place where Eli wouldn't look. He'd look at the innocent, cheesy Elizabeth Perrier writings. Never would he wander to the back of my journal where Jude lurks.

> Jude arched her back to look up at the Sandhill Cranes. Their long legs trailed behind them as their giant wings stretched out across the blue Nebraska sky. It was Jude's way of saying good-bye to Nebraska. Her way of saying good-bye to Alison Bouchard.

I look out at the Mississippi, how it curves around the bend to the left, and how it disappears from sight to the right. There are one, two, three, four, five ships that I can see, and two barges. I look back down on the page. I cross out the last line I wrote with three strong stokes of my pen.

> Jude lived in a box car the next three days. Three days while it moved south through Kansas, Missouri, Arkansas, and finally Louisiana. She packed light, but well. She had a few cans of tuna, some warm cans of soda, and a few candy bars to keep her going.
>
> The train followed the Mississippi. During the hot days, Jude would open up the boxcar door and hang her feet out, watching the river get broader and more dramatic as they travelled south. When the train stopped once, in Hannibal, she jumped out and found some water at a pump along the river. She looked out at the island where Huckleberry Finn hid out and she felt satisfied about the turn her life had taken.
>
> There were no more bad dreams about her father finding her. There were no more fears that Alison Bullshit would leave her behind.
>
> She peeled a candy bar wrapper. It was here, in Hannibal, that she learned how to stop stealing. She simply sat down on the sidewalk and waited. When she saw a couple of motherly women walk past, she said, "Excuse me, do you have a dime, or even a nickel? I'm hungry." That's all. When they saw her, dirty and alone, they forked over enough change from the bottom of their purses for Jude to buy a little bit of the shaved

ham that comes in an air-tight package for fifty-nine cents and a candy bar.

As she took the first bite of the candy, the train whistle sounded. Jude quickly put the bar back into its wrapper, grabbed her tattered duffle bag, and hopped into the train car.

I look back at the river and stretch my hand. "This sucks," I say to myself, frustrated at the disjointed crap I keep writing. Why can't I get one story written? Just one story from beginning to end?

A shadow crosses over my notebook, blocking out the sun. It disappears, then crosses again. I look up and see a man staring at me with a big grin on his face. He paces back and forth while he's looking at me. His blond hair is kind of wild looking, but his beard is trim, his clothes are clean.

I start to feel uneasy, so I close my notebook and put it away with my pen. I glance back at him and he's still grinning. He has a bit of a wild look in his eyes. He's not exactly homeless—he's too well-kept for that. He looks clean—from his hair to his clothes—but his whole being is in a state of disarray. His clothes are baggy and bulky. He takes another step closer as he mumbles something.

"Excuse me?" I ask him defensively. Stupidly. What was I thinking?

"Miss Hawkson won't let you go out and play?" he says, giving me a boyish grin.

I stand up and pull my backpack over my shoulder. "That's right," I say, "Gotta go."

"That's right," he says with a giggle and I can't decide whether he's innocent or dangerous. I walk away from him quickly, back toward Jackson Square.

He yells after me, "Who you gonna be?" Now he sounds innocent, like he wants to play a game of make-believe.

I ignore him and he yells it one more time as I race down the steps, "Hey! Who you gonna be?"

I try to find some people, a crowd, as I look over my shoulder for any signs that he's following me. I manage to get across the street. Standing among the artists and palm-readers, I look back at him. He stands at the top of the stairs with the cannon behind him and he's still looking at me. His eyes are sad, like Jude's. I brush off his stare and keep walking.

I walk into Jackson Square, glancing back at him one more time. He's still there, watching me. Who you gonna be, Ally? I hear Jude's voice this time. I feel like I want to cry.

Tourists are taking pictures of the Cathedral and the statue of Andrew Jackson. I wait for the photo to be taken before crossing in front of them. I look behind me and the man is gone.

Heat rises from the body-to-body contact inside Preservation Hall. There must be more than a hundred people crammed into the small club. Some sit in a few chairs down front, some sit on the floor, others stand in the back (usually the first-timers)—ready for a quick escape. But it's hours before they will leave. They never expected to experience jazz quite like this.

There are seven performers onstage tonight and they've just called Eli up to sit in with them. He takes a seat at the piano. His home away from home. I sit up straighter and look around to see people's expectant faces. They know he's a professional. I smile and look back to Eli. My Eli.

He runs his fingers across the keyboard, as if he's acclimating himself to new territory. "Every keyboard plays different," he told me once, "they all have their own lives."

His fingers push down on the keys, delicate, strong. He begins to massage the keyboard, his pinky plays with the high notes. The bass player, Eli's buddy Dave, joins in, thumping his fingers on the strings. The drummer begins a ching-cha-cha-ching kind of rhythm. One sax joins in, then another, and another. I see toes tapping down along the first row of chairs. People are crammed into this tiny room as if history were unfolding right in front of them. People peer in the dingy windows, trying to see the show for free. But they can only truly experience this if they come in, pay the price.

The fans whirring above our heads do nothing to cool off the room. Sweat drips off Eli's forehead onto the keys. In the old days, Eli would have sought me out in the crowd. He would have managed to take his eyes away from the music for one moment to gaze at me, sitting off to the side in the front row. He always found me smiling broadly at him, unbelieving this was my life. Listening to my boyfriend, an accomplished musician, playing music in the home of my fantasy life.

The music swells, the crowd is moving, nearly dancing to the rhythm. Dave thumps thumps on his bass, Eli trills out a melody, the sax lifts the tune up and lets it fly over the heads of the crowd, spilling it out into the streets over innocent, drunken passersby. I feel suspended by the sound. Held up, held present, held by all the history played here.

The piano trills and I drum my fingers on my thigh—just like Jude used to do. But no, I'm not thinking of Jude now. I'm here. With Eli.

He bites his bottom lip as his head bobs, bobs, bobs. The music swirls and dances around us, envelops us, makes us part of it. A sax player stands and Eli stops. The notes spill out of the instruments and are laid at the feet and hands and hearts of the audience. Gift accepted. Loud applause. A camera flash goes off outside the window. Eli digs into the keyboard again. A trill. A tinkle. A tease. The drum solos. Beating. Swishing. Rolling. Everyone joins in again. Applause. "The bass!" the music almost seems to say. And the thrumming, thumping sound reverberates in my chest. I want to close my eyes and let it live there for awhile. The saxes rise up around the bass again and the piano joins in. I look at Eli. Happy. When was the last time I saw him this happy? He takes off on his solo. Eyes bright. Fingers alive. Twirling, twirling, twirling on the keys. Applause. The sound rises again, louder, higher, faster. My heart quickens. A few people whoop from the back. No one can help but want to be part of the music. Everyone's moving now, in their own way. Tapping, thumping, bobbing, moving.

And then the song slows, trickles off into the slow afterglow of an orgasm. Suspended momentarily in the air and then dropped, back down into the piano, into the bass, into the drum, into the sax, the sax, the sax. And we are all present again, clapping our hands together in a feverish passion for the music. The music Eli wrote. It brings us down to earth again.

Eli stands, bows, and holds his hand out to the other guys in the band, letting the audience show their appreciation for each one. Then he puts his hands together, as if in prayer, and bows to the piano player who gave up his spot for this one song.

Eli jumps off the stage and lands next to me, the sweat glistening on his brow. I lean into him and plant a kiss on his hot, moist face. "I love you, baby." I say it without thinking. I haven't said it in a long time and I feel shocked in that moment—as if I've said something I shouldn't have said. As if I hadn't thought it through.

"I love you too, baby," he says and smiles at me. "Maybe we should go back to the hotel?"

I hold his hand before it caresses the side of my breast. "It's early," I say quickly. "Dave would be so disappointed if we left."

Eli looks back toward the stage and smiles. "Yeah, he's good, isn't he?" And I see Eli's mind wander away from sex and back to the music. I see it in the way his eyes glaze over again.

And I know I've done it again. I've managed to get exactly what I want from our relationship. From our friendship.

* * * * * * * * *

We get back to the hotel around three a.m. Too late to make love. Too tired—both of us. "We're not getting any younger, are we Ally?" Eli's voice cracks from fatigue. "Remember when we used to stay out 'til the sun came up?"

I flush the toilet. "Yeah. Those days are gone."

He squeezes toothpaste out onto his travel toothbrush. "See, that's why we need to start thinking about kids. What're we gonna do—adopt when we're sixty?" This isn't rhetorical. I can tell by the tone of his voice.

Do I want to start this conversation at three a.m.? Not really. I squeeze past him to wash my hands, then leave him staring at me with a dollop of toothpaste perfectly poised on his upraised toothbrush, still waiting for an answer.

I drop back onto the bed. "God, I am exhausted," I say to break the silence, but Eli can't hear me. Either that or he's ignoring me now.

The water turns off with a squeak. There's a silent pause, then the sound of urine hitting water. I open my eyes. I suddenly realize that I hate the force with which men's pee lands in the toilet. It really annoys me and I actually gag. I wish he'd stop sooner than he does.

I try to block out the sound by looking at a photo next to me on the wall. It's a close-up of one of the iron rails in the French Quarter. Its intricate pattern winds around and around.

I close my eyes as the water runs in the bathroom and I try to imagine Elizabeth Perrier glancing out over that rail.

Where was it that I had Elizabeth living? At the end of Royal? Or did I make that up later, after I first visited New Orleans? Well, no matter—I place her at the end of Royal Street. Among the balconies with planters hanging down, cascading above the sidewalks. I picture her walking there way back after Spanish rule—after the French Quarter was rebuilt into what it is today. After the Good Friday fire that burned down all the French architecture. That's where I place Elizabeth and it somehow comforts me.

Eli shuts off the light in the bathroom and I quickly turn on my side as if I'm fast asleep. He rustles around in the room, then settles in. No good nights. No "aren't you going to take your clothes off?" He doesn't even seem to mind that I'm lying on top of the covers. He just manipulates his way under his side of the king bed then shuts off the light.

I look out into darkness. I haven't even taken my shoes off. Eli seems to be sound asleep. "Eli?" I whisper. No answer.

I kick my shoes off and they roll to the floor, then I unzip my pants and wiggle out of them. Eli is snoring. He's such a deep sleeper. I wish I could sleep so easily. I take off my bra. Then I button my shirt back up and lie down.

I should get up and get into my sleeping t-shirt, but I'm too tired.

I shouldn't sleep in this dress shirt, but I don't want to sleep naked.

I should want to sleep naked.

I should want to put my skin next to Eli's.

I somehow drift asleep and before I know it, I'm watching Jude. She's sitting in the incinerator, holding the drawing of the sandhill cranes. She's looking at it, turning it over in her mind, wondering how she could make it better. She wants to give it to me. She wants to say, "Let's go see the Sandhill Cranes, Ally." She hopes she can get me back.

She folds it up, puts it in her pocket, and walks out into the alley. She starts the mile and a half to the store, but then she makes a turn at the edge of downtown. Instead of walking south, she walks east. She walks toward Emma's barn.

Eli's snoring wakes me. I'm shaking. My head is pounding. My ears are humming. I take a deep breath, but my lungs only expand so much before they stop. They won't let me take in as much breath as I want to take in. Another breath. No luck.

Fuck! I'm wide awake. It's fucking three-thirty a.m. and I'm wide awake. My shirt is tight around my arms. What's wrong with me? *Deep breath, Ally. Deep breath.* No way. My lungs are tight. Probably from being in a smoky club.

Part of me wishes Jude would've walked straight to Emma's barn.

But she didn't.

She came to see me. And now my thoughts flood with the memory that I've tried to keep out and I see her, walking into the store that day, her hand in her back pocket, her head down. I ran to the back room. "Beth, tell me when she's gone."

Beth chuckled like it was funny I was screwing over my friend. My best friend.

I sat in the backroom, waiting to hear the all-clear from Beth. We had a code phrase. When all was clear, Beth would get on the store intercom and say "Clean up on aisle four."

So I sat there, feeling shitty about myself, hiding away in the back, sitting on a stack of the paper bag stock when the announcement came, "Clean up on aisle four."

I took a deep breath, then walked out onto the floor and up to the front of the store. Beth was smirking.

But then, the automatic doors opened up and Jude walked right in. Her eyes were on me. Her hand was still in her back pocket.

"Sorry kiddo," Beth put her hand on my shoulder and still had that smirky lilt in her voice.

I swallowed down a big lump in my throat. My hands were shaking. I tried to relax my eyebrows.

"Can I talk to you, Ally?" Jude's voice was soft.

"Yeah, sure," I didn't want to go somewhere more private with her. What was I so fucking afraid of? But we went back to the breakroom. Jude knew where the breakroom was; she'd sat with me on more breaks than my manager would've been comfortable with. On all those cold nights when she hung out in the store trying to keep warm while I worked.

I wanted to say something, I wanted to take control, but I couldn't.

"How've you been?" Jude's eyes looked hopeful.

"Good." Part of me wanted to tell her all the things that had been going on; how I was scared of college, how my dad came home drunk the other night, how I missed her. But I didn't say anything more than "good."

Jude fidgeted. She pushed her hair back behind her left ear, then looked at her feet. She cleared her throat. "Ally?"

I looked her in the eye, then quickly looked away. I didn't say a thing. Why didn't I say something?

She cleared her throat again. "What…? What happened to us?"

I looked around for Beth, but she was nowhere in site. I was hoping she'd come and save me. Geez. Save me. "What do you mean?"

"I thought—" her voice quivered a little and I remember thinking when will she just go away? "I thought we were friends."

"Yeah," I looked at my feet. A piece of cash register tape was stuck to the bottom of my shoe. "We were." We were, I thought, things change, people change, I'm going off to college.

"Did I do something wrong?"

"No."

I glanced at her face. It was soft. It wasn't tense like when she was on edge.

"I should get back to work." That's what I said.

"Yeah." She followed me out to the cash registers. She stared at me for a minute, and then she walked out the doors.

I never saw her again.

And now it's so freaking hot in our hotel room that I want to strip off all my clothes, but I don't think even that would help. Eli is sound asleep, snoring off the few beers and shot of vodka he had.

I can't fucking stand it here anymore. What time is it?

The clock next to the bed glows 3:58.

I want to get out of this bed. I want out of this room. I want out of this body. I want out of this life.

And then I hear Jude's voice, as if she's standing right there next to me. *Who are you gonna be, Ally?*

The voice is so clear I quickly squeeze my eyes shut, just in case some vaporous mist is forming next to the bed. My heart is pounding. *What the fuck is going on?*

Eli turns over. He snores. A muscle starts to twitch in my back. I turn over and Eli stops snoring. I don't want to wake him. The muscle still twitches. Okay, this is silly. There are no ghosts in the room. I open my eyes and peer into darkness. There's no vaporous mist. No disembodied voice.

Eli snores again.

Okay, that's it. I push my body up and realize that my chest feels tight. I can't catch my breath. Oh my god. I put my hand over my heart. It seems normal; there's no pain. *Breathe.* Can't—quite. The breaths I do catch are so loud, I'm afraid I'll wake Eli. *Okay, get up.* Legs on floor, try not to think about bare feet on hotel carpet, and walk—watch toes and shins, feel around in darkness, bathroom light on. Sit on toilet. I'm okay. Just tired. But I'm not going…back to bed. I just need…fresh air. Deep breath Ally. Take a deep breath. I rub my sternum as if that's going to help. Okay.

Who are you gonna be? Jude's voice again. Loud and clear.

My breath shudders. "Leave me alone, Jude."

She doesn't deserve that, but I say it into the cold bathroom air. Just like that. And I'm not going to cry. I'm not going to lose control here.

That's it, a quick shower and I'm out of here. Get moving. That'll help.

Eli is still sleeping when I leave the room at 4:50 a.m. I don't wake him. Part of me wants to run out of the hotel lobby, into the street, and walk. Just walk. I don't know where to, but away. Away from myself.

But I can't. My legs are rubber, my body can't move anymore. I sit down in the hotel lobby at a table in the coffee shop and open my journal. At five a.m., there's only me and a business woman here; she's typing on her laptop. Click, click, clicking away. I bite on the cap of my pen while my coffee cools.

"Tell me a story, Ally." Jude's voice again, whispering in my ear, but this time I have a vision of her, leaning into me, shoulder to shoulder, a flirty smile on her face.

I drop my forehead into my left palm and exhale. It feels good to rest my head. For a minute, I think I could fall asleep right now. Why is that? If I were to lie down in bed, I'd be wide awake.

Tell me a story.

I keep my forehead in my hand and stare down at the blank page.

"Elizabeth Perrier," I write in almost a scribble.

Tell me a story.

I slam the journal shut and the business woman stops clicking on the keyboard. She looks at me as I apologize to her.

I open the journal and print in block letters, "You fucking tell me a story, Jude."

What the fuck does she want from me?

And then it comes. The story I have dreaded to put down on paper. The story I have dreaded to speak. The story Jude told me so long ago.

She stared at the concrete wall of the incinerator as she told me. Her eyes were fixed on a section of wall that was broken and crumbling; the metal rods inside the cement were visible. Jude told me how she shook and trembled and wanted to say the words when her father lay on top of her night after night, pushing himself further and further inside, but the pain she felt silenced the words. The shame she felt held them inside. Instead, she gasped the words in the middle of the night when she was alone and crying. No more.

"No more." I write on the page. And then I keep writing.

> "NO MORE! She screamed in her head on that day she ran away, when she bit down so hard that blood filled her mouth. Her father fell to the floor in pain—writhing and crying as he held himself, and Jude stood over him—numbed and shocked. She wiped the blood from her bottom lip and then swished the mixture of semen and blood and saliva in her mouth. She looked down at her father, who was crying in pain. Feeling only anger, she spat on him. A pink sticky blob landed on his neck.
>
> Jude grabbed a pack of cigarettes from the table; she pulled $52 from his pants, laid neatly across the arm of the couch. She calmly tucked the cigarettes and the money in the pocket of her flannel shirt. "B-bitch," her father cried when he was able to breathe again.
>
> She looked down at him, blood staining his hands as he

held onto his damaged penis. His blue eyes pierced her flesh. Those sparkling, blue eyes she saw when she felt love for him.

I try hard not to edit the story Jude told me, even though it makes me sick. How she ever felt love for the man she called father, I could never understand. But she told me so I keep writing.

Sometimes his eyes were all she could see—like when he called himself the master chef and made a dinner that would make her feel special and cared for. She'd sit and watch him sauté the chicken breast in garlic and oil, then he'd carefully make an alfredo sauce to perfection—a magician in the kitchen, that's what her mother used to call him. Or so he said. Jude knew he was happiest in the kitchen, his eyes sparkling like a child's at Christmas. That was her favorite time to be with him. That's when she felt like her father was like other fathers, when he wore her mother's old apron and cooked for his daughter.

Looking down at him, with those eyes looking up at her, she suddenly felt guilt rise up in her heart. He had taken care of her all these years since her mother died—he had given her shelter, food, clothes, and sometimes—just every so often—he was the father she longed to have. She knew in that moment she had killed all parts of her relationship with her father.

Sweat rolled across the bridge of her father's nose; his face was bright red. She suddenly panicked. She squatted down to him and put her hand on his calf. "Dad?" She wondered if she should call an ambulance or could she, herself, fix this? She let herself feel for him just long enough that she didn't see it coming. The heel of his foot smashed into her nose with blinding force. Her head hit the floor as she fell backwards; she held her hands over the stinging pain. Blood filled her mouth once again.

"Get the fuck out of my house!" her father screamed. She felt another kick on her legs, and another and another. She scooted away from her father and watched as he cried in pain with each kick. He yelled again, "Get the fuck out! You fucking fucking bitch!"

She wouldn't let herself cry—no pain was worth that. She

stood up, rubbed the pain in her face, wiped the blood from her nose, and said the words she had practiced day and night after night after night after night.

"No more!" She yelled it loud and clear, her right hand was curled into a tight fist. Her father only groaned. And then she left. With the clothes on her back, her father's old army jacket, and the $52 she'd taken from him. And she never went back.

I tap my pen on the paper, then drop it on the page. I arch my back over the chair and close my eyes when they meet the high open atrium of the hotel.

This is the story I've always wished I could get out of my head. It's the story I wished I hadn't asked Jude to tell me.

I tried to fix it for Jude. I put my arm around her waist and held her tight. Then I said, "Elizabeth Perrier and Jacqueline Montalban lived in the French Quarter of New Orleans." That made Jude smile, a kind of half-smile that snuck out from the depth of despair. Of course, she always wanted Elizabeth and Jacqueline to end up together.

"It was in the French Quarter, on Royal Street, that Jacqueline opened a dress shop. She and Elizabeth lived above it."

"In an apartment?" Jude asked hopefully.

"Yeah, in an apartment they shared."

And of course, Elizabeth and Jacqueline had to live and work in the French Quarter; it's where they would have been accepted. Living with the outlaws, prostitutes, and thieves. They couldn't have lived with the upper crust in the Garden District like Elizabeth and Walden had.

That's where the story ended because, in that moment, Jude kissed me. She kissed me in a way that thanked me for the gift I had just given her. She kissed me in a way that was enjoyable. She kissed me in a way that scared me down to the core of my being.

I gave Jude hope and then I took it away. That's what I did.

I look back down at my notebook. Maybe the best thing I can do is write about Elizabeth and Jacqueline. Put them back together in New Orleans, just like Jude hoped would happen.

I open up to the page where I weakly wrote Elizabeth's name. A sharp pain runs through my lower teeth. That's when I realize my jaw is clenched.

I grasp that page firmly in my fist and I pull, I rip it out of the notebook and crumple it into a ball. I toss it across the room at the garbage can; it bounces off the edge and rolls across the floor. The businesswoman looks at me in shock and when I look back at her, she returns to her laptop.

The bar back comes from behind the counter and tosses the piece of paper in the trash.

"Sorry," I say to the bar back.

She manages a small smile and says, "Don't worry about it, baby."

I suddenly wish I could talk to Dr. Vonda. I wish I could sort out all of this crap with her. Why did I cancel my last appointment?

It's six a.m. There's only one person awake this early who I can talk to. I pick up my phone and dial. It rings.

"Hello." A rattling cough follows the greeting.

"Hi, Mom."

"Ally? What's wrong?"

I killed my best friend, I slept with a woman, and I want to leave Eli. "Nothing. Does something have to be wrong?"

"You never call me this early. Aren't you in New Orleans?"

"Yeah. I guess I'm not used to the time change." Mom doesn't need to know there isn't a time change between New Orleans and Minneapolis.

"Oh. How are you?"

"Fine. How are you, Mom?"

"Oh, I'm doing okay. I haven't been feeling well this week. I've got a cold or something."

"Really?" It's unlike Mom to complain about not feeling well. "Maybe you should go to the doctor."

"No, I'll be fine. How are things going in New Orleans?"

"Fine." But I don't sound very convincing.

"What's wrong, Ally?"

"Mom…" What do I want to say?

"Yeah?"

"Did you ever feel like leaving Dad?" It's such a stupid question.

"Are you and Eli having problems?"

I start to cry, right there in front of the businesswoman and the bar back at six a.m. in the coffee shop at the hotel.

"Oh sweetie, all married couples have their problems you know." She forgets we're not married.

"I know, but this feels different." I blow my nose into a scratchy napkin.

"Different how?"

"Different like…" like I might be a lesbian different. "…like we don't want the same things anymore."

"Well, honey, you'll just have to work through it somehow."

What does that mean? She wants me to stay with Eli? Just like she stayed with Dad?

"Yeah."

"Well, you and Eli try to have a good time. You're in New Orleans for pity sake."

"Yeah, I will Mom."

We say our good-byes and I click the phone shut.

So that didn't help at all.

I look at the businesswoman and she is still glancing my way, I'm sure she wants to see if I'm still crying. But I'm not. I feel hung-over, but I didn't drink at all last night. There's a heaviness in my head and lungs. I'm just getting older, that's all. I can't stay up until three a.m. anymore without consequences.

"Here you go, sugar," the bar back is beside me pouring me a fresh cup of coffee. When do they ever do that? I must be in bad shape.

"Thanks," I try to smile at her.

"No problem, baby. You just relax." She pats my shoulder before she walks away.

I grab my stuff and move to a high-backed cushy chair that looks out on Canal Street. More importantly, it faces away from the businesswoman and the bar back.

I lean back and let the chair encase me. I hold the coffee mug in my cold hands. I just want to sit with myself for a minute. I just want to be alone for one minute.

I stand on Canal Street and all is quiet. It's eight a.m. on Sunday morning and I know exactly where I'm going. I walk to Decatur Street, past Jackson Brewery. It's a quick walk without all the crowds around. There's the cannon where the guy asked me that question, "Who you gonna be?" I feel so weighted by it.

Just let it go, Ally. Okay, there it is: Café du Monde. A small crowd is there. Mostly people over fifty, who weren't out late last night listening to jazz at Preservation Hall. But Sunday morning at Café du Monde—what could be better? Sitting at the open-air café, eating a plate of beignets. I feel better now—back to normal. I sit on the side furthest from the street, where the morning sun warms my back.

The waitress brings a plate of beignets to my table and sets a mug of hot chocolate next to it. This is what will make me feel better. I know that already. I breathe in. Easier this time. Deeper. I'm going to enjoy this day.

A slight breeze blows powdered sugar off the table and it lands like snow on the black sweater of a woman sitting close by. I panic for a moment. The dust just sits there, spotting her sweater. If I tell her and she wipes it, there will be streaks of white and she'll look like a zebra. Jesus. What do I do? Well, she'll never know and her husband, with a thick southern accent, won't say, "You've got some been-yay dust on yer back honey." By the end of the day, she'll never know where she picked up the white streaks on her black sweater.

Another woman sits close by with her husband and two kids. Her hair is chopped short. She's portly, but solid. And the first thing I think is "lesbian." I've been around so many gays and lesbians over the years, I can even begin to see who is and who isn't. So there she is, with her husband and two kids and I think that she must be miserable.

I wipe a cloud of powdered sugar off my hands and try not to cry at myself. Or laugh. I'm stuck somewhere in between. My whole fucking life is being stuck somewhere in between.

A street musician begins singing a rough rendition of "Only You," his voice broken by the sound of his trumpet. The lesbian with the husband and two kids is focusing on the children, and only the children. She hasn't exchanged one word with the husband since they sat down.

Maybe that is what I need to do—have kids who consume my attention.

Jesus! What am I thinking?!?

I don't want to think. I don't want to go back.

And then I see a homeless girl, standing across the street from the trumpet-playing musician. She can't be more than twenty years old. She's sitting against the French Market building with a banjo case and a dog. It's a big, well-fed dog and I'm glad she has it. Maybe it will keep her out of harm's way. I can see from here that a tattoo runs along the side of her face and creeps down around her neck. It ends somewhere down the back of her shoulder, under her dirty t-shirt.

And then a familiar yearning inside me kicks in. Every time Eli and I came to New Orleans, I would look for Jude. I always did imagine that maybe she ran off to the Big Easy. I thought maybe she would have become a street musician, playing the washboard or just tapping drumsticks on an old tin wash basin. She lived happily somewhere between Bourbon Street and the St. Louis Cemetery in a row house. It would have been a little run-down, but it would have had running water and a refrigerator and a stove. All the things Jude needed. And she would have been safe there. Her nightmares about her father would have disappeared. And she would have stopped playing with fire.

I haven't thought about that in a long time.

My eyes land on the white powder on the woman's black sweater as I trace that memory. My eyes are fixed as I open my notebook and think about what I might want to write.

So many nights Jude and I sat in that incinerator, she on one end of the bed roll, me on the other, facing each other, sitting with legs crossed, or knees pulled up to our chests. Jude would pull out a matchbook that she stole from a liquor store or bar. Whenever Jude got scared—or so full of fear that rage took her over—she got real quiet.

She would lean back against the wall that once burned boxes and egg cartons and she would hold a lit match up in front of her face. The flame would rise above her eyes, then fall again.

I would sit with my arms draped across my knees, resting my chin on my forearms, and I would watch her. I was as entranced by the flame as she was—and I'd watch her raise the sleeve of her jacket above the flame, dangling a tattered edge to the fire. Most times it would curl up and singe. Sometimes it would catch fire and Jude would watch it burn dangerously close to her arm or leg before she'd blow it out.

I always held my breath—waiting to yell at her, to beg her to put out that fire—but I knew the only thing I could do was watch. Watch that flame burn so close to the point of danger.

Funny thing was—I never felt afraid for my own safety. Even though I was furthest from the only exit. Even though Jude was between me and the door. I was never scared for me—only her.

And always, she started to burn her clothes right before she'd start talking about her father.

I blink the burn out of my eyes, look down at the notebook, and begin to write.

> In dreams Jude watched him walk through doors. Always the same dream. Closed doors. Locked doors. Hidden doors. He walked right through them—just like a ghost. She hid behind doors, hoping he couldn't see her, wouldn't find her. But he always did. It was as if he could smell her—like a dog. In these dreams, Jude made herself as small as she could. She would wrap her arms around her legs and she would suddenly become as small as a cat. Just a tiny little being, hiding in the corner—hiding in the shadows.

And then his figure would appear as a mist through the door. He was just glowing at first, just a hazy figure seeping through the thick cement wall. But then he appeared; solid, whole. She squeezed her eyes shut and hoped he couldn't see her, but he always did. He approached her in his solid form.

"Hi baby girl," his voice was always sweet and tender when he wanted this.

And then she would wake up.

"But it seemed real, you know?" she would say as she watched the flame rise on her sleeve.

"Yeah," I said, my eyes focused on her arm. But I didn't really know. How could I?

"I wish I had a locked door here." She looked at the cement walls around her.

"But he won't find you here. No way," I said, not knowing how to reassure.

"He could if he wanted," she blew out the flame. "See, I've been thinking about this. He has to know I came into town. Where else would I go? All he'd have to do was call the school. Find out if I've been to classes. Then he could start asking around. What if he went to the 7-Eleven or the Y? They might tell him they've seen me around."

"But they don't know you live back here," I wanted her to feel safe, even if it wasn't true.

"What if he asked you? What if someone said they saw 'that girl at the grocery store' with me and he found you. What would you say?"

The thought of meeting Jude's molester—rapist—face-to-face sent a chill down my spine. I tried not to let on. "I would tell him I didn't know where you were."

"What if he watched out for me at the grocery store? And he saw me there and he grabbed me? Who would stop him?"

"The police," I said ignorantly.

"Yeah," Jude laughed, but tears started to roll down her face. "Guess again. He would tell them he was my father and I was a runaway. Think they'd ask why I ran away?"

"Well, then—Beth, my friend at the store, and I would stop him."

"You couldn't stop him, Ally. You couldn't."

> "Then you'd stop him. You stopped him before, didn't you?"
>
> Jude leaned back against the wall and pulled her knees to her chest. She rested her chin there and said nothing. I felt ashamed for asking such a horrible question.
>
> Jude's whole body quivered. But she never cried. Instead, she picked up her lighter and held it once again to the frayed edge of her shirt, letting the flame rise dangerously close to her skin.

As a waitress passes by with a heaping plate of beignets, I look up from the page and breathe in a shuddering breath. I can hear a banjo playing faintly from across the street. The trumpeter is taking a break, so I guess the girl thought she had the opportunity to start entertaining. I look over at her and she's now standing with the banjo, her dog lies close by, and her banjo case is open.

I close my notebook, put my pen away, and pack up my backpack. I wipe the fine dust the beignets left on my jeans and leave little white streaks. Not as bad as the dust on the woman's black sweater, anyway.

The banjo is keeping a rapid pace, kind of like a gallop, and like all banjo players, the girl looks calm while the music seems almost frenetic.

I cross Market Street and throw a couple of dollars in the banjo case. Then I glance at the girl in front of me. She looks nothing like Jude. Then I look for signs of burning on her clothes, but there are none and I think that might be a good sign.

She finishes her song just after I throw the money in her case.

"Thank you," I say as I rub her dog's head then turn away from her.

"Hey," the homeless girl calls out to me again. I turn and look at her. "Do you have a cell phone I can use real quick?"

"No. Sorry." Give my cell phone over to her? I don't think so. As I walk away, I feel it tucked safely away in my jacket pocket.

Another banjo jig flies up behind me. I stop and watch the girl from a distance, wishing she was Jude. Wishing Jude would have made it.

The bells of the St. Charles Cathedral sound off one, two, three, four times... They ring above Jackson Square and sound out over the Mississippi.

Shit, what time is it? Eli could be up by now. And I'm filled with dread again. *Take a deep breath, Ally.* But the breath skids in my lungs.

I look back at the girl with the banjo; she's happily tapping her feet to the music she plays. And I wish I were her right now. I wish I could be anyone else right now. I feel a rise of tears in my chest, my throat, my eyes.

"Hey, are you okay?" The banjo girl is standing right next to me, her hand on my shoulder. How did she get here? There's a young guy with a nose ring and a tattoo on the side of his face holding the dog leash and guarding her banjo case.

"What? Oh yeah," I wipe the tears from my face.

"Yeah, you need to release some shit."

"Excuse me?"

"Whatever you're carrying. You need to release it."

What? She's a fortune-teller too? Well, it's possible in New Orleans. Anything to make a living.

"Let it go, baby. It's not worth it. Life's too short." And with that, she leaves me again and goes back to the guy and the dog.

I disappear behind the gates of Jackson Square, behind the high plants and trees, so the girl can't watch me anymore. Funny, I thought I was watching her.

What does she mean I should let go? What do I let go of? Jude? Softie? Eli?

I'm shaking just as much as Jude was shaking that day she set herself on fire. It's got to be 80 degrees out, but I shiver as I walk toward the arches of the Cabildo.

On the plaza, a group of musicians begin to set up. Obviously none of them played at a club last night. These guys are a lot older, with white shoes and white shirts and big bellies.

I pause to stand in the sun to warm up. To stop shivering. I watch the life around me move slowly this Sunday morning. Only the families and people over forty are out walking around. The shops are closed, but mass at St. Louis Cathedral began at ten.

I realize I don't want to go back. I don't want to go back to the hotel. I don't want to have a talk with Eli about not wanting a baby, about cheating on him with Softie. I don't want to start over.

I walk somberly past Le Petite Theatre and down St. Peter Street. I've heard Le Petite is haunted, but I've never been in. I wish I could go in right now and sit in the wings, in the darkness, and listen for creaks and ghostly moans.

Maybe Jude would speak to me there. Maybe she would tell me what to do.

I walk down the cold, shadowed St. Peter Street toward Royal. I walk fast as if I can escape. The smells of trash and stale alcohol begin to tickle my nose as I turn onto the sun-warmed Royal Street. I walk slowly, past Orleans Avenue, St. Ann Street, Dumaine, further away from our hotel.

I end up on the residential end of Royal Street, a few hotels, a few B&Bs, and a lot of the Spanish-style buildings that are now apartments. Many of them are three stories, with the ornate railings and lots of big, luscious plants hanging from the balconies. This is where I always imagined Elizabeth and Jacqueline would have lived. I told Jude they would have sat on their balcony early in the morning sharing coffee, or late at night sharing wine. They would have talked to their neighbors down below, speaking French to some, English to others. And if they lived here, they would have taken evening walks down Royal Street, over to Jackson Square, and back around again. Jacqueline's dress shop would have been on the lower floor of their building and people would have come all the way from the Garden District to purchase a Jacqueline Montalban original.

As I scan the fronts of each building, a sign catches my eye. It hangs from a chain overhead a door, underneath a balcony. There's a phone number.

I take out my cell phone and dial.

As the phone rings I wonder why the hell I'm doing this.

I watch the sign swing in the gentle wind. It creaks as it sways between plants that cascade off the balcony.

"Hello?" A woman answers.

Part of me wants to hang up right then and there. I half-expected to get a machine.

"Hello?" the woman says again.

"Hi, I'm Alison, and…I'm standing outside your place on Royal Street, where the studio is for rent?"

"Yes?"

"I'd like to see it." My heart pounds hard in my chest.

"I can show it to you right now if you'd like."

"Oh, uh—really?"

"Yeah, I'll be right down."

We both hang up and I wonder where she's coming from. I feel an adrenaline rush as I look down Royal Street; we're just a few blocks from my favorite coffee shop. I can see all the way to Canal Street where taller, newer buildings stand at the end of all this exquisite history.

"Hello? Alison?" I expect the woman to come from inside the building where the studio is, but instead, she comes from a Bed and Breakfast across the street.

She has to be a transplant here. There's no southern accent, no "come on baby, let me show you around," but she is very hospitable. I'd say she's in her late fifties. She has short hair and is dressed modernly casual.

She carries a big ring of keys that jingle in her hand as she opens the front door, which makes the place even more romantic. Like she's opening the doors to a castle.

"Have you been looking long?" she asks and I detect a slight New England accent.

"What? Oh, uh, no, just started."

"Where do you live now?"

"Oh, I…" and then what I'm doing hits me. "I live in Minneapolis, but I'm thinking about moving here." I feel something unfamiliar rise in my chest. At first I mistake it for fear, but it's not. I'm actually happy.

"Oh," she sounds disappointed and a bit annoyed, like I'm putting her out. "You don't have a job lined up or anything?"

"No, I—I'm thinking of going to Tulane to study writing." What the hell am I talking about?

"A writer? Well, that's not going to pay the rent, is it?"

Geez. She must be a New Yorker.

"No, it's not, but I'm part of Actor's Equity. I'm a stage manager. So, it's easy to get things lined up." Kind of.

"Actor's Equity? Well, they don't pay rent either do they?"

Geez. What's with this lady?

"Don't worry; I've got lots of money in the bank." And I do. Thanks to Eli. He made me save and save and save. "What's the rent?"

She's opening the door to the apartment with the same jangling of keys. When she tells me how much it rents for, I'm surprised that it's not much more than I pay Eli for utilities and some of the mortgage. It smells kind of musty in here, but it is an old place. Dark halls, hardwood floors. "It's a studio with a view of the courtyard," the woman says.

She opens the door and I see a shallow little apartment with all the charm of the old world. Rich dark wood, tall windows that open out to a small step-out balcony where I could place maybe two plants, if I'm lucky.

"There's a small bathroom and a small kitchen. Nothing to write home about. Where did you say you're from?"

"Minneapolis." I look into the small bathroom with white tile that has little pink roses in every third or fourth tile. White sink, slightly stained, big bathtub (no shower), and toilet right up next to the tub.

"You get a lot of snow there, don't you?"

"Yeah, not as much as we used to." I look in the kitchen. Sink, slightly stained, a few cabinets, stove, small fridge.

It's not the most exciting apartment I've seen. "Do you allow pets?"

"Cats, and dogs under fifteen pounds as long as they're quiet. If they're not quiet, they don't stay. And in a place this size, only one pet."

She seems slightly annoyed with me, but I don't care. "I'll get back to you later today if I decide to take it."

She isn't at all surprised and has that look like, "I won't hold my breath." On the other hand, I'm completely surprised.

We shake hands, exchange the "it was nice to meet you" courtesies, and she goes back into her B&B.

But I stand looking down Royal Street, feeling like I know what's next. For the first time in forever, I feel like I know who I want to be.

It's not Eli's girlfriend or some baby's mother. It's not Alison Boooshaaar or Alison Bullshit or Softie's one-night stand.

And I think I could swing the rent. If I could get some work, it'd be no problem.

I start walking, more sure of myself now. I pay attention now. To "For Rent" signs; and there are a lot of them—hanging from balconies that belong to old, wonderful buildings, or sitting in windows with fancy curtains. One is hanging on an old beautiful door that belongs to a Creole Townhouse.

As I ponder all of the choices, I think about how all of this amazing architecture was built after the fire. One massive catastrophe allowed this city to start over.

And then I remember the story of how Elizabeth Perrier died. It was after that Great Fire that burned down 700 homes in the French Quarter, and Elizabeth, who was by then married to Walden Bouchard, vowed to help in the recovery.

In those days, a woman helping the in the recovery was unheard of—unless they were cooking meals for the men or setting up a makeshift infirmary.

Elizabeth was not that kind of woman. So, without her husband's knowledge, she searched through his wardrobe, finding an appropriately fitting costume. She found a baggy shirt to hide her bosom. She found knickers that slightly hugged her hip so that they would stay up, but had enough room so that they hid her figure.

She admired herself in the mirror, front to back. And for a brief moment, she thought of her beloved friend back in Paris. This was the closest she felt to Jacqueline since she left. She felt her heart pound and an old familiar excitement rush up her thighs.

She tucked her hair under a hat, pinning it tightly to her head so that it almost hurt. The outfit was complete—all except the shoes. But her ten-year-old son had plenty of shoes—and he had to be close to her size.

Yes, a young man—that's what they would think she was. But they could use all the help they could get and wouldn't look at her closely enough to know she was anything other.

Elizabeth walked into the destroyed French Quarter, side by side with the men. And I imagined her heroism; I imagined her thoughts and her death. None of this is accurate. I consulted no history books; I just imagined.

I imagined she stepped over ashes of buildings and broken merchant signs. She sifted through the rubbish to find charred remains of old neighbors and friends. She took these remains, these delicate random body parts that would crumble in her arms, and she'd place them on stretchers to be carried out of the burned quarter.

And then it happened. Elizabeth took one step and felt a sharp pain in her foot. She took another step and the pain increased. She didn't cry, though. She found a plank to sit on, something from a porch perhaps, and she raised her foot with her hands. A nail had lodged into the heel of her foot. And then she walked on, limping, through the French Quarter, picking up the remains of her friends and neighbors. She walked on because she was running. She was running like I was running.

And she had to die.

This was the final story of Elizabeth Perrier and I wrote it the summer Jude went missing, right before I went to college. I had to kill my old life. I had to leave Harmony with none of this in my head. No Elizabeth. No Jacqueline. No Jude.

But even in the imagining of Elizabeth's death, in her bed, sweating and shivering with a fever that no doctor in New Orleans could cure. I couldn't imagine her with anyone other than Jacqueline. Walden Bouchard was not at Elizabeth's side. She didn't want him there.

So Elizabeth died in 1788 after she stepped on a nail in the French Quarter. How unromantic. But that's what I wanted it to be. Unromantic. Real. Stupid. I wanted to purge Elizabeth Perrier and Jacqueline Montalban from my thoughts. I wanted it all to go away.

I wanted to leave Harmony firmly planted in reality so I couldn't hurt one more person like I hurt Jude.

And now look where I am—standing on the corner of Dumaine and Burgundy looking at another "for rent" sign on a beautiful Spanish-style home, just around the corner from Tennessee Williams's final dwelling. I dial the number as I look at the grand balcony that curves around the building where huge plants hang down toward the street. I don't even hesitate. I don't make up reasons. I just dial.

The building sits on the corner and instead of a squared edge where two walls meet, this building is rounded at the street corner. A rotund, balding man in white pants and a white shirt steps out of the doorway that sits right at the corner of the building. The minute he extends his hand to me, I know he's gay.

"Alison?" he shakes my hand. "I'm Jesse. Come on in, honey." His face is round and friendly. He wears a smile that complements his red face.

He leads me up the stairs to the second floor and opens the door with the great old castle keys like the ones at the other place. Unlike the other place, this apartment is bright when the door opens. It has high ceilings with crown molding, yellow walls, white curtains. French doors open onto the balcony where sunlight pours into the big room. There's a small kitchen and bathroom and that's it. A big, bright studio with lots of sunlight.

"I don't have a job here yet, but I can give you first and last month's rent plus a security deposit." The words just come out, smooth and easy, without fear.

"Oh honey, we'd love to have you here," Jesse says as he squeezes my shoulder. He doesn't ask me any questions about where I came from or where I'm going.

Even as I'm signing the one-year lease agreement, effective immediately, I know I should check in with Eli, at least to tell him that I'll be back at the hotel soon. Now my message light is flashing. But I'm not ready yet. I want to feel happy for just a little while longer.

I take the keys from the man, who gives me a hug in return. He walks me to the door and says, "You're gonna fit right in. There's a lot of us in the French Quarter."

A lot of us. I know exactly what he means. I don't argue.

The man closes the door to return to his life, but I want him to come back. I want him to be in that moment with me for awhile longer because if he leaves the moment, then I have to as well. I'm left out here on the street alone.

I walk toward Bourbon Street. I consider for a moment to just disappear, like Jude disappeared. It would be so much easier for me to just walk off into the labyrinth of the French Quarter. To leave my life behind. My heart is pounding from excitement and from fear.

I can't do that, though. I'm not Jude. I can't just leave Eli like that, not after all we've been through, after everything he's done for me. Then it hits me; I can't help but hurt Eli because I can't stay in this relationship without hurting him and I'm going to hurt him by leaving the relationship.

So, there it is.

I look at the face of my cell phone and I dial the numbers.

"Hello?"

"Mom?"

"Ally, twice in one day? Are you sick?" She says it as a joke.

"Mom…I'm leaving Eli." There. I said it. It feels terrifying and exhilarating all at the same time.

"Really?" She's not joking anymore.

"Yeah. It's not right to stay with him anymore. I…I think…" I'm a lesbian stays in my head. One bombshell today is enough. I just know I have to leave. Even while I'm talking with Mom, I walk back toward Royal Street.

"But honey, you've been together so long—you have such a good life."

"I'm moving to New Orleans."

"Oh honey, you're what? They had that horrible hurricane and there's all those people there."

Those people. God! "Mom," I scold.

"Oh honey, I'm not racist. You know what I mean."

That you're racist. "Mom." A stronger scold.

"Well, what about the hurricanes?"

"I found a place in the French Quarter. It's the highest ground in New Orleans." Okay, she's taking all the joy out of it for me. "Anyway, I have to go. I have some things to do before I talk to Eli."

"You haven't talked to Eli yet? Well, honey, you can still change your mind."

"No, Mom. I need to do this. I need to be on my own for awhile."

"But what are you going to do for work? How will you take care of yourself?"

"I'll just do it. That's all." The Jazz Festival must need professional stage managers, right? Well, I'll have to make a call to some of my contacts and see what I can come up with. Maybe I go on tour every now and then or maybe I go back to Williamstown in the summers, or some other East Coast festival. Until then, I have quite a bit of money saved, thanks to Eli.

"Why don't you come home to Harmony. You can stay with me."

Okay, is she serious? She's not laughing. "Thanks, Mom, but I want to try out New Orleans."

"Okay, but you can always come home, you know."

"Yeah, thanks."

She takes a deep breath. "Okay, well, call me if you need to."

Wait. She's the one who wants to get off the phone first? That's new.

"Okay, Mom, I love you." The words come out so easily. For the first time, they come out easily.

"I love you too, honey."

I hang up and get my bearings. I'm back on Royal Street. If I turn right I'll end up at the hotel on Canal Street.

I become more determined now. Now that I've said it out loud.

I walk past a scooter parked on a sidewalk and I decide—I'm going to buy a scooter. I'm going to sell my car and buy a scooter. It's New Orleans; what a perfect place to own one. And Eli would never let me buy a scooter; he says they're too dangerous.

The possibilities make my heart beat stronger.

Chapter Twenty

As I step onto Canal Street, dread fills my chest and the soles of my feet burn. I feel like I've been walking and walking and walking. I'm tired of walking. There's really nowhere else to go except back to the hotel to face Eli.

The elevator is so slow in this hotel. I hear it ding on other floors, the doors opening and closing and it seems like no one will ever get out at the lobby. I feel like I'm in a hurry for the first time today as reality sinks in. What's Eli been doing all day? He probably got up around eleven. Then he maybe went down to the fitness center to ride the bike because at that time he thought, "oh she just went on one of her walks." Then he came back and showered. At a little after one he tried my cell phone and probably left a message. Then he read the paper, turned on the tv, called a few friends, paced toward the window, tried my cell phone again at two. By two-thirty, he was getting pissed off.

The floors light up as the elevator climbs. I'll just tell him I lost track of time. That I was so engaged in everything I forgot to turn my cell phone on. That I thought he'd sleep late because he worked so hard last night. I slide my key into the door. The tv mumbles on the other side. I see Eli's stockinged feet as the door opens and he jumps up off the bed.

"Hi?" I feel terrified. Terrified of being caught.

Eli comes toward me. His face wears determination and I almost want to run out in the hall and scream bloody murder. He shuts the door behind me, his arm stretched out over my shoulder.

"Eli, I—" but before I can say any more, he pushes me into the door and his lips are hard on my lips. His teeth click on mine. His breath is heavy and he practically sucks the air out of my lungs. I want to turn my face, but I can't. His hand is firmly planted on the back of my head.

I want him to stop. I want him to turn and go back to watching tv. I want him to say, "Where the hell have you been?" But I don't want this. Anything but this. I force my arms up between him and me and I begin to push. Push harder against him than I ever have before.

He falls backwards a few steps. His eyes are wide, disbelieving. He gasps in air and releases it deep in his lungs.

He looks down at his hands, those beautiful music-playing hands, turning them over thoughtfully, rubbing his thumb up across his index finger, and then he looks back up at me. "What's going on with us, Ally?" his voice is soft and quavering.

It takes me by surprise. Us? He's still using "us"?

In that moment, I want to turn around and leave this room with its sugary disinfectant smell and its coffee-stained carpet. I want to push him far enough away from me so that I can open the door and escape. But at last, there seems to be nowhere to go.

"It's not what's going on with us, Eli. It's what's going on with me." I somehow think this will make it better.

He releases a little laugh and then I see that his eyes are filled with tears. "I don't know what else to do." He shrugs. "Tell me what to do."

I swallow down an aching lump in my throat.

He stands looking at me, waiting for me to say something more. He's still trying to hold on. He's still trying to make something out of nothing.

I can't hold the tears anymore. I have to do this quick. No excuses.

"Eli, I think I may be a—I may be gay." Wow. I said it. I said it to Eli.

"What?!?" He squints his eyes at me.

I take a deep breath for the first time in forever. "I love you, you're my best friend, and I, I've been trying to figure this out. I don't want to lose you—"

"Ally, what the fuck are you saying? You're gay? And—what? Where…?"

His hands are laid out like Jesus's on those etchings in the sides of churches. The "Come Unto Me" pose. I wish I could just fall into his arms and change this feeling. I wish I could make things better.

"You're gay?" he asks it quickly, almost as if I'm playing a joke on him.

I nod and my eyes seem fixed on a stain on the carpet.

"Just overnight. Just like that."

"No, not overnight. I—" And I finally release everything. I can't control the tears, the sobs, the way the truth comes out from deep in my belly. "I can't pretend anymore."

I don't think Eli knows what to do because I've never heard him swear so much. "What the fuck Ally?" His voice is shaking. "How long have you been hiding this? How many years has our relationship just been a mask for you?"

"It wasn't a mask, Eli. I—I loved you. I love you."

He lets out a little disbelieving laugh, then turns his back as he yells, "Jesus! Christ, I'm the guy who put up with someone who wouldn't marry me! What was your excuse for that?" He turns toward me and walks quickly up into my face, "Oh yeah, 'my parents had such a bad relationship, I don't want to jinx us by getting married,'" his voice in falsetto. So now he's making fun of me too. And I can't stop the tears.

"Eli…" Part of me wants to say "what about all of those nights you just left me at home while you went out? What were you doing?", but I know that I've hurt him enough already.

"And the baby thing? You don't remember us talking about having kids way back when we lived in Brooklyn? That's bullshit, Ally. You never intended to have kids. You just wanted to live this lie as unencumbered as possible. And now—what? I'm freaking forty-two years old and I'm supposed to start over with someone else? Have kids with someone else at fifty? You're so fucking selfish! I don't even know you. Twenty years together and I don't know you."

"I didn't plan for any of this to happen," I almost whisper it as I look down at the stained hotel carpet. I almost whisper it because I feel like anything I say won't help.

And then the door slams. Eli has grabbed his shoes and is out the door.

I wait for it to open. I wait for him to come back to keep talking. Eli, the man who always wants to talk.

But the door doesn't open.

I stand there for a long time. Just looking at the closed door. And now the tears won't come, even though I want them to.

Finally, I pull my suitcase out of the closet and open it on the bed. I go to the dresser and pull out the small stacks of clothes I have there. I go to the closet and pull my clothes off the hangars. I try not to rattle the hangars as if doing so will disturb the thick air around me. I pack methodically. Slowly. Waiting for him to return. I put the underwear and socks in the bottom of the suitcase, trying to leave some room for the dress shoes

I brought. Then I put the shoes in. I fold and refold and refold again my pants, jeans, and shirts. I don't want Eli to come back and find me doing this, but I don't know what else to do. It doesn't seem like Eli will be back anytime soon. That is, until I realize that his wallet is still here.

He can't even get over to Dave's house, or into a club. He can't have a coffee at the coffee shop or a drink at the bar. For the first time, there's nowhere for Eli to go.

I'm sitting on the soft chair in the hotel room watching the door. It's starting to get dark in the room as the sun begins to drop.

Then, a rectangle of light from the hallway spills into the room, slowly, it broadens and Eli's shadow follows it in.

He clears his throat. His voice sounds raw, like he's been crying. "Have you ever…?" He looks scared. It's the first time I've ever seen him scared. But then his voice becomes determined. "Have you ever slept with a woman?"

"When I was a teenager." I say it softly at first, trying to get the words out.

"What?" he asks, but his voice doesn't sound as angry now as it did when he left.

"When I was a teenager." I say it quickly and loudly. "But I thought it was just a phase. Something girls go through."

"Jude." He says her name loudly.

I nod.

"And that's it? Or have you slept with someone since we met?"

I look down at my hands. Not nearly as pretty as Eli's, not as artistic. In fact, I hate my hands right now.

"Ally!"

I don't look up. I don't say anything.

"Jesus!" His voice quivers at the edge of tears. "Ally, what the fuck?"

I start to pull off a hangnail. The pain bites all the way under my fingernail.

He falls onto the edge of the bed, his back to me.

Blood beads on my finger, so I kiss the blood off, but it comes back. Just the tiniest little dot. I watch it rise higher and higher.

"When?" Eli asks.

I wipe the blood off my finger. I take a deep breath. "I'm staying in New Orleans, Eli."

He ignores me and continues with his question. A question I didn't expect. "When did you sleep with this woman, Ally?"

"Eli—"

"No! I want to know." He sounds resigned.

"A few months ago."

He gives a muffled snort, a half snicker, then turns toward me.

"Was it Softie or Jane?"

"Jesus, Eli."

"You guys were acting weird that night. Now I know why. Who was it, Ally?"

"Eli, does it really matter?"

He just does the half snicker/snort again. And then there's silence for awhile while I pick another hangnail off my other hand.

I take a deep breath and the air comes in easily.

He sits on the bed again, looking out the window, over the horizon of the French Quarter. "I want you out by Thanksgiving, Ally." He says it without anger. He says it softly, with sadness.

I sit on the other side of the bed, my back to him. I'm facing the door. "Yeah," I say.

I look at the fire exit route on the door. I follow the red line to the stairway. Maybe the stairway would be faster than the elevator now. But I make myself sit there in the silence, wondering how I'll break the next news item to him. I look at the picture of the French Quarter balcony rail and wonder where that rail is. Once I hear his sniffles subside, I say, "I'm staying in New Orleans."

Silence. I hear him shift around on the bed, then he stands and moves toward the window. I can see his reflection on the glass of the framed picture I'm facing. His back is to me.

"Where will you stay?" His voice is more in control now.

I turn to face his back. One curl is twisted onto his ear. I want to tuck it back behind his ear, just like I have this past twenty years. "I found an apartment on Dumaine," and suddenly I think of Betty, and of Jude. "It's small, but it'll do." I don't tell him I already signed the lease.

He nods his head as he looks out the window. "Good."

I take another deep breath and it feels as if my lungs touch my ribcage, there's so much space inside me now. The tightness is gone.

"I should get ready to go out. Remember, we were supposed to have dinner with Donna and Ted?"

"Oh yeah…" I stand up.

"No, Ally. I'll go alone. You can stay here and pack."

"Oh," I blush and look at my suitcase in the corner by the dresser.

His eyes glance over and then he stands and faces me, a big king-size bed between us. "We don't need to pretend anymore. I'll see if there is another room in the hotel for you."

"Oh, I—"

"I'll pay for it for a few nights. When do you move into the apartment?"

No, I'm not going to hurt his feelings even more by telling him I can move into the apartment tomorrow.

"November 15th." I lie.

"Okay, well," Eli thinks for a minute and then says, "I'll pay for the hotel for you for until then. Okay?"

How do I get out of this? I don't want to take more from him. "That's really generous, Eli, but you don't have to."

"No, really," he says apprehensively, "I'll pay."

I don't know how to get out of my lie so I just say "thanks." I wonder when this will all sink in for him. I wonder when this phase of kindness ends and the ugliness begins.

"What will you do for work?"

"I don't know yet. I—" Jesus, here I go again, no-plan Alison. "I was going to call a few people, see what I could pick up here and there, you know."

"Yeah." I can hear his voice quiver again. "I'll give you some names of people here. Maybe they can help you, okay?" His voice is scratchy.

"Yeah. Thanks."

He looks at me for an awkward moment, then goes into the bathroom and shuts the door. He's never shut the door before. In fact, when we first started dating, he laughed that I would shut the door to the bathroom; he said he'd seen all of me anyway and wondered why I was shy about the bathroom. Even to take a shower.

I know I could leave now and never look back, but it doesn't seem like we're finished. Then I realize I will have to go back to Minneapolis and get the rest of my stuff, sell my car, move my bank accounts, sort out money in my account with Eli. Jesus.

Maybe that's why Eli is being so civil to me, because he knows all of this. He thinks ahead. He's always a step ahead of me, even when I blindside him. He's the grounded one.

I go to the desk in our room, Eli's room, and I start to make a list. Who's going to keep the cat? That's when I start to lose it. I start to cry.

Okay, Eli gets to keep Mozart. It's only fair to the cat, after all. I don't need to drag her all the way here when I don't know what's next. I can get another cat, or dog, when I'm ready.

Still, the tears come even harder and I try to control them, to gulp them down so Eli doesn't realize. But he comes out of the bathroom.

He doesn't say anything, he just looks surprised that I'm crying.

I quickly say, "Eli, you should keep Mozart. She'll be better off with you." And then I really start to cry.

He bends down next to me and grabs my hand. "Hey, hey. You don't have to make that decision now. She's more your cat than mine. You get settled and then let me know, okay?"

"Eli, how can you be so…"

"I don't know. I was thinking, this hasn't been a real relationship in awhile, you know?"

I nod my head as I blow my nose.

"I'm sad, Ally. I'm really sad. And it sucks that you slept with someone—someone I know, even. But—"

My head is pounding. My thoughts are spinning.

"But, I haven't really been happy either."

I blow my nose again. "Why didn't you say anything? Why did you just let me think it was all about me all this time?" God!

"I don't know. I guess I just threw myself into work more and tried to forget about the rest. You know, it's a guy thing."

"So, we'll work this out?"

He looks at me, surprised.

"I mean, we'll work out this breakup. We'll settle things."

He stands up. "Yeah, of course we will." He rubs my back. "Don't worry about it."

"Eli…?"

He waits for me to continue.

"I already signed a lease with that place on Dumaine. I move in tomorrow." It seems to be time to tell the truth. To stop being afraid of the truth.

"Oh," he looks shocked. A little confused. "Okay. Well, then you'll only need a room here tonight?"

"Yeah. I mean, I can pay for it."

"No, no—don't worry about it."

He goes back into the bathroom and I return to the list. Now I realize I need to start another list. I write down: pots and pans, bed, iron, ironing board, table—Jesus. I have a lot to buy.

I take a deep breath. Freedom is fleeting.

I'm still writing lists as Eli comes out of the bathroom, dressed and smelling like my favorite cologne. He picks up the phone and calls the front desk, getting me a room for the night.

He hangs up. "Okay, well, you can go down and pick up your room key. I'm going." His voice quivers as he says it. Then he leans in and kisses me on the lips. He pulls back quickly. He's blushing. "Sorry. Habit." He wipes his mouth as if that will take it away.

"It's okay." I gulp down tears again. I feel empty, even though this is what I wanted.

As he closes the door, I almost want to cry out to him. To beg him not to leave me here alone, but I don't. Because he's letting me go. And I have to let him go too.

Before he left for the airport, Eli called to say good-bye. His voice was still shaky. "I'll miss you, Ally."

I wanted to say, "Don't worry, we'll still be friends," but I didn't want to throw that cliché at him, even if I hope it's true. After he hangs up, I say "I'll miss you too" into the phone.

Now, a cool breeze ruffles the white curtains by the French doors in my new place. I'm still trying to put my new home in the French Quarter together. I call the bank to see how much money I have in my account before I buy more furniture.

Turns out, Eli has put $20,000 in my bank account.

"Alimony," he says when I call him. "It's the least I can do."

I know I should say no thanks, but we were kind of like a married couple, and I have helped us get through some tough times too.

"Hey," he says, "call me, will you? Maybe after the weekend?"

I try not to cry, but I do. "Yeah. I will." And I mean it.

After we hang up, I sit and look out the window onto Dumaine. People are strolling around, some walking dogs; a couple of tourists; and some people coming home from work.

It's four o'clock. I put on a jacket and head out the door. I walk down Dumaine toward Royal Street. The sun is just beginning to disappear behind the buildings on Canal Street and a soft glow settles over the French Quarter.

I stop to say hello to my landlord, who is sitting at a neighborhood watering hole with a friend. He stands and gives me a hug and a kiss on the cheek. "So Ally," he says as the conversation progresses, "do you have a special someone?"

I shake my head no.

"Oh honey, we have GOT to find you a girlfriend," he turns to his friend, "do you know anyone?"

"That's okay," I say, "I need some time alone for awhile."

"Oooooo—a broken heart. Who was she?"

Jude flashes in my mind.

I give him a slight smile and say, "Good-bye, Jesse."

He hoots as I walk away. "See ya later, sugar pie!"

I wave back at him and laugh to myself. I wonder when the collisions between past and present will stop.

Jude is always on my mind. Because I've begun to write down our story. Every day, I write it. And the more I write it down, the less she seems to haunt me. So now it's just me—Alison Bouchard, the daughter of Eric and Mary Bouchard of Harmony, Nebraska—walking down Dumaine Street, where I live in the French Quarter of New Orleans.

No more ghosts.

No more lies.

No more bullshit.

Acknowledgements

I am deeply grateful to the following people who helped this book come of age:

To my mother, Joan, who lives on in the small details of Mary Bouchard... a half-whistle, the rustling of slippers on the floor, the banging of pots and pans early in the morning, and small kisses when she thought I was sleeping. Thanks, Mom, for so many memories.

Jamie Willan (1977-2004) was a talented musician who touched many lives in his short time with us. His lyrics are used with permission from his parents, Richard and Lindsay Willan. I thank them for their generosity.

Thanks to my family and friends, who took the time to read the book, and give thoughtful feedback and encouragement: my amazing partner, Marian Martin-Moran; my niece, Shannon Malloy Whitus; my great friends, Carol Anderson, Nanette Stearns, and Sally Heuer; and to Chrystal Teachout and Gary Schiess.

Thanks to my niece Jacque Wikowsky for searching out barns in the Nebraska countryside for the cover photo (and to my sister Jean who went along for the ride). Thanks to my talented friend Janet Mills for the author photo.

Thanks to Lindsey Thomas for forensic information/insight. Thanks to the kind caretaker at the Fremont Opera House in Fremont, Nebraska, for a priceless tour of a beautiful building.

Thanks to my musical heroes, Bette Midler and Cyndi Lauper, for keeping me company on countless drives from Minneapolis to Nebraska. I'm sure I've entertained many fellow motorists on I-35 and I-80 over the years because of your music.

Finally, a special thank you to Pam Carter Joern and Felicia Eth.

NORMANDALE COMMUNITY COLLEGE
LIBRARY
9700 FRANCE AVENUE SOUTH
BLOOMINGTON, MN 55431-4399